# THE MAFIA'S BLACK OPAL

## TIFFANY RANSIER

INDIGO HEARTS PRESS LLC

# THE MAFIA'S BLACK OPAL

Valerio Marchioni

Six years ago, I got the job I never wanted—being the head of the Italian Mafia. There's no room to take my position lightly. I do whatever is required of me, according to the rules passed down from my father, including marrying someone I'm not in love with. I hold respect for her as the mother of my children and a former member of another Italian family. It only takes one night for us to be split apart forever. One vulnerable moment when I leave for a business trip gives someone the chance to attack my family. Now my pregnant wife is gone without a trace to be found. I will find who's responsible and make sure their blood runs through the streets of New York City. First, I have to send all the women I find in the process, home. Except for *her*, the woman with nowhere to go.

Her

THE MAFIA'S BLACK OPAL

It only takes one night for me to be taken. I should've been safer than anyone. Yet I end up on the circuit, bounced around from place to place. It's only on the day I decide to escape that I'm rescued by *him*, Valerio Marchioni. A man I should hate with every fiber in me. But then I get to know him. I see him for who he really is. And by then, it's too late. I can never leave, not even if I wanted to. If he discovers who I really am, I'll be dead before the men who took his wife.

Ebook ISBN: 978-1-949079-09-8

Paperback ISBN: 978-1-949079-11-1

Hardback ISBN: 978-1-949079-12-8

Published by: Indigo Hearts Press LLC

Editing: Mad Hatter Press

Proofreading: Clever Girl Literary Services

Cover design: Lori Jackson Designs

❀ Created with Vellum

*To James, thank you for writing this with me. I couldn't have done it without you. I love you always.*

*To Tiffany, thank you for always inspiring me. I love you always.*

# PROLOGUE

## Valerio

Life has never been normal for me, and there's no changing that. I was born into this life, and I've accepted my role in the world. It isn't an easy job, but there's no way I'm going to disappoint, or even worse, disgrace the family.

I straighten my tie while looking in the large mirror at my reflection.

With that, I finish in the master bathroom and walk down the wide hallway to our master bedroom. My wife lies asleep in our massive custom bed, big enough so we don't have to sleep anywhere near each other. Exactly the way we both want it. It keeps up the lie, and that's good enough for me.

Before leaving, I approach her side of the bed and stroke the roundness of her stomach. The belly that's been carrying our twins for eight and a half months. The doctor said she would be due any time now, because there are two. Even with her stomach as large as it is, her body is still attractive to me.

I move my hand away before I wake her up, watching her expression change from a frown to a smile as she sleeps. Her long brown hair is splayed all over the place from the constant tossing and turning she does every night from being uncomfortable with the twins.

The only thing I can't see are her piercing bluish-green eyes.

Once upon a time, I had hoped that I'd come to love to look into those eyes. It hasn't happened yet and I doubt it ever will. The only thing that's changed is that I've learned how to smother my own feelings. This sham of a marriage I was forced into at the age of eighteen was a huge mistake. There's no time for love in this business. Sure, my parents got lucky, but that's them, not me.

After one last look at her, I straighten the cuffs of my suit and stroll out of the bedroom to go to the small room to the right of ours.

Every time we have a baby, this is the room the baby temporarily stays in. Right now, it's empty, waiting for its new occupants. It makes it easy for her to hear them cry at night, and it's all the more convenient to just walk next door. After peeking inside to check that nothing is out of place, I close the door and head down the hallway, walking as quietly as possible across the Travertine tile into the entryway where the double staircase is.

It wouldn't be right for me to leave without saying goodbye to them.

I take the right half of the double stairway, easily going up two-by-two and turn to the right hallway. I avoid the telltale creak in the floor and walk down to the farthest room. The biggest room and the one that used to be my room when I was a child.

I open the door as quietly as possible and quickly dart inside to make the least amount of noise.

My phone starts to beep, and I mutter a curse, hurrying to silence it before it wakes him up.

With careful steps, I approach the bed of my first born, my boy Vincenzo. The spitting image of me. He continues to sleep soundly without realizing I'm in the room. He'll be angry that I didn't wake him up to say goodbye, but he knows I'll be back. Reluctantly, I leave him to let him sleep and do the same for each of my boys.

Nicolo, Vittorio, Emilio, and Aurelio.

My father wanted us to have children, so like the obedient son I am, I put five boys inside her. Leagues better than what he himself did since I'm an only child. *Her* fertility turned out to be better than I had ever imagined. Five boys. Soon enough, they'll learn the business, just as I had to.

After seeing my last boy, my almost-two-year-old, Aurelio, I leave the long hallway and listen to the sounds of silence. My phone buzzes again in my pocket.

*Damn it, I need to hurry.*

I walk briskly past the stairs to the left hallway and enter the first room. This hallway has plenty of bedrooms, just like the right hallway, but only one of them is occupied. The largest one on this side. I open the door, quieter than all of the others. Apparently, it's not quiet enough because I immediately hear the sweetest baby giggle.

Even with the rush I'm in, I have to see her.

I approach her crib, and her little fingers immediately reach out for mine. My darling princess, Valeria. She turned one only yesterday. Her curly brown hair, the same shade as her mother's, bounces as she puts her arms up for me to pick her up. Her bright blue eyes pull me in, begging me to stay and play with her. But I have to leave.My phone buzzes again for the third time, and this time, I really do have to go.

I back out of the room and watch Valeria's grin turns into a pout as her bottom lip pokes out like she's about to cry.

*Shit. Not good, not good.*

After closing the door, I run down the hallway and back down the stairs, on the left staircase this time. *I'll be back soon enough. Just please be good for your mother so I don't have to hear about how I need to be around more.* My position prevents me from being home as often as I'd like. I button my suit jacket and open the front door to find my men waiting outside for me.

"You're late, boss," Luca says, smirking.

He's my second in command, my right-hand man. We've known each other our whole lives, and I already know what he's thinking.

"No, I'm not late because I was banging her. I'm late because I wanted to see my kids, you horny fucking asshole," I remark, shaking my head.

I know I can be myself around them, if no one else. No one else needs a piece of the real me except my kids, not even my wife.

At that, the other two break their serious expressions. Luciano gives me a rare smile, and Alessio bursts out laughing. They sober up after a minute and put their neutral expressions on.

"Ready to go, boss?" Luciano asks, gesturing toward the waiting car.

"No. I want the three of you to stay with my family," I order, looking at each of them.

4

"Boss, you should take at least one of us," Alessio speaks up, looking concerned.

"I said no," I respond, deepening my voice to emphasize the seriousness of this task.

They all close their mouths, forming tight lines, and nod. They know I mean fucking business.

I try to soften my expression. "I won't be alone. Father is coming with me this time, unfortunately. I'll be back in one week."

They look at each other in shock. Yeah, I didn't want him to come either, but he was forcing his way in. I know how to stay under the radar, but he couldn't risk having his one and only son vulnerable. If something were to happen to me, who'd run the business after he's dead and gone?

He still doesn't think I can take care of myself.

The driver opens the door of the car for me, and I slide in. We drive away around the circular driveway, and I look back at the mansion that officially became *mine* at the age of eighteen.

A funny feeling forms in my stomach, but I shake it off. I've been gone for longer than a week before. Nothing bad will happen as long as the men do their job. We drive down the long driveway and out the front gate, heading toward the airport. It doesn't take long for us to get there, one hour before the private jet leaves.

To my surprise, Father isn't here waiting. He never likes being late.

I frown and glance at my phone to check for a message but find none. One hour, that's all I'll give him. I go over some business plans to pass the time and by the time I'm done, he hasn't arrived.

Well, he knows how I am. He shouldn't be fucking mad when he does finally show up at the airport. I get on the jet alone and look out of the small window, thinking he might show up at the last second.

"Are you ready, sir?" one of the pilots asks.

"Yes," I reply without hesitation.

I'm not waiting for him any longer. I don't have to. I'm the Don now. You're not in control anymore...Father.

# ONE

## Valerio

I hate being away from my kids for any amount of time, but this meeting is too important to miss. In my line of work, I have to focus on my people first and my family second. The other families would turn on me faster than the snap of a finger if they sensed any amount of weakness. In other words, I can only trust the people around me and myself. Many people say that they have my back, but at the earliest instance, they will plunge a knife in, and deep at that.

Thinking back, I've never really been able to rely on any of the other families under me. I'm on good terms with two of them, and even then that's something that can change. They all want my position. They want to be my the main family.

But truth be told, none of them are smart enough to try to take me down. I don't fucking fear them. As for our biggest threats, the only groups I've had to worry about are the Russians, who've always been in an off and on war with us, and the Cartel, who keep flooding drugs into my city.

While I know the leaders of each crime family, I know hardly anything else about them, and the same can be said for what they know about me. That Russian bastard and Cartel asshole and I all took over from our fathers at the same time. I don't even know if they have heirs, though I'm assuming they both do. It's our way of life to always have someone who can take over if something were to happen to us.

And though I don't love my wife, I love my kids. If I did have the choice though, I would've married someone I actually love, like my father, but that choice was taken away.

I knew as a young boy that I would have to marry to keep the line strong and keep my family secure. Even if the woman I was marrying has nothing in common with me at all. To anyone else, they'd see a wonderful, beautiful woman and find a way to love her. Well I fucking tried, but we're just too different, if not the same in some ways. That doesn't change the fact that she's the mother of my children.

The plane hits a patch of turbulence, causing everything around me to shake. I shift a little in my seat, relaxing and sinking back into my thoughts, back to my early days. I would follow my father around whenever I could, but he would often send me out because he didn't want me to know before it was my time to be taught. At the time, I didn't understand, but now I do. I don't want any of my kids seeing the business I do.

As soon as I became a teenager, I started learning the family business. At first, it was a little shocking to learn, but now I can't see myself doing any other job other than running the family. I don't like taking orders from anyone, so

I could never work under someone. I might be able to run a company, but I rarely do things the legal way. The government is always trying to stick their nose into our fucking business.

My only normalness as a teenager was a girl named Sarah. It was refreshing talking to a normal person. She was a daughter of one of the women who worked as a maid. She was beautiful, kind, and didn't care who I was. On the days my father allowed me to leave, we always went to the mall and I was able to act like a normal teenager. We never talked about it until I was seventeen. After a year of being together, I wanted to ask her to marry me. But that wasn't in my father's plan. He said I couldn't marry the help because they aren't part of the core families. I was told right then and there that I was going to marry a daughter from one of the other families to strengthen our bond with them and make our own bid for the top even stronger. Maybe I loved her, maybe I didn't. I saw her as the only girl who I was able to be myself around. It was heartbreaking either way having to accept that my wife would be chosen for me. That was the first big argument with my father. Like the rebellious teenager I was, I decided to run away with her.

We were supposed to meet up away from the estate, but after an hour of waiting for her, I heard a car pull up, and my father stepped out. He motioned for me to get into the car with the stone-cold face he always has when people don't listen to him, so I complied to avoid a further argument.

The car ride back to the house was quiet and nerve-racking. Once we arrived back home, I found out exactly why she didn't show up to the meeting. My father had not only fired her mother from the compound, but also said that if he ever saw them again, he would have them both thrown in jail. I know he was only doing it to get me to where I needed to be for this family, but I hated him for it.

From that point on, I refused to ever let my emotions cloud me, or make me fall for a woman ever again. In the end, I decided not to fight him anymore. It would only distract me from the job I have to do.

I fucked around a lot until my father put an end to it. He told me he found the woman I was to marry and a few days after I turned eighteen, I got married. I came to the realization that if I wanted to have a decent life, then I would have to deal with her and my father on their terms. If nothing else, I could always marry her and then find someone else on the side, but that might only cause more trouble for me down the line.

Since marrying her almost seven years ago, I've let her and my father do what they wanted, while I do my own thing, making my own moves on the proverbial chess board. I needed my own pawns and my own knights, so I quickly built up a small family of loyal men around myself who I could bet my life and future on.

I will be strong. Stronger than my father ever was.

---

AFTER ALL THE thinking and reflecting on my past, and maybe the mostly calm plane ride, I start to drift off into a deep sleep. Within minutes, I'm on a small porch swing watching as a car pulls up into the driveway.

My father gets out of the car and walks around to the back door. Opening the door, he reveals my future wife, who steps out of the car, with a scowl on her face. She stares right into my eyes, not looking away for a second. Not even when my father motions for her to go into the house. Eventually she walks in, sitting down at the kitchen table where my mother's "first meeting" lunch is to be served. Our one chance to get together before tying the knot, but all she does is stare at me with a blank look from across the table. The only thing she says is, "Hello."

I learn next to nothing about her, but my parents tell her all about me and what to expect from being a part of our family. She continues to listen and nod, but I feel as though she has already been told everything that she needs to know.

When the lunch is over, my father asks her if she has any questions, and she pauses for a second, and then shakes her head no. I watch as my father brings her back to the car to take her wherever he picked her up from. It almost slips by me, but I notice that as soon as she thinks that she is out of my sight, she drops her neutral expression and looks sad.

From that moment on, I knew this would be a complicated marriage. It was only the first time I had ever seen her, yet I understood that while we would be married, it would not be a happy one. We went on a few dates by ourselves, and I gradually got to know her, but it never once changed that we were not a good match for each other. We never wanted the same thing at the same time, and it was more than just food, we completely hated what the other thought was fun. She wanted to see plays, while all I wanted was to play video games. The one we had in common was always wanting to get away so people would leave us alone. In time, we grew to learn each other's patterns so that we got to keep out of the other's way. No matter what we did or didn't do, for that matter, we would always end up smiling for the outside world while feeling dead inside. We did what we had to do to keep my parents happy with our engagement; we made the best out of what we had.

During our dating stage, we tended to end up at the mall

frequently because neither of us had to worry about money due to my parents giving us both credit cards with almost no limit. It was there that I'd hang out with my three best friends, at least until my parents got wind of it because they were prominent members of the mall's board of directors. One of the kiosk workers ratted us out, and that caused my parents to sit us both down and tell us they don't care whether we like each other or not, but we need to appear to when we are outside of our house. It would make us look weak if we didn't appear to be in love with each other to the public.

Suddenly, my dream fades. But I don't wake up. Instead, it comes back in on the day that I proposed to her.

We were taking a walk at the botanical gardens. We had just gotten to a small garden with an archway that had a small bench underneath it. I got down on one knee and pulled out a small ring; it wasn't fancy, it was simple. I felt like a fraud giving it to her because no love came from that gesture. But at the botanical gardens, she said yes to my proposal.

My parents were excited that I had finally caved in to doing what they wanted me to do. We were excited that they were happy because my parents being happy meant they left us alone, and when they left us alone, we could pretty much do whatever we wanted, which meant whatever we wanted without the other one. At this point in our lives, we would hang out watching terrible old movies. She would actually enjoy them, but I would only enjoy making fun of them, Mystery Science Theater 3000 style. It pissed her off a little bit, but I'd have to get my enjoyment somewhere, and by doing just little things, I wouldn't create a rift between us that might cause her to do something we would both regret. It wasn't long before our lives were taken over by the wedding. My mother made it this huge deal and caused us both to be a part of the planning because if her little baby was getting married, then he was going to get married the right way.

We went through ten different venues because none of them had something that everyone wanted. It took forever, and it was a pain in the ass, but we finally found a decent place to get married as well as having our personal chefs be the caterers for the wedding. That only left the cake and the wedding dress, which was being taken care of by my mother and fiancé.

And then I'm at the altar. After all the stupid planning was done, the wedding finally came, and we said our vows to each other. Vows that meant nothing in both of our hearts. We end up going to the hotel from the reception and consummating our marriage. That night, I'm almost positive Vincenzo was conceived. The honeymoon cruise lasted a little over a week, and we didn't have that great a time other than fucking. When we got back from the cruise, I found that my parents had already moved out of the large house and left it to us.

That part, I was glad about. In a way, it made me officially the Don at the same age as my father was, eighteen.

It wasn't long before our first child was on the way. I was nervous. I mean, even if I didn't love my wife, I was certain I would love my children. After all, they are my flesh and blood, and they will be the ones that my legacy will be built on. Vincenzo was the hardest to deal with. He never wanted to fall asleep, and when he did, he would sleep for thirty-minute intervals. He made sleeping difficult because we had to sleep in shifts to make sure that our child was taken care of. My men asked me whether I should just find a nanny, but I refused to lose any time with my kids.

It took us a while to get into the swing of it, but we did eventually get into a rhythm together and with our child. However, the bliss of one kid was soon replaced when she turned out to be pregnant again. The second time was easier to go through, she gave birth not only easier, but without much of the pain that she had the first time. Once our second child was born, things again became easy for a while. We fell into a lull with each other, where I was only focused on work and our kids, while she was focused only on our kids. We would fight occasionally, but it was always over something stupid. Frequently, we would go for days in between fighting to making up, at least in a small degree.

It didn't take long until we were forced to by my parents, who said they wanted me to have a large family, and that two kids weren't nearly enough. She wasn't very happy at the thought of having more kids, but she knew that we didn't have a choice in the matter. We ended up enjoying it after a while, but it didn't make us like each other any more than we did.

Life took many turns for us. We almost lost Emilio and Aurelio, but they kept fighting, and so did we. We made sure all of our children were healthy, and because of that, they were all born without any major complications.

My parents were happy when we announced to them that we would be having our seventh child, and then to my surprise, an eighth. Twin girls. My mother was always ecstatic to show that she was a grandmother with a large family. After all, I was an only child.

---

SUDDENLY, something shakes me out of my dream. Glancing around the plane, I find everything to be fine, but there's a tugging sensation at the back of my mind. It feels as though something is very, very wrong with my current situation. I close my eyes again, tossing and turning for a few minutes, but I can't shake the feeling that I'm missing something important.

I might as well check my messages since I can't sleep. As soon as I unlock my phone, I see multiple missed calls from my mother. What the fuck is going on? My mother never calls me on my work phone, it's always my father who calls this phone. If my mother is trying this hard to reach me, something terrible must have happened.

I feel my stomach drop as I can't wrap my head around what could cause her to call me on my work phone. Something must have happened to my father, which is in itself a scary thought because if someone is going after old mafia bosses, then it's not too far a stretch that someone might come after me. My mind races to my family. What if something has happened to my kids?

Shaking my head, I dismiss that thought. No. That can't be. If anything is wrong with my family, one of my men would have called me to let me know. Only one way to find out. I click *her* name in my phone's directory and wait for the phone to pick up, but it rings through. I call another three times, but she never picks up, causing my fears to only get worse.

Just calm down. My anger and worry threatens to leak out and I fight the urge to scream at the pilot. *It's going to be okay.* She's probably just busy with whatever is going on, and she'll fill me in once I get back or even before that. My gut tells me something is terribly wrong, so I make the decision to get back home as quickly as possible. I get up and out of my seat to make my way to the cockpit, where the pilots are.

"Hey Frank," I say to the pilot on the left. "We need to

turn around right now and go back to the airport." My fingers nervously start clicking against the border of the door.

"No can do Valerio. We are about to head into a storm, and if we turn around now, we may not be able to get there until later this week," he replies.

"Look, this isn't a question or a debate. It's a damn *order*, we need to go back right now."

"Your father said that you need to go to this meeting no matter what."

"God damn it, Frank! I don't give a fuck what my father said. You either turn this plane around, or I will take control and turn it around myself," I shout at him, slamming my fist against the wall.

His eyes go wide, and he quietly nods and tells me to take my seat.

We quickly bank and turn back toward the airport. I keep calling to see if my mother will answer the phone and tell me what the hell is going on, but she never picks up. Furious and scared, I throw my glass at the back door and shout out in rage. It shatters, and I glance at it. If someone even dares to hurt my family, that glass will be exactly how they will look. Broken.

As soon as we make it back to the airport, I hop into the first cab that comes.

"Step on it," I growl.

The cab driver glances back at me, and we race down the street. On our way, I notice that a car has been tailing us since shortly after I left the airport.

"I don't have time for this," I say, grabbing my hair angrily.

For now, I'll ignore it.

When we almost reach the road that we turn down to get

to the long driveway that leads to my house, I notice that the car tailing me has turned a different way. We go down the lane, which ends at my house, and I can't help but shake the feeling that once I get there, I'm going to see something terrible. Something that is going to bring out the side of me I keep locked away. That car tailing me...something isn't fucking right.

We go up the long driveway and pull around to the front of the circle and stop. I don't need to get out to see the French doors are wide open.

*Shit.*

Without saying a word, I throw money at the cab driver and get out. I carelessly throw my bags on the ground.

Getting prepared, I pull out my custom Glock 17 and switch the safety off. Walking up slowly to the door, I notice right away a trail of blood on the floor. I quickly clear the entryway and move in slowly, keeping my head on a swivel, looking around for not only my wife and children, but my men. The amount of blood only seems to increase the farther into the house we get. Not one body is seen. I clear most of the downstairs and make my way to the kitchen when I hear a noise.

I follow it until I get to the sink and stop to stare.

There, in our stainless-steel sink, are two newborn babies. My newborn daughters with blood still covering them. They make small noises, and I breathe a little easier knowing they're okay.

But what about my boys? And Valeria? My heart starts to hurt.

Whoever did this is going to wish they had never been born.

I make a snap decision to leave my daughters where they are, only for a few minutes, as I finish clearing the bottom floor. I call out to anyone who might be inside the house but get no reply.

Just as I'm about to go upstairs and start clearing the other floors, I notice movement outside.

I move to the window and stare outside in the trees. Just as I'm about to pull my gun out, my head maid peeks her head out.

She breathes a sigh of relief and comes fully out of the trees, followed by, to my relief, the rest of my children.

She's holding Valeria in her arm and motioning for the other children to go ahead of her.

Vincenzo is carrying Aurelio on his back, who is sucking on his thumb.

They run inside through the sliding glass door, and I hastily put my gun away before being tackled by them.

Their faces are dirty and tear stricken. They must have been terrified. They shouldn't have to go through something like this.

But where is *she*?

"Bernadette, where is my wife?" I ask as she puts Valeria in my arms.

Bernadette's hopeful smile falls. "I'm sorry, sir, but she was taken away by the men who broke in, right after giving birth."

Fuck...

The children start to cry, and none of them will calm down, so I bring them all to the living room and have them all sit down while I call my men. This time, they actually pick up and come back to the house. When they arrive, they give me a small rundown on what had happened.

It was a normal day until these men in masks showed up and killed my men watching the gate. They busted the lock on the door and came in shooting. The shootout happened quickly and didn't last very long. The only person taken was my wife, who the men tried their hardest to retrieve but lost her trail. They assaulted my mother, who was moved to the hospital to verify that there were no permanent injuries.

This can only mean one thing. It was an organized hit, which means that they meant to take my wife the entire time, and the shooting was just enough to distract everyone from what they were after. They tried to chase them to at least get a license plate, but it was no use. The guys and my wife were gone, my mother is in the hospital, and my house is a complete disaster.

Without any leads on who it is that took her, all I can do right now is clean up and take care of my kids.

Even though he was the last person I want to talk to, I call my father, who picks up on the first ring.

"Hello?"

"Father, is Mother okay?"

"Yeah, how are you and the kids? What about your wife?"

"My wife is gone, but the kids are fine."

"You need to find her and take these fuckers who did this down. Make them regret ever being born, and then end them with extreme prejudice."

"I will. I don't care how long it takes me, but I will find these people and end them."

"Good." With that, my father hangs up the phone and leaves me to my rage and frustration.

I make a call to our doctor to come and check my newborn daughter's out.

While I'm grabbing them from the sink, the men finally arrive back at the house and try to keep my kids calm and make a call to a cleaning service to make sure that the house is spotless in a short period of time.

I head back into the living room where my kids are and sit down with them.

My oldest looks at me, "Dad, is Mom going to be okay?"

"Don't worry about it, Vin, leave it all to Daddy to take care of this."

"I need you to be strong, kiddo, and take care of your siblings for me. Make sure that they are safe and that they stay calm."

"I can do that, Daddy. I just miss her already. Why did she have to go away? Who were those men that took her?"

"I wish Daddy had those answers for you, kiddo, but I just don't have any."

The doctor comes after a while, and I hand my daughters off to him. He'll let me know in a while whether everything is fine.

I hug all of my children before leaving and head straight for the living room, where my men are.

"Luca," I say to get my second-hand man's attention.

He moves toward me, and I lead him down the hallway to my office. I close the door roughly.

"Where do we begin the search, and how long before we find the fuckers who did this to my house? Who had the fucking audacity to come into my home and scare my children?" I shout at him.

"I don't know, sir, but if we're going to start somewhere, we should probably start with slavers. They tend to kidnap women, and if they had her then, we need to hurry before she is sold off."

"Let me make a few calls before we do anything, I don't want to go out half-cocked and end up messing everything up."

He nods and leaves me alone to sit in my office. I slowly fill a tumbler full of whiskey, which I then proceed to nurse. I know I need to try to rescue her because she is the mother of my children, but honestly, a small selfish part of me hopes that we don't find her...

Maybe this is a way out, but...

But then again, maybe this is all my fault, and she deserves better than me.

I call my other men into my office and sit in my chair behind the desk.

They file in, and I stare into each of their eyes. "It's time to find her and get her back."

# TWO

*Her*

Pain. Gloom. Exhaustion.

I know it's time to wake up, but I don't want to open my eyes and stare at the steel bars of the cage.

The room is cold from the terror and anxiety of the other women with me. All of the windows are boarded up, and the air is stale from the lack of air circulation. The buckets in the corners of the room are full and desperately need to be emptied as our waste starts to leak over the tops of them.

This has been my life for at least three months. I stopped counting after ninety days. Instead of focusing on how much time I've been here, I should focus on the amount of time until I get out.

Any day now. It has to be.

I suck in a deep breath and slowly open my eyes to see the dirty black bars. My legs hurt from being curled in the same position for hours. The cage is only big enough for me to lie on my left or right side.

It's always dark, so it's hard to tell how much time has passed. Every day, it's the same thing. We get one meal of the nastiest slop I've ever seen, and we're allowed to use the bathroom in a corner, in front of everyone else. Then we go back in our cage, and hours later, we get one more meal of the same thing and get one more bathroom privilege before being shoved back into our cage.

That's if you're lucky.

If you aren't lucky, like Daria, a blonde, petite girl who looks younger than me, you'll be kept out of your cage after the last meal and taken by one of the men who keeps us in our cage.

It only happens every once in a while, because I'm pretty sure they aren't supposed to be doing it with how nervous they act when they take us out of this room. I've been lucky enough to not be taken.

I shiver at the thought of being forced to have sex with any of them. There are three men who cycle through. Glasses, Pudgy, and Angry. Glasses took Daria, and she didn't come back until the next time we got to eat. She was crying and had bruises all over her body. She cried for her mother and father.

It made me think about my own family. I know they're wondering what happened to me, and more than anything, I want to get back to them. I just need to be patient and wait.

My papa's poor heart will be broken, and Mama will be beside herself and my—

no. They'll be okay. Everything has to be okay.

My bladder feels like it needs to explode, but at the same time, I'm dying of thirst. My lips are dry like sandpaper. Two glasses of water a day is nowhere near enough.

I miss having the freedom to do whatever I want. Sleep, eat, and drink whatever I want.

Being treated like a human being instead of an animal.

At the beginning, I hoped that I'd somehow be able to escape. There'd be some opening. But these men, they're meticulous in their watch over us.

I don't even know where I am. All of these men have Russian accents, so it's possible that ... maybe ... no. There's no way that would ever happen.

Before I found myself in this room, I was shipped around. Moved from place to place and constantly drugged. Random men spoke other languages. The drugs only stopped when I was placed inside this cage.

I haven't had a bath in so long. I can't remember the last one I had when I was at home. My own stench makes me gag, and it seems worse than the smell coming from the other women in the room.

At some point, I was changed out of the dress I was wearing when I got taken, and now, I just have a shirt on. The shirt was once plain white, but it's now a much darker color that's almost black.

Maybe that's not even the worst part. It might be the wig that's glued on the front to my normal hair. My regular light brown hair is covered with a cap and then on top is an ugly black wig that's now grimier than the shirt.

It will make it difficult for anyone to ever find me. They won't be looking for me with a black wig. They'll be looking for me with my natural light brown hair.

I'm no longer scared about what happens to me next. I'm cold, so very cold.

No, that's not the right word. Numb.

It's best to stay numb.

The relaxed breathing of the girls surrounding me in their cages slowly stops, signaling they're waking up.

Suddenly, in the far back corner of the room, I hear the sound of one girl sniffling. It has to be the newest girl. She cried all day yesterday after she was put into her cage after our first meal.

Her sniffling turns into loud sobs, and the other girls stay quiet.

My heart aches for her and her family. Who knows what might've happened to her before she got here? A few girls whisper to her to try and comfort her.

She starts to quiet down, and I breathe a sigh of relief, glad that she can save her energy for something else. Crying only gets you noticed by the men who watch us.

My attention turns to the doorknob as I hear it jiggle until it clicks, and the door creaks open.

The man enters the room, and by the heavy footsteps, I'm able to tell it's Pudgy. My eyes watch as he walks deeper into the room, going cage to cage to see if we're all still alive. He walks right past me until I hear him stop in the corner of the room where the new girl is. She starts crying again, and I dig my nails into my palm in worry for her.

"Hey, shut up," he grunts.

She keeps going, and he kicks his foot out and hits her cage. "Keep quiet or you're coming with me."

The crying stops, and I breathe a sigh of relief.

Pudgy chuckles in a way that makes chills go up my spine. "I'm taking you with me anyway."

The new girl gasps, and I hear her cage open, followed by a distraught scream. *I'm sorry, I wish I could help you.*

No, I have to do something this time. I take a deep breath and gather all the courage in my body.

"You don't want her," I say out loud as confidently as possible.

His heavy feet stomp to my cage and stop in front. My gaze shoots up from his feet, and the cruel smirk on his face is the first thing I see. I glance at his big, meaty hands and see his hand is tightly gripped around the new girl's arm.

"Well, you are a pretty thing, much prettier than her," he comments.

I stare at the new girl and see she has bright red hair with freckles and green eyes. She gives me the smallest of smiles. I have no idea what he's talking about, but if this is what's going to save her, I'll go along with it.

"Exactly," I proclaim.

I stare into his eyes and watch as his eyes change. He turns away and shuffles back to the corner.

"Oooof," the new girl says.

Being thrown back in a cage might be the worst part. I hear the click of him locking the cage, and I watch as he comes back quickly and unlocks my cage. His hand grabs my arm and yanks me out. I let my body hang as limply as possible, so he thinks I'm fully cooperative.

My legs ache like they always do when I get out of the cage, and I walk next to him shakily and get pushed through the doorway. He locks the door behind him, and we continue down a short hallway that curves around to another hallway. He stops in front of a door on the left and pushes the door open, shoving me inside. I flop on the small single bed right in the center of the small room.

"You're going to stay here, girly, while I take care of business. There's no way for you to leave, but in case you try to, it's the last thing you'll ever do."

He slams the door closed, and I stare at the plain white wood. Plain white. So different from home. After what seems like hours frozen in place, I stretch my legs out. If I can't make a plan happen, I'll be forced right back in that cage.

I sniff the musty air and study the iffy-looking blanket covering the bed. What can I do? How can I get out? I guess it was too easy to assume there would be a window in this room.

There has to be a window in this house somewhere. It's either that or the front door. If I try the front door, I'm sure to get caught. What are the chances that I find a room that has a window though?

One night is all I have...

---

I WAKE up to the sound of the door opening and perk up in the chair. Pudgy closes the door behind him and comes immediately toward me. He didn't lock the door.

"Now, let's have some fun," he says, eyeing my body.

Without even missing a beat, he pushes me against the wall, causing the wooden chair to hit it. He smiles creepily and pushes his mouth against mine. Chills go up and down my spine as I try to stay still. He moves his hands along my breasts and grasps them firmly, squeezing to the point of pain.

*Don't let him see how much it hurts.*

He pulls me against him harshly, and his tongue pushes into my mouth. My breath speeds up as his mouth and hands steal the last bit of my control.

*Home with my family. I'm home with my family, not being assaulted by a man I don't know.*

Pudgy removes his tongue from my mouth only to bite

my lip so hard, I know it's bleeding, and seconds later, the taste of copper hits my tongue.

I can do this. *I can do this.* It'll be over soon.

Suddenly, everything starts to get hazy, and his face starts to swim. The room seems to spin, and then everything goes black.

---

HUNGER. Why am I so hungry? My eyes shoot open and find myself in complete darkness. The heavy snores of someone next to me make me jump, and then it all comes back.

I'm not in my cage. I'm in the room with Pudgy. I glance down at myself and squint hard, but I still can't see. Please let me still be in the same nasty shirt. I touch the front of my body and find it to be just as rough as my usual shirt.

At least that's a good sign. I relax and stay still when it hits me.

This is it. This is my chance. I need to take advantage of it. Right. Now.

My eyes start to adjust to the darkness, and I watch Pudgy snore away as I inch out of his bed until I'm standing up.

*Please let the door still be open. Please tell me he didn't lock it.* I slowly turn the doorknob, and it turns easily. Yes!

I hold my breath and listen for noises and hear silence. If I take it one step at a time, maybe I can make it out. I tiptoe out of the room after making sure Pudgy is still snoring and softly close the door. I walk across the hall and put my ear against the door, and after hearing nothing for a few minutes, I slowly turn the knob and open it up to find an empty room. Good, but still no windows.

I close the door and stay in the same spot while I decide what to do. Should I go back down the hallway and start where the room of cages is? Or should I go the other way where the front door is? There might be rooms off the main area too.

It makes more sense for the other two to be closer to the cage room, and maybe whoever runs this place too. With resolve, I turn the corner, going right, and walk to the main area I vaguely remember. There's a small table right in the center with four chairs around it. The front door is straight ahead, and there are five different locks on it. The windows in this area are all boarded up.

Suddenly, I notice right in the corner there's another hallway. Do I dare go down it?

I hesitate for only a few more moments before walking over and darting down it. This might be the only chance I have. I listen against the only door at the very end, and after hearing nothing for a while, I carefully open it. Right away, I can tell it's bigger than the other room Pudgy has. But even better, there it is. Right above the double bed, a single window. Not a huge one, but big enough for me to go through. I take a step inside and study every corner of the room. No bathroom, just a small closet. I relax a little, but keep my ears open when I step on the bed and walk to the headboard.

This is it. If I can just get this window open.

I stand on my tiptoes and pull the piece to open the window. The window slides up and makes a sharp scraping sound that makes me hold my breath. Crap. I wince as I slide it up the rest of the way as the sound seems to echo throughout the room.

Fresh air floods into the room, and I rub my hands over my arms to get rid of the newly formed goosebumps on my arms.

Shakily, I grasp the windowsill and hoist myself up by putting my foot on the headboard. I put my other foot next to it and look outside.

Oh shit.

Snow. The ground is covered in it, and it's still coming down. All I have to do is find someone to help me, and then I'm out of here, I'll make it. Maybe it won't be too far away... It's better than being here. Plus, the other girls are counting on me. I've come too far to just go back to that nasty room with Pudgy.

I climb halfway out, and just when I'm about to get completely out, I feel someone grab my legs and pull me back.

My first instinct is to scream, but instead, I kick back and hear a groan when my foot connects with something. I scramble quickly to get away, but this time, I feel them grab my hips and pull me back.

A tear slips out of my eye as my only hope of freedom is gone forever.

The hands grabbing me shift to my hair and yank it back.

"Did you really think you were going to escape?" an evil voice asks calmly in my ear.

Perfect English, but with a slight Russian accent.

Tears start clouding my vision, and he pushes me onto the bed and puts his body on top of mine. The man who cost me my freedom has bleach blond hair that's slicked back. There's no kindness in his ocean blue eyes, and his skin is pale, like it hasn't seen the sun in years.

"No one ever escapes from here," he says, studying my face and then my hair. "Now .. .which dumbass let you almost escape?"

I stare at him without saying a word, and his face twists into anger, and he slaps me across the face. "Tell me."

When I still don't reply, he slaps the other side of my face harder than he did the first. His angry expression changes to a cruel smile, and he gets off the bed and yanks me to the floor by my hair. He throws the door open and drags me behind him.

I desperately want to cry out in agony at the feeling of my hair being pulled out of my scalp, but I hold it in. He pulls me back down the hallway, where the room I came from is, and throws that door open.

"Was it you, Pashkov?" my captor shouts, waking up Pudgy.

I guess I can't call him Pudgy anymore.

Pashkov groggily makes noises and sits up in bed. He rubs his eyes, and then they shoot open in horror at seeing me in the clutches of who I assume is the boss.

The man holding my hair sighs. "I told all three of you to be careful. Now, we have to teach her a lesson."

He shouts down the part of the hall that leads to the cage room. "Pelevin! Lazarev! Wake your asses up!"

Immediately, two doors open, and within seconds, the other two are standing next to the boss.

"Yes, boss," they both say in unison.

Their boss yanks me up to face them. "Look who Pashkov almost let get away."

They eye me, and their eyes widen slightly.

"Now, it's time to punish her." Their boss lets go of my hair and throws me over his shoulder. He takes his time walking back the way we came, and I watch as the three of them follow him.

As soon as he gets back to the main area, he throws me off, and I lie there, watching as they all start taking their pants off.

Please...this can't happen.

Pudgy reaches to the bottom of my shirt and starts to pull it up, I hear something hit the front door. They stop and turn their attention to the front door. And then after a pause, the door flies off its hinges, barely missing hitting us, but mostly me.

I stare as ten men in suits come in with guns out, pointing them at my captors. The men part in half and another man walks through. Please let it be...

But it isn't.

I stare right into his eyes and see the heat blazing in them. He shifts his gaze to the boss. "I'm sure you know who I am. So, tell me...where is she?"

He stares down at me, and my body shakes at the intensity of his gaze. Who is this?

"We don't have her," the boss replies tersely.

"I'll find out soon enough. Search the whole property," the dangerous man orders his men.

His men walk around us in the center of the room, and the dangerous man advances inside, crossing his arms as he stops next to me.

"I will make sure you get far away from here," he says without looking at me.

Pudgy makes an annoyed sound, but I don't care.

I stare at the open door and can't help the small smile that spreads across my face.

Freedom.

# THREE

## Valerio

I stand and watch with annoyance as my men break down the door into the master bedroom. She wasn't in any of the past three places that we've already searched and burned down. Once the door is blown off its hinges, I can see into the room over my men. Staring back at me are four ugly Russian bastards and a woman, who even under all the dirt and unkempt hair could easily be a model. My men march into the room and then split apart so that I can walk calmly up to the scumbags in the middle of the room.

"Where is she?" my voice comes out unwavering, yet inside, I am seething with rage.

"We don't have her," the man who is their obvious leader replies.

"I'll find out soon enough. Search the whole property," I

bark out to my men as I pace over to the woman, stopping beside her and crossing my arms.

I can't bring myself to look at her anymore, so I just mutter, "I'll make sure you get far away from here." After saying that, I turn my attention back to the four scumbags standing in front of me.

"Take her into the other room and bring in the tools, it's time to see what these *stronzi* know."

After watching carefully that she has been escorted out of the room, I slowly crack my knuckles and smile as the men that aren't searching the premises bring in an assortment of power tools.

"I'm only going to ask this once, so I want to make this perfectly clear. I will let you go if you give me the information that I want, no questions asked. Do you all understand?" I ask, as I nod my head at them.

"We don't know where she is! Please, just let us go, you can have the girls and the money...we'll even help get you more girls. Please, just let us go," the chubby Russian man begs.

A slow laugh rumbles deep within me until it bursts out and I can't control it. I wipe tears that come to my eyes due to their hilarity. *As if I'd let them go.* I motion to my men for them to start torturing the Russians.

As I'm walking away, Luca comes in to brief me on the situation of the building.

"I'm sorry, Valerio, we looked everywhere, but she just isn't here," Luca says dejectedly.

"It's alright. Right now, we just need to wait for the screams to stop, and we might still end up with information on her."

"Can I ask something boss?"

I shoot him a look and nod.

"I mean, I understand that she was the mother of your children, but you didn't really seem to like her? So, why are we doing all this?"

After a deep sigh, I turn to him, and he flinches reflexively.

"I'm not going to hit you, and to answer your question, it's precisely because she is the mother of my children that we are doing this. It's because my children don't deserve to be without their mother. But I know where you are coming from. I think it's about time to let it go."

"Alright, boss."

Shaking my head, I start to wonder myself. *Is that really why I am doing this? Or am I doing this just because this is what my father would expect of me?* This is what the other families would expect of me. Even if it was a loveless marriage made to strengthen my claim and to make sure that the other families didn't try to overthrow me.

I just don't know anymore. I want to say that I'm a good person, and that I'm trying to save my wife, and that even if I don't find her, I'm saving all these other lives in the process. But I know I'm not a good person. If I was a good person, this whole mess never would have happened. If I was a good person...I sure as hell wouldn't be the boss of the mafia.

Anger starts to ripple through me. I can feel my muscles begin to tense up, and I know that I need to just go in and make a statement to these fuckwads.

I walk back into the room where the men are being tortured, and I look at the fat fuck who begged for his life before.

"I'll let you go. But I want you to go find whoever you might know that is a part of the sex trade. Tell them that all of their lives are over because they decided to mess with Valerio Marchioni!"

With a look of shock and amazement at his good fortune, the fat man goes to run out of the room. I pull my gun out and shoot him down in front of the others.

"Oops, I lied. Now, do any of you have actual information on my wife or are you all useless to me?"

They all begin to blubber and babble incoherently, none of them actually offering up what I want to know.

It figures. While I hate these scum-sucking low lives, they do tend to keep each other's secrets, even in death. I guess their reasoning is if you could easily flip them then the whole organization could be brought down, but this way each piece is independent enough that no matter how many I kill, two more take their place. I'm sick and tired of this whole game, and I want to give up. By this point, my wife is either dead or she is too far gone for me to be able to bring back.

I know that some of my men are talking about me behind my back. Whispering that this is a fool's errand, and instead of being at home and working on our territory, I'm out here looking.

"Kill the rest and burn this house down. Bring the girls to the jet. We're going to make sure that they all get to where they want to be."

I watch as my men gather all the scared women together and load them into vans to take them to my jet. They put the one who was undoubtedly about to be raped into a van, and the van takes off. After she's gone, I turn back to the task at hand, which is erasing this blight from the light of day for good.

"Luciano, is the kerosene in place?" I ask while tapping my foot.

My friend, and the most serious of my group of men, gives me a look and nods his head.

"Good, get everyone into the cars and on their way to the

airport. We need to be out of here before any police show up."

My men clear out and leave only Luca, Luciano, Alessio, and myself. Alessio hops into the driver's seat of the SUV, and Luca follows him in the passenger's seat. Luciano strikes up a cigarette and offers me one, which I gladly take.

Watching the glowing embers of the lit cigarette, I flick it outside into the kerosene, igniting it. The fire spreads and quickly becomes an inferno as the entire property is engulfed with flames.

I get into the back seat along with Luciano, and we pull out of the driveway and begin the long trek back to the airstrip.

"I'm done. This was the last time and the last straw!" I exclaim out loud to nobody except myself.

Luciano just turns to stare at me with a puzzled look on his face, while Alessio, my blood cousin, leans his head toward me to share his look of disbelief. Luca starts to laugh as he turns to me with a smile.

"Now, you're talking my language, I told you before that you needed to find someone you actually cared about. Since you're ready to settle down and all, I could introduce you to a ton of women that I know," Luca says.

"I'm not interested, Luca, I just want this mess to be over. I'm done looking, and I'm done wasting time," I reply.

"Wait, but what about the other families, won't you look weak in their eyes?" Alessio asks.

"I couldn't give less of a fuck what those other families think. They can try to come at us, but it won't work. It didn't work before when they came at my dad, it won't work against me."

"I normally agree with you, but on this one, I have to agree with Alessio. Unless you have some sort of support from the other families, we are vulnerable," Luciano says softly.

I let out a sigh and throw up my hands.

"I have their grandchildren, even though their daughter is gone. I'm pretty sure I still have their support. As for the others, I don't think they would be dumb enough to fuck with us when we can destroy them easily."

The rest of the ride passes in relative silence as we make our way back to the airstrip.

Once back at the airstrip, we all pile out of the car and focus on getting all the women onto the plane. On the airplane when everyone is on board with a total of ten women, my men plus myself, and the two pilots, we embark for New York City and then to my mansion. There, I'll schedule transportation to take the women wherever they want to go.

As a last ditch effort, I decide to ask the women about my wife and pull a photo of her from my wallet to show them. "Please, have any of you seen a woman who looks like this? Has anyone seen her? Please, pass the photo back and maybe one of you might remember something."

As each and every girl shakes their heads or tells me that they have never seen her before, all I can do is focus on the beautiful woman in the back who has not said a word the entire time that she has been on the plane.

Once the photo gets to her, handed to her by a woman with red hair, she again looks me dead in the eye and shakes her head. She looks back down at the photo, and I see her face drop just a bit. She looks sad for a second, like she might have someone who is looking for her much like I am looking for my wife.

"Well, thank you all for answering me honestly, I have some water in the back as well as some food. Once we get back to my mansion, you all can clean up, and then we can focus on where you want to go," I tell the group of women.

The woman with red hair looks up at me and asks, "So, you don't plan on selling us or using us for yourself or your men?"

"I do not. I *abhor* rapists and sex traffickers. They make me sick, which is why those men that were holding you captive are dead as well, and that entire complex burnt to cinders," I reply.

"Why would you do this from kindness? I know of you, mafia you are, aren't you?" another woman says in broken English.

"I'm not doing it from kindness, nor am I doing this for any other reason than I want those bastards to pay, because I think that they took my wife."

"You didn't answer if you were mafia or not?" another woman asks.

"For your safety, I am not going to answer that. Now, regardless of who I am, you are all free now. I will make sure that you all make it to wherever you want to go."

"So, we can go anywhere we want? Even if we want to go to a new country or something of that sort?" a woman asks.

"As I said, I am willing to give money and travel anywhere you want to be, but once there, you are on your own. I am not a bank nor am I going to babysit any of you. I just want to make sure that everyone here can get back to living a life that doesn't include being raped every day."

The girls whisper among themselves, except for the women in the back with red hair, and the other that doesn't speak.

Luca's eyes are on me, watching as I keep staring at the girl who doesn't speak. His face forms a huge smile until I give him a glare. He comes up to me and sits down in the seat next to me.

"I didn't know you were into models? I mean, you can clearly give her a ride, if you know what I mean," he says with a chuckle.

"Luca, I will kick you out of the plane with a parachute full of holes," I whisper to him, and he pales quickly until he starts laughing.

"Valerio, you're my best friend, and I say this because I love you. You need to get laid, and badly."

I laugh at that and put my head back to relax for the rest of the plane ride. The girls keep talking amongst themselves, and my men keep talking to themselves, so I can't help but feel a little lonely.

Even when I was with her, I felt alone, I guess I wanted her back so one of us could be with our kids, that way I wouldn't have to do it alone. And with my decision not to go looking anymore, I'm a single father.

I hate the fact that I have to do this alone, but I have to come to terms with the fact that she's dead and gone. If I need help, I have my men, and I can always use my mother or Bernadette to keep my children safe at home.

"Valerio," a voice rings out over my own thoughts.

"Yeah?" I tilt my head down to see that Luca is staring at me.

"You have been quiet since you threatened to throw me off the plane, are you sure you're okay?"

"Yeah, I'm fine. How is everyone doing?"

"Well, the women are all fed and have used the bathroom to freshen up...all except that woman who looks like a model. She's barely moved and hasn't said a word since we left."

"I wonder what her story is. I wonder if she has someone looking for her or if she has somewhere she wants to go."

"Well, when she finally talks, you can ask her yourself. Until then, why don't we figure out a plan for everyone else and make sure that these women get taken care of."

"I have a plan. I want you to have the pilot radio ahead and make sure that nobody is at the house just yet, I will let them clean up and then give them whatever plane tickets and cash they need to make it to their next destination. After that, we are done with them, and I just want time to myself because this entire situation has been extremely stressful. I need something to go my way for once."

"Are you sure? I mean, the longer we wait, the less of a chance we have of finding her," Luca replies.

"For right now, I'm sure, and that's all there is to it."

We make one stop to fuel up and then continue on our way. Hours later, one of the pilots pokes his head out of the cockpit and alerts us that we're going to be making our descent soon and that the cars will be waiting to take us to the mansion.

The girls start chattering louder when they hear that we're landing. It appears that their nightmares are finally over, and that's something that I made happen.

*Not bad for a bad guy.*

"Once we all land, I want you all to follow the instructions of my men and get into the cars in an orderly fashion. The cars will bring you up to the main building in which I will have clean clothes and showers ready."

The women mutter in agreement, and they all shuffle in their dirty torn clothes.

"You have my word that my men will not touch you and will leave you alone."

Once the plane lands and all the women are loaded up into cars, we get into a car and head back to my home.

The women take turns using the various showers in my house until everyone is clean and fresh.

The group of girls all gather in the front parlor, each of them asking or demanding to go to their various homes or countries.

"Luca and Luciano, get the details from each person about where they want to go and then arrange travel for each of them to wherever they say they want to go."

"Yes, boss," they both echo.

I turn to the women and clear my throat. Once I have their attention, I scan the group slowly.

"I shouldn't have to say that this is our secret, I did not save you. You have never seen me, nor did anyone from this house ever save any of you. You escaped because they were incompetent, and they ended up meeting their makers due to a fire that broke out. Now, I don't want to hear from any of you ever again. Nor do I want to hear about me being a hero or a savior because if I do, and trust me, I will, I will find you, and you will not be able to say anything again. Do I make myself clear?" I threaten.

The women, now frightened, murmur and nod their heads.

They continue to give Luca and Luciano the information. All except for the woman who hasn't said anything at all. Oh well, let her be quiet. If she doesn't want to leave yet, she can stay in a room here for all I care. Just so long as she stays away from me and my children.

Once everyone is done, we quickly make the arrangements for them all to depart from my personal airstrip, and my plane will drop them off at a random airport nearby. That way they can all be safe and sent on their way.

After I manage to get all of the women out except for the model, who still won't say anything, I have her brought to a room on the main level, where she will be kept until either she wants to talk or I find a place for her.

As I sit down in my family room, I'm quickly bombarded by my children who have decided that it is a perfect time to jump on their father.

"I'm sorry, Mr. Marchioni, I didn't mean to let them get away from me. They were supposed to be in the back room until you were ready to have them come out. They really missed you," Bernadette says, holding my two youngest daughters in her arms.

"It's fine," I assure her.

My oldest child comes up to me at the same time that Luca, Luciano, and Alessio come into the room.

"Are you going to leave and look again?" Vincenzo asks.

"Yeah, are we going to go back out and look for her? I mean, giving up really isn't like you," Luciano comments.

"She's out there somewhere, you have to believe that she's alive. I mean, giving up is not like you, and if you feel like she's not, then you need to just keep trying," Alessio begs.

All of my children quiet down and stare at me, even Valeria, who stares with a sad look.

"Look, I'm sorry, but I don't want to talk about this in front of the kids, and my choice is mine to make. I don't want to make this a major deal, but after six months, there is no way for us to actually find her, so it's time to stop looking."

"If you give up, I will hate you for the rest of my life, and I will make sure that you'll never have a restful day," Vincenzo says angrily.

"Vincenzo, you will understand one day that this is for the best. She will always be your mother, but after six months of searching without a hint of her anywhere, it's time to stop. At some point, you have to give up."

He stomps off, and I feel like my heart is being ripped out. No, he needs to understand that this is for the best, because in this world, hope is something that can easily get you killed. If you keep hoping, people can use that hope against you to manipulate you. They will use it all against you until they either use you up or kill you. That is something that we can't have in our family because every one of our enemies will be out to get us.

"I'll be in my office, I don't want to be bothered so please just leave me be."

I march to my office and slam the door behind me. I pour myself a glass of whisky with a couple of cubes of ice from the refrigerator.

My mind goes back over the past six months to all the places we've been, and the things that we've done.

The first stop was a place in Siberia, the people there were really fucking sick. They were drugging the girls with a hallucinogen to get them to enjoy sex first then breaking their minds. That way, they didn't fight back at all.

We couldn't do anything for the girls because by the time we got there, they were too far gone. We killed the men and sent the women to a rehab facility that would maybe be able to give them some semblance of a normal life someday.

The next stop was in the Ukraine. It was a little shithole run by some fat fucks who thought that they were God's gift to women, and any woman that rejected their advances had to be punished and taught that they were only breeding cows. When we got there, we tortured the men for info but didn't get anything out of them because they were acting alone without the backing of some bigger buyer or group. We left them at the hands of the women because they were all locals. Once the women were done with them, they burned the place down and went home, wishing me luck on the quest to find my wife.

All of this seems like a lot to do to find a woman that I don't even love, but I know that my children love her, and that's enough for me.

The next spot was Bulgaria. It was a government official, which meant that we had to take care not to be caught. But after we were done, that guy will never be able to fuck a woman again. I personally made sure that he was caught with his pants down by his own people and government. They threw him in jail, which last I heard, he killed himself.

I can't keep doing this though. Eventually, I'm either going to get caught or someone is going to come for me while I'm not here, and my kids are going to pay. And I will *not* allow them to be harmed. I need to let it go and focus on the future with my children and my job. Without warning, my door bursts open, and Luca comes in.

"That model woman is still in the spare bedroom, maybe you want to go find out where she wants to go so we can get rid of her?"

"Fine, Luca, I'll handle it."

Making my way to the spare bedroom, I open the door and see her sitting on the edge of the bed. She quickly turns her attention to me, and I feel a sense of déjà vu as I see the same sad expression my wife had in the beginning of our marriage. This woman must have someone she loves or someone who loves her. Her blue eyes study me, and I finally speak.

"I need to know where you want to go. I can take you anywhere in the world. Just tell me what you want."

But once again, all I'm met with is a sad look and silence.

# FOUR

## Her

On the ride back to this mysterious man's mansion, I give a lot of thought about going home. How long exactly has it been? My family...they miss me, but maybe they're fine without me. Maybe I shouldn't.

No. They need me. I have to...even though I don't want to.

Home. The place I'm wanted, yet not wanted.

After we land and get in a car to go to the mansion, I pay extra attention to where we are. The closer we get, my stomach starts to sink. I know where we are.

We stop outside of the gates, and I feel myself shiver when it hits me, I'm looking in the face of death. I can't go home. If he finds out...he'll kill me.

The rest of the girls tell his men where they want to go while I stay completely silent. When the girl with the red hair leaves, I feel a small sense of dread that I'll be completely alone now. She must have noticed my expression because she stops and takes a pen from a table and writes her number on my right hand and squeezes my other one. I commit it to memory so I won't panic when it rubs off.

After they're all gone, I'm brought to a room on the same level, and the door is locked behind me. I take a deep breath and try to relax. He'll only know if I tell him...there's no other way for him to find out.

I sit on the edge of the full-sized bed and take a look at the small room. No windows, but there's a bathroom. It looks like no one's ever lived here, but it's been kept clean. There's no dust, and it doesn't smell stale like most rooms do without people living in them. After glancing back at the door, I make my way to the bathroom and see a crystal clean counter with generic shampoo and conditioner near the small shower. The whole bathroom is white with gray accents, including the cold tile on the floor. But the thing I pay attention to the most is the window. It's only just small enough for me not to crawl out of.

*Damn it.*

I walk dejectedly back to the bedroom and lie on the bed. The sheets feel itchy against my skin, like they're brand new. I sit up when I hear the door unlock and watch as *he* walks in. He looks none too happy that I'm still here.

A look of something passes across his face before he says, "I need to know where you want to go. I can take you anywhere in the world. Just tell me what you want."

I stare at him, into his steel-gray eyes with a hint of blue. They draw me in, and I struggle to get back out. This man. I know it's *him*. How can he have eyes like those and yet be the most dangerous man I can be in the same room with? I've heard the stories of his cruelty, of his family's cruelty.

Finally, I look away. I look at anything else but him.

"Tell me," he insists.

I clench my hands into fists and stare at the floor. After a moment of silence, he sighs.

"If you don't tell me, I'll be forced to tell you who I am. And then, well, things will change. Is that what you really want?" he asks.

I'm never going to be able to go home anyway.

"I'm—" hesitation comes out on his voice.

*Valerio*, I think. *Valerio Marchioni.*

"—Valerio Marchioni," he finishes with resolve.

I knew it. It really is him. I meet his eyes again, and he looks at me as if I'm going to say something. His eyes flash angrily, and I stay rooted in my spot on the bed as he starts pacing back and forth.

Suddenly, he stops in front of me and leans down to my level. He places his finger under my chin and forces my eyes to lock with his.

"This is a dangerous place. I am a dangerous man. Do not stay here. The longer you do, the less likely it is I'll let you go," he angrily states.

My eyes don't waiver, and I stare back into his. After a few moments, he lets go and backs off with a curse.

"I'll be back," he mutters before stomping out and slamming the door behind me.

He doesn't lock it, and I stare at it in confusion before getting lost in my thoughts. He comes back a few minutes later with one of the men who was with him when he rescued us in Russia.

"This is Luciano. He's going to be standing outside your door guarding you, but also making sure you don't try and escape for your own good. Periodically, he will come in and make sure you're okay."

Luciano's face stays neutral as he regards me and nods at his boss in agreement.

Luciano has blue eyes that strangely reminds me a little of Valerio's. His brown hair is on the longer side and stops just above his shoulders. He looks a little more rugged than Valerio with his slight beard and mustache. Under the suit he's wearing, his muscular arms are bulging. I glance away and lie back in bed.

Valerio mutters and curses under his breath before leaving. He won't be back for a while.

With that, I turn on my side, away from Luciano, and wait for him to leave.

"Miss, the maids will bring your dinner in three hours. I'll come in when they do to check on you."

He exits the room and closes the door softly.

I stare at the wall and think about how my life used to be. *I wonder if I'll ever see them again.*

They'll be happier without me.

And then it all starts to pour out, all the pain from being locked away for so long. The ache of not being with my family. The hurt from being taken away. I sob and cry until I'm all cried out and finally fall asleep.

---

"MISS?"

I jolt awake at the voice and find Luciano standing in front of the wall I was facing.

My eyes feel dry from all of the crying, and my nose still feels stuffy. It's probably red.

Luciano speaks in Italian, and a maid comes in with a food tray.

"Miss, we have chicken with rice and vegetables for dinner. Is this okay?" the woman asks with a comforting smile.

I nod, and she sets the tray at the end of the bed.

"I'll come back and get the tray when Luciano calls me back."

She leaves the room in a hurry, and I sit up and take the top off to find a juicy piece of grilled chicken with white rice and green beans and carrots. So much better than the nasty stuff I've been forced to eat these past months. I wish I knew how long it's been. It's cold outside, so it must be sometime during the winter.

Luciano stands in one spot and watches me eat food. I savor the deliciousness of it, and when I'm finally done, I put the lid back on. Eyeing the tray, Luciano strolls to the door and calls for the maid again. He moves away as she comes in, and she smiles in my direction before taking the tray away.

My stomach feels fuller than it has in months, and I was just barely able to finish it. I clutch my stomach.

"Are you okay, Miss?" Luciano asks from his position next to the bed.

I nod, and he turns to leave when I clear my throat and wet my dry lips.

"Lu-Luciano," I stutter.

He turns around with a slightly shocked expression that he tries to hide. "Yes, Miss?"

"What month is it?" I carefully ask.

"February," he replies.

I cover my mouth. Six months. I've been gone for six months. Tears start to well up in my eyes, and I turn away.

"I'll be outside your door," he says quickly and steps out, closing it behind him.

*Just like her.*

I cry what little tears I can from the unfairness of it all and go to the bathroom. Just as I grab a tissue, my stomach rolls, and I rush to the toilet and throw up the contents of my stomach. All that yummy food...gone.

When my stomach is completely empty, I start to dry heave, and the clenching of my stomach makes me clutch my stomach in agony. As soon as I'm done, I flush the toilet and wipe my face with the tissue I came to get. I lie on the cold tile and try to calm down. *Things will get better.*

Before leaving the bathroom, I splash cold water on my face and stare at my reflection. I took a shower earlier, but I still feel dirty and nasty. Maybe I'll take a bath before I go to sleep.

I leave the bathroom and come to a stop when I see someone standing in my room. Hesitantly, I walk out and eye him. It's a boy, no more than seven.

He has an angry expression on his face, and he crosses his arms at seeing me.

"Who are you?" he asks.

This has to be one of Valerio's sons. I shouldn't talk to him.

"I said, who are you? You're in my house, answer me," he insists.

"My name...is Kat," I reply.

Just speaking it out loud makes me feel strange.

He cocks his head at me as a strange look goes over his face. "With a C or a K?"

"With a K," I answer.

He doesn't say a word as something seems to be going through his mind.

"Okay, Kat. Why does my father have you here? No one's ever in this room. He doesn't think I know, but I pay attention. You know I'm going to be the boss one day."

Oh, so this must be his oldest. I stare at him, and for a moment, his look of determination...reminds me...

"I was supposed to go home, but truthfully, I really don't remember anything besides my name," I lie.

He narrows his eyes. "You don't?"

"No."

He seems to accept my answer. "Well, if you don't know, where are you going to go?"

"I don't know," I answer.

He frowns and looks at the door. "You're one of those girls that my dad finds while he's trying to find my mom, right?"

I nod.

He swallows back and looks at me with serious eyes. "Do you think my mom is okay?"

I blink and note his clenched fists. "What's your name?"

"Vincenzo, now please tell me."

"Okay, Vincenzo..." I start and move toward him.

He backs up, but I take another step forward until he's standing right in front of me. I bend down to his level. "Your mom was strong, right?"

He nods and seems to listen closely.

"Then I'm sure she's okay. She's somewhere out there, thinking of you, wishing she was here with you. Someday, you'll see her again, I'm sure of it."

He blinks quickly and puts his arms around my neck. "Thank you, Kat."

Suddenly, the door bursts open, and Vincenzo lets me go immediately. I stand up straight and stare at first Luciano and then Valerio.

"What are you doing here, Vincenzo?" Valerio booms, glaring at him.

"Father, I—" Vincenzo starts.

"I did not give you permission to talk to her. What have I told you about wandering the house? Stay in your designated area!" he yells.

Vincenzo nods quickly and stares at the ground.

"Now, go to your room. Right now," Valerio says, pointing out the open door.

Vincenzo glances back at me and then walks out the door. Valerio slams it behind him.

"Now, Luciano told me you talked to him."

Luciano looks at me with a slightly guilty expression.

"You asked him what month it is. Why?" he asks, although he has to already know the answer.

I bite my lip nervously and talk to him for the first time. "I wanted to know how long I'd been locked away."

His eyes change for a second at the sound of my voice, but then he goes back into questioning mode.

"Oh? And how long has it been?" he asks, studying me to see if I lie most likely.

"Months," I reply, telling a partial truth.

"Okay, and where did they take you away from?" he asks.

I glance at him and then Luciano. "The street."

"The street? In Russia? You don't have a Russian accent," Valerio says.

I gulp. "No. The street here."

His face starts to relax with every question that gets answered. "And what about your name? What's your name?"

He asks the last question with emphasis and so much seriousness that I quake a little bit.

"Kat," I reply.

Valerio's mouth drops a little bit, and he glances at Luciano, who gives him a look.

"Okay, Kat. What's your last name?"

"I...I don't have one."

That answer doesn't satisfy Valerio because his face twists into anger. "Even someone who lives on the street has had a last name at some point. So, what is it?"

If I told him the answer, he'd shoot me dead right now. Or maybe even accuse me of being a spy since he saw me with his oldest son.

"I don't have one," I calmly say.

"You do!" he shouts.

"I don't," I reply.

He glares at me and starts mouthing off in Italian. "Come, Luciano," he says, stalking out of the room.

Luciano follows him, and I hear the click of the lock. That's all of the truth he'll ever be able to get out of me. *Maybe I should go home.*

I slip under the covers and try to get my first restful asleep in the new clothes I was given today. The only face that lingers in my head is Valerio's angry expression. His face follows me into my dreams.

---

The next morning, I wake up to the sound of the door unlocking and flip over to find Valerio standing in the doorway with the key. I rub the sleep out of my eyes, and he clears his throat. "Here's some toothpaste and a toothbrush," he says, pulling it out of a bag from his pocket.

"Thank you," I squeak out, having complete morning voice.

"The maid will bring you a change of clothes, and then you can come and have breakfast with me and my men," he states.

I nod, and he stares at me for longer than he should. I stare back and notice his eyes again, so very gray, but also blue. "I'll let you get ready then," he says with a hint of reluctance.

I nod, and shortly after, the same maid comes running. "Here you go, miss." She hands the shirt and pants to me.

She turns to leave. "Please, call me Kat," I comment before she leaves.

She smiles and pats my hand. "Kat, dear, do you have any food allergies?"

"No, none that I know of."

She brightens. "Great, be ready for bacon, sausage, ham, scrambled eggs, biscuits, hash browns, waffles, pancakes, and French toast."

I get a little teary at that and nod. "Thank you, I will."

She rushes off, and I go right into the bathroom to take a shower. After I get out, I dry myself and brush my teeth. The clothes I put on are almost about my size, so they don't fit too badly, just like the ones from yesterday.

Cautiously, I walk out, even though I know Valerio knows I'm coming. He invited me, I shouldn't be so nervous to leave this room. I walk through a few hallways before I finally come back to the entrance of the house and walk past the double staircase, past the living room area, into the kitchen, where there's a massive table with lots of men seated.

I get a little misty eyed and sit in the only chair left, which happens to be between Valerio and Luciano.

"Bernadette will get you whatever you want," Valerio explains as he shoves a piece of bacon in his mouth.

The maid comes over. "What would you like, dear?"

"Sausage, eggs, and hash browns, please."

She smiles, getting me a plate of food, and sets it down in

front of me. I eat and feel like all eyes are on me, especially Valerio's. Bernadette piled my plate up, and I take my time again, eating. When you're used to slop, it really makes you appreciate real food. Most of his men leave way before I'm done, and I eat a little easier knowing the eyes of strangers aren't on me.

The man he seemed the closest to sticks around and keeps shooting him weird looks. He winks at me.

"Luca," Valerio barks.

"Yes, boss?" Luca asks innocently.

"Stop looking at our guest and get your ass to work," Valerio orders.

"Yes, boss," Luca replies, getting up from his chair promptly and leaving.

"You too, Alessio," Valerio says.

"Yes, sir." Alessio smiles in my direction and leaves.

Now, it's just Valerio and Luciano.

"Have you had enough to eat, Kat?" Valerio asks quietly.

I nod and eat the last bit of hash browns from my plate. "Yes, I'm done."

"Bernadette and the other maids will come and clean up. Let's get you back to your room."

Bernadette gives me a gentle smile as the three of us go back to my room. This time, Luciano stays outside and Valerio comes inside with me.

I sit on my bed, and Valerio stands in front of me. "I appreciate you actually talking to me, and telling me who you are, but I need to tell you again. You shouldn't be here. It's not safe for you, and I'd hate to keep you away from the ones who love you."

My family's faces flash in my mind, and I almost come out with it. I almost say it, but I stop myself. As much as I love my family, I wasn't happy. I want to return and have everything go back to normal, but that also means accepting everything again. I love them...

But I think I also need to find some love for myself, especially after everything I've been through. That's it, then. This is my decision. I'm not going back...ever. Sometime down the line, I'll go back and apologize for being gone for so long. But right now, I need to enjoy my own life. That starts now, leaving here and just enjoying my life.

Finally, I just blurt it out, "I don't have anywhere to go. I don't remember my last name because I lost the memory of my family. I don't know who I am, besides the fact that my name is Kat. I've lived on the streets of New York City for a few years now, and then one day, I was in an alley looking for food and someone put a bag over my head and grabbed me. The next thing I know, I was being trafficked around. A few months ago, I ended up at the house you found me in."

I take a deep breath, and Valerio's face changes, and he seems to be thinking about everything I said. *Please believe it so I can start trying to move on with my life.* He inches close to my face and stares me right in the eyes. Blue-gray eyes to my light crystal blue ones. "I'm sorry that that's happened to you. I will believe you, but if you're lying to me about any of your story, well, you'll never leave here alive. I have to protect my kids and everyone who lives here on this property. For now, you can continue to stay here until you decide where you want to go."

He stares into my eyes a little longer and finally backs up. "It's nice to meet you, Kat."

Valerio smirks. "Cat got your tongue?"

A flush goes up my neck. "It's actually Kat with a K," I tell him, and his eyes widen a little. "Thank you, for allowing me to stay here."

He nods thoughtfully. "I'll see you later at dinner time. Please, tell Luciano if there's anything you need."

I nod, and then he's gone again. As soon as he is, I place my hand at the back of my neck to feel how hot it is.

"I've never felt like that around anybody," I mumble ot myself.

Valerio Marchioni. Something about him is so sincere, but also dangerous, and yet...those eyes of his.

# FIVE

## Valerio

Good, that woman. Something about the way that she looks just draws me to her, and I feel like a moth to a flame. There's something so innocent and good about her. Something that makes me want to know more about her.

Physically, she's stunning. When she came here, she had black hair, but I'm guessing that was a wig because the next thing I know, she has light brown hair that stops just below her shoulders. There's a certain strength about her, that shows that despite what she says she went through, she can take it. If I'm being honest with myself, she's everything I would look for in a woman. If I was going to hook up with someone, it'd be someone like her, but I can never do that. I doubt that I could ever do that sober, I would never want someone to just use me for sex, so why would I ever do that to someone else?

Kat's blue eyes flash in my mind. It's been a while since I've had sex, which is probably why I'm having these thoughts. She might have her own family or someone out there looking for her. But I can't think about her like that. I can't live for myself, and I will never be able to. Not as long as I'm called boss. I will stand by my family.

It's better for me to be alone. Look what happened to the wife I did have. I'd just be in danger of losing someone again anyway. How would my kids even feel if I moved on? My youngest could easily deal with a new mother, but my older children wouldn't be able to. They had more time with her, they're more connected to her. I can't do that to them. I can't and won't do it.

I call out to Luca and tell him to bring my older children into my office so I can speak with them about Kat.

A few short minutes later, Vincenzo, Nicolo, and Vittorio are all gathered in my office in front of me.

"As you all know by now, there is a woman staying with us right now. She is staying in the guest room and under no circumstances are you allowed to talk to her alone. Do I make myself clear?"

I stare right at Vincenzo, who meets my eyes. They all nod back to me, and I dismiss them back to Bernadette.

I rise from my chair and pour myself a drink before sitting back down.

I don't need a woman in my life in order to make myself feel normal, if anything, after the six months that I've spent looking for my wife, it would be a detriment to me. There's more time for me to focus on my job and keep my workers and the other families happy. My kids will never lose anyone else in their lives. The first three months after she was gone, they were all inconsolable, except Vincenzo. Vincenzo was just angry.

*He reminds me so much of myself. By doing this, I will be able to keep everyone safe.*

After downing my drink, I head out to the kitchen and wait for dinner to be ready. The other maids make dinner alone now while Bernadette watches the kids. Once dinner is ready and set on the table, my men and my children sit in their seats. My attention draws me to the end of the table when I notice that *her* chair is back. Someone had to have made a mistake. Bernadette removed *her* chair so no one would have to sit in it months ago. But tonight, there it is. Empty. Kat approaches the table and pulls out the only chair available, *her* chair. I look over at the chair she sat in earlier, only to find no one there. In its place are high chairs for my two youngest. She sits down in the chair that always used to be situated at the very end of the table, right across from me in what was my wife's chair. The table is silent, and I can't help but notice how she fits so perfectly in this picture, and yet, she doesn't belong here at all.

It's been hard seeing her wear clothes similar to my wife's, and now, she's sitting in my wife's seat. Her blue eyes stare into mine, and she smile slightly. So slightly, I want her to smile more. And her name...Kat. I can't help but wonder if it's short for something? If it was...that'd be...

"Valerio?" Luca's voice rings out.

"Yes, Luca?"

"I asked if you wanted us to eat somewhere else instead of eating here."

"Why would I want any of you to leave?"

"Well, you're just sitting there, not touching your food," Luciano replies.

"No, everyone is fine, and I don't want anyone to leave. I

don't want to bother any of you, I just have quite a bit on my mind right now."

"Is it because of my presence? I mean, I can't help but assume I'm in your wife's spot at the table," Kat asks softly.

"It's fine. You are fine. Everything is fine. Now, can we please just get back to dinner?" I ask, glancing at everyone.

Everyone is quiet for a while, and we turn our focus to the plates in front of us.

"I'm tired of this, man. You need to keep going instead of just locking yourself down in your own mind. I understand that this isn't exactly my place, but you need to stop. You need to actually free yourself from this whole thing," Luca says, slamming his fists on the table.

There's a moment of silence, and I sigh as I stuff a piece of potato in my mouth.

I wish everyone would just mind their own fucking business.

"Dad, I can't believe that you're just going to give up on Mom. Are you really thinking about replacing her with Kat?" Vincenzo cries out.

Kat looks at me with wide eyes like a deer caught in the headlights.

I drop my fork onto my plate, causing a clattering sound that makes everyone jump.

"Excuse me, Vin! You have no fucking right to say anything as long as you live under my roof and eat *my* food. I am your father, show some respect. You are going to listen to me! I hate to tell you this, but chances are your mother, *my wife*, is dead. I've looked for her these past six months, and I can't do it anymore. You kids need me here to keep you safe."

Vin goes to argue but stops at the last second.

"I'm sorry, Father, and I'm sorry, Kat. You didn't deserve

what I said because you are a guest and you didn't do anything wrong."

"Thank you, Vincenzo. Now, I want you to finish your dinner and go to bed. I'll be there in a bit to talk to you, alright?"

He holds his head down and solemnly replies, "Alright."

For the rest of the dinner, everyone stays quiet, and Kat won't even look at me. I hope she doesn't feel too uncomfortable around me now. After dinner is finished, my men go to their respective rooms, and Kat leaves before I can apologize for my son's actions. So, I decide to go up to Vin's room and take care of this whole situation once and for all.

Once I get to his room, I notice that the door is closed. I knock softly, and I crack the door open to see Vin sitting on the edge of his bed.

"Dad, is Mom ever going to come back?"

I sigh and sit next to him on the edge. "Vin, I'm not going to lie to you. This talk is going to be from father to son, and it's going to be completely honest. Is that what you want?"

"Yes, Dad, I need to know what's going on. I'm the oldest, and I want to be there for you."

My strong boy.

I put my arm around him and hold him close to me.

"I love you so much, son, but I don't need you to be there for me. I'm supposed to be there for you. I don't know if your mother is ever going to come home, I spent the last six months searching for her all over the world, and yet, I found nothing about her anywhere. It's like she's completely disappeared. Lots of women all over the world disappear like this. If I had found some sort of evidence, then maybe I could keep looking in that direction, but I can't make evidence appear out of thin air."

He nods. "But, I mean, if you don't find her, then what if she's trying to get home? What if she's just scared and lost?"

"Buddy, she was taken. She isn't lost or scared. I've found and rescued many women, and none of them were able to save themselves. Once these men get a hold of them, it's impossible to escape without someone's help from the outside, like what I did."

His lip starts to quiver, and he hides his face in my arm.

"You aren't just going to replace her, are you, Dad? I mean, you aren't just going to get remarried to Kat, are you?"

"No. I'm just trying to figure out a place for her to stay or go, and right now, this is the only place she has. I'm doing what any good person should do, alright?"

"Alright, I miss Mom."

"I miss her too, buddy." Only a half truth, but it's what he needs to hear.

I tuck him into bed and head out into the living room where Luciano is waiting for me.

"What is it, Luciano? It's already been a heavy night. I just want sleep."

"Valerio, I love you like a brother man, and I very rarely try to tell you that what you are doing is stupid. But I have to tell you, keeping her here instead of just forcing her to go somewhere else is kind of stupid."

"She said she has nowhere to go, and it's unlikely that she's a spy or working for a different family or crime syndicate. I just feel that she needs some place that she can stay for a while where she won't be raped or hurt. Also, keep in mind, I don't have to explain myself. She is going to be staying here, and that is it," I spit out at him.

"Valerio, I'm telling you that this could come back to bite you in the ass if you aren't careful about this. You need to make sure that she isn't a relative or something from another family or a Russian one, because if she is, then we are in deep trouble," Luciano says, standing up and straightening his clothes.

I stay silent because he's right. If she's a member of a family or a girl of one of the Russians, then I'm breaking a treaty that is keeping us out of war. I tap my fingers in frustration.

When I get back to my room, all that occupies my mind is wondering if she could actually be from a rival group.

No, I'm not going to think like that. Every single time something happens, Luciano goes off the deep end with the worst possible outcome, and I can't think like that. He can't help it, but I've been the boss long enough to get vibes off of people and know if they have good or bad intentions. I don't feel any bad ones from Kat.

I pull back my sheets and slip out of my daily clothes and into a pair of silk pajama bottoms. After settling down in my empty bed and my bare room, all I can think of is how alone Kat must feel in this huge house where she doesn't know anyone.

How can she feel comfortable here when I barely do? It's empty and cold. It doesn't feel like a home. I sit up quickly in horrible realization that this has never been a home, it's always been cold even when my wife was here. Slamming my hand into my face, I shake my head and tears well up in my eyes. If I'm ever going to have a chance at real happiness, I'm going to make this house my actual home.

I stand up and pace around my bed, struggling to think about how I can make this house feel more open and warmer.

Fucking hell, what am I supposed to do with how dark this house actually makes me feel now?

I slip out of my bedroom and head to the kitchen as

quietly as possible. I make my way to the fridge, and the dark is flashed away by the light of the fridge. I feel the presence of someone else in the room and jump when I realize it's Luca sitting at the counter on a stool, eating out of the container of ice cream.

"Really, Luca? Eating out of the container?"

"I can't help it, man, you know that mint chocolate chip has a control over me that I can't fight against."

I grab a spoon and pull up a chair next to him.

"Valerio, why can't things just go back to normal. We're all fighting each other, and we should be standing together. That way we'll be strong enough to take on anyone. I don't care who they are, we will take out the world if we have to."

At that, I stop my assault on the container of ice cream.

"I don't know if things can ever actually go back to the way they were before," I tell him frankly.

He stares blankly at the ice cream container, and with that, I get off the stool and leave him to it.

I head back to bed and fall asleep thinking about finding out more about Kat.

THE NEXT MORNING, I wake up, determined to find out something about her. After all, I can find out more than she ever could as the Don of the New York Italian Mafia. Maybe if I can find a missing person who fits her description than maybe I can find out her actual name and find her family.

My children are taken to my parent's house, and I'm alone other than my men and Kat.

I eat a quick breakfast and head out the door. My BMW is the vehicle I choose today and head toward a bar that's known to frequent cops on my payroll.

Once there, I sit down at my table and wait for one of the detectives to come over to me and sit down. It doesn't take long seeing as this is a shit bar and there aren't many other people in it.

"What do you need Mr. Marchioni?"

"I need to know if you have missing persons reports for a woman fitting this description," I hand him photos and a brief description of her.

He grabs everything and nods.

"I'll see what I can do, but I'm not sure if I'll be able to find anything."

"Look just do this for me. I know you couldn't find my wife, and I know that you're also having some gambling problems at one of my establishments, so please just do what you are told and don't argue with me. Or else, I might actually get mad," I snap.

The detective looks visibly shaken and gets up quickly. "I'll do what I can right away."

I nod and wave him away. I have a few more people to meet and such a long day to go. A beer or a stiff drink will only cloud my mind for what needs to come. So, while I really want to, I don't stick around. Instead I hop back into my BMW and head off for my next location where I'm meeting a member of Interpol. They know that I'm a crime boss, but this member also knows that I try to keep my streets as clean as possible.

"What? Could it be that you're actually asking *me* for a favor?" Agent Clarkson asks as she sips on what appears to be a frappuccino.

"Look, I need to know if you have any missing persons matching this woman." I hand her the packet that has the pictures and the description of Kat in it.

"Well I'll be honest with you, I'm going to give it a look

but don't expect to hear from me. We can't be seen together ever again. If something does come up, you will find a dead drop location with your information. Otherwise have a good day ,Mr. Marchioni," she says dismissively.

I quickly leave because I'm sure she has a team at the ready to try to arrest me if I linger for too much longer after she already stated her intentions.

I feel her watch me as I make my way back to my BMW parked across the street.

*Well, that's all I can do. I hope that's enough.*

As I'm heading to my next meeting, I get a call from Luciano who I put in charge of one of my biggest clubs to get him out of the house and out of my hair. I had Alessio stay and attend to Kat, I hope that wasn't a mistake. He's a year and a half younger and a little less experienced than the rest of my men.

I answer my phone and put it on speaker.

"What's up Luciano? What's the problem?"

"Yeah soss can you just get down to the club so we can have a little talk about business?"

"Yeah, I'll be right there," I reply and hang up the phone.

I turn the car around and speed over to the club in record time, making sure to avoid any police officers because the last thing that I need is a speeding ticket. Once I arrive at the club, I park in the back and slip through the employees' entrance.

"Hey Boss," Luciano greets me while sipping an ice-cold soda.

"What's this business that we need to talk so desperately about that you dragged me away from my other appointments?"

"Well first I wanted to tell you that I had already put out feelers about Kat and found absolutely nothing. I'm sorry

Valerio, but we can't find out anything more about her until she decides to tell us."

I roll my eyes and glare at him. "That's not club business, and I hate when you do that freaky all-knowing shit. So just tell me about the business."

Luciano smirks. "I just know you, that's all."

"Anything else?" I ask impatiently.

"Okay well we had some merchandise go missing, but it was quickly recovered, and the perpetrators are being punished as we speak. As for the nightclub, we have some new girls including one named Elenore," he says, saying the name with a hint of fascination.

"And...?" I ask and gesture for him to continue.

He clears his throat. "The net income is pretty good, and we should be having no problems in the foreseeable future as long as you keep all the other families happy. There is some dissent that you can't be trusted as you let your wife get kidnapped."

"Find the fuckers who are dissenting and let them know that I'm not to be trifled with, nor am I someone who they can bully around. Teach them a lesson then make sure each family is notified that I will put a bounty of 3 million dollars for the head of whoever attacked us and kidnapped my wife."

With that Luciano leaves and alerts the rest of my men that are nearby to go and take down those dissenters. I get up and look through the ladies and notice that I don't even care how they look anymore. I'm not interested in any of them, even though every other time I would be.

I drive back to my house and decide that I need to take a break from everyone for a while, so I stop by a small sandwich shop on the lower east side. My dad once told me that this place had the best hoagies in the entire city. I make my way in and sit down at the greasy counter. It looked as though cleaning isn't the biggest priority on the owner's list. After ordering and waiting for what feels like an hour, I get my sandwich, and I'm forced to agree with my father. This is the best sandwich I've ever had.

Speaking of my father, I need to go pick up my children from my parents. It's been a day full of business, and I need to spend some time with my kids.

Their house is a mansion but is a little smaller than mine. When I pull into their driveway, Vincenzo opens the door and looks at me. As soon as I get close, he tells me that Grandpa won't stop farting, and it smells awful.

"Well little man, Grandpa has always been like that. Just don't tell him I told you that alright?"

We make our way inside and go straight to the kitchen where my mother is cooking up a storm.

"Hey Ma, what's cooking, because it smells good?"

"Oh Valerio, I didn't hear you come in. Why don't you come over here and taste this sauce? I think it might need just a dash of sugar to lessen the acidity but otherwise I think it's perfect," my mother states as she stirs the sauce.

I make a path through my swarm of children and sample the sauce to find she's right as always. Just a dash of sugar and it'll be perfect.

I leave the kitchen and go into the living room where my father is sitting in his reclining chair. Immediately I'm assaulted by the worst smell I have ever dealt with. Trying not to retch, I make my way through the cloud of toxic gas and plop down into a chair.

"Took you long enough to get here. Now why don't you tell me what the fuck you think you are doing by giving up?" my father asks while flipping the channels on his 80-inch TV.

"Father, I can't keep putting myself and the kids through

this. It's hard enough to know that their mother was kidnapped, but the fact that she's most likely not among the living anymore is something that I don't want the kids to have to think about and the longer this drags on, the more that becomes the stark reality."

"Son you need to know that you have true power at your fingertips. If you don't use it, then you don't deserve to keep it. So, either you do something about it, or I will make sure that you never lead this family ever again do I make myself clear?"

"Father, once and for all, I need you to know that I'm not your lackey anymore. Stop fucking trying to boss me around or else you will feel the entire might of our family do you understand?"

A look of surprise quickly crosses over his face and as soon as it's there it's gone.

"Good boy, I taught you well. Fine if that's what you want, then that's what you get. I will not interfere with you anymore."

My father hands me an envelope with a bunch of different dollar bills, with a few different coins. "This is the allowance from the old family. I want you to put this toward the children's futures."

With that, I say goodbye to my mother and load my children into the van that was left here by Bernadette. I leave my BMW to get later and drive them all home.

Once home, I play a few games with them in their room and put them all to bed. Feeling restless and itching to talk to Kat, I decide to head out to a large bar near my house. I know that I can easily go down there, and nobody is going to fuck with me while I just want to have a drink.

At the bar, I sit down and wait for someone to come over and take my order. A waitress with black hair and freckles by the name of Barb quickly makes her way over and talks to me. Barb has taken my orders the past four times I've been in this bar.

"Hey honey, haven't seen you in a while. What have you been up to?"

"Well I've given up searching for my wife because it's been six months with no trails or evidence of where she went. I don't think I'm ever going to find her, and I feel like at this point in my life, I need to focus on my kids and myself instead of chasing a shadow all over the world without any actually hints as to where she could be."

"I'm sorry to hear that, honey. I mean seriously from the bottom of my heart, I wish you the very best."

"It's okay, I just want to live a life of peace now and maybe someday I will find a new bride, but until that point my kids are going to be the only thing on my mind. So, can you bring me over a rum and Coke, light on the Coke?"

"Yeah no problem, it's on the house, babe."

I down the first one in no time and ask the bartender to keep them coming. I soon notice that a waitress with light-brown, straight hair who has been near the whole time is the only one bringing me drinks now which I don't mind because she's easy on the eyes.

Before I know it, I am hammered and tell everyone nearby that all their drinks are on me and that if they want some food to get that too.

My head starts feeling fuzzy, but the next thing I know, I'm being brought into the back room by the waitress, and she is stripping all of clothes off. Is this real or am I dreaming?

She slaps me lightly in the face. "Hey sugar, you can have me for your new bride if you want. All you have to do is have your way with me. So, come on, have your way with me. I'll never leave you like your wife did, I promise. Just get me out of this shitty bar."

She quickly tears off her panties and hikes up her skirt while I fumble with my pants until I'm able to take my dick out, which leads me to look up at her.

I stumble back and sober up quickly when the waitress suddenly looks exactly like Kat.

"Get the fuck out of here! Now!" I shout as I put my dick away and pull my pants up.

She shrieks and quickly grabs her clothes and bolts, leaving me reeling. I tap my head a few times. Maybe I need to have a talk with Kat...

# SIX

## Kat

It's been a few weeks now since I've been staying with Valerio. I still don't know what to do or where to go. I seem to be stuck in limbo. Every time I think about going somewhere, I always change my mind and never go through with asking Valerio to let me go there.

Maybe it's because I'm scared. I'm scared because I don't know if I'll be okay by myself. If I'll ever truly be able to call a place *home*. That's all I want...

I haven't eaten dinner with Valerio since that night because I don't want his kids to get the wrong idea. The only time I venture into the kitchen is when I know no one but Bernadette is around. She lets me know when it's safe to come out, and I immediately hurry to grab the plates she makes me. There've been times when I'm returning a plate and I'll see him. He only gives me passing glances, but every time, I can't help but admire how good he looks in his suit. All the men around here wear them all the time. There's just something about Valerio that catches my breath every time. Of course, I can't avoid his men who check on me every now and again. However, I've managed to stay completely away from his children. I'm not staying here forever, and I don't intend on taking the place of their mother. The wrongness of that resonates in me deeply. I'd never want...

My stomach abruptly grumbles. God. Bernadette is running late tonight. I wonder what's going on.

I get out of bed and walk to the door. I crack it open and peek out. The hallway is clear. No Valerio on his way to his office. He might not even be here right now. No Bernadette on her way to my room. I hope she's okay. Anyway, it's well past eight, I should be okay to go and get food. I step out of my room and quietly close the door behind me. The house is completely silent, and I stride down the hall on the cold tile. As I'm about to pass the double staircase entryway, I hear the soft cries of a baby.

They stop me in my tracks, and I stay completely still as I wait for them to lessen, for any signal that there's someone who's trying to soothe the baby. And then suddenly, I hear the cries of another baby.

Bernadette must help sometime. I stalk down the hall and hurry to the kitchen area and there's not one soul around. I go all the way back to my room, still hearing the cries of babies and frantically knock on Bernadette's door. My heart starts beating faster when she doesn't come after a few minutes. That's not like her. I probably shouldn't invade her space ... but I turn the knob.

It doesn't open.

*God, what should I do?*

I go back to the stairway and hear the cries continue on,

most likely unheard by anyone else, making me take a deep shaky breath. My hand shakes as I grasp the banister and before I can stop myself, I start to ascend the stairs on the right.

When I get to the second level, I follow the sound of their cries and walk to the hallway on the left. I don't want to get this wrong. I might open the door of one of his other children.

As I get closer, it's easier to tell their door is the second from the end.

I inhale quickly and turn the handle before changing my mind. Gulping, I peek inside to find both babies in their cribs crying.

*Go inside*, I tell myself.

I've already come this far. With one last glance behind me, I step in and close the door. The first crib I approach is the one on the right. I glance up above the crib to find her name. Carina.

Tears immediately well in my eyes, and I tremble as I look down at the beautiful baby girl in her crib. She can't be more than ... six or seven months old. I hold my hands out in front of me and look at them. *Just do it.*

Without another thought, I gently pick Carina up and turn her around to smell her diaper. I don't smell anything, but I better check anyway. I place her on her changing table and open up her diaper, but it's not wet in the slightest. Nope, she doesn't need a change. Crap, I should've gotten a bottle. Suddenly I notice two empty bottles sitting right on top of the table near the door.

Her face is completely red, and she keeps crying. "Hold on Carina," I say setting her back down in her crib.

I walk across the room to the other side and see her twin sister crying in her crib. I don't know her name either, so I look at the wall to find the name Ilaria. "What about you little one, do you need a change?" I pick Ilaria up and take her to the changing table, but find she's completely dry too.

"Do you girls just need some cuddling?" I ask softly.

I keep Ilaria in one arm, holding her to my chest, and then grab a sitting Carina and hold her with my other arm. It's no easy task and my arms start aching with the amount of exertion.

To get them to sleep, I sit in a chair in the corner and start rocking them in my arms. Tears start to fall from my eyes watching both of their little faces as they start to calm down. And then almost at once, they stop and stare at me with bright blue eyes.

Ilaria's pouty face turns into a smile, and she makes a happy sound. Carina just blinks up at me with her big eyes. Her chubby cheeks look so cute, and my emotions get the better of me as I start bawling my eyes out.

They start looking at each other and wanting to play so I place them both back in their cribs. I wait for a little while in the chair, until I'm sure they're asleep.

When I go to leave, I look back once at their cribs and sigh with relief.

Curiosity gets the best of me when I walk out and hear noises coming from the room next door. I peek in to find the occupant of the room on the floor of her bedroom, playing with her toys.

Valerio's oldest daughter who isn't even two yet. She looks at me with a sleepy expression on her face. "Play."

There's no name on the walls of her room, but I already know her name. I remember it because I remember Valerio. "Valeria," I say softly.

She perks up and gets up on her little legs and tries to hand me her toy. "Play."

"I think your Dad would want you to sleep right now."

She frowns a little and pokes her bottom lip out. "Play."

"Valeria, it's sleep time."

She blinks and starts to cry. "Wait, shhhh," I urge.

I pick her up and place her in a larger crib. She must have climbed out because she wanted to play. Valeria cries even harder, and as I pick her back up, the door opens.

I set her down carefully and turn around to a gasp.

"Miss Kat! You must not be in here," Bernadette says.

Sorrowfully, I glance at Valeria who suddenly stops crying. She glances at Bernadette and says, "Berna."

Bernadette smiles sweetly at her. "Valeria, sleep time."

She hastily pulls me out of the room and closes the door behind us. "We must get to the ground level right now."

We leave the girl's hallway and go back to the stairway to go down the left flight of stairs. I gasp in horror when I see Valerio coming up the stairs.

Oh. Shit.

Bernadette's eyes widen as she looks at me nervously. As Valerio gets to the top of the stairs, we stand, unable to move anywhere without being seen. His cool face becomes murderous when he spots us. "Bernadette, what is she doing up here?"

"I- I- I let her come up and..."

"What!" he yells.

"No," I interject. "No, she didn't. I came up on my own. I heard the babies crying and I couldn't help but—"

"I don't care what you thought," he thunders, stalking toward me. "You stay the fuck away from my kids. All of them."

His eyes flash dangerously, and I glance at Bernadette.

"I'll take her downstairs, sir," she states in a precise tone.

She pulls me away and down the stairwell on the right and pulls me into my room.

"What were you thinking, Kat?"

I sit down on my bed and stare down at my hands.

"I'm so sorry, I didn't mean to get you in trouble," I tell her regretfully. "I just couldn't help it."

She takes a few steps toward me and places her hand on my shoulder. I look up at her and her face softens. "It's okay."

"I just ... out of all of the nights I've been here, I've never heard them cry like that. There was no way for me to stop myself."

She nods thoughtfully. "It's my fault. I was outside emptying the trash, and when I saw a bunch of gum stuck on the bottom, I decided to scrape it all out. It took longer than I thought it would. Usually I help them get to sleep before I come to get you so you can get your plate."

"I didn't mean any harm."

"I know you didn't, but Valerio is very protective. Even more so over his princesses. Valeria was his one and only princess until Carina and Ilaria came into this world."

She sits next to me. "Their mother delivered them on the day she was taken."

My heart tumbles all the way to my stomach. On that day...

Despair rises in me. It builds and builds, and I cover my hand with my mouth to keep it from spilling out, but I can't stop it.

I let out an earth-shattering sob and Bernadette puts her around me. "Kat, why are you crying honey?"

I shake my head. I can't say it.

"Nothing," I murmur.

"It's obviously something if you're crying this hard," Bernadette softly replies, rubbing my back.

"It's nothing."

She looks at me with sadness in her eyes. "I know you'll tell me when you're ready." She pats my hand.

"Let's go to the kitchen so we can get you something to eat."

We walk to the kitchen and when we get there, she pulls a plate out for me from the heating tray and places it in front of me at the table. A quiche this time. I'm too hungry to take it back to my room so I eat it right away. I take a bite out of it and taste the flavors of ham and cheese. Mmm, it's so good.

I'm almost done when a certain angry person walks in. He leans up against a counter in the kitchen near the doorway and stares me down. I don't meet his gaze, but it completely makes me lose my appetite. I push the plate away, getting up from the table and begin to walk out of the room. I'm determined to get past him, and just as I'm about to, he grabs my arm and pulls me up close to him. A spark of electricity shoots up my arm. He leans down and pushes his face right against mine. Feeling uncomfortably close to him, I try to wrench my arm away, but he keeps it locked tightly in his hand. "Tell me exactly what happened."

I shrink back. "Ask Bernadette."

Turning around, I found Bernadette is nowhere to be found. She must be in the pantry.

"Kat." The sound of my name on his tongue makes me shake nervously. He seems to notice as he lets go of my arm. "Come, let's go your room."

He gestures for me to lead the way, and I walk ahead of him. I swear I hear him make a noise behind me but ignore it as we make our way into my room.

I sit on my bed and he stands in front of me with his arms crossed. "Tell me exactly what happened."

His look of determination tells me he won't stop until I

tell him. "I went to get my food for the night, and I heard the sound of your children crying. I waited to see if someone would go comfort them, but no one came. So, I went up to see what they needed, and when I got there, they only wanted someone to put them to sleep, and I did exactly that. Well, I didn't exactly get to finish with Valeria."

He grunts. "Valeria is a little spoiled. Please don't feel compelled to help me out in any way with them. I have others who can help, and I myself try to do it when I can."

I nod soundlessly and clasp my hands together anxiously. He stares at me with a weird expression on his face, and his eyes quickly bounce down to the rest of my face before locking on my eyes again. He shoves his hands into his pockets and leaves my room.

I'll never do that again. I just have to force myself not to, if something like this were to ever happen a second time...

---

The next night, I get the usual knock on my door and expect to see Bernadette, only to find Valerio.

"You can eat in a second, but first I want you to come with me."

I hesitate, but I can tell by his eyes that I'm not in trouble. To my utter shock and surprise, he leads me to the stairs, and I follow him up to the left hall where we enter the room on the end, Valeria's room.

She's already in her larger crib and when we walk up to her, I see her thumb in her mouth.

"Dada."

I watch Valerio's face change from his neutral expression

to a genuine smile. The very first I've seen from him. It looks weird on him for a moment, until I really start to see him. His eyes seem to brighten the longer he looks at Valeria. "Valeria, it's sleep time."

"No sleeeeep Dada. Play, play!"

He rubs his hand through her hair. "No play. Valeria, this is Kat."

I gasp and glance at him, but the same look of happiness decorates his face.

She stares at me and reaches her hand out.

"May I?" I ask Valerio quietly.

He's silent for a moment. "Sure."

I allow her to touch my hand, and she grasps it. She giggles and I start to pull my hand away.

"Now, it's sleep time, Valeria." She pulls her thumb out of her mouth and pouts, but he hands her a teddy bear from the corner of her crib.

She grabs it and holds it tightly to her. "Teddy."

"Yes, Teddy. I love you, Valeria. Sleep well."

She closes her eyes while holding the Teddy and her sleeping face makes my heart skip a beat.

Valerio gestures for us to leave and we walk out. He opens the door immediately next door after closing Valeria's.

We walk in to find Carina and Ilaria already fast asleep. We exit the room and walk outside the left hall to the stairway.

I keep my eyes turned away from his, until he says my name in the gentlest tone I've ever heard. "Kat. Thank you for meeting my girls. I know I yelled at you yesterday about it, and I apologize. You didn't do anything wrong."

I nod. "I love kids. Especially babies."

"I realize that now." He runs his hand through his hair.

"If that's all, I'm going to go back to my room until Bernadette tells me my plate is ready," I tell him softly.

A stormy look passes over his face, and I start to go down the stairs.

"Kat," he whispers, but I still hear it.

I turn back toward him. He stomps down the few stairs I went down toward me and backs me up into the wall. I awkwardly stand with one foot on one stair and the other on the one above it. He puts both of his hands on either side of my face on the wall and places his face inches away from mine. "You have the most beautiful eyes I've ever seen in my life. They haunt me every night, and I don't know why."

I gulp and stare right into his bluish-gray ones. His eyes move down to my lips and stay there long enough for me to definitely know he's staring at them.

"I don't know what I'm going to do," he murmurs. "I want to kiss you more than anything right now."

I gasp inwardly and watch as his face gets inevitably closer to where his lips gently ghost over mine. His scent invades my nostrils, and I can't help but breathe it in. His spice mixed with the sweat of a day's work. His eyes hold mine as his mouth finally moves the half inch keeping our lips apart. He presses a soft kiss into my lips and my face completely heats up. My heart bursts, and he moves his lips over mine a few times, like he's searching and hoping for a response. I finally give it to him when I can't stand it any longer and kiss him with everything in me. He pulls back suddenly and stares at me with wide and...anxious eyes. He backs away completely, pushing himself off the wall and doesn't give me another glance as he heads down the stairs taking them two by two.

I rub my fingers over my lips and close my eyes, still

feeling his lips against mine. I've never felt that kind of fire before. *His* fire. I inhale the air, and I can still smell him.

I place my hand over my fast-beating heart and continue down the stairs to my room. A minute after I get inside, I hear a knock at my door. This time when I open it, I find Bernadette.

"Kat, I have your plate ready."

"Please, bring it to my room," I tell her quietly.

She nods but looks concerned.

A minute later, she comes back with the plate and fork. "I'll come back for your plate tomorrow."

She shoots me a worried look, but she doesn't say anything and closes the door. I'm not annoyed with her or even angry. I'm nervous and confused, and it has nothing to do with her. It's about *him*.

Valerio...

What are you thinking? What am I thinking? What are we *doing*?

# SEVEN

## Valerio

I can't believe I actually kissed her. What the hell was I thinking? I can't get involved with her. Not now, not ever. But her eyes are with me every night when I close my own, and she invades my dreams. No woman has ever affected me this much before, yet I can't bring myself to go any further than what I just did. I don't feel that guilty for doing it either since I've wanted to be with her since the moment I saw her eyes. Something in them called out to me like a siren's song. As much as it shouldn't have happened, I don't regret it either. It wasn't a long kiss, but it was more explosive and fiercer than any kiss I've ever had in the past, from both my wife and ex-girlfriend. If I were to have one last wish on my deathbed, it would be to experience that kiss once again. I wanted to make it last, but while I was doing it, the sheer look of shock in her eyes made me panic. She looked like she was into it, but at the same time, there was a hesitation that made me pull away.

I could feel that same hesitation in myself. While it's not guilt, I'm afraid that if I get too close to her, I am going to lose her as well. She's only just come into my life, and she's already bonding with my children. I really didn't expect that to happen. I don't think I can just throw that away now.

She has this peace inside her that I feel like I've been looking for for my entire life. It's like a white-hot flame has washed over me and has burned away all the weakness that came before. This white-hot flame formed a tornado around us and it's not going to be easy to escape from without something going wrong or one of us getting hurt or worse. She deserves better than any life I can give her. This life will always be dangerous to those that I love and care about. She doesn't deserve to be stuck with someone who can't provide her with the basic level of care and safety that she needs. Just look what has already happened to *her*. Anything can happen.

At a time like this, the only thing I can turn to to end the incessant noise in my head is alcohol. I walk down the hall and straight to my office. I can be alone and not have to deal with a crazy waitress who wants me to knock her up. I don't have to deal with hundreds of different people who tell me how sorry they are for my loss.

All I need to do is move on. Act like nothing happened. That's probably what she expects from me. She'll believe me and then will act like nothing happened herself. This way everyone wins in the end and nobody gets hurt, though my heart wildly tells me otherwise.

As I'm sitting in my chair, nursing a cold beer, the building goes into lockdown mode and from the monitors on my wall, I can see Luciano at the front gate with a man in a black hood. Luciano buzzes up and says five words that change my stance on whether I should give up on my wife or not.

"I've got one of them."

That's it. We can finally find out not only how they did it, but who the hell has been behind it the entire time.

I watch from my desk as Luciano and my men bring him inside the house and down to the basement.

I shudder with anticipation because I now know I'll be able to take out my frustrations on this man. Now I have everything I need.

Slamming my can of beer down onto my desk, I force myself up and crack my neck slowly. This is going to be a long night. If Luciano brought him back here instead of just bringing back the info, then this man needs to have it extracted from him by any means necessary.

Before I make my way down to the basement, I make sure that Bernadette has the kids under control and make sure they stay up on the second level no matter what. Once I am sure of that, I pass by Kat's room where she still has the door closed then finally make my way to the basement.

As soon as I'm down the stairs, I close and lock the basement door behind me.

"Luciano, you said you found one of the guys who was involved with the kidnapping of my wife?" I say, my voice shaking with excitement.

With a smile Luciano replies, "Yeah boss, I found one of the fuckers who took her. He was bragging about it at a bar on the other side of town. Just so happened that we had one of our boys there who overheard it. He brought him out into the back alley and beat the hell out of him. Then he called me to come pick them both up."

I turn to look at the man and see that his left eye is

swollen, and he's covered in bruises and cuts. He couldn't be much older than twenty-one, and yet he is covered in gang tattoos, though I can't tell where they were from or what language they were in.

As I lean in to get a better look at his tattoos, he tries to spit in my face. When he goes to spit, one of my men grabs his face and squeezes to prevent him from spitting.

"So, you thought you could just spit on me and get away with it? I mean why not, right? You already came in here, assaulted my mother, and stole my wife, right?" I snarl into his face.

"Look man, I was just a driver. I didn't know who she was. I didn't know it was you we was targeting," the gang member begs.

"What's your name?"

"Frankie."

"Well Frankie, you're going to tell us everything we want to know, and you're going to tell us without any problems, alright?"

"Look man, I already told you I was just a driver," Frankie whines.

"I don't believe you. My man heard you bragging about kidnapping my wife, so you obviously knew who you were fucking with. Now I'm going to ask one more time, what do you know?"

I motion for Luciano to bring out the tools to begin the torture.

"I don't know nuffin'."

"Alright then. My friends here are going to talk to you for a little while about some power tools while I go get a drink."

Luciano brings out a power drill and gives it a few test squeezes. When he brings it close to Frankie's head, Frankie lets out a small whimper.

"Last chance to actually give us an answer," Luciano states.

Frankie starts to whimper, and I turn around and head into the back room where I pour myself a glass of whiskey with two ice cubes.

When the screams die down just a little, I head back in and watch as Luciano shoves the drill into Frankie's foot. He shoves the drill in and out as Frankie continues to scream, flesh and muscle being torn away and he can do nothing but scream his lungs out.

"Have anything you want to say now?" I ask, motioning for Luciano to stop drilling.

Letting Frankie catch his breath, he pants and looks up at me with an angry face.

"I ain't tellin' you shit, man."

"Okay." I dump some of the whiskey from my cup into the hole in his foot.

Frankie screams again as the whiskey burns inside the wound.

"So how about now, Frankie?"

Frankie spits onto the ground.

"Well, I'm going to continue more of this until you give me all the information I want," I say while motioning for Luciano to start again. I head upstairs and decide that I'll go to bed while they handle the questioning of Frankie.

Once upstairs in my bedroom, I get out of my suit and change into a pair of silk pajama bottoms. After getting dressed, I decide to go and check on my children. They're all sleeping soundly. Seeing them all asleep while one of the men who kidnapped their mother is downstairs fills me full of a rage that I can't even begin to describe.

SOON IT'S the third night that we have Frankie, and we're still getting nowhere with him so it's time to go big.

I make my way down to the basement and pull out a large bottle of lemon juice as well as a large container of smelling salts.

"Well Frankie, regardless of what you wanted out of life, you never should have crossed me and mine. Tonight, will be your last night on earth. There is no way out, and there is no escaping your fate," I growl out at him.

Luciano and my men transfer him from a chair to a table with leather straps.

Once he is strapped onto the table, I have a few of my men take scalpels to his legs and slowly peel the skin away from his leg. We continue until he passes out, and when he does, I use a container of smelling salts to wake him up.

"You aren't getting out of this that easily, Frankie. We are going to keep going until we have taken everything from you, now what do you know about the kidnapping of my wife?" I yell at him.

"Okay! All I was told was it was going to weaken you. If you're still searching for her, it looks like it's working."

"And who did this? Was it the Russians? The Cartel? Where is she now?"

"I ain't gonna say, so you might as well just kill me!" Frankie screams.

Wow, this fucker really doesn't want to give up the info I need.

I open the bottle of lemon juice and dump it all over his leg wounds. He screams so loudly it echoes throughout the room.

Once the bottle is empty, I pull out my .45 ACP and put a bullet into his head.

After putting my pistol back into its holster, I adjust my

tie and tell my men to dispose of his body. When I turn around, I see the door open and Kat at the end of the stairs.

At the same time that I see her, Luca does as well. He marches over to her and grabs her arm. With one last look back toward me, he leads her back upstairs. I follow them to eavesdrop and make sure that Luca doesn't say anything stupid, but also so I can find out what Kat is thinking after seeing this side of me.

"What the hell were you thinking Kat?" Luca asks.

"I was curious as to why everyone had been going into the basement for the past three days," Kat replies. "I didn't mean to see anything I wasn't supposed to. I just kept hearing noises from downstairs."

"Kat, I can understand a lot, but I can't understand how you're okay since you just saw someone get killed in front of you. I mean that's some pretty messed up shit for someone who isn't used to it."

"Can I ask you to keep a secret? I don't think even death can scare me more than those months with the sex traffickers. I was pretty sure I was going to die there so I made peace with that fact."

"I'm sorry you had to go through that, I can't imagine how hard it must have been to think that no matter what happens, you were probably going to die," Luca says quietly.

"It's okay. This is why I asked you to keep it a secret. Valerio shouldn't worry about me seeing that and developing PTSD or something," she replies without a hint of fright in her voice.

"Sure, yeah. You know...I've never seen Valerio take to someone as quickly as you. He doesn't like people near his kids, and yet he let you close to his princesses. That's a big accomplishment," Luca chuckles. "Well I'm going to go back down. I'm sure that Valerio is going to be up here soon, and I don't want to be here for that."

"Thank you, Luca."

I wait in my hiding spot and watch as Luca leaves her room. After he is gone, I wait for a few minutes and knock on her closed door.

"Come in," Kat calls out to me.

I open the door, seething with rage over the fact that she could just come and interfere with what I was trying to do.

I enter her room and as angry as I am, I can't bring myself to flat out scream at her.

"I can't have you coming down and getting into my business. That's very dangerous. I don't want you getting involved when you could easily be brought into this world. You don't deserve to have to deal with any of this. I can't keep rambling like this, but what I'm trying to say is I don't want you to have to deal with a problem that has nothing to do with you."

"I understand, Valerio, I didn't mean to get involved. Like I told Luca, I just heard everyone going downstairs, and I wondered what was going on."

"You need to be more careful around here. Things like this could get you killed, which is something that I'd rather not have happen."

"I'd rather not have that happen either," Kat says with a giggle.

"Wait did you just crack a joke while I'm trying to be serious here?"

"I'm sorry," she says, all laughter out of her voice.

"No, it's fine, it's just that I've never had anyone other than Luca try to crack a joke with me while I'm being serious."

I try to choke back a laugh, because I can't understand

how someone who has been so quiet and so meek at times could crack a joke while I am trying to be serious and angry.

"Things are different with you here. What you saw tonight can happen at any point, and that wasn't even the worst of it."

She nods and hesitantly asks, "Valerio, did he give you any information about your wife? Do you know anything about her whereabouts?"

"No, he didn't give me any information. I meant what I said when I told everyone I gave up on looking, it just so happens that he was in the wrong place at the wrong time. I thought I'd give it a try one more time, but I'm done."

"Are you sure, shouldn't you be still trying to get her back?"

"After this long, the odds are that she's either dead or too far gone for me. But you...I can still give you money to go wherever you want to go, but please take all the time you want to think about it. I'm not rushing you."

I widen my eyes at the words coming out of my mouth.

"I understand what you are going through, at some point during my capture I just gave up on the fact that I was ever going to be free again."

"Okay. Again, just stay out of the basement."

"Okay," she responds.

I leave her room and head back up to my own room where I get changed and ready for bed.

Of course, she knows exactly how I feel. She went through the same exact thing that I'm going through, just from the other side. She must have gone through a lot just to survive.

I better get to sleep. Tomorrow is Sunday, and while normally that means absolutely nothing to me, I think tomorrow I'll actually go to church and confess for the first time.

---

I LEAVE EARLY in the morning to beat the rush and make it to the little church that my mother took me to when I was a kid. She brought me here because unlike my father and grandfather, she wanted to make sure that I had some form of conscience. I don't want to have to worry anyone, and I don't know what to do anymore.

I'm haunted day and night by her face and when I should have been able to snap at her and blow up, it felt like all that rage left as soon as I was trying to take it out on her. It hurt to think of what I was trying to put her through, and all I could think about was how she had already been through enough.

She has made her way into my life, and I don't even know if she'll stay. *I don't think I want her to go.* She's someone I want to keep safe and sound, yet I also want to keep her with me.

I stay in the back and watch as the pastor commences his sermon. He continues to preach and the more I listen, the worse I feel. *It's not cheating, it's not.* She is dead or worse, and there is nothing I can do about it. So why do I feel so bad about this whole thing? Maybe it's not because I have a family, maybe it's because she might have one looking for her somewhere. I sit and wait patiently until the sermon is over. Once it is, I make my way over to the confession booths and sit in one.

Eventually I hear the little door slide open.

"Forgive me Father, for I have sinned."

"What is your sin my child?"

"I have kissed another while I have a wife, but my wife has been missing for seven months and is presumed dead. I don't know if it's enough time to move on or if I should even move on."

"Well, it sounds like you are having a conflict of conscience. You want to remain faithful to your wife, but you don't know if you even have a wife anymore. Is that about it?"

"Yes, Father."

"Well, has she been marked as dead as in a death certificate that has been printed?"

"Yes Father, no government agencies were able to find anything about her whereabouts."

"Did you love your wife?"

"It's not that I didn't love my wife, it's that we were sort of forced to be together, and I don't even know if she loved me."

"Is that so my child?"

"Yeah, we have children who I love more than anything, but I can't bring myself to keep fighting. I feel so guilty."

"Well my child, I think you are being too hard on yourself. I want you to relax and think about what it is that you want to do. Now because this is your first time in a long time that I've seen you Mr. Marchioni, I want you to give me three "Hail Mary's" and feel forgiven for your kiss."

I almost choke on my own saliva at that. "How did you know who I was, Father?"

"I know your mother and she has been very good to this church, and she has shown your photos constantly because she is proud of who you grew up to be and this meeting has just proven her point even more."

Of course, my mother has been keeping these people up to date with me. My mother is way too proud of me, and she's always showing off the fact that I'm a good Catholic boy.

"Thank you, Father. I will forgive myself for the kiss and I want you to know that I'm going to start coming every Sunday."

"There is no need, but I appreciate the fact that you would want to come to church to be closer to God and closer to your community."

"Anything for the community, Father."

Leaving the church, I decide to go home.

Arriving back at my house, I open the door and I'm greeted with a sight that I have only seen once before, which was at my wedding.

Standing in my foyer is my two uncles, Domenico and Oliverio. But even more surprising is that next to them is my aunt, Evelina. Both of my uncles are dressed in suits and my aunt has a short light-yellow day dress on. Her hair is in a bun, and she looks exactly the same as she did over six years ago.

"Valerio, how come no one told us?" Uncle Domenico asks as he approaches me with a concerned look.

"Yeah, you know we would've come right away if you had told us," Uncle Oliverio says with a frown.

"I don't even know what's going on, these two just told me I had to come...despite my wanting to stay away," Aunt Evelina says glaring at them.

"Well, since you're all here I'll just say it. My wife was kidnapped from here six months ago, and no matter where I searched, I couldn't find her anywhere."

Everyone is silent until Uncle Domenico starts swearing in Italian.

"What the fuck are you going to do about it then? Do you know who fucking did it? Once we find those fuckers, we will make them fucking pay," Aunt Evelina swears, clenching her fist.

"Look, I've stopped looking. After six months of searching, I wasn't been able to find any information about it besides the fact that they did it to weaken me. This little punk was bragging about it at a bar, and he wouldn't tell me the gangs name, nor if they still had her or not."

"Those sons of bitches, I'm going to fucking *maim them* once we find out whose gang this is. I'm going to make them scream for their fucking mothers and once I'm done, they will know the wrath of the Marchioni family," Aunt Evelina swears again as she paces around the foyer.

"Evelina you need to calm down. Valerio, you said that you had no leads?" Uncle Oliverio asks.

"I've hit multiple sex trafficking rings and taken them all down. I've had multiple government agencies work to find out where she is and yet nothing has come up at all."

"Then the only thing we can do is keep our own feelers out there to see if we can find some sort of information," Oliverio says.

"I don't know if I can keep putting my kids through all this. I don't know if *I* can keep going through all of this. I burned myself out and let the other families start talking about how I couldn't keep my own wife and mother safe."

"Speaking of your mother, I'm surprised *they* didn't come here to try and help figure out who did that to her," Domenico murmurs.

"My mother talked them out of it," I assure them.

I shake my head and think about all I've had to go through in the past six months, and I just can't think about going back to searching place after place.

"You don't have to do anything anymore. Let your family

TIFFANY RANSIER

take care of this now while you continue to hold down the fort," Domenico declares.

"This isn't your fault, Valerio. There isn't a place in this world where we won't be able to find her for you. I promise, we all promise to find her for you," Oliverio says.

"I don't know if I want to find her. It was arranged by my father, and it wasn't a marriage of love but one of ease. It was easy for me to marry her for duty instead of being with someone I love and care about."

"So, you are saying that you don't even want us to attempt to look for your wife? That's a little suspicious if you ask me. Why would you not want us to try? Unless...you found someone else," Evelina ponders.

"Maybe I did find someone who I care for, but that's my business and that's only my business. If you can find her, good we can get her back safely, but if not it's alright. I just want things to be semi-normal for my children, and I need to get on with my life."

My uncles and aunt nod their heads. and they all hug me. Before my aunt leaves, she whispers in my ear, "Love will always win over duty, never forget that."

# EIGHT

## Kat

In my room, I'm just getting out of the shower and putting more borrowed clothes on when I hear loud voices. Voices that I haven't heard before here. His main three guys, Luca, Luciano, and Alessio, are the only voices I can recognize right away. The rest of his men always talk quietly to him.

But right now, all I hear is him yelling.

Oh well, it's none of my business. I put the clothes on and turn the radio on. Valerio gave it to me, so I don't have to just sit in my room in my own thoughts all day. I don't exactly feel comfortable going outside in his backyard yet. What I wish he'd have given me is a good book to read.

I sit on the floor and become entranced with the music on one of my favorite stations. Sometime later, my stomach starts protesting, and I know it's almost time to eat dinner.

A sharp knock on the door makes me sit up. "Come in," I say as I turn the radio off.

I expect to see Bernadette with my plate, instead I'm surprised to see it's Valerio. The look on his face is more serious than usual. He closes the door behind him.

"Is something wrong?" I ask carefully, hoping I'm not upsetting him by asking.

He shakes his head. "No. I know you don't really venture out of your room a lot. I had planned to tell you that you can go out of your room more. Go outside to the back and walk around the property, but I hate to have to tell you now, but please stay in your room during the day. If you wish to come out at night, ask Bernadette and she'll know whether you can."

I shrink back nervously. "Why?"

He eyes me and indecision flits across his face. "I have visitors, and I don't want them to see you just yet. I have no idea when they'll be leaving. Either one of them could tell my father that you're here, and I can't have that."

He frowns and runs his hand through his hair. "I had no idea they'd come, I'm...sorry. I don't want you to think I'm trying to cage you. I'm not."

I look down at the floor and then stand up. His eyes lock with mine, and I take a few steps in his direction. "I know, Valerio. I'll stay here, don't worry."

His shoulders seem to sag in relief, and he opens his mouth to reply. Whatever he was going to say is interrupted by a small knock. Valerio turns toward the door and opens it. First a little, and then all the way.

"Your dinner is here. I'll see you later."

Bernadette walks in and Valerio walks out. "I hope I didn't interrupt anything."

I shake my head and stare at her. For the first time, I really look at her.

She's slightly taller than I am, and she isn't that old. Probably around the same age as my own parents, early forties. But the thing I never really noticed before is she has sad, blue eyes, the color of the rolling ocean waves when there's a storm.

"You didn't interrupt anything, Bernadette. Thank you so much for helping me."

She smiles at me all the same, and it masks the sadness in her eyes a little. "Happy to help, honey. I'll be back for your plate later, as usual."

I need to really talk to her one day. She leaves me to the yummy food that I devour all too quickly.

After I'm done eating, I go back to listening to the radio. With the combination of a full stomach and the sounds of the sweet music, my eyes start feeling heavy, and I feel compelled to get in bed and go to sleep. I didn't sleep very well last night, but not because I saw him kill that kid, but because for some reason, I've been thinking about the cages again. I lie with my back to the floor and close my eyes. Just a little nap . . .

*Alone in the room with him. He watches me with dark, shining eyes.*

*"I'm going to enjoy you a little bit while you're here."*

*I close my eyes and start hyperventilating when I hear the obvious lowering of a zipper.*

*He groans and I feel his grubby eyes on me, on my dirty, naked body. Tears make a path down the dirt on my face, and I cover my body the best I can with my hands.*

*"Now don't do that, beautiful," he purrs, and I hear the sound of him getting off of his bed.*

*No, please don't. With quivering hands, I lower my arms and move them to my sides.*

*I hear the creaking of the bed as he gets back on it.* "Ah, that's right." *He moans as he touches himself again and I shudder.*

*I'll never be free again. Let me go. Let me out. Please.*

"Kat, Kat."

I jump out of my skin and pop my eyes open.

Bernadette is staring down at me with her hand on my arm. "I'm sorry to wake you. You were moving around, and it seemed like you were having a nightmare."

Tears well up in my eyes, and I take a deep breath in and out. "It's alright, thank you Bernadette. I was having a nightmare, but they don't come very often."

She rubs my arm in a comforting way for a minute and then reaches for my tray. "Is there anything I can get you? A cup of tea?"

I shake my head and sit up to hug my legs under me. "Thank you, Bernadette, but I'll be okay."

"If you need me, I'm right next door," she reminds me.

Footsteps interrupt me before I can say anything else. I look behind Bernadette to find Valerio. He looks from Bernadette to me. "Did I hear something about a nightmare?"

"Yes, but I'm okay now," I state, hoping this will be the end of talking about it.

*The sooner I forget about it the better.*

Bernadette nods at Valerio and with a wave, she exits the room, closing the door behind her this time.

Valerio holds his hand down for me to take. I allow him to help me up, and he puts his arm around me and holds the front of my body to him. He leans down and whispers in my ear, "I wish I was the one to wake you up and chase that nightmare away."

I gasp and my stomach flutters. *Why?*

He lets me go and backs off. His bluish-gray eyes stare into my icy crystal ones. They start to draw me in, and I uncontrollably move in his direction.

A knock breaks through the connection and Valerio's eyes flash angrily for a second. "Come in."

The door opens slightly, enough for Bernadette to stick her head in. "Sorry to interrupt sir, but Valeria is out of her bed again. I just saw her climb out on her monitor. Would you like me to try and put her to sleep again?"

Valerio chuckles. "My stubborn little princess. I'll put her to sleep, don't worry. Thank you, Bernadette."

She smiles and shuts the door.

He turns to leave but stops and turns back to me. "Would you like...to help me?"

He nervously smiles and shifts on his feet. My heart swells and my breath catches. How could I say no? "Of course."

He opens the door and walks out. I follow closely behind him, and we go up the stairs and head straight for Valeria's room. Just like Bernadette told us, she's in the center of her room, playing with one of her stuffed animals. Valeria looks up at Valerio immediately. "Dada. Play?"

He laughs. "Sweetheart, it's time for bed. Didn't Berna put you here?" he asks, placing his hand on her bed.

She pokes her lip out. "Want to play. Play."

He steps over to her and leans down to pick her up. He holds her ever so gently in his arms. "I love you Valeria, but it's time for bed. There's plenty of time to play tomorrow. You know Berna, Anna, and Rosa will play with you tomorrow in the playroom."

Her eyes blink. "No. Want Dada, play."

My eyes well up with tears and Valerio shifts his eyes

away from her to look at me. I can see the guilt leaking from them.

"Daddy will play with you tomorrow princess..."

I smile as she puts her tiny arms around his neck.

"...and so will Kat."

"Kat?" she says, pulling back and looking at me.

"Hi, Valeria," I say softly.

She stares at me and Valerio looks back and forth between us. "Well that's enough for tonight, let's get you in your bed."

He sets her down inside, and she immediately stands up. "Now come on Valeria, you need to sleep."

Her eyes start filling up with tears and she cries. "I don't want to, Dada."

"If you don't go to sleep, how will we play tomorrow?" he asks with a smile.

She blinks and a smile forms on her cute, chubby face. "Okay sleep."

She sits back on her butt and puts her thumb in her mouth. We both stand by her bed and watch as she sucks her thumb.

"Night, night, Valeria," he says softly.

She looks at me. "Good night."

Her blue eyes light up and she pops her thumb out of her mouth. "Kat...mama."

I cover my mouth and turn toward Valerio nervously. His eyes are wide and frantically looking from her to me. "No, Valeria."

"But...mama..." she says and reaches her smaller arms out for me. My stomach clenches and bile rises up in my throat.

I shouldn't have come.

"Your mama isn't here," Valerio says, his mouth forming a thin line.

Her mouth quakes and she stands up. "Mama, I want Mama."

She moves back into a sitting position and stands up. I move back as she tries to reach for me. When she isn't able to touch me, she starts sobbing.

Valerio turns away from both of us, and I don't have to see his face to know this is killing him. So to stop her crying I move forward and pick her up out of her crib. I put my arms around her and feel her wet tears on my shirt. Right away she quiets down and hiccups. "Mama."

"Shhhhh, okay Valeria."

Valerio doesn't turn around once. After rubbing her back for a while and I'm sure she's fully calm, I place her back in her bed. She lies down without complaint, and I put her blankie around her. Her eyes drift closed, and I place my hand on Valerio's shoulder.

He doesn't meet my eyes. Instead, he walks directly out, and I follow behind, closing the door.

He stays silent the entire way down the stairs until we get inside my room.

"I'm sorry," he whispers with a catch in his voice, still avoiding my eyes.

"Don't be. She was young when her mother was kidnapped, but she still remembers and misses her. It's...okay," I say and hide my right hand behind my body as it clenches into a fist.

He finally turns toward me, and his eyes are stormy, filled with sadness and anger.

My eyes fill with tears and one of them leaks out. "Hey, it's okay," Valerio says, and steps closer. He reaches a hand out and wipes the stray tear from my face. "Thank you for comforting my daughter."

I nod and he stares into my eyes. "Is there anything you want or need?"

I bite my lip and look around. "Actually yes. I love the radio, I do, but is there any way I could have some books?"

He raises an eyebrow. "What kind of books?"

"Any kind of fiction book." I gulp and start in on my lie. "I've been trying to think about my life before I was on the street, and I keep thinking about books. I think I really like reading."

His face brightens. "Yeah sure, I'll see what I can scrounge up. One minute."

He leaves the room and I collapse back on my bed. *How long can I keep this up?*

"Hey Kat, I know it's not much, but I found—"

I sit up and his eyes widen a little at me lying on the bed. My face feels a little hotter and I respond, "Yes, you found?"

"Ah, *Little Women, Jane Eyre,* and *Pride and Prejudice.* I know nothing about these, but I hope that you'll enjoy them. I'll have my men grab some more books for you the next time they go out."

I jump up and pick them from his hands. I almost hug them to me. He has no idea that I've read all of them several times and enjoy them. Especially *Pride and Prejudice.* They're like old friends I haven't seen in a long time. "Thank you, Valerio."

He nods. "Good night, Kat."

I watch as he turns around to leave, and I remember how he reacted when he saw me lying on my bed. My eyes are drawn to his wide shoulders and my eyes travel down to his arms. *I wonder what it'd be like to have those hold me at night.*

The door closes softly.

I lie back in my bed and close my eyes to picture the expression he had on face. My face grows hot, and I open my eyes to make sure he actually isn't standing there watching me.

But it's just me.

I grab *Pride and Prejudice* and start reading. And just as I suspected, it's like meeting an old friend again.

---

THE NEXT DAY, I'm finishing up *Pride and Prejudice* when I hear the loud voices again.

To my utter shock and surprise, they start moving closer to my location. I listen as they seem to stop right outside of my door.

"Valerio, I told you I'm fine with staying in your house. I don't have to have my own on the property."

"Yes, but not this—"

My eyes shoot to the doorknob as it twists and then the door swings open.

I stare as a woman I've never seen before steps into the room. She jumps out of her skin when she notices me, on the bed. "Oh!"

She shoots a look back at Valerio while the other two men he's with look from me back to each other.

All at once, they start chattering.

"Valerio, who is this?"

"Valerio why is there a woman who isn't your wife or the maids living in your house?"

"Is this the woman keeping you from going to look for your wife?"

Valerio starts swearing in Italian. "Get out of her room."

"Oh, so it's her room," one of the men says with a smirk on his face.

"I'm not leaving until we get some answers, Valerio," the other man says.

I stare at Valerio and try to communicate that I don't want to be interrogated. That I did what he asked and stayed away.

He rubs his hand down his face and sighs. "Fine."

My heart drops to my stomach as he walks in between them and approaches me. "This is Kat. She's one of the women I rescued while I was trying to find my wife."

They look at each other. "Kat you say..." the woman says, trailing off with a glazed look in her eye.

"Yes. Kat."

"And...how long has she been here?" one man says.

"About a month and a half," Valerio answers. "Now listen, do not interrogate her while you're here. She's here as my guest, and she will leave when she's ready to leave and not a moment before. Do you understand me?"

The woman scoffs and walks around him to me and holds her hand out. "Hi dear, I'm Evelina, Valerio's aunt. These two are my brothers, Domenico and Oliverio. I mean no harm child, but this is a dangerous place you're in. Do you understand that?"

I nod and I can see the sympathy in her eyes. "As long as you're aware."

I glance down and watch her walk out in her black high heels and black and white dress. Her golden blonde hair is pulled back into a tight, high bun. "Valerio, I'll take any house on your property. I don't want your guest to be too overwhelmed."

"It's really fine," I tell Valerio and his uncles.

One of his uncles stops in front of me. "Hi, I'm the youngest brother, Oliverio. Don't be in too big of a hurry to leave, okay?" He winks and turns his back to Valerio and points over at him.

I smile a little and the other one offers his hand. I gently shake it, and he places his other hand over mine. "I'm sorry for whatever you went through before getting here. Please let me know during my stay if I have to slap my nephew for being inappropriate."

"Uncle Domenico."

He grins and then shrugs.

"Please wait outside with Evelina you two," he tells them.

He shuts the door behind them and then comes over to me. "I guess you staying in here didn't work so well. I hope they don't bother you when they wander into the house at random moments." He laughs a little half-heartedly and I place my hand over his. "Valerio, this is your house. If you have guests come and go, it's okay. They're your family. And...if you have female guests...that's okay too."

I gulp and hope I don't offend him by saying so.

His eyes harden and the fire in them seems to ignite. "No female guests, *ever.*"

His eyes drop from mine to my lips to all the way down my body.

My mouth drops open as he turns to leave the room. "And don't ever say that again. There's only one woman I'm interested in...and she's already here."

The door slams behind him, and I turn my attention back to the books. I go back to the page I left off at, but no matter how hard I try, I can't seem to concentrate. I read the same sentence over and over.

*Only one...and she's here.*

I laugh a little to myself. *Out of all the women it could have been...it had to be me. How will I ever tell him the truth?*

WHEN IT COMES time for Valerio and his men and kids to eat dinner, I hear a soft knock on the door.

I close my book, memorizing the page number, and open it.

It's Valerio, and he looks a little annoyed. "My aunt and uncles want you to have dinner with us."

I bite my lip. "I don't have to. I'm fine with staying here."

"No. Come on, it'll be fine." My heart beats out of my chest as he holds his arm out. I link my arm with his, and he leads me out to the hallway. We walk slowly to the formal dining room. I've never sat at this table before. Where do I sit? Did his wife have a specific chair at this table? My breathing ceases as I eye the table full of his men and children.

I don't have to agonize over it too long as he pulls out the chair for me at one end of the table and helps me in. An excited giggle interrupts my nervous thoughts, and I see Valeria is seated...next to me. Quickly, I blink them away.

"Mama."

I feel a flush go over my face as his men struggle not to stare in my direction.

Valerio clears his throat. "We're just waiting for them to get here from their houses."

I stare at the table and notice there are still six empty chairs. I gaze around the table and notice there's no Luca, Luciano, or Alessio. *That's strange.*

Suddenly, I hear the sound of the front door opening and the distinct sound of heels clicking on the floor, followed by two other softer sounds.

"Sorry we're late. Oliverio couldn't get off the phone with his girlfriend," his aunt says as she walks into the dining area and takes a random seat in the middle of the table. His two uncles take two more seats.

Bernadette and two more maids rush out with huge platters of food and set them on the table going back and forth a few times. When they're finished, the other two maids excuse themselves to the kitchen for their own meals while Bernadette gets all of the kids' plates prepared. Carina and Ilaria are both on each side of Valerio. They're in their high chairs, watching with their pink and purple pacifiers jutting in and out of their mouths.

"Kat, please make your plate next."

I grab some of everything I can reach and ask for only one farther away so I don't take up too much time.

"Now you Aunt Evelina, Uncle Domenico, and Uncle Oliverio."

They grab lots of food, but there's still plenty left for Valerio's men.

After everyone gets their plate, his aunt says a quick prayer and we start to eat. Then out of nowhere, the front door opens.

I glance up at Valerio, whose face turns pale. He turns toward the entrance way, and we watch as Luca, Luciano, and Alessio come around the corner.

They stop upon noticing us and everyone is completely silent. Valerio clears his throat. "I thought I told you to do—"

"We did what you asked," Alessio interjects with venom in his voice. "What is the meaning of this, Valerio?"

"Boy, have some respect for your boss," Domenico says.

Alessio's hands clench into fists.

"Alessio, I was going to tell you when you got home. I didn't think you'd get it done so quickly."

"Boss, I like completing your orders in a timely manner," Alessio spits.

Luca tries to clasp his shoulder, but Alessio wrenches it away.

"Alessio," Luciano starts.

"Alessio, stop being dramatic. Come and give me a hug," Domenico says.

Evelina looks back and forth between them, sipping a glass of white wine.

I shift uncomfortably in my seat, and Valeria bounces in her booster seat.

"No," he replies, glaring at him.

"Just do it man," Luca mumbles.

"Shut up!" Alessio screams. "You don't know what it's like to have your father be ashamed of you. And neither do you." He says the last part looking at Luciano.

Luciano's mouth forms a thin line. "Of course, I don't Alessio. I don't have one, *remember?*"

He sighs and guiltily looks away. "Just stay away from me as long as you're here," Alessio says, with a note of finality.

"As long as I'm here?" Domenico asks. "I'm moving back home, son."

Alessio's fist slams into the closest wall to his left. "Fuck you!" He stomps off and I watch as Luca and Luciano follow him.

Valerio leans back in his chair and looks up at the ceiling. It's quiet for a second, except for the sounds of Carina and Ilaria sucking on their pacifiers.

"That boy..." Domenico spits.

Evelina catches my eye and holds up the bottle of wine.

*Yes, I would love some.*

# NINE

## Valerio

It's been a few nights and things seem to have settled down here once again. Even with all the relative silence, I still find it hard to sleep. I still see her face every time I close my eyes and now every time I see her, I can't help but feel the urge to kiss her. She's started coming out of her room more, so I'm seeing her even more frequently. It's hard to fight myself. I'm worried about jumping into things with her and having the children think I'm just trying to replace their mother. The girls seem to be okay with her, but my boys, I don't want them to misunderstand. I want to be with her because I feel like I have an actual connection that goes beyond anything I've ever actually felt before.

God, I have to get her out of my mind, I need to start focusing again. If I'm not focused, I might make a mistake like I did last time, and I swear to God that if anyone ever touches a fucking hair on my children, I will kill them and their entire family and then salt the fucking earth that they are buried in so it will never grow anything.

Sitting up in bed, I reach over to my nightstand and open up the top drawer. I grab the large Bible that's in the center of the drawer and then close it. Opening the Bible halfway, I pull out the bottle of thirty-year-old Irish whiskey that my Dad gave me as a wedding present. He thought it would be funny if he gave me the whiskey in a Bible due to Mom always preaching the Catholic way.

I open the bottle and take a whiff of the woody smell that drifts from the open bottle.

I walk outside to my balcony and bring it with me.

"I said I would drink this bottle on the day that either my father dies, or the day I found a chance to live a life that would make the younger me proud," I speak into the cold night air. "Dad is far from dead, but the chance is there for me to take. Do I want to put someone I could actually care about into the dangers that are associated with my life? Regardless, Saluti." I take a large swig and immediately feel the burn is just a bit different than usual.

I don't know if I can put her through this, and it's selfish to think about...but I am beginning to want it more than wanting to keep her safe.

I hear a soft knock on my door, and I walk over to answer my bedroom door.

Luca is leaning against the doorframe with two glasses and a bottle of Jack.

"Luca, it's the middle of the night. What the hell are you doing?"

"I heard what you said, and I'm here to celebrate with you."

THE MAFIA'S BLACK OPAL

"How the hell did you hear what I said?"

"I was just checking things out on the main level before going to sleep."

"So, you were eavesdropping?"

He shrugs. "Call it what you want."

"Look, Luca, I'm not going to take that risk with Kat yet. She deserves better than me and you, and I both know how dangerous it is."

"Oh well, at least you know that. Ol' Valerio actually does have a heart under that cold exterior," he replies in a joking tone.

I chuckle and head back into my room where I stay until the morning.

---

AFTER GETTING ready in the morning, I walk out of my room and down the hallway. From the front of the mansion, I hear my princesses crying upstairs. Rushing up, I find Bernadette in the twins' room, trying to soothe them, but they seem inconsolable.

"What's wrong with them?" I ask softly.

"They're just a little fussy right now, why don't you try to get them to calm down, and I'll bring your coffee up here for you?" Bernadette asks with a smile.

I nod my head and gently take Carina from her and rock her back and forth as she starts to calm down.

"Hush little Carina, Daddy is here now, and he's got his eyes on you. Please forgive me for not being here more often but whenever I see you two, all I can think of is that day. Your daddy does love the both of you very much. Daddy loves his Carina and Ilaria. You two along with all your siblings are the most important things in Daddy's life. More important than his empire or his own life," I say in a soft sing-song voice.

Once Carina is asleep, I gently lay her down and pick up Ilaria.

"You don't like to sleep like your sister, but I know exactly how to get you to." I make weird faces at her, sticking my tongue out, and bulging my eyes until she stops crying and starts a little gurgle that I assume is a giggle. Once she has calmed down, I rock her for a bit until she too drifts off.

As soon as both of them are down, I sit down in the rocking chair and wait for my coffee which only takes a few more minutes.

"Oh, I see you got them both back to sleep. How did you do it?" Bernadette whispers.

"I have my ways as a father," I reply with a whisper.

"Here is your coffee, sir. The babies have already been fed and Miss Kat has already eaten her breakfast. Do you want me to make you an omelet or some bacon or something?" She whispers again.

I shake my head. "I think I'll just pick up some food later. For right now, the coffee will get me through my day until lunch."

She nods and takes her leave.

I linger and watch my two princesses sleep. They remind me so much of Valeria when she was a baby. They remind me so much of *her*...

I slip out of their room quietly and into the nearest bathroom. I stare at myself in the mirror and see a man who doesn't look like Valerio Marchioni. I see a man who has buried what he wants and feels.

"This is why I spend so much time away, I don't even know if I'm cut out for doing all this. Any of this."

I sigh and head out of the bathroom and run] right into Vincenzo.

"Oh Dad, I actually wanted to talk to you, and I was wondering if we could do that right now?" Vincenzo asks.

"Yeah, no problem, Vin. Do you want to talk right here, do you want to go back to your room, or would my office be a better place?"

"Can we talk in my bedroom?"

"Sure, Vin."

He leads me by the hand back to his room even though I know exactly where it is. I think he might be afraid that I don't want to actually listen to him.

Once there, he practically shoves me in and closes the door behind us.

"Dad, I don't want you to go anywhere anymore. I mean this is the longest you've actually been here since Mom was kidnapped, and I'm tired of being the man of the house. I want you to stay home, and I want things to go back to normal," Vincenzo shouts at me while tears are quickly welling up.

"Vin, I..." I start, but Vincenzo cuts me off.

"No. You already told me you're giving up...and I guess I have to be okay with that. I'm not stupid, she's probably dead and searching isn't going to change that, but that doesn't mean you get to disappear too. Before Mom got kidnapped, you were hardly ever home, always away on business."

"Wow Vin, I didn't..." I go to start again, but once again, Vin cuts me off.

"That's right, you didn't know because for the past six months when you were here, you ignored us because we reminded you too much of that day and when you weren't here, you never even called to check in with us."

"Vin, did one of my men tell you to say these things. I

mean how are you even...you're only almost seven...how do you know all of this?"

"Dad, you paid for the best teachers and wanted us to all learn as quickly and as early as possible remember?"

I'm floored by how Vincenzo feels, I didn't think of it like that. I figured that it was always supposed to be like this. I mean I was okay when my Dad was gone because my Mom was always there, but my children don't have their Mom anymore, so it's just me. Well fuck. I have been an absentee father, trying my best to find their mother and in the same span of time fucked up by ignoring the needs of my children. A maid and a teacher are not substitutes for an actual parental figure.

"Vincenzo, you have my word as a man and as your Dad that I will start staying home more. I will only go on trips when absolutely necessary and even then, I will stay in contact with you guys so that you all understand I'm not going to disappear like what happened with mom so please, can you forgive me?"

"Yeah, Daddy," Vin says with a gulp. He wipes his eyes and shows off a beaming smile.

"Well Vin, I have something to tell you. I guess since you're getting to be a big boy, I can tell you the story of my childhood."

"Okay!" Vin yells excitedly.

"You know Grandpa, my dad, had the same job that I have now. I barely got to see him because he was off on business trips and constantly dealing with business instead of being here with me and Grandma. He would be gone for days or even a week or more at a time, and it happened all the time. I never really missed him because I had Grandma to keep me company, and she was a lot of fun. She taught me how to be a good person which is something that I want to teach to each and every one of my children including you, Vin. I know you love Grandpa, but he is not the nicest nor is he really a good person which he will agree with."

Vin keeps quiet but nods along with my story.

"Well, the first thing that you need to know is that someday, my job will probably pass to you. As much as I don't like it, and as much as I wish it wasn't this way, this is how the family business works."

"Oh, cool! I've always wanted to be just like you and Grandpa when I grow up. Punishing the bad people and making them all pay if they don't listen to us."

"Vin, that's exactly what I'm talking about, Grandpa taught you that stuff right?"

"Yeah."

"That's what a bad person does. I don't look forward to punishing anyone, and if I can get away with it, I'd rather not punish anyone."

"Then why did you want the job?"

"Because unlike you and Grandpa, I didn't really have a choice. I didn't have a sibling that I could pass it off to. I *had* to take it because I'm an only child and that's it."

"Oh."

"I didn't want this job, Vin. This job...it's hard to stay a good person and that's all I ever wanted to be when I was sitting in church with my mother. I hated the thought of my dad off and around the world doing whatever he was doing and hurting people along the way."

"Do you hurt people now Dad?"

"I only hurt the people who threaten my kids. So, watch out bullies," I joke.

I smile and ruffle Vin's hair. He's a good kid, but he worships his Grandpa a bit too much and this is what this story is for.

"I had a girlfriend before I got married to your mom, did you know that?"

"No. What was she like?" he asks, tilting his head with a curious look.

"Well, she was what I called my first love, but my dad stopped by her parent's house and said that if she didn't stop coming over, that he would have them all given an Italian neck tie, and that they would end up in the bottom of the Hudson river. The point of this story Vin is that I don't want you to end up like Grandpa or me. If you find something that you like to do or you find someone that you love, I will always support you."

Vincenzo seems to understand a bit more, and I give him a hug before leaving his room.

I head downstairs and start toward my office, almost knocking Kat over as she's coming around the corner.

"I'm so sorry, please forgive me. I wasn't looking where I was going," Kat says in a rather meek voice.

"No, you have no need to apologize. It was my fault, so please forgive me."

She smiles a little nervously, and I notice she's wearing some borrowed clothes that don't quite fit her.

"Kat, why don't we go shopping today? I'll take you to get some clothes of your own and you can pick up as much as you want for yourself. Especially books, I know you've already finished the ones I gave you."

Her face turns pink, confirming my suspicions.

"Oh, you don't really need to do that. I mean I'm okay with the clothes that I'm borrowing really. I don't want to be any trouble. You've already done so much for me."

"Kat, I'm not taking no for an answer. Now I want you to get ready, and we are going shopping."

"Just one thing...is there any way you could get me some

black hair dye?" She's staring a little anxiously at me, and I think she expects me to say no.

Whatever her reason for wanting it, I'll give her what she wants. Maybe she thinks she'll be taken by someone again.

*I'll never allow that to happen.*

"Sure, I'll have my men pick some up for you, and then we can go."

Kat nods and as she turns away, I swear I can see a genuine smile spreading across her face.

---

A FEW HOURS LATER, after Kat dies her hair, it's noon and we get ready to leave the mansion. Her dark hair makes her skin look a little paler than usual, but I don't hate the color on her. She looks beautiful either way to me.

I cough and help Kat into the passenger side of my BMW. I get into the driver's side and follow Luca in his Range Rover. We're followed by Luciano and Alessio in Luciano's Range Rover. We arrive at the large strip mall quickly and find three consecutive parking spots.

Kat looks a little uncomfortable as I help her out of the car, and I'm not sure why. Maybe because she hasn't been to such a large public place in a long time. I hope she isn't frightened.

"Are you okay? I mean you seemed happy before, but now you seem off?" I ask Kat.

"Yeah, I'm fine. It's just that big places tend to freak me out a bit. That's all," she replies.

"Alright, well my men are here, and I'll make sure that nothing happens. You'll be perfectly safe."

We make our way into the mall, and the first stop is a female clothing store that Kat picks out.

It takes a little while, but she grabs a large stack of clothing and brings them into the dressing room. One by one she comes out with the new outfit on and each is more beautiful than the last.

After she has tried on all of the clothes from the rack she chose, she brings out all of the clothes and turns to me.

"Can I get all of these? I mean I really like them all."

"Yeah, no problem. I have a tab here. Just tell them that Mr. Marchioni wants these on his tab."

"Can one of your men bring these up? I'd rather not have to talk to anybody."

"Yeah sure." I turn to Luca and ask him to bring these up.

"I need one other thing. I need some more black hair dye. This will last for a month and a half, but I need more...if that's alright with you."

I nod and motion for Luciano and Alessio to come over to me. We walk just out of earshot of Kat.

"I want you two to keep an eye on us but don't stay too close alright? I want you guys to watch out for anyone who might look suspicious. Also, while you guys are at it, I want you guys to find some more black hair dye and bring it back to the house with us alright?"

They both nod and head off in different directions so that they can get more hair dye and keep an eye on us.

We make our way to another store where she picks up some necessities like panties and bras. While she's skimming through the section that's her size, without even thinking about it, I grab a matching set of black lace bra and thong and hold it up to her.

"You would look amazing in these."

Kat looks at me and color floods her cheeks as she takes them from me and quickly adds them to her pile. My eyebrows raise a little and a vision of her in them floats through my thoughts.

Kat leads the way as we pay for the undergarments at the front and then make our way out of the store.

"Are you hungry? I'm starving and I know this great little place nearby that sells the most amazing crepes," I ask as I rub my stomach.

"I didn't think you'd be into crepes. I mean that's a French pastry and you're Italian. I thought you might take me to get spaghetti or something," she replies with a small smile.

"Another joke, huh? You know keep it up and I might just force you to wear those things I picked out around the house. That might be a good enough punishment."

She quickly looks at me wide-eyed and her face turns beet red.

"Relax, that was a joke. I'd never force you to wear something like that around the house in front of my men. I didn't even think you would get them, I just thought you would look good in them."

She nods and looks away although the redness in her cheeks still remains.

"May I take your hand so I can lead you to the crepe shop?"

She nods again and I wrap her small delicate hand in mine.

Once at the shop, we both order our crepes. I order a crepe filled with strawberries and whipped cream while she orders one with mixed berries and chocolate sauce.

We sit down to dig in. I start to eat and watch as she eyes mine, so I cut off a piece with some strawberry and whipped cream.

"Open your mouth," I tell her.

She obediently opens her mouth for the crepe, and I push

the forkful in. While I do so, I accidentally get some whipped topping on the corner of her lips.

"Kat, you have some whipped cream on your lips."

"Where? What side?"

She tries to get it, but she can't seem to fully get it.

"Here let me get it for you."

Using my thumb, I gently brush the whipped cream off of her lips, and I stick the tip of my thumb with the whipped cream on it in my mouth.

Her eyes widen and a blush hits her cheeks as she watches me stick the whipped cream into my mouth. I watch as she shifts slightly in her seat and lick my lips for good measure.

"I'm sorry if that was too much, I mean I don't want to make you uncomfortable."

She shakes her head and bites her bottom lip.

God, I love teasing her. She's so perfect for me. She's everything I want out of a partner and yet the deeper my feelings get, the more I become aware that her life is in danger with me. If I wasn't in the Mafia, then I could make her my wife, I would bend over backward to make sure that she was always happy and well taken care of. We'd have an entire library of books just for her.

That's a pipe dream though, she's in danger the longer she stays, and the deeper we get, the harder this is going to become when she has to leave. And now with Valeria calling her Mama, it just breaks my heart. I'm sure she thought I was angry when I heard her call her that but the truth is, all I could do was hide my real feelings.

We both finish our crepes in silence, and I throw both of the plates away.

"Would you like to accompany me while I stop at the toy store? I wanted to pick up something for Vincenzo, and I was thinking maybe you could pick something out for Valeria. If that's alright with you?"

"I would love to, Valerio."

With a smile, I grab her hand gently and lead the way to the toy store where we both search for a while. I find a toy that Vincenzo has been asking for recently which is a remote control Ferrari while Kat comes up to me with a stuffed, pink bunny clutching a small heart.

"It's perfect," I whisper.

She smiles brilliantly at me, and my heart starts to ache because we have to end our little shopping trip.

We check out our gifts and find Luciano, Luca, and Alessio not too far behind us.

Once Kat is in the BMW, Luca whispers into my ear, "Vasya is at the new club. What do you want us to do?"

I clench my hand into a fist as my mind starts running wild. "Nothing, let me handle it. I'll go straight there and leave her in the car."

We drive in silence while I let the rage build up inside me. I can't go into this without bringing up that monster inside me. If anyone is as much an equal in this job it's Vasya, the leader of the Russian Mob. He is as dangerous as he is cold and violent.

"I need you to stay in the car, and no matter what do not open the doors for anyone other than me. Do I make myself clear?" I say without even looking at Kat.

"Crystal clear, but what's wrong?"

"Just stay in the car. If anything does happen, there is a gun in the glove box. It's loaded..."

I pull up at the club and get out of the car, locking the doors behind me.

I look at the four black SUV's that aren't mine and for some reason, I feel a pang of guilt go through me.

This is the kind of situation that Kat would have to deal with. I could very well be walking into a death trap.

Walking in, I quickly notice that Vasya and his men are set up in the middle of the place to make it nice and open without either of us actually having an upper hand.

I make my way over to them while my men follow right behind me.

Vasya's light brown eyes are mostly concealed in the low light of the room. His dark hair is cut neat and short, and he sits in a high-end, grey suit waiting for me to sit down.

"Vasya, what do I owe this unexpected visit to?" I ask, feigning a smile.

"Valerio. Why, I've just been so worried as to whether or not anything has changed with you recently. I've had reports that you've stopped going all over the world, did you happen to find what you were looking for?"

"We've had reports as well that you've stopped traveling all over the world as well so the same goes to you."

We both sit and stare at each other, neither giving the other the edge until someone coughs.

"Oh, where are my manners, Luca why don't you bring out a bottle of vodka, and we can toast to good health and fortunes with our...friends here."

Once Luca is gone, I turn back to Vasya whose expression is as cold as ever. He barely seems to show emotion and that gives him one hell of a poker face.

"So, Vasya anything new with you recently?"

Two of his men start whispering in Russian which I can barely make out, but it's something along the lines of not trusting the Italian bastard.

"I can assure you that everything is completely normal on my end of things, and I intend to keep it that way. This was just a courtesy meeting as we are both back in the city and neither of us wants another war on our hands now, do we?"

"I couldn't agree more, war between us would just leave us both ripe for some other gang like the Cartel or something to come in and try to take us out."

Luca arrives with a large bottle of Russian Standard Gold.

"Only the best for my friends from the cold of Eastern Europe. Please everyone, have a glass."

Once everyone has a glass of vodka in hand, I turn to Vasya.

"Saluti."

"Na Zdorovie, thank you for the vodka," Vasya replies, and gulps it down.

"Don't mention it. Now if that is all you have to discuss with me, why don't you take the rest of the bottle for your trouble of coming over here and have a wonderful day."

"Before I go...a little warning. A storm is coming. Whether you are caught in it or not is up to you. Don't fuck with the Russians, and we won't have to fuck with you."

He gets up without another word and leaves with his men.

"I hate those fucking Russians," I mutter.

# TEN

## Kat

The whole time Valerio is inside, I'm full of dread. I worry that maybe he won't come out unharmed. Those Escalades...I know who it is. My stomach clenches uneasily when I start seeing the men come out. I unbuckle my seatbelt to get under the glove compartment. We're all the way at the very end so it's likely they won't see me. I hear the sound of the SUVs speeding off, but I stay in place before Valerio comes back.

I hold my breath as time seems to tick on. All of a sudden, I hear footsteps and then the driver's door opens.

Valerio gets in the driver's seat and closes the door. "Kat, it's safe."

I pop up and get back in my seat. Valerio starts the car, and I buckle my seat belt quickly as we zoom off. I look behind us and watch as Luca, Luciano, and Alessio drive behind us in the Range Rovers.

"Russian asshole," Valerio mutters.

*I shouldn't ask, but I can't help it.* "Is...is everything okay?"

He sighs. "Yeah. Just a Russian bastard invading my club. Don't worry, I'll never let him near you."

A chill goes down my spine and my hands start to shake uncontrollably. I put them underneath my legs to stop the shaking and nod. Valerio doesn't notice as he keeps his eyes on the road and takes us back to the mansion.

---

After the mostly wonderful day with Valerio, I finally feel comfortable enough to sit and eat with his family and men. Valerio says his aunt and uncles are staying away for now, finding three mansions for themselves, but I think it'll be awhile before they have dinner here after the last incident.

Valerio ushers me into the seat to the right of his. Bernadette brings the babies' high chairs, and then proceeds to place the girls in them with Ilaria sitting in between Valerio and me and Carina on his other side. All of his sons come down, and Vincenzo takes the chair on Valerio's left. The chair next to mine has Valeria's booster seat, and I watch as the other maid brings a giggling Valeria and sits her in the chair next to mine.

She smiles at me. "Mama!"

His sons don't say a word, but I can feel their eyes on me. I can't help but smile back at Valeria's happy expression. Bernadette sets the food on the table, and we start making our plates, getting a little of everything.

"The men won't be joining us tonight?" I ask curiously, glancing at all of the empty seats.

"No. I have them all watching the property right now. Just in case that Russian bastard tries something...I can never be too careful now," Valerio replies, worry etched into his face.

I make Valeria's plate while Valerio helps make sure his sons have theirs. They look at him with so much admiration, and I can tell how much they love him.

Only one bite of food is in my mouth when Vincenzo says, "Miss Kat, are you going to stay here?"

I cough a little and hesitantly meet his eyes. Eyes just like his father's. "I um...I don't know Vincenzo," I reply.

It's the truth...I don't really know. As much as I would like to, do I really deserve to be happy with Valerio? Can he find room in his heart for me?

"If you do, you'll never be my mom. Not even if that's what Valeria calls you." He crosses his arms.

"Vin," Valerio snaps.

"No, it's okay." I hesitate for a second. Is this the right time to just come out and say it? "Vincenzo, Nicolo, Vittorio, Emilio, and Aurelio." The three younger ones may not quite understand what I'm about to say, so I focus most of my attention on Vincenzo and Nicolo.

"I like your father. A lot. At first, I could never think about staying here. And I know your father didn't want me to. But this place...and you guys are growing on me. Please don't be mad at me if I decide to stay. I'll never replace your mother, I promise." I take a deep breath and look back at my plate nervously.

Vittorio, the closest one to me says, "Okay."

I look up in shock and watch as Emilio starts eating his food and nods.

Aurelio smiles at me.

But Nicolo and Vincenzo both look unsure.

"Now, with that being said, let's enjoy our meals. Okay boys?"

I lock eyes with Valerio, and he winks at me. "Thank you," he mouths. The rest of the dinner is full of nothing but happy talking and baby giggles.

---

After dinner, Vincenzo suggests watching a movie together, so we all sit down to watch *Back to the Future Part 1*. I sit on one long couch and Valeria sits next to me. Valerio holds Carina and Ilaria in a chair while the boys sit on another couch themselves. Valeria doesn't understand, so I play with her and watch the movie at the same time while Valerio tries to keep the twins' attention.

When it's over, Valerio tells his boys it's bath time and then to bed. None of them protest, however the girls are a different story. Valeria is fussy as usual, and Valerio gives me the task of making sure she gets a bath while Bernadette gives the twins a bath.

It doesn't take me long, so I have Valeria in her room, ready to go while Valerio takes longer with the boys.

To pass the time, I read her a book that she picks out from the bookshelves built into the wall. By the time Valerio comes in, she's almost asleep.

He places her blanket over her and looks down at her lovingly. "Good night Valeria."

She closes her eyes completely, and we leave to go next door.

Bernadette already has both twins asleep and tucked in, so Valerio only peeks at them and we leave.

"Thank you, Bernadette," Valerio says as Bernadette shuffles down the stairs.

"Good night, sir," she calls softly.

Valerio turns and fixes me with a smile. "Thank you, for what you said at dinner. For what it's worth, I like you too. Good night, mi tesoro"

He walks me to my room, and then continues down the hall and around the corner to his room.

My face heats up and I close the door. I glance around my room as if the object I want is going to appear out of thin air. That's what I should've bought when we were out, an Italian dictionary. How else am I going to know what that means?

His words whisper in my head until I fall asleep.

*Mi tesoro.*

---

A FEW DAYS LATER, I'm in the living room reading a nice book when Valerio's men come in.

"I'm starving. Is it lunchtime yet?" Luca asks with a stretch.

"We still have another forty-five minutes of guard duty left. Don't be so impatient," Luciano says rolling his eyes.

They pause when they see all spot me at the same time.

"Hi Kat," Alessio says with a wave.

"Sorry to disturb your reading," Luciano says.

"Oh. It's okay. You aren't bothering me," I say with a reassuring smile and close my book.

They go in the kitchen and come out a few minutes later with bags of chips.

"See you later, Kat," Luca says.

I study all three of them and it hits me, I don't really know anything about them. Well besides the fact that Luciano doesn't have a father. That moment at dinner replays in my mind and all I can think about is how unemotional he seemed about it.

"Hey, wait. Can you guys tell me something about yourselves?" I ask just as they're about to leave the huge family room.

They stop right at the threshold and turn around.

Alessio sticks his hands in his suit jacket and straightens. "Well, I'm Valerio's oldest first cousin. His others are my brother and sister, Soren and Caelia. You'll be meeting them soon since my father and mother are moving back here now."

His eyes seem to darken at that, and I can't help but wonder why he doesn't get along with his dad.

"What about you?" I ask Luca.

He seems to think for a moment and sighs. "My old man is Valerio's old man's right-hand man. He's the only reason I have this job. I'm his only son. Valerio and I have been friends since we were babies. I grew up knowing I'd have this position."

He doesn't mention his mother, so I assume she probably passed away. The thought makes my heart pang a little.

I turn my attention to Luciano and he states without hesitation, "I have no father. My mother disappeared a long time ago. I don't know whether she's alive or dead and frankly, I don't give a shit. No siblings. Valerio picked me up as a kid on the street."

Oh, Luciano. My heart aches for him, but his face doesn't hold an ounce of sadness. *Looks can be deceiving.*

"Well if that's all, we have to get back to guard duty. See you later, Kat," Luca says as he leaves with Luciano and Alessio in tow.

Twenty minutes later, Bernadette comes out from her room and starts making ham and cheese sandwiches for everyone. I close my book and rise from the couch.

"Would you like help Bernadette?" I ask.

She looks up from the counter where she's putting slices of bread down on pieces of paper towel. "I'm okay, dear, but thank you for asking."

I smile in her direction. "I'll help anyway."

I walk to the kitchen and pull out the mayo and a knife.

"Thank you," she says, absolute gratitude leaking from her voice.

After I mayo each piece of bread, she puts a piece of ham and cheese on each piece of bread, and I assemble each sandwich for her.

She folds up a piece of paper towel around each of them and pulls out bags of chips, like the ones Luca, Luciano, and Alessio grabbed.

As I start washing my hands, and I hear the sound of sniffing like someone's crying. I dry my hand quickly and find Bernadette sitting at the table alone eating one of the sandwiches we made.

"Bernadette?"

She looks up and I immediately notice the tears streaming down her face.

"Bernadette!" I rush over to her and put a comforting hand on her shoulder as I sit next to her. "What's wrong?"

She puts her sandwich down and gulps down the piece she had in her mouth.

"I'm sorry to do this in front of you. Today just isn't a good day."

I rub her shoulder and she cries onto her sandwich. "What's wrong?"

She wipes her face and looks at me. "I just miss *her*...we

used to make sandwiches together like this, and it just reminded me."

"Why won't anyone say her name?" I ask carefully, hoping that I'm not putting my foot in my mouth.

I've been wanting to know for a while, but I've been too afraid to ask Valerio.

"After a few months passed, and it seemed more and more like she wasn't coming back, we were asked not to talk about her again. And well, when you came, we knew we really weren't allowed to say her name. Her identity is a secret, just like the other wives of the other crime families. The women are their greatest treasure."

I nod, understanding completely, and she seems to calm down.

"I guess I should make myself another sandwich," she says with a laugh.

I smile at her and get up from the table to grab a sandwich to eat in the family room. "Oh, one more thing. Would you happen to know what *mi tesoro* means?"

Her eyes widen and a smile lights up her face. "My dear, it means my treasure."

I cover my mouth and she chuckles as she starts to make another sandwich. "You don't have to tell me who said it to you because I'm positive I already know. I wish you all the happiness in the world, dear."

When I get back to my room, I hug my book to my chest as my heart races uncontrollably. I never knew it was possible to be this happy about a man.

---

THAT NIGHT, I've just gotten out of the shower when I hear a knock at the door.

I peek outside to find Valerio.

"I'm coming out for dinner in a minute, I promise."

His eyes trail up to my hair wrapped in a towel and lower to my face. He smirks. "Actually, I wanted to do something with just us. Let's go out to dinner."

My stomach flutters a little nervously, yet I feel excited to go out on a date for the first time in years.

"I'd love that. Let me hurry and finish getting ready."

His bluish gray eyes start to shine with extreme interest as my towel falls a little so the edge of it is seen through the crack in the door.

"I'll be in the car," he responds, looking back into my eyes.

His hot gaze starts to melt me, so I shut the door quickly and rush to my closet. Okay, what do I have? Not much, I don't think. I think I only bought two dresses. One day, and one evening.

The day one is a long white and yellow dress with flowers on it. Nope, definitely not. Has to be the evening, no matter what it looks like.

I pull out the short black dress with a V neckline and a halter top. I eye the only dressy shoes I bought and sigh with relief at seeing they're black with a sandal heel. Less of a chance for me to trip and stumble over myself. Without even trying, the many times I've stumbled and fallen over flash through my brain. It's been so long since I've worn heels.

I pull them on and get in my dress, zipping it up in the back.

In the bathroom, I comb through my hair and brush it until it's straight and sleek, and put it up in a low ponytail. The black is still very present, so at least I don't have to worry too much.

The last thing I do is add some a smoky eye shadow and a nude lipstick.

*I hope I look okay...*

Casually, I step out of my room and walk slowly down the hall, hearing my black heels click with every step. My face turns a bright red as I come around the corner and see all three of Valerio's closest men waiting near the front door.

Luciano looks me up and down while Luca whistles and Alessio grins at me. "We'll stay in the parking lot while you guys go in," Luca says, opening the door wide for me.

Just as I'm about to step out, I hear the gasp of a woman. I turn around to find Bernadette.

"Kat, don't you just look amazing." She's holding Valeria in her arms and Valeria reaches her arms out to me.

"Thank you so much," I say, blushing from all of the praise. "It's okay, I'll give her a hug before I leave."

She hands Valeria to me and Valeria kisses my cheek. "Mama, you're...pwetty."

"Awww, Valeria," I say, as my eyes start filling with tears. I hug her tightly to me. "Daddy and I will be back soon. Be good for Bernadette, okay?"

She nods and gets a mischievous look on her face. I chuckle and give her back to Bernadette.

"I guess I shouldn't keep him waiting any longer," I comment and walk outside to the circular driveway.

The car in front of the door is a Range Rover, so I carefully open the door and get in. "Thought it'd be nice to be in something different," he says and takes off down the long driveway. When he pulls out to the road, he looks left and then as he turns right, his gaze locks with mine and his eyes seem to burn with pure want as his eyes drop down to my front.

"Maybe we don't need to go out at all," he murmurs, but turns on to the road anyway.

I blush all the way to the restaurant, which turns out to be a place I've been before. It's a popular steakhouse and the steaks are known for having the best grade of beef around this part of the city.

We walk in and the hostess immediately recognizes Valerio. "Mr. Marchioni, right this way," she says with a nod and leads us to the back of the restaurant.

Our two-seat table is far enough in the back that no one can really pay attention to us without turning around.

As soon as we sit down, the hostess leaves us with the menus and our waiter comes almost right away.

"Water for me," Valerio says, opening the menu.

"I'd like an iced tea."

The waiter nods and leaves.

"What are you thinking about ordering?" Valerio asks, the menu covering up his face.

I pull mine open and glance over the pages. "I'll just go with a steak and lobster."

He closes his menu. "I'll have the same." His eyes stare into mine until the waiter comes back.

"What will be it be, sir and ma'am?" he asks holding his pencil and notepad.

"Two steak and lobster dinners. I'd like medium-rare." Valerio turns to me and I shyly say, "Well done for me, please."

"Right away." He leaves and I watch as he goes right to the kitchen.

My stomach growls and our waiter returns with our drinks. Valerio waits patiently for him to leave and then stares right at me. "Kat, we need to talk."

I shift in my seat as my anxiety starts to creep up. "Okay, sure."

"I know you've only been here for a short amount of time, but I don't want you to leave. Please tell me you'll stay." His voice breaks a little at the end and my anxiety disappears as the only thing I can say comes out of my mouth.

"Yes. Of course. I've...grown so used to everything. I've grown to love Bernadette. She's such a sweet lady. And your kids...I know I'll never be their mother, but please know I'll never harm them. And Luca, Luciano, and Alessio are great men. Honestly, I tried to figure out where I should go, but no matter where I thought of, nothing ever really seemed to fit in my mind. I think my home is with you. I want to stay with you."

His mouth drops open and his eyes start shining, and he looks away as he takes a sip of his water.

"I don't know if I deserve you. Or any happiness besides my kids, but I'm ready to move on. I'm ready to try for this happiness *with* you," I start to reply but get interrupted when our food comes.

"Enjoy," the waiter says and with a bow leaves us to our food.

We both grab our steak knives and start to eat. "Don't take too long eating," he states. I look up and watch as he seems to undress me with my eyes.

My whole body heats up, and I bite my lip.

In no time at all, he's done, and he watches as I finish my meal. I take a few sips of my iced tea and he calls for the bill.

He slams a few bills on the table, and we walk out of the restaurant. When we get to the car, he helps me get inside quickly and goes around to his side and hops in. He turns the car on and speeds out of the restaurant parking lot.

"In a hurry?" I ask with a giggle.

His eyes turn to mine, and he starts loosening his tie, speeding down the road.

"Yes," he says bluntly.

It takes half the time to get home than it took to get the restaurant.

"Baby, I'm going to make sure the kids are asleep and then I'll come find you."

He races inside and as I get out; three Range Rovers pull up behind us.

Luciano gets out of the first one. "What the fuck is going on? I could barely keep up."

I shrug and go inside with a blush staining my cheeks.

Well, I'll just go out back and wait. It might take a while before he comes out.

I walk to the back of the house and go out the back door. I glance at the gigantic pool sitting square in the center of the yard and go around it through the grassy area.

The spring breeze is a little warmer tonight, so I venture a little farther on the property that stretches for acres. I go through a patch of trees and follow a stream, listening to the sound of an owl off in the distance and crickets.

*Why didn't I come out here sooner? I guess I should go back inside.* I realize I've been out here long enough.

I turn around abruptly and start on my walk back to the house. As I go around the first tree, I step on a rock and it slides right out from under me as I go to take another step.

In what seems to be slow motion, I fall backwards and hear a thump as my body reaches the ground.

For a second, I'm able to make out the dark night sky with a few dots of stars and then everything suddenly goes black.

# ELEVEN

## Valerio

"**V**alerio!" I hear just as I close Aurelio's door.

Sounds like Luca. He knows better than to be yelling at this hour when the kids are trying to sleep.

"Valerio get the fuck downstairs now!" His voice echoes throughout the whole mansion.

My blood starts to boil, and I run down the stairs quickly to get to the bottom of the yelling.

"What the hell is going on?" I exclaim as I reach the bottom and make my way to Luca in the family room.

"About time!" Luca screams upon seeing me.

"What the hell is going on, and why are you fucking screaming at me? There had better be a damn good reason that you're yelling when the kids are trying to sleep," I growl with a glare.

"You need to call all the men surrounding the property. Kat is gone."

A buzzing starts in my ears and I blink at him, trying to process what I'm hearing.

"What the fuck did you just say Luca?"

"It's true. We saw her go inside the house, but we haven't seen her since. The back door was open when we came inside. She's gone."

My heart starts racing, and the buzzing in my ears grows. No, this can't be fucking happening.

She just told me she wanted to stay.

*I think my home is with you. I want to stay with you.*

Did she change her mind already? Something has to have happened.

"Boss, we aren't sure that she isn't on the grounds. We just know that right now she isn't in the house. Why don't I lead the search, and I'll update once we search the entire grounds," Luca states.

I should trust him enough to search for her...I should trust my men to do this for me and yet the only thought that is running through my head is that I need to do this myself. If she's trying to leave, I need to find her and ask her why. There's no way she's gotten through my men. I hired more after the kidnapping of my wife. She has to be here somewhere, trying to find a way out. But, why?

"No, I'll lead the search and look for her. What I want you to do is get Alessio and Luciano and meet me here in five minutes. We're going to ask everyone we can."

"Can do boss, I'll be right back with them."

I nod and watch as Luca leaves to go and fetch the others.

Just when I thought I found someone who might truly accept me, the whole me and actually care about me...they're gone just like that.

In the meantime, I go to the liquor cabinet and grab a bottle of whiskey and pour myself a few glasses. The burn of the whiskey going down my throat distracts me from the situation at hand. It gives me back a little control somewhere in my life. My drinking is interrupted by Luca coming back.

"Hey boss, I got Alessio and Luciano. Where do you want to search first?"

"First, we're going to go talk to the guards at the front gate to make sure that they haven't seen her and then we'll go and talk to Bernadette."

As we march our way out the front door and down to the big gates that separate my house from the outside world, I feel the gravel biting into my bare feet and remember I left my shoes by the stairs when I first went in.

"Boss, do you want my shoes? I mean if you keep this up, you might actually cut open your feet," Luciano says.

"The only thing I want is answers. I want to know exactly where she is, and I want to know why she's trying to leave me. I need to see that she is safe. Until then, fuck my feet," I bark at him.

As soon as I say it, I know it isn't fair to Luciano. He just wants to help, but I can't focus on that, I need to keep going. I need to see her.

We reach the gatehouse and I see one guard reading a magazine and the other eating a doughnut while watching the cameras.

"Can you two really be any more stereotypical?"

"Oh boss, sorry we were just taking a small break." The guard with the doughnut drops it and quickly starts monitoring the cameras more.

"Look I don't give a shit what you were doing, I just need you to answer one question. Have you seen Kat? Black hair, blue eyes. You know who I'm talking about. Look through the footage and see if you see her leaving through the back door!" I yell at the men in the booth.

Luca puts his hand on my shoulder and pulls me to the side.

"Look, you need to calm down just a bit that way we can get through this okay?"

I take a few deep breaths and nod my head. He's right, I can't just keep yelling and screaming at everyone. I need to work with them to get what I want.

"One second, boss. Okay it looks like she went out the back door into the backyard and then she disappears out of the angles of any of the cameras."

"Is she alone?" I ask.

"She was alone when she left, and we don't see anyone else come onto the screen."

"She could be anywhere on the property. Damn it! It hasn't been that long. She couldn't have found a way out."

"Boss...there is that spot in the area with all of the trees. It's not too far into the property yet. If she could somehow climb over the wall, she could be up and over it before anyone suspects anything," Luca whispers.

My stomach clenches in fear. *No, it can't be.*

It still doesn't make sense to me. After what we discussed over dinner...how could she just try to escape like this? Did she think I was going to force her to stay? The thought leaves a bad taste in my mouth.

"She must be lost in the dark or something. I can't believe she would just run after our dinner."

My men give me a questioning look, but I'm not going to tell them a word of what we said to each other.

"She and Vincenzo don't really get along. I also heard her talking with Bernadette and she said that she missed your wife," Alessio speaks up.

Maybe that's what did it. Bernadette was really her first friend here and to hear that must have sent her over the edge with everything else that has been going on.

"So, now we need to go and talk to Bernadette. Maybe Kat said something to her, something that would tip us off that she wanted to leave. Let's go," I say and lead the way back to the house.

As we walk back to the front door, we pass by men who've gathered around to search for her. I hear Luciano bark out orders behind me and when we get to the front door, I wrench it open and stomp inside.

"Bernadette," I call out.

I hear the sound of a soft reply from the kitchen and head straight there.

Bernadette is waiting in the kitchen, warming up some bottles of formula.

"Bernadette, we need to talk and we need to talk now," I grumble.

"What can I help you with, Mr. Marchioni?"

"What did you say to Kat yesterday, and what did she say to you?" I ask as calmly as I can.

"Well I just told her that I missed your first wife, which I do. She was always nice to me and we had lovely talks together."

"Okay and how did she take what you said? Did she seem sad? What did she say back to you?"

"Well I mean I think she took it well. I didn't pressure her or get mad at her or anything. I just wanted to vent to someone because I can't very well vent to you, now can I?" she asks.

"I'm sorry. I don't want you to feel like you can't talk to me. But I'm only asking because Kat is missing, and I need to know if maybe she mentioned something to you...like she was going to run away or something of that sort?" I ask, touching Bernadette's arm softly.

"Sir, she was not in a bad mood when I talked to her. I doubt she just ran away. No matter what you might think of her, she is an incredibly strong woman to have made it through what she did and to come out the other side without being completely broken by it. So just take that into mind that she might have just gone out for a walk or something." Her eyes shine with the truth of a worried friend.

"Thank you, Bernadette," I reply.

"Don't mention it, Mr. Marchioni."

I motion for my men to follow me out the back door and when they do and the door is shut behind us, I turn around.

"It's possible that our talk at dinner scared her away. I wasn't trying to rush her, but maybe she felt like she couldn't say how she really felt at dinner."

*Shit. Please don't be gone.*

"Boss, it's not your fault. If she wanted to run away, I'm sure she had made up her mind long before you asked her on a date," Alessio responds with a smile.

Right after it leaves his mouth, he realizes what he said and quickly clamps his hands around his mouth.

Luca's quick to diffuse the situation. "Valerio, what he's trying to say is that it wasn't your fault if she decided to run away, you shouldn't beat yourself up for it if she is gone."

"Yeah boss, let's just do what we can," Luciano says with a nod.

I exhale a heavy sigh and start the walk to the wooded area.

We walk through the grass and brush towards the area that she was heading. We continue through for quite a while and nothing seems out of the ordinary. No Kat to be seen at all.

Fuck. The bottoms of my feet start aching as we start walking over the small rocks littering this section of the property.

"Hey, boss, how far are we going to go? All the way to the wall or what?" Alessio asks.

"Look, we are going to keep going until we either find her or we get to the wall. I do not need to stress this again. I need to find her."

While we continue walking, I hear a faint groaning sound coming from nearby.

The next thing I know, my legs are moving on their own and I bolt around each tree looking for her, when I finally get around one and see Kat lying out cold on the ground, her dark hair strewn around her head on the ground. There is a small pool of blood next to her head near a rock and while my heart bursts in excitement that we found her, my heart sinks once I see the blood.

I pick her up gently, cradling her head as much as I can. Without wasting another second, I race into action.

"Alessio, Luciano, go back to the house now and call Dr. Rosen. He needs to get here ASAP. I can't lose her like this. Get that fucking doctor here now!" I order.

They bolt off to the house, and Luca helps me carry her all the way back to my house and to my room. Once there, I gently lay her on my bed and start to pace.

God, please let her be okay. I'll do anything if she's alright. I'll...start going to church every Sunday. I'll donate as much money as I can to charity, and I'll be a better person. Just please let her be okay.

While I restlessly walk around my room, the door opens and in comes Dr. Rosen.

"Doctor, you need to check her. You need to make sure

that she's okay. I heard her breathing, but she's been unconscious since I found her."

"Well, first off what happened to her?" the doctor asks.

"I think she hit her head on a rock in the back. She had some blood around her head where she fell. Please tell me she'll be okay."

He pats me on the shoulder. "Let me take a look at her."

After feeling her head and noting a lump, he uses a small penlight to check for reactions to the light. He concludes that she's just unconscious and that she must have hit her head pretty hard.

"She seems to be alright overall. She just needs her rest right now as she is suffering from a minor contusion to the back of her head. Pay attention to her when she wakes up. Luckily all of her responses are within the normal range so she should be alright as long as nobody pushes her down the stairs or she doesn't fall and hit that same spot again. I'll check on her again in a few days," Dr. Rosen says and leaves.

My shoulders sag in relief. I had no idea how tense I was.

"Thank God she's okay. I actually fucking prayed to God that she would be alright can you believe that Luca?"

I laugh a little to myself and try to shake some of the worry off.

"Valerio, we were all worried. Honestly, I think even Alessio has grown to like Kat and you know how he is with anything that might disrupt the business," Luca responds with a chuckle.

"Really? Wow, I didn't know that she was really growing on anyone else besides the girls and me. I really wish that things had been different, and I could have met her somewhere else, but I have to admit, she is the only woman I have eyes for."

I stare at Kat and watch as she breathes steadily. The door opens again.

"The guys are all back and want to talk to you Valerio," Luciano says with a serious expression.

I glance down at her one more time and head outside of my room while Luca stays behind to watch Kat. As I head to my office, I suddenly notice the splotches of dirt left behind on the floor after me. Oh well, I'll just have to clean my feet later.

I enter my office and stare at each of my men. Some of them don't seem to want to be here, but others seem to be bothered by something. "So, everyone wants to talk to me now?"

"We want to know the real story about Kat. Why do you keep her around, and why did you freak out so much when you thought she left?" one of them asks carefully.

"Well as I have told Alessio, Luca, and Luciano. She is someone who has become close to me during her stay here. She has become close to my daughters and that means she is an important part of my life. As you all know, I was never truly in love with my first wife. I never thought I'd find someone that I'd be interested in again since my ex-girlfriend, but miraculously I did. I've tried to deny myself, but I can't fight it any longer. She cares about my children like they're her own. I can see it in her eyes. Does that answer your question?" Tapping my fingers, I narrow my eyes at the man who is just a grunt in my army. He is not even a true made man yet, and he has the audacity to question me.

"If anyone has any other questions for me, I expect them to take it up with either Alessio, Luca, or Luciano. Now, I want you all out of my fucking house until I say otherwise.

Patrol the grounds and make sure everything is safe. Do I make myself clear?"

Everyone nods or mutters in agreement.

Good. Assholes questioning me...they should be lucky I'm not my father. As I walk out of my office, I notice that Vincenzo is outside waiting for me.

"What can I do for you Vin?"

"Dad, I need to talk to you in my room okay?"

"Is everything alright Vin?"

"Yeah, Dad."

We go upstairs to his room, and I notice that he's been pacing around a lot as his normally messy room has an unmistakable line right down his walking path.

"Are you sure everything is okay, Vin?" I ask looking down at him.

"Is she going to be okay, Dad?" he asks quietly.

"Is who going to be okay?" I ask, already knowing his answer.

"Is Kat going to be okay? I'm really worried about her. I saw you carry her into your room, and she wasn't awake. Then I saw the doctor come, and he only comes when someone is hurt."

"Kat is fine, the doctor said that she would be okay with some rest. Why are you so worried about her though? I thought you didn't like her because you thought she was replacing Mom?"

"Just because I don't want anyone to replace my mom doesn't mean I want to see her hurt. I don't want you to be unhappy Dad. I want you to be happy and if you are actually happy with her, then I won't be so angry about it anymore. But I still don't want to hang out with her like my parent or anything, okay?"

"You know Vin, you are pretty grown up for someone

THE MAFIA'S BLACK OPAL

who is just six and a half." I tussle his hair with my hand until he tries to throw it off.

"Cut it out, Dad. You know that I need to be the man here when you are busy or gone so I need to be mature."

"Alright Vin. Well Kat is going to be fine, and I asked her out on a date. I don't know how things are going to go, but she does make me happy and that should make you happy too. Because when I'm happy, that means more toys for the most important people in my life." I wink at him.

"You guys are my world, but I need someone I can spend my life with, and I think that person might just be her. I'm not going to rush it, I promise. Tonight, kind of changed everything. I know now that I need her in my life somehow. Do you understand, son?"

He nods. "Alright Dad, well you go stay by her side then."

I get up and watch as my son goes back to playing with his toys like nothing ever happened.

I head back downstairs and go to my room, gently opening the door. Kat is sleeping still, but she's moved a little and is now clutching one of my pillows in her arms as she sleeps soundly.

Luca leaves with a silent wave, and I pull up a chair and wait for her to wake up. What a night. I hope she wakes up soon.

As I watch her sleep, I slowly feel my eyes relaxing and listening to her soft breaths as she sleeps, blissfully unaware that I'm right here, just a few feet from her sleeping form.

She's like an angel given human form, she's perfect for...

My thoughts slip away as I pass out in my big armchair.

---

A BRIGHT BEAM of sunlight shining through my window hits my face, waking me up.

Oh God, sharp pains shoot through my arms and I stretch them out to relieve some of the tension. I stare over at a still sleeping Kat. I hope she wakes up soon. As I'm staring, I notice her form start to stir and all of a sudden, her eyes peek open. Her eyes widen when she sees me.

"What happened? Why am I in your room? The last thing I remember was being out in the backyard taking a walk," she mutters while holding her head.

"There is some Tylenol next to you and a bottle of water. It's been waiting for you all night long. Now that you're awake, I can tell you everything that happened."

"Why does my head hurt?" she asks, wincing when she touches the lump on the back.

"You tripped or slipped on something in the back of my property and hit your head on a rock. It knocked you unconscious, and it also caused a minor contusion to the back of your skull. I already had my personal doctor come in and take a look. He said you would be fine as long as you rest."

"Who found me back there?" she asks, gazing around my room.

"I did, along with Alessio, Luca, and Luciano. I carried you back here and placed you in my bed so I could keep an eye on you. I will admit though that at first I thought you might have been running away."

She giggles softly and clutches her head.

"Why would I want to run away?"

"I thought you ran away because you changed your mind. I thought you wanted to run away because of all my children and how Bernadette said she missed my first wife. There was so much that it could have been that I was just nervous that I had scared you off."

"Well I'm sorry that I frightened you, and I'm sorry that it looked like I ran off, Valerio. I'm not just going to run away from you. I'll tell you if I want to leave, don't worry. But know, I don't plan on going anywhere." I smile at that and rise from my chair.

"Do you want any breakfast? I can have Bernadette bring some up for you."

"No, I'm okay. I probably should've told you how much of a klutz I am. Now you know not to worry so much if I disappear again. I'm not going to run away, and I'm not just going to leave without at least saying goodbye to the twins or Valeria," she says with a smile.

"I'd have to kill you if you left without saying goodbye to my little princess," I joke.

She keeps the smile and stares at me and suddenly I am struck with the urge to kiss her. I need to make her mine and show her that I care about her.

I walk over and sit on the bed next to her. I gently take her head in my hands and lean in for the kiss that will seal both of our fates. Our lips are about to brush against each other...

The door opens and I step back quickly.

Luca coughs. "Boss, you have some business that you need to attend to at one of the clubs. It's urgent and it can't wait any longer."

I look her in the eyes and see a spark of something there and smile broadly.

"I'll be back soon, Kat. Make sure to get plenty of rest alright?"

"I will, Valerio. Have fun in the city taking care of

whatever business that you have to attend to, I'll be here," she says, staring at me with her bright blue eyes.

"Trust me, I never have fun at these things."

I leave my room and go upstairs and say goodbye to each of my children in turn.

Once I get to the twins' rooms, I smell the fact that they both need a diaper change. I quickly take care of them and dispose of their nasty diapers in the bin.

I kiss them goodbye and head downstairs where my briefcase has already been packed for me.

I go outside and hop into my car. The only thing on my mind is getting back from this business and making Kat mine. We were *so* close to kissing if only Luca hadn't interrupted. I'll have to think of a punishment for him later.

*It sucks being the king. To have all the power, and yet I still can't use it to get some damn peace and quiet.*

# TWELVE

## Kat

Ever since my accident, Valerio and I have grown closer. With each passing day, we're falling into an actual routine. He sees his children in the morning and does his work. He gives me all the books I could ever want. The good days are ones where he stays home, and he's able to have all three meals with me. Sometimes he even shows me how to play a few video games. Other times, he's off with his men for almost the whole day.

We have dinner around the same time with his men and children. The babies are growing every day, which makes me happy and sad at the same time.

Sometimes I put them to bed at night, sometimes I don't. Valerio never questions me on the nights I don't. One day I'll have to tell him why.

And then we talk for hours. Out on the patio, in my

163

room, in his room. Some nights in his room are tempting. They make me think back to the night of the accident. If I hadn't had the accident, would I have actually slept with him?

I've only ever slept with one man before.

*Maybe I would have.*

Anyway, today is one of those good days since Valerio's doing work at home today. I step out of my bedroom to get a snack before having lunch with him. On my way to the kitchen, I run into Evelina, Valerio's aunt.

She looks just as put together as she always does. Her blonde hair is in the same tight bun and she wears a blue business dress and black stilettos. She smiles upon seeing me. "Just the person I was looking for."

"Oh. How can I help you Ms. Marchioni?" I ask politely.

"Please, call me Evelina. I'm going to my hairdresser today, and I wanted some company. Would you like to come?"

I touch the front of my hair and think back to how it looked in the bathroom earlier. It could use a touch up at the roots.

"I'm sorry, I don't have money to pay," I tell her.

She laughs. "It's on me, dear. Now let's go! I don't want to be late for my appointment."

Her heels click across the floor as she moves toward me and grabs my arm.

Suddenly, an idea pops into my brain. "Wait, I'll only be a minute."

She lets go of my arm as I rush down the hallway and into Valerio's office.

I haven't had my hair done by a hairdresser in so long, but I always used to...

I come to a stop outside of Valerio's office and rap my knuckles on the door.

"Come in," his voice rings out gruffly.

Opening the door, I see him behind his desk, writing something down. He sets his pen down and looks up. Seeing that it's me, a slow smile spreads across his face. "Kat, it's not time for lunch yet, is it?"

I shake my head. "Sorry to disturb you. I was just invited out with your aunt."

A look of surprise flashes across his face. "Go ahead, by all means. She's harmless."

I grin. "I was planning on it, but I have a request."

He raises an eyebrow. "And that would be..."

Nervousness keeps me from telling him right away, so I hesitate and then blurt it before I lose all my nerve.

"I just...can I take Valeria with me? I promise I'll keep her safe and you can have your men follow us, but I'm sure Evelina has her own, right?"

I bite my lip and wait for him to reply. He stares at me for a second, unblinking, when his lips part. "I think she'd love that. I trust you."

He doesn't say anything else as he looks down at his papers.

"Thank you," I reply, closing the door so I don't bother him anymore.

Not wasting another second, I break out into a run and stop in the foyer where Evelina is waiting. "Are we leaving now?" she asks.

"Please just one second," I say, racing up the stairs.

I come to a stop in the large entertainment room in the second level and go all the way to the back of the room, stopping at the stairs. Taking them two at a time, I get to the top quickly and go straight ahead to the largest room.

Opening the door, I find all the kids, Valeria included, playing with their toys.

Bernadette looks up at me. "Oh, hi Kat."

"No time to talk," I tell her. I walk right over to Valeria and pick her up. She's dressed in a cute white and yellow dress with matching shoes and a bow in her light brown hair.

She drops her toy as I put her on my shoulder.

"Mama, we going?" she asks.

"Yes, baby. We're going somewhere," I tell her before looking at Bernadette. "Valerio told me it's okay, don't worry."

I carefully hold her and go all the way back downstairs to the entryway.

Evelina beams at me. "What a great idea. Now I get to spend time with you and my little niece."

Right as we're about to walk out the door, I stop. "Wait, we need a car seat."

All of a sudden, from behind us we hear running and turn around. One of Valerio's men comes around the corner holding a car seat.

"Boss told me to bring it," he says.

I smile and picture Valerio in his office. That wonderful man thinks of everything. "Thank you."

We walk outside to Evelina's Mercedes. I insist on putting the car seat in myself and placing Valeria in it correctly.

As soon as I get in the passenger side, Evelina races down the driveway.

"Thanks for thinking of me," I say, looking at her.

She places a pair of Coach sunglasses on her face. "We have lots to talk about my dear."

That statement makes my stomach roll, but I stay calm all the same. No one follows behind us, so I assume she likes doing her own thing. In the backseat, Valeria stays so quiet, I look in the mirror to watch her and find she's just admiring the world as it practically flies by. Behind us, I can see a black Range Rover keeping pace.

*Protection for his princess.*

---

Evelina's hairdresser turns out to be in a very nice corner of town. There's only one other woman inside when we walk in. Her auburn hair looks smooth and shiny with tight curls, so I assume her appointment is over, and she's on her way out.

Angela, the hairdresser, insists it's no trouble doing both of us at once, so I sit in one chair while Evelina sits in the other.

I keep Valeria on my lap, so she doesn't wander through the shop getting herself into trouble.

As the woman with the previous appointment walks by us to get to the door, she stops. She gazes down at Valeria with a warm smile on her face. "You have such a beautiful daughter."

My mouth drops open and I don't know what to say.

*No, she's not my daughter? Thank you? That's very kind?*

"Thank you. Say thank you, Valeria."

She looks up at her. "Than' you."

The woman smiles at me and then leaves.

I keep Valeria busy, playing with her until it is my turn for her to start on my hair.

"So, this is Valerio's daughter then," Angela says when she gets to my chair. "I've never met Valerio's wife, but it's very nice to meet you."

Evelina coughs a little, and I immediately catch the hint. "Thank you, it's very nice to meet you."

She colors my roots with a fancier black hair dye than I use at home. She finishes Evelina's hair, making it straight and silky. It flows all the way down her back and stops at her butt. Angela does beauty curls on me. The whole time, I manage to keep Valeria entertained and when I finally let her down, she runs wild.

"Come again," Angela says as I race after her while Evelina pays the bill.

After getting situated back in the car, we head back to the mansion. I watch as the black Range Rover follows closely behind.

"Can I get pretty hair like you, Mama?" Valeria asks.

Evelina chuckles. "She's precious."

She is. This little girl has such a strong hold of my heart like she really is my own daughter. "Your hair is already pretty, baby. One day you can get it done like us, just wait until you're a little older, okay?"

As she murmurs a reply, the car jerks forward and races off faster than even when we were running late to the beauty salon.

I glance over at Evelina. "What's going on?"

A grimace forms on her face. "We're being followed," she grits.

In the side mirror, I see an Explorer racing after us with no Range Rover in sight.

*Shit.*

"Call Valerio," she says as we race past the road leading to the mansion.

She takes jerky turns as I pick up her phone and go straight for her contacts, finding Valerio's name. The phone rings once. "Evelina? Is everything okay?"

"It's...it's me Valerio."

"Kat? Is something wrong?" Panic rises in his voice.

"There's a car following us," I admit, waiting for the blow up. The one time I take Valeria out, this happens.

He mutters a curse, and I hear the sound of his fist slamming against what I assume is his desk. "I knew I should've sent more than just Luca. Where are you?"

"It looks like we're circling around, going down side streets trying to lose them."

He grunts. "Don't worry, I'll take care of this."

The phone clicks, and I look at Evelina. "He said he's going to take care of it."

We go down a side street, around a main street, and through a parking lot. When we pull back on to the main road, we're on our way back to the mansion when two Range Rovers get on each side of us, keeping pace.

I glance behind in the mirror and my mouth drops open as I see an endless amount of them trying to catch up to us. The Explorer peels off down the first possible street it can turn on, and I watch as half the SUVs follow it while the rest follow us back to the mansion.

"That's a relief," Evelina says with a sigh. "The last thing I need is for something to happen to you or his princess."

I laugh a little at that. "You mean, just his princess."

She stays quiet. "No, I said exactly what I meant. You're irreplaceable now. My nephew has it bad. He hasn't let anyone into his heart like this in a long time. You are very important, Kat. I hope I'm not overstepping by saying, you're the future Queen."

Heat crawls up my neck at hearing that word. *Queen...*

We turn into the driveway and go around the circle when the doors to the mansion open and Valerio stalks out, coming right to my door.

He opens it and his bluish gray eyes stare into mine. "I'm glad you're okay." He helps me out of the car and then opens Valeria's door.

She screeches, "Daddy!"

"Yes, my princess." He unhooks her from her car seat and holds her in one arm while he goes around to open the door for Evelina.

"Thank you," she calmly says.

"Thank *you* for your driving."

She smirks and leads the way inside as Valerio takes my hand and pulls me in with him.

We go straight to the living room and sit on one long couch with Evelina sitting on the other.

Valerio opens his mouth to speak when his cell phone goes off on his pocket.

He drops my hand and sets Valeria down on the floor to answer. "Well?"

A moment passes and he mutters in Italian under his breath and then says, "Okay."

He glances at Evelina and then me with blazing anger in his gaze. "They got away. I can't believe they got away."

Evelina snorts. "We'll find those fuckers one day. They'll be daring enough to try something again, don't worry. Next time we'll be ready to catch them."

Her words don't calm Valerio down one bit as he seethes in anger.

Valeria runs around the room while we sit in silence until finally he sighs. "Fine, well I might as well get back to business."

Were they after Valeria? Or Evelina? Did they watch us go in the salon?

The doorbell interrupts my thoughts, and I look toward

the entryway. For a second, fear grasps ahold of me. *I don't want to go back.*

Rationality comes back when I realize his guards had to have let whoever it is in. Valerio rises to answer the door and comes back with both of his uncles, Domenico and Oliverio.

"Did you know they were coming?" Valerio asks in Evelina's direction.

She nods. "The three of us have to talk to you."

Valerio takes his seat next to me while they sit next to Evelina, with Oliverio sitting closest to her. A wave of uneasiness flows through me. Valerio seems to sense it as he leans back and places his left arm around the couch behind me. It makes me feel a little better, although I know his family is friendly.

"Is this woman going to stay Valerio?" Domenico asks.

"Yes, is she going to be the new Mrs. Marchioni?" Oliverio asks, shifting his gaze from him to me.

Evelina's face remains neutral.

"I don't have to tell you anything," Valerio replies crisply with an air of annoyance.

Evelina clasps her hands together. "We can help you with Salvatore. You know, you'll have to tell him sooner or later."

There's a moment of silence before Valerio snaps, "If Father thinks he can deprive *me* of the happiness I deserve, he's mistaken. I will not allow him to do it again. I was a boy before, barely eighteen. Not this time." He grabs my hand. "This woman is my only want, my only desire. She keeps the fire in me burning brighter than it ever has before. I'd *love* to see him try and get in my way again."

Domenico sighs. "You know how he is though, Valerio. He never stops until he gets exactly what he wants. Do you remember how thrilled he was that I gave up my spot? This mansion, this life, it should all have been mine. Alessio should be in your position right now. But the thrill I saw in his eyes the moment I gave up, he relished having that control. That was never me, I could never bring myself to do it. Father was livid, but what could he expect when Salvatore was more interested than I was right from the start."

Valerio clicks his tongue. "None of that matters now. It doesn't matter what Father thinks, it doesn't matter what Grandfather thinks. I am the boss of this family now, and I will do whatever the fuck I want to do."

His tone sends a chill down my spine and Valeria stops running abruptly to sit next to me on the couch.

"Are you Italian my dear?" Evelina asks.

I chew on my lip before answering softly, "No."

She smiles. "Well as long as you aren't Russian. He'd really do everything in his power to stop your relationship."

My face pales as I think over the lie. I was on the street when I was taken by the men. I don't remember who I am. *I don't remember.* My name is Kat, just Kat.

"I-I lost my memory and the men who took me found me on the street. I'm sorry I can't tell you more than that. I was on the street for at least five years before they got me."

"So, you see. She is no threat to us. She stays."

They nod and look at both of us. "We support you all the way, Valerio," Oliverio states, getting up to shake my hand and leaving.

Evelina and Domenico get up and follow him, nodding in my direction.

They believe it too. God, I'm the worst. I'll never ever be able to tell any of them the truth. What would they think of me if I did? Valerio would never trust me again, and I can't lose him now.

Valerio squeezes my hand. "You're so quiet, is something wrong?"

I shake my head. "Nothing...nothing at all."

*I'm just a lying bitch, that's all.*

He lifts my chin up with his finger. "Look at me." I stare right into stormy eyes swimming with emotion and heat. "No one is going to separate us. I'll talk to my mother soon, and she'll help this go over a little easier. They'll love you, I promise."

I open my mouth to reply, but he silences me with a heart shattering kiss that shakes me to my core. I kiss him back with everything inside of me, trusting his words, and knowing deep in my heart that he means everything he says.

We break the kiss when we hear a giggle. We turn in the direction of the sound and see Valeria watching us with smiling eyes. "Mama and Daddy kiss."

"Yes, we kissed, now come over here so we can kiss you," Valerio says.

She gets up from next to me and hops into the tiny space in between us. Valerio and I proceed to shower her with kisses. "We love you so much princess."

He looks at me as a happy tear leaks out of my eye. *What a change.*

---

I grab a small bag of chips from the kitchen since I missed lunch and head back to my room. To keep myself from thinking about my problems too much, I grab a book I've been dying to read. Werewolves are so hot. I bite my lip and get lost in the pages.

All of a sudden, things start getting fuzzy, and I stop being able to concentrate on the words on the page.

*The sound of the front door banging open makes me shudder. I can feel his presence before even seeing him come through the door. He stalks in, eyeing me. I turn away and cry. "Please, I don't want to go. I'm in love for the first time in my life. Don't make me do this."*

*"You're coming home," he screams.*

*His large hand grabs my arm, holding it in a tight grip as he pulls me to the door. I try to keep my feet planted on the ground, but his strength is too much. He pulls me to the doorway. As a last-ditch effort, I cry, "Valerio, please, don't let him take me back. I love you. Don't you love me?"*

*It's all for nothing because I'm yanked promptly out the door, and it slams right in my face.*

*"No."*

*"Yes," he whispers in my ear.*

*I sob and cry, chanting, "No, no, no, no."*

Inhaling, I'm jolted awake and realize I'm still here, in my bed. A weight falls off of me as I sit up and realize it was the book I was reading.

I place my hands over my eyes and take a shaky breath. It was only a nightmare. Nothing has changed. Valerio hasn't let me go, and *he's* not here. I get off my bed, walk to the bathroom, and run a bubble bath for myself.

Oh! That book and this bath would be a nice combination. After the bath fills up halfway, and the bubbles are big and plentiful, I go back to get my book.

The bath is just what I need. Relaxing in it for an hour and reading my book. Although, being in this water actually makes me want to go swimming. It's still a nice sunny day, and the sun won't go down for a few hours.

I get out of the tub and rush to get into the only bikini I have. In the full-length mirror, I look at my stomach and self-consciously rub over the stretch marks.

Oh well, I still look hot as hell. I study my backside before leaving my room and walk straight to the backyard where the Olympic-sized pool is.

Valerio says it's three feet on the shallow side and twelve on the deep end. It's nice and clear, except for a few shapes of something on the bottom. Not a leaf or bug in sight. I hate bugs. Time to check it out.

I jump right in, making a huge splash and sinking almost to the bottom. The coldness of the water bites at me a little, making me regret not going down using the bars and inching in slowly like I usually do with a pool. At the bottom of the pool, I reluctantly open my eyes. The chlorine makes my eyes sting a little, but the burn slowly goes away. Immediately, I notice there are a few cars littering the bottom.

Those must be Vincenzo's.

I swim back and forth for a long time, enjoying the feel of the water. Only coming up when I need air. When I get tired, I float on my back and allow the water to move me. It's not as cold as it was when I first got in.

Still, I think it's time to explore that jacuzzi. I eye it across the pool and swim to the edge of the pool and lift myself out of the water. As I walk to the jacuzzi, I leave small puddles of water. Now, where's the switch for the bubbles?

After a careful look around, I spy the machine in the bushes and press the button to start the bubbles. The jacuzzi immediately starts doing its thing, rumbling low and making bubbles in the water. With a satisfied nod, I turn around and slip into the hot water of the jacuzzi. Immediately it soothes every tense muscle in my body, and I close my eyes, fully allowing the feeling to calm me.

I wish Valerio was here to enjoy this with me. Every worry flies out the window, and I focus on the feeling of the

TIFFANY RANSIER

bubbles and get off the little jacuzzi seat to swim around in the water a little. My foot touches something hard at the bottom and I frown, looking down and trying to glimpse the thing through the water. The bubbles keep me from seeing exactly what it is, but my foot feels around it, trying to discern what it is.

A toy car. So, Vincenzo was in here too. I sit back on the seat in the jacuzzi, closing my eyes.

All summer, this is where I'm going to be. Maybe Valeria can get in the jacuzzi with me. I'll hold on to her, so she doesn't drown. The warmth of the jacuzzi starts getting old and I feel the need to go back to the cool pool.

*Going back to that pool is going to be hard,* I remind myself. The shock of that cold water—

Suddenly, I feel hands touch my shoulders. "Can I join you?"

I shiver as I tilt my head back and Valerio's eyes come into view. His eyes shift to my bikini top, shining as they shift back to my blue ones. "Don't move," he breathes, getting up and going back inside.

I watch his retreating back, my face flushing as I think, *I've never had sex in a jacuzzi before.*

# THIRTEEN

## Valerio

I t feels like a lifetime since I left Kat at home. I've fallen for her hard and fast, and I don't want to keep waiting, I don't want to keep things slow. Slow is for those who don't know what they want.

Pulling into the driveway of my house, my driver states, "It's been quiet since you've been gone, sir."

I nod and wait for him to pull up to the front door.

Getting out, I go into my house and sure enough, it's quiet. Dealing with crazy people and guys who think that the women are prostitutes tends to get a little tedious. Dirty douchebags who think that these women belong to them just because they can wave a little money. The funniest thing is most of those girls probably have more money than the men who frequent my establishments.

Everything is quiet as I come into the house. My best

guess is either the kids are with their tutors or playing together, but whatever the case, nobody seems to be doing anything right now.

I rub my shoulders as the tension in the muscles is causing a dull throb in them. Every step I take sends a small shock wave through them, causing even more pain. I walk through the foyer and into the kitchen. Once inside, I see a pot of spaghetti on the stove with a pot of sauce next to it.

"I'm betting the meatballs are already in the oven then?"

"Oh, har har, whether or not you'd eat this in Italy or not doesn't matter when this is what your immigrant forefathers would have eaten," Bernadette says sarcastically.

I grin at that. "I'm just messing with you. Spaghetti and meatballs sounds delicious."

"Why don't you go relax, Mr. Marchioni, while I finish with dinner?"

*Sounds like a good idea.* I head to the sliding glass door leading out to the back patio and pool.

Casually, I check out the landscape. My eyes are suddenly drawn to a moving figure, leading to the most beautiful sight I've ever seen. Kat is swimming back and forth through my pool. Her beautiful black hair is flowing behind her as she swims. Suddenly, she stops swimming and pulls herself out, moving over to the Jacuzzi. I stand back and watch as she struggles to find the switch to turn it on, bending over a little bit and giving me the best vision of her beautifully round ass.

Oh, how I'd love to get a nice grip of it; my cock rises in my pants at the thought. I sneak outside while her back is turned before I can stop myself.

I go around the bushes where she can't see me. When she finds the switch, she happily gets in the Jacuzzi and leans back to relax. Coming around from behind her, I eye her shoulders. She doesn't seem to realize I'm here at all. Hopefully I don't scare her too much.

I lean down, place my hands on her shoulders, and whisper in her ear, "Can I join you?"

She looks back at me in surprise and my eyes are drawn to her bikini top. I stare back into her eyes. "Don't move."

I head back inside and quickly make my way to my room. Once there, I practically throw off my clothes and put on my swimming trunks.

When I get back outside, instead of Kat being in the Jacuzzi she's in the pool, swimming in the deep end.

I dive in smoothly, push off the bottom and slide up against her when I surface behind her.

"Now, what do I have here in my pool? A beautiful woman in a sexy bikini. It would be enough for anyone to want to ravage you. So, what should I do with you?"

"Well, you could always let me go," Kat replies coyly.

"I don't think I'm going to let you go. Especially since I have you so close right now. I mean why give you up when I could easily just take you right now."

"What would your kids think if they saw?" she asks.

"I don't think they'll be able to see what we're doing in the water. Anybody else would know what we're doing, but I don't give a fuck what they think. I know that I want you with everything that I am. So, I'm going to make you mine and nothing and nobody is going to stop me," I state, staring into her blue eyes that widen with every word.

"Well, then I'll just have to escape from you," she teases back.

She tries to swim away, kicking quickly in the water, and I follow close behind. It's not until I pin her to the wall of the pool on the other side that she turns around to face me.

Leaning in close, her breath quickens, and our air starts

to mingle. We stare into each other's eyes, and I can see the want and need flooding hers. It's all I need to move that extra space and lock lips with hers. Her breath hitches in her throat at the feel of my lips and she presses her lips into mine.

Her lips taste so sweet against mine, like the sweetest honey I've ever tasted. She wraps her arms around my neck, pulling herself closer to me. In the water, I feel my cock growing harder. *Fuck, I want to be inside her so bad.*

Suddenly, she pulls away and pushes me off slightly.

"Wait...we need...dinner will be done soon," she says her voice husky with want.

"Are you sure you want to stop?"

"Yes. We need to go and eat dinner." She says it so firmly and yet, her eyes are filled with lust, and I watch as her eyes shoot down beneath the water and back up to my own.

But she's right. Dinner is almost done, and I may be fine with an audience, but she isn't.

I'm willing to wait for however long it takes. Whenever that perfect moment is, I'll be waiting for it. I smirk and swim away, climb my way out of the pool, and then turn around to help Kat out after me.

Instead of going through the kitchen, we go through another back door which leads to our pool room. I grab a towel for her and myself. As she dries off facing away from me, I pinch her ass and laugh softly as she jumps at my touch.

"Why would you do that?" she asks with a gasp.

"I couldn't help myself," I say with a shrug.

She giggles and smiles ear to ear.

We finish drying off, and I go straight to my room to take a quick shower and change into some regular clothes for once.

Heading to the kitchen after, I hear a mix of children and men talking.

As soon as I turn the corner, I see everyone but Kat sitting at the table. A few minutes later, I hear her walking quickly as her feet hit the tile.

The chair my wife previously sat in is gone, and Kat and I agreed her place is here, next to me. And that's exactly where she sits, with Ilaria between us in her high chair.

Of course, Valeria sits on Kat's other side.

"Everyone can eat now," I say, helping my children fix their plates and then fixing mine.

"So boss, how was your day at the club? Everything okay?" Luca asks me.

"Yeah, some assholes were causing some trouble getting handy with the girls. But I took care of them, they won't be back to the club at all."

"Are the girls okay? I mean none of them were harmed or anything?" Luciano asks with a slightly panicked tone.

"Yes, the girls and everyone else are fine. I threatened those guys that if they ever came back to the club that I would cut off their balls and feed them to my pet Komodo dragon."

"...but you don't have a Komodo dragon," Luca responds.

"We know that, but they sure as hell don't."

Kat stifles a giggle and soon the entire table is in uproar, laughing uncontrollably.

After the men finish their food, they leave to either switch with the guys who haven't eaten or to go back to their homes. Bernadette takes the kids upstairs for their baths while the other maids clear the table off.

"Hey Kat, I was wondering..." I start.

"Yeah?"

"Would you like to watch a movie with me while the kids are getting washed up and ready for bed?"

Excitement flashes in her eyes. "What movie did you have in mind?"

"I was going to let you pick. I have a huge collection of movies, and I figured that since you are always reading in your room that you might want to watch something for a change instead?"

She bites her lip and then gives me a huge, appreciative smile. If I had known she'd like the idea this much, I would have suggested it ages ago.

We move into the family room where the large flat screen TV is. While Kat picks the movie, I turn the TV on. I wonder what she'll pick. Action? Fantasy?

Kat finally picks one, a love story called *Crazy, Stupid, Love*, and we both sit down to watch it.

"Normally I don't watch these. All those action films are mine. These belonged to my wife. Well, some of them belong to Luca as well. He won't admit it, but I'm pretty sure he watches them and cries sometimes, but you didn't hear that from me, okay?" I whisper in her ear.

She shoots me a look of disbelief but giggles all the same.

The movie winds on as my men end up moving into the room, surrounding us as we watch the movie.

"I love this part. This is where his wife calls him to fix something at their house, but he's already there and sees that she was just missing him instead," Luca whispers with a wistful tone to Alessio who looks at him like he's insane.

I snake my arm slowly around Kat's shoulders and pull her close to me while the movie is going. She snuggles into me and makes a noise of contentment.

Honestly, the only thing that could make this better

would be a large tub of popcorn. The movie is halfway over when suddenly Kat jumps up out of my arms.

"I can't stand this anymore!" she exclaims.

My stomach drops a little as I can't read her expression. "What's wrong Kat? What do you mean you can't stand it anymore?" I manage to get out.

She sighs. "I can't keep watching this movie without popcorn. I need something to munch on while we're watching this."

The look of shock on my face must have been visible enough because she bursts out laughing.

"Why do you look so scared? What did you think I was going to say?" she asks.

"Nothing. Don't worry about it. I'll go make some popcorn quickly okay?"

As soon as I'm in the kitchen, I take a shaky breath and attempt to calm down.

*Thank God she just wanted popcorn, I thought maybe...she wanted to leave. I should stop thinking the worst, but what else can I do when I've finally found the woman of my dreams?*

I make some popcorn and bring it out to her, sitting back in my seat. The movie starts back up, and we eat popcorn while watching the film. The ending of the movie comes about, and it unexpectedly makes me a little teary eyed to see both partners ending up with their happy endings. *I'm working my way to a happiness just like theirs.*

Kat turns toward me with small tears in the corners of her eyes. "That was a really good movie. Thanks for watching it with me."

Luca tries to slip away with the other men, but before they can fully get away, I remark, "Enjoy the movie, guys?"

Luca turns around and shrugs with a sheepish look and walks away with the rest of the men. With that, I turn to Kat.

"I think it's time to give Carina and Ilaria their bottles and then it's time to put all the kids to bed."

Kat stands up and grabs my hand, leading me upstairs to my daughters' room.

Once we get up there, we find Bernadette waiting with the bottles. "Oh, Mr. Marchioni and Kat. What a pleasant surprise. What brings you two up here?"

"I'd like to feed my daughters tonight Bernadette, you do plenty of work for me."

She smiles gratefully. "Of course, Mr. Marchioni."

With that she leaves the bottles for us to feed my daughters.

I happily take Carina out of her crib, cradling and supporting her while giving her the bottle. While I do this Kat is doing the same thing with Ilaria. Once they're completely done, they make happy noises and attempt to get out of our arms to play.

"You really do have some of the most adorable kids, Valerio," Kat comments quietly. A weird flash of guilt passes across her face that leaves me a little puzzled.

"Thank you, Kat," I reply quietly. Sometimes when I look at them, all I can see is *her*, and I'm reminded again of my mistake in not keeping her safe. "So, do you want to help put all the other kids down so we can have some more alone time or would that be too much?"

She grins. "Of course, I'll help."

Gathering up all of the kids in the sitting room, we sit down and pull out a book. I go to grab the book, but Aurelio stops me and hands it to Kat. She looks surprised and a little nervous, but he smiles. "Can you read tonight?" he asks.

I stare at her and watch as tears start forming in her eyes and she nods, opening the book to the first page. Valeria leans against her as she reads, her beautiful and melodic voice floats through the air, and I become engrossed in listening.

Everyone seems to enjoy it, even Vincenzo. The closer she gets to the end, the more their eyes start to glaze. When she's done, they've all almost drifted off, and we help them off to their beds.

I pick up Vincenzo and bring him to his room, tucking him in and kissing him on the forehead.

"Daddy...Kat read a good story," Vincenzo says in a sleepy state. I smile at that and go back to help Nicolo and Vittorio to their beds while Kat finishes helping Emilio and Aurelio.

We meet back up in the sitting room. "So, what do you want to do now? The kids are asleep and my men normally take over the family room at this point in the night so that they can play video games or watch movies of their own."

"Well I was thinking that I would go to my room and you could go to your room and then we could both have a quiet night without each other," she replies while smiling sweetly.

I can't help but feel my heart sink a little. "Is that really what you want? You're just going to go to your room and that's it?"

Her sweet smile turns torturous and flash down to my lips. "That's it."

Two can play this game. "Okay, I'm going to my room then. It's gonna be a long day tomorrow," I say nonchalantly.

"Why? What do you have to do tomorrow?" she asks.

I shrug. "Something always seems to happen. That's one thing you can never count out in this life. Anything can happen at any time."

She nods and I turn around and stride to my room. I feel her eyes watching me as I leave, and I'm tempted to look over my shoulder at her. Tempted to go back and throw her over my shoulder and carry her to my room, just so I can hold her.

Once I get there, I tear off my clothes and throw on my silk pajama bottoms. I wait a few minutes, enough time to let her think we're not going to see each other. Eventually, I make my way to her room. Across the mansion I can hear the distant sounds of Luca talking in the family room about the romance movie and Alessio groaning in frustration. I knock on her door and she opens it in a plain nightgown that hides all of her curves. *How I'd love to take it off of her.*

"What are you doing here?" she asks as her eyebrows furrow.

I put my finger up against her mouth and move with her into her room, closing the door behind me.

"Valerio?" she asks with a note of nervousness in her voice.

I stare into her crystal-blue eyes and place my forehead against hers. "We never seem to get enough alone time before someone interrupts us. I want to talk to you more with no one else around."

Her lips form a smile. "So, late at night is the only time we can be alone like this?"

I get her meaning, but as much as I want her, I'm not going to rush this. My eyes flick down to her lips. "I'm not here for that, unless you want to. I really just wanted to talk to you. I really care about you, and I want to know everything there is to know about you."

Kat looks from me to the door and then motions for me to join her on the bed. "Tell me about yourself first."

We sit on her bed and I tell her about my childhood. That at one point I was in love or at least I thought I was, but my father forced me to give her up.

"Do you think he's going to force you to give me up too?" Kat asks sadly.

"Over my dead fucking body. He can't make me do anything anymore. I'm the Don now, and I promise you, you aren't going anywhere."

She sighs happily. "That makes me happy to hear, I don't want to leave. I...I like it here, and I like you and your family." She lets out a small yawn that grows steadily.

She stretches her arms out and lies down. A similar feeling comes over me and soon I'm falling asleep right next to her.

---

SUNLIGHT STREAMS through the curtain and bathes the room in an early morning light. While turning slightly, I feel a smaller form curled up next to me.

I sit up and stretch, feeling the muscles in my shoulders pop. I crack my neck and attempt to get out of bed as quietly as possible.

"No…" Kat's small voice squeaks out.

No?

"No..I...I...hate…"

What kind of dream is she having? I reach over to her and almost grab her shoulder to wake her up. "I hate you...Valerio..."

Oh. I stop in midair and yank my hand away before it can touch her. So, that's how she must feel then. Even if she is sleeping, aren't dreams subconscious thoughts? I heard her loud and clear. Why the fuck is she leading me on? Making me think… I could actually fall in love. Why would she use me and my kids? All of my kids were just getting used to her. Poor little Valeria. And what about Vincenzo? He was just getting used to her. All of these thoughts only make me angrier. A knock on the door rouses me from my growing anger.

Luciano pokes his head in. "Boss we need to talk in the office right now."

I nod, wiping the sleep away from my eyes. Standing up, I hear Kat begin to move on the bed, her sleeping frame stirring. Her harsh words echo in my brain, and I don't stick around to ask her anything. I walk out as soon as I hear the creak of Kat getting out of her bed.

Slamming the door behind me, I plop down hard into my seat. I fold my hands together and stare straight ahead at Luciano.

"What the hell is it now?" I ask with an exasperated sigh.

"What's your problem boss?" Luciano asks, folding his arms.

"Nothing I want to talk about."

"Alright well then, we have big problems. First off, there have been whispers of the traffickers coming to New York again really soon. Second, you have to leave for California in a few hours."

"Why the fuck would I want to go back to Cali?" The last thing I need to hear is it has to do with him.

"Julio wants a meeting." Fuck. I rub a hand over my face.

"So, the head of the Mexican Cartel wants to meet me in person. Why the fuck would he want that?"

"He didn't say only that it was important."

God what the fuck does that fucking Mexican want? We only just fucking settled the war and now he wants to meet? "Fine, let me get the tutors in order and then you and I are going to California."

He nods respectfully. "Alright boss, I'll see you on the plane."

With that he's gone, and I'm left alone with my thoughts and my phone. After making the necessary call to the tutors, I leave my office and quickly gather my children to spend a little time with them before I leave.

Fuck. How could I have been so clueless? Of course, she's just using us, just using *me* for safety. Fuck this. I'm done playing games. I stomp down the hallway and when I get to my office, Luciano is waiting for me.

"Dad why do you have to go? You said you wouldn't anymore," Vincenzo remarks indignantly.

"I need to do this for the business, something you will understand when you are older," I reply and ruffle his hair. "Take care of your siblings, Vincenzo. Make sure that everyone is safe since you're the man of the house while I'm gone. Okay?"

He nods his head and starts to pout.

"No don't pout. Luca and Alessio will both be here to watch you guys so just try not to be sad until I get back. Okay?"

He nods again and gives me a long hug. I don't exactly want to leave either, though maybe I do after Kat...

I can't waste any more time. Heading downstairs, I grab the suitcases Luca packed for me. Out of the corner of my eye, I see Kat is waiting for me by the door, but I quickly move past her and walk out the door to my waiting car. If she wants to hate me, let her hate me. I'll give her something to hate. God, things were going so well too. I told her everything, more than I've ever told anyone. I let her inside and she set me on fire, only to put me out just as quickly.

I stare out the window as my driver brings me to the airport. We pass through the city, and I get lost watching the streets of people so focused on their own lives that they lose track of everything around them. I've been lost in this but no more. From this point forward, nice Valerio is dead and gone. Like he should be.

"We've arrived sir, I'll load your bags while you board."

I nod at the driver and get out of the car, making my way over to the plane and notice that Luciano is waving at me from inside the jet. The jet is luxurious, mahogany paneling along the walls and the seats are plush and comfortable.

"Well five and a half hours with me in a jet, what do you want to do boss?" Luciano asks me his voice more chipper than I care to deal with right now.

Usually we play a game of cards, or just talk, which can be nice, but I'm not in the mood. "Nothing. I need to think out my next move. I can't go in there without some sort of plan or that asshole is going to blindside me."

Luciano blinks, but I know he understands. The most subdued of my men, he understands silence. "Okay, boss."

AFTER THE PLANE, we get into the waiting limo. It takes us to a rather large corporate building. The building otherwise is unremarkable, no logo, no signs. Nothing to denote that the head of the Cartel is sitting inside of this building with most likely his elite forces. Stepping out of the limo, the heat is the first thing I notice. It's hot here and I rush to the door opening it to meet a blast of cold air.

"Mr. Marchioni. Welcome to California and welcome to Cartel country," the receptionist at the desk greets.

"Thank you. So, can I go in now?" I ask, adjusting to the cold temp of the waiting room.

"Yes, please go in right now, but your man has to stay out here in the waiting room."

I stand up a little straighter, already annoyed by having to leave him behind. "Fine. Luciano stay here and wait for me."

He nods his head and sits down, picks up a magazine, and leafs through it. Luciano may not say much, but I know deep inside, there's a monster waiting to come out. If need be, he'd kill everyone here to make sure we both get out alright.

I walk past her into the conference room where Julio is set up at one side of the table, with a smug expression on his face. I sit across from him and lean back in the chair.

"Welcome, Mr. Marchioni." The sound of that bastard's voice already makes me want to punch him in the face.

"So, what is it that this meeting was supposed to accomplish?" I ask, unable to keep the annoyance from leaking into my tone.

"This meeting is just touching base since we inked out our treaty. We haven't seen hide nor hair of each other. I missed you, *vato*."

"Stop fucking around with me, Julio. What the hell do you want with me? I came here out of respect to the treaty and that's it. If you just want to fuck around, I'm leaving."

He smirks. "Easy now, easy. Chill out. How's that pretty wife of yours doing? I haven't seen her at your house in a while," Julio says, licking his lips.

The mere mention of my dead wife makes my blood boil and I stand up. "Treaty be damned, I might just kick your ass now."

"Hold on, hold on. Fine. Enough games. I called you here because someone has been fucking with my men and my territory. I wanted to confirm it had nothing to do with you."

I grit my teeth and stare him right in his eyes. "I have not and will not break the treaty unless provoked myself. Since you haven't done anything to me, at least not that I'm aware of, it's not me."

Julio nods his head, snapping his fingers. Four Hispanic women in nothing but thongs come out of the back doors. "Pick a woman, I promise they will please you, unlike that wife of yours."

"No thank you. I'm fine," I reply, clenching my fists behind me.

"No. I think you need to accept, or I might be offended."

I've had enough. I turn around and walk straight out of the meeting.

God, I hate the fucking Mexicans. We have rules to what we do. No kidnapping women and no selling to kids, but these fuckers have no limits no rules to what they do. It's despicable, and they make me sick to my stomach.

Walking out, I motion for Luciano to follow me. We hop into my limo and have them drive us to my California home. On the way there, I think about his words of someone messing with his territory, but I shake the thought away. I don't care what's happening with him. Pulling into the driveway, I realize that this is the first time that I've been here since she was taken.

She always loved this house. She felt too alone in the New York house, but this one was small enough that she could make it her own.

I head inside, with Luciano behind me. Other than a layer of dust, everything is how we left it the last time we came out here to visit. The smallest inkling of sadness fills me, but I push it away. I take out some cardboard boxes and start putting all of her things away. Packing up every single thing she owns into boxes. Everything that reminds me of her. Everything that proves that she was a part of my life other than my children. All into boxes where it can't be seen by anyone. This house needs to be cleaned out. That way I can sell it and forget about it.

I go into my room and see her everywhere, on the bed and in front of the mirror. She was the one who loved this place. She wanted it to be her permanent home, but I guess she'll never get the chance to fight me on that again.

My mind wanders to Kat. Will she find a place she loves more than New York? Or will she want to stay in the New York mansion? Then it hits me. No, she doesn't really want me. She doesn't want to share our lives together. My anger grows all over again.

"I'll feel better once this is done," I say out loud.

"Hey boss, who are you talking to?" The voice shakes me out of my thoughts. I turn and see that Luciano is standing in the doorway.

"Sorry to eavesdrop, but I don't trust Julio and you've been alone in here for a while. I can help you, you know."

I sigh. "I'm going to sell the house. But first, I need to clean this stuff out and send it to storage in New York. I can't just throw it away. I'll lock it away where I don't have to see or deal with it anymore, but the kids can see it when they're older."

"That's fine, boss. I'll hire a mover then and we can be back in New York in a few days."

That last part throws me off. "Why a few days?"

"With how you were earlier," he coughs, "a break from everything might be good for you. So, that's what this is going to be."

For a split second I'm torn. I could go back to my kids right away. I'm sure Vincenzo would be happy. But at the same time, this is time away from Kat, time for me to figure out if I should make her leave and tell me the truth. "That sounds like the best idea you've had in a while."

# FOURTEEN

Kat

The sound of a loud knock on my door jolts me out of a dead sleep. Sitting up quickly causes blood to rush to my head. I wince as my head starts to pound from lack of sleep for the past ten nights.

Another knock sounds on the door. "Coming!" I yell.

I swing my legs out of bed and rush to the door, pulling it open. Bernadette smiles brightly, and I feel the urge to smile back even though I don't feel like it.

"Good morning Kat, I just wanted to let you know it's already almost noon."

My eyes widen. "But Bernadette, I wanted to be woken up early so I could help get everything ready for today."

She shakes her head firmly. "I know you wanted to help, but you haven't looked well since...well..since Valerio left."

I shift my feet on the soft carpet and rub my hands over

my sleep filled eyes. "I'm okay." Her light blue eyes study my face and she grabs my hands. "Kat, things are going to be fine. Valerio should be back soon."

I nod wordlessly and go back over the last time I saw him. I thought everything was great. We even slept in the same bed together all night long. And then he walked right past me to leave without saying a word? As if I didn't exist. Like I wasn't standing by the door, waiting and hoping for a kiss goodbye.

Remembering makes a stray tear slip out of the corner of my eye. What did I do to deserve that? No matter how many times I've gone over that night in my head, I can't remember doing anything out of sorts. Before going to sleep, he gave me no indication that anything was wrong. I don't know what to think. He hasn't called, and even though I begged Luca to call and see if he's okay, he said he was under strict orders not to bother him. The only thing I can do is wait for him to get back and ignore him as soon as he does for leaving me in the dark. I'll see how he likes it. More than likely, today will be the day he'll come back. I don't think he'd miss today for anything, even if he doesn't want to see me.

With a sigh, I let go of Bernadette's hand and give her a tight hug. "Thank you for letting me sleep."

Her flowery perfume reaches my nose as she rubs my back soothingly, reminding me that I always have a friend in her. If there's anyone I can always count on, it's her. "Exactly how much got done while I've been lazing about, asleep?"

"We decorated the backyard, put the tables up, picked up the cake, made lunch and strawberry lemonade, and got the children dressed and ready. They're still upstairs right now finishing up their studies for the day."

"Bernadette! What you're saying is, everything has already

been done and I don't need to do anything?" I ask, unable to keep the surprise out of my voice.

She laughs. "All that's left to do is for you to get ready. Hurry now! Party starts in an hour." My heart swells with gratefulness for Bernadette as I watch her turn around and leave. After she's out of sight, I close the door gently and walk to my bathroom to get ready.

Twenty minutes later, after a scalding hot shower and my usual morning routine, I'm finally ready to slip on my brand-new dress, a bright yellow sundress, perfect for the summer. I brush through my hair quickly and leave it down, letting it flow straight down my back. In the mirror I stare at my roots and notice my brown roots are starting to come through. Maybe it's finally time to ditch the hair dye. It's been six months, and I miss my tawny brown hair.

A bright fire engine red is my lipstick choice, and I hurry out of my room, so I don't waste any more time. A rush of nerves flow through me as I go up the stairs.

Today is not just anyone's birthday. It's Vincenzo's. I'm still not exactly sure what he thinks about me. He's been so quiet around me since his father left. I'm not sure how today is going to go. And what if Valerio doesn't come back today? That'll only make Vincenzo feel worse.

I take the left to the girl's' hallway and go inside the twins' room to find them and Valeria with one of the maids.

A look of surprise flashes on her face before she smiles. "Good afternoon." Before I can reply, she's already out the door.

Valeria runs to me and grabs ahold of my leg. She's wearing a cute, pink dress that goes just below her knees and cute, pink sandals. "Are you ready?"

She nods and toddles over to her sisters who are playing

on the floor with their toys. "Rina and Ria let's go," she tells them.

Neither of them gives her any indication they heard her, which makes her frown and poke her lip out. "Don't worry," I say to Valeria.

I bend down and grab one in each arm. They both make upset noises and just when their breath hitches and their faces crumble into a cry, I kiss both of their cheeks and make funny noises. It distracts them enough for me to leave their room, with Valeria following close behind.

We walk back to the main area past the sitting room and find all of the boys in their long schoolroom with the tutors. "That'll be all for today," I announce.

They look to the doorway at me and almost all of them jump out of their chairs, rushing past me to get downstairs. Valeria runs after them with her little legs keeping her at the back of their group.

The tutors get up and leave with a nod in my direction and the only person left in the big yellow room is Vincenzo.

Hesitantly, I walk toward him. The twins giggle in delight as I get closer, straining against me to get down and get to him. "Hey Vincenzo," I say softly.

"Hi," he murmurs staring dejectedly at the paper on the table.

"Why don't we go downstairs and start the party?" I ask.

"It's not the same with Dad gone. He's never missed *my* birthday, and it's not fair. And Mom isn't here either. She'll never be at another birthday." He sniffs and my heart starts to sink to my stomach.

"That's true, but don't you think she'd want you to have a good day? I'm sure your father is doing something super important. He'd be here if he could."

He nods a little but stays sitting in his chair.

Come on, Kat. Think. *Think.* What would get him excited enough to go downstairs? Would anything?

My eyes move over the nice, white, collared shirt and pants as an idea forms in my head. This will basically ruin all of Bernadette's work, but...

"Why don't we make this a pool party instead?"

His eyes brighten as they meet mine. They look so familiar. *They're Valerio's.*

"I've never had a pool party for my birthday." He jumps up and grabs me around my middle and hugs me. "Thank you." He quickly lets go before his sisters can grab his hair and runs off.

I stare after him and it hits me. This is one step in the right direction. Now, I just have to make sure today is a good day, even if Valerio doesn't come.

I walk all the way back to the stairway and yell down, "Bernadette!"

It takes a few moments for her to come, but she does and smiles up at me. "Yes, Kat?"

"Do you think you could get the kids back up here? I'm so sorry, you went to all that trouble, but I decided we should have a pool party instead."

Her smile widens. "No trouble at all," she says happily before walking back to the family room.

Feeling satisfied, I step away from the staircase and look from Carina to Illaria. "Let's get you girls in your swimsuits."

---

After everyone has changed into their swimsuits, they all put floaties on. Bernadette changes into a swimsuit and holds Carina and Illaria while I keep Valeria in my arms. The boys all know how to swim, but they stay in the shallow area, splashing each other to their heart's content. Aurelio has had practice swimming, but since he's the youngest, I keep a close eye on him. All of them seem to be strong swimmers for their age though.

Valeria's eyes watch as her brothers swim back and forth in front of her, and she pushes off of me to try to get away. "Sorry sweet girl, you don't know how to swim yet so you have to stay with me. But we should get the instructor here so you can start learning."

She blinks her big eyes at me and frowns. I splash her gently with water. "See, you can still have fun with me."

Her frown disappears and she starts plopping her small hands in the water, splashing my chest with it. "Fun."

I swim through the water with her firmly attached to me. We stop right where her brothers are in the five-foot-deep area and swim back. "'Gain, 'gain."

"Okay, okay." I swim back and forth many times, making sure not to run into Vincenzo and his brothers as they swim around the whole shallow area.

After a few hours, we all take a break and get in the jacuzzi. It doesn't last long because the boys much prefer the cold water to the hot, bubbly water. The twins are put down for their nap by Bernadette. During our second round of fun in the pool, the twins wake up. Almost two hours later, we've been in for a long time and my stomach is starting to rumble as the sun starts to set. Valeria is a little cranky from missing her afternoon nap, but she brightens up when she sees the food on the table. Chicken nuggets and French fries, her favorite, and possibly all the kids' favorite, except for Carina and Illaria.

I feed them their baby food, switching between them,

while the kids finish their dinner. Vincenzo's laughter fills the air, and I watch as he talks animatedly about something. Relief bubbles from deep within me. I've been watching him all day and his smile hasn't left his face.

"Everybody, look who's here for Vincenzo's birthday dinner," Bernadette says as she steps outside.

My head shoots up and I know Vincenzo is looking the same direction and hoping the same thing I am.

From behind Bernadette steps are Luca and Alessio followed by Valerio's aunt, uncles, and a boy of about thirteen and girl of about eight. I wonder who they are. My heart sinks in my chest when no one else steps out, and I glance at Vincenzo to find him holding his head down, looking at his plate.

*Valerio, how could you not show up for him?*

His aunt and uncles come over and each give me a hug. Evelina and Oliverio go to talk to Vincenzo, but Domenico hangs around, motioning the boy and girl over. These must be his children.

"Kat, this is my son, Soren, and my daughter Caelia."

"Hi," they chime at the same time.

"Nice to meet you. Help yourselves to the food."

Domenico nods at me and shoos them toward the food.

They immediately walk over to Vincenzo who seems to perk up a little at seeing his cousins. Breathing a sigh of relief, I finish feeding the girls and wipe Valeria's mouth when Bernadette brings out a three-layer, white, birthday cake decorated with race cars on the side with a number seven candle at the top. Bernadette quickly lights his candle and we all sing happy birthday to him. He closes his eyes and then quickly blows out the candle.

Vincenzo's gaze abruptly meets mine, and I smile at him.

*Whatever you wished for, I hope it comes true Vin.*

Bernadette and I hand out the slices. Emilio immediately starts stuffing the cake in his mouth, getting icing all over him. "I'll be back," I tell Bernadette and rush inside to get extra napkins.

I grab them from the kitchen table and turn around when I bump right into a chest. "Excuse me," I say instinctively.

My breath catches as I find myself looking into *his* bluish-gray eyes and immediately step away. "So, you only came for the cake."

He frowns. "I came though, didn't I?"

My mouth tightens into a thin line. From behind him, Luciano shifts an apologetic look at me. Rolling my eyes at Valerio, I turn around and saunter outside, clearing my throat as I step out. Everyone stares at me, and I move aside for Valerio. Chairs scrape on the concrete and all of his kids rush up to him and hug him, with Vincenzo being the first to get to him.

A smile sneaks out as I watch icing cover his nice suit jacket, but I quickly smother it and place the napkins on the table.

"My wish came true," Vincenzo cries to Valerio.

I dig my fork into my slice of cake and vaguely hear Carina and Illaria's upset cries at me eating something that they can't have.

*What was the plan?* Right, ignore. Cold, dead, silence.

---

It doesn't take long to clean up and as soon as it's done, I find the boys playing amongst themselves upstairs in the playroom.

"It's time to go to sleep," I announce as I enter the room.

All of the boys grumble, except Vincenzo who comments, "I hope Dad comes up to say goodnight."

"I'm sure he will," I assure him.

Going down the hallway, I wish each boy goodnight. When I get to Aurelio's, he stops me before I can leave. "No story?" he softly asks in a sleepy tone.

"Of course, how could I forget?" I reply, walking into his room.

Aurelio always seems to enjoy my stories slightly more than the other boys. By the time the story is done, he's fast asleep, breathing deeply. Quietly, I back out of his room and bump against something hard and firm.

I close the door quietly and spin around to find Valerio. "I was just coming to say goodnight to him."

"Well he's already asleep," I snap and walk past him and head to the girls' hallway.

"I put all of them down already, you don't have to," he says in a monotone voice.

I turn around without looking at him and go back downstairs and go straight to my room and close the door. Immediately, it bangs open and Valerio slams it behind him.

"Don't walk away from me," he threatens.

Instead of responding, I ignore him and flop onto my bed. A long silence follows while he stands and waits for the response that I'm not going to give to him. I don't feel like arguing, especially when he won't even tell me what I did.

"Kat," he murmurs.

I turn my back to him and stare at the wall. *Maybe he'll leave soon.*

Minutes tick by, and my eyes are starting to grow heavy

from lying on the comfy bed with a quiet room around me. Just as I'm about to fully drift off, I hear him sigh. "Thanks for taking care of the kids while I was gone."

I grunt in reply and a sound of anger comes from him. I watch as he comes around to the other side of the bed and faces me. "Look, you're the one who started this."

"Started what?" I exclaim and sit up, confusion filling me.

"This," he says, motioning from him to me, "space between us."

"What are you talking about?"

He looks up at the ceiling and back at me. "Do you remember the last time we saw each other?"

I nod.

"You said something," he says with hurt and anger in his eyes.

"Me?" I ask, placing my hand on my chest. I never said anything to him that day because he left so abruptly. "I didn't."

"You did," he says in a firm tone and sticks his hands in his pockets. "You said...you hate me."

"What? No, I couldn't have, and would never say that."

"But you did," he says and chuckles darkly. "I knew it was too good to be true."

"Valerio. Listen to me, was that..." my mind tries to grasp at straws, "was I still asleep?"

"Yes, but you've never talked in your sleep like that before."

My mouth drops open as I feel a sense of relief. I move off the bed and stand directly in front of him. "I don't hate you. If anything, I was having a bad dream where I just so happened to be talking out loud about it."

"So then...those aren't your true feelings about me?" he asks, staring deeply into my eyes.

I shake my head, and he gently cups my face in his hands

"I'm sorry for how I treated you then. I should never have walked past you like that. Instead, I should've done this."

He inches closer, until his lips press against mine gently. A tingle goes through me and I immediately respond, moving my lips on his. With a groan, his tongue slips out and ghosts over my lips, and I open them to accommodate it. Our tongues immediately dance, making me gasp as pleasure shoots to my toes. He slowly pulls away and presses his forehead against mine.

"I couldn't stop thinking about you the whole time I was away," he admits.

"Neither could I."

"Then why don't we get some rest?" he asks as he starts taking off his tie.

"Sounds good to me," I reply.

And for the first time in weeks, I know I'll get a good night's sleep.

# FIFTEEN

## Valerio

It's been one month since Vincenzo's birthday party. The party that I basically missed. I still feel guilty about it, but Vin doesn't see it that way. He's just happy that I'm home. I'm glad to know that Kat's real feelings aren't ones of hate, yet this day is still one that is going to haunt me no matter what. Staring at the calendar hanging on the wall, my eyes lock on the date circled in red marker. The day that changed my family forever. Today is the day that she was taken. I can't believe it's been one year.

Shaking my head, I try to chase the thoughts away. I'm going to have to find a way to get out today and at least get a drink, something to stop myself from thinking about how I failed my kids.

Begrudgingly, I get up and quickly put on my clothes for the day. The silk of the shirt slides down my body easily as I grab my pants and pull them on. Heading out into the morning light, I go straight to the kitchen to grab a cup of coffee before I leave for the day but find Luca sitting at the breakfast nook.

"Hey Boss, I'm sorry about today, but we have some things to handle in town before you can relax."

"I understand. I just want to get things done so I can go to the bar for a quick drink that I don't have to pour myself," I reply.

"I understand, I mean today is the day that..."

I clench my fists and grit my teeth just thinking about men entering my home without my permission. Men that decided to rob my children of their mother.

"I don't want to talk about it, Luca. We both know what happened, let's try and move on."

The only good thing that came from that day is the birth of my twin girls.

Luca nods slowly and sips on his coffee. I grab the coffee pot and pour my morning coffee into my travel mug.

"Hey, uh, Boss?"

"Yes, Luca?"

"I'm sorry we failed you. We were supposed to keep everyone safe. We were supposed to get her back." He hangs his head as the apology slip from his lips.

"I know..." I finish screwing the lid on my mug, and I walk out to the front door.

My thoughts drift to the woman that's come to fill my head all day, every day. Kat has been avoiding me all week, so it's not like I have anyone to worry about today. I wish she'd tell me what's bothering her. Maybe today, I'll finally ask and get an answer. I want her to feel like she trusts me as much as I trust her.

As I slip into the back of one of the SUV's, I gaze at my

house and the only thing that runs through my head is how easily that house was taken.

"Luca," I manage to get out of my dry tight throat.

"Yeah boss?"

"Triple security today. Nobody in or out without my permission."

"Why, boss? Are you worried it might happen again?"

"Better safe than sorry."

Luca nods and radios in to my men to triple security.

The morning passes pretty quickly as the things we have to do mostly involve dealing with some money that came up short. We finally find it in the register; it had slipped under the drawer. The next step is to drop by my parents' place so I can drop off some papers for my mother to sign when they get back in case something were to happen to me.

After dropping off the documents, I have Luca drop me off at the local bar so I can just get in a few drinks. Heading inside, I find it to be pretty empty, luckily. I don't have to deal with rowdy people or women who know who I am and are trying to get into my pants.

*The only woman I want is waiting at home for me.*

Annoyingly, I become aware of a rather loud Russian guy in the corner by himself. Russians. The image of that smug Russian bastard running things here comes to mind. It'll be too soon before I have to see him again. I sit down as far away as possible from him and order a Jack and Coke. As I'm minding my own business, nursing my drink when I feel the eyes of someone watching me. That Russian guy must know who I am. I look up intentionally to meet his gaze, but he glances away before I can. Coward. Taking a sip, I see him grabbing his glass and taking a sip as well out of the corner of my eye. Gripping the glass firmly, I tap on the bar with my other hand to get the barkeep's attention.

Once he comes over to me, I flip my eyes over to the big Russian guy.

"Is he a regular here?" I gruffly ask.

"Not usually. He's been in here a few times. Always asking about some of the local Italian families."

So, the fucker has been looking for *me* most likely. They always like to come after the main family. A chuckle escapes me. He picked the wrong damn day to find me and start something. This just so happens to be the only day of the year, I don't mind starting a war. One thing I'm not going to do is go after the fucker. I'll let him throw the first punch so I can kick his ass without any recourse. The smart way.

Downing a few more Jack and Cokes, I find the guy is just milking his beer. Finishing up, I pay my tab and go to leave. I only get two steps away when the Russian guy shouts at me. "Where the fuck do you think you're going?"

"I'm going fucking home, what the fuck do you want?" I yell at him.

"I'm going to kick your ass, that's what I want," the Russian guy drunkenly yells back.

I'm not nearly as hammered as he is.

The bartender cocks a shotgun and screams at both of us. "Get out of my bar *now*!"

Not a problem at all. I crack my knuckles as I walk out of the bar first and wait for him to come out. A few moments later, he stumbles out and laughs as he approaches me.

The guy has me by at least 50 pounds, but I know I can kick his ass no problem. I've gone up against bigger. His ratty, greasy hair stands out as he gets close, matted with what I can only assume is sweat. He glares at me and his mouth forms a nasty toothy grin. "I'm going to fuck you up so bad that your kids won't even recognize you. Then I'm going to find your family, and I'm going to make them my fucking bitches."

The pounding in my ears is almost deafening as I glare at this big Russian guy. The blood rushes to my head and my mind grows fuzzy. He wrenches off his jacket.

"What the fuck did you just say?" I ask, in a low tone.

"I said I'm going to find your family and make them..."

His sentence is cut off as my first punch smashes into his jaw. The punch knocks him off his feet, and he falls to the ground.

"I'm going to fucking kill you!" he screams as he pushes himself back up onto his feet. Throwing his fists in a flurry, he tries to land a punch. I duck and dodge his more obvious punches as I smash my fists into his stomach.

Moving in to finish him, he sneaks a punch in, smashing me in the face. It feels like my jaw explodes. Immediately I know that he busted my lip open when I taste copper in my mouth. Spitting out the blood, I watch as he smirks, moving his hands to beckon me to attack him again.

"You little chickenshit, I'm going to make sure your daughters call me daddy tonight!" he screams.

I hesitate, stopping in my tracks. I can't let him coax me into doing what *he* wants. I need to be smart about this, think rationally instead of just smashing his fucking face into bits. Controlled rage, that's the way to go. Moving back in and sidestepping his punch, I throw a jab into his ribs and smash my fist directly into his nose. When I feel the sickening crunch of his nose breaking, I lash out with my leg tripping the drunk, Russian asshole.

Quickly pouncing on him, I throw two more punches left and right into his bloodied face. "Take it fucking back! Take what you said back or I'm gonna beat you to death you drunk, Russian fuck!" I scream in his face.

As I haul back my fist to punch him again I get sucker punched. Scrambling to my feet, I assess the situation. Someone else has shown up, another Russian guy who is checking on the guy on the ground.

"Look, I don't want trouble. I'm sorry for whatever my comrade said, but he's drunk and I know that doesn't excuse it, but still... can't you show a little bit of leniency for the fact?" the new Russian guy blurts out in somewhat broken English.

I can make him out, but things are starting to get fuzzy again, so I reach up and touch my eye to feel the puffy swelling of it. "The guy said he was gonna make my kids his bitches and make my daughters call him daddy. No one gets away with saying that. If I ever see his fucking face around here again..." I leave my threat open-ended as to not actually say anything that might get me in trouble. Witnesses are everywhere.

"I completely understand, I will make sure that you never have to see him again."

I spit out the blood that has been pooling slowly in my mouth and brush myself off.

"Boss, what the fuck happened to you?" I hear someone call out to me.

Turning around, I see Luca standing with a look of disbelief.

"I leave you alone for just an hour and you get into a bar brawl? This is why I wanted to keep an eye on you today. God dammit. Was it a fucking Russian? Do you want to start a war? Is that what you fucking want? To go to war over someone you never even loved?"

"Luca?" I ask abruptly.

"Yes, boss?" Luca replies hesitantly.

"Shut the fuck up for a second. I didn't fight him because

he was Russian. I beat his ass because he threatened my family."

"Oh. I see. Well, I'm sorry for judging you but still you should try to avoid conflict as much as possible with the Russians unless you want to start another war," Luca explains.

I nod slowly and make my way to the SUV waiting behind him. A gentle breeze blows as I walk, causing me to wince when it blows over my split lip.

We ride back in silence.

"Boss, maybe we should have a doctor look at you," Luca continues, "I mean you have a bleeding split lip and a pretty serious black eye."

"I'll be fine. Now I just want to be left alone for the rest of the day alright? Can you handle everyone?"

"Yes, boss."

I get out of the SUV, nod, and go inside. God this sucks, I want nothing more than to break down Kat's door and force her to tell me why she hasn't wanted to spend any time with me at all. I want to know what's so bad that she's willing to just flat out avoid me. I can't wait any longer for her to tell me herself. Fed up with waiting, I march to her room and knock on her door.

"Can I help you?" I hear her voice call out from the other side of the door.

"Yes, I'd like to come in and talk. If you aren't busy," I say my voice dripping with sugar, hoping that she doesn't turn me away.

"Come on in, Valerio."

I enter her room quickly and as soon as she sees me, she jumps off her bed. "What the hell happened to you? Did you get jumped? Were you robbed? Do you need to go to the hospital?" she runs through her questions quickly, with the sexiest worried expression on her face.

"I got into a minor fight. No, I didn't get jumped or robbed. I also don't think I need to go to the hospital. This really isn't that bad. You should see the other guy." I smirk.

She frowns and her crystal-blue eyes stare into mine. "Valerio, that's not funny. I need to patch up your lip at least. It's bleeding pretty badly."

"I'm telling you, it really isn't that bad. But if you really want to fix me up, go ahead."

I sit on the edge of her bed and watch as she pulls a first aid kit from her dresser.

"You really shouldn't be getting into fights when you should be here with your kids. I don't know what's going on, but you really should be more careful. I mean what if you had gotten hurt? What if someone killed you? Your kids only have you left," she says softly.

Everything she says rings true. "Kat, I've just been having a bad day."

She smiles sweetly and continues patching me up.

I wince as she cleans my lip thoroughly. Might as well ask the hard question now. "What's been going on with you recently? For the past week you've been avoiding me and everyone else. Even the kids. You've been eating alone in your room. What's changed?"

"I spent lots of time with them today to make up for it. It's the twins' birthday and though they won't remember it in the future, I tried to make it as happy as I could. But don't worry about me. I'm fine, and it's not that big a deal," she says, avoiding my eyes.

"Thank you for that, but it is. I feel like I did something wrong, and I don't know what I did. I want to make whatever it is up to you, but I won't know what's wrong or how to fix it unless you tell me," I insist, fervently.

"I want to, I really do Valerio. I just don't think I can right now, it's too hard to talk about."

"I get it. Just don't fucking pull away, okay? Let me be your shoulder to lean on. No weight is too much for me to carry. Whatever you're going through, I'll gladly listen. I'll always help you no matter what," I reply, placing my hand on her soft thigh.

She bites her lip. "I know you just want to help. Right now, the only way you can help is by giving me some time to deal with it. Eventually I'll tell you..." She trails off.

"I understand, it's alright. Just know that whenever you want to talk, I'll be here."

She smiles and lowers her head slightly, brushing her hair back over her ear. My eyes travel downward to the outfit she decided to wear. An orange, polka-dotted sundress that gives me an eyeful of her cleavage. I look past and down to her shapely legs. Legs I can't wait to wrap around my waist. Fuck, I need to get out of here.

I get up abruptly to leave, but stop at the door, dipping my head slightly. "I never told you why I had problems with the Russians did I?"

I turn to see her shake her head. Her face turns slightly pink and her eyes widen. "No, you never did. Why do you hate the Russians so much?"

Sighing, I sit back down on the bed next to her.

"Since the days of my great-grandfather, the Italians and the Russians have been at war with each other over territory. They've committed crimes...horrible crimes against us. We've retaliated. I don't know how it started, only that it's been raging for as long as I can remember. Every time I've come across one, it's always ended in trouble. Like, today.

Somehow, the last time I managed to keep my cool when I met with their boss. I don't know who's worse, him or Julio. During my father's time, he set the groundwork to stop the fighting, but it took till my generation for us to at least come to some sort of cease fire. It has been tenuous at best."

"But why have you been fighting over territory instead of just dividing everything equally?"

"Because there is no equality between the Mafia and the Mob. There will never be true peace between us. We both want control of the city. Control is everything."

"That doesn't really explain why you hate them if you aren't at war anymore."

"The Russians had to be behind my wife's disappearance. They wanted to cripple me, make me unable to keep my mantle and hand it over to another member of my family. They might not have done it themselves, but I wouldn't doubt that they hired someone to do it. It has been a bloody war with both sides, killing a lot of the other side. I never really understood when I was growing up because we're all just people, but today I got another reminder of the kind of people they keep in their Mob. He threatened my family and I couldn't take it, so I beat his ass down."

She gasps and looks at me with this terrified look.

"He said he was gonna make my daughters call him daddy. So, I made sure he wouldn't be getting back up on his own any time soon. And no, I didn't kill him even though I wanted to."

"Is that going to start another war or is everything going to be okay?" she asks with an anxious expression.

I shake my head. "I doubt it will. We haven't been on the best of terms, but we haven't been at war for a while now. Unless something major happens, we won't be. Their boss...he freaks me the hell out. He's a silent, deadly, loose cannon and honestly if it wasn't him in charge, I would willingly try to take them out."

I can't help but shake in anger as I manage to tell Kat everything that I have been hiding from her.

"I've been dreading telling you any of this just because it's been so hard. It's been hard dealing with this situation especially now because while I might think that they took her, there's no evidence. It's been a year since that day. And now, I want something completely different. I want to stay here and protect *you*. You will never suffer at the hands of another man again."

She smiles slightly and tilts her head down. "I really appreciate everything that you have done for me here. You didn't have to take me in and give me a place to live. You didn't have to let me get attached to your kids. You didn't have to let me get attached to you," she says softly. "But you did, and now I don't want to go anywhere else." Her face reddens. "And I don't want you to find anyone else. I know a lot of women want you because you're the boss, but I'm not like that. I know that it sounds selfish, but I really like living here with everyone and it makes me feel a joy that I've only felt a few times before."

Her words make my forehead start to sweat and my heart quicken. Gritting my teeth, I clench my fists and keep them at my sides to prevent myself from grabbing her and showing her just how much that means to me. The image of her milky white thighs parted makes my growing erection ache.

"You have no idea how happy that makes me. Thank you for being a part of my children's life. They really like you. You've made them a lot happier in the six months you've been here than in the six months after she was taken."

"I'm glad to hear that—" Kat starts.

"You've awakened something inside me. Something that I've never felt before. This fire inside me, it stems from you. I'll let it blaze inside of me as long as you want me to, but right now, I need to let some of it out."

Her eyes widen as her breath catches. Slowly getting off her bed, I take a few large steps to the door and lock it. Turning around, I stare at her beautiful face with her plump pink lips and the only thing I can think of is how much I want to taste her.

I walk back to the bed and pull her into a deep kiss. Her mouth opens slightly, and I take advantage of that split second to dart my tongue in. Our tongues dance together, letting me get the smallest taste of her sweetness. It's nowhere near enough. I slip my hands around her back, holding her close. She wiggles against my arms as I break the kiss away and move my head down to nibble on the nape of her neck. The smell of her body wash only makes her smell sweeter than she always does.

"Why are you doing this?" Kat moans as her breathing falters.

"Shhh. This is because I can't wait any longer to taste you. I want you and *nothing* is going to stop me now."

She moans again as she lets me kiss and bite her neck softly. All the while my hands roam lower and lower until I manage to slip a hand up her dress. To my surprise she's already soaking wet. I slip a finger under the fabric of her underwear and slowly tease up and down her soaked slit.

Breaking away from her, I push her softly onto the bed, lift her dress, and slide her panties all the way off.

"Wah...wait...I'm not sure—" she pleads.

"*Amore*, I have no intentions of that yet. I'm going to show you how much I appreciate everything you've done for the kids and me. This is all going to be about you, Kat," I interrupt huskily.

I slide my head down leaving small kisses down to her little patch of light brown hair just before her pussy. Once there, I slowly kiss up and down her inner thighs making sure to take my time to build up the tension. While kissing her inner thighs I use my fingers to rub her clit, causing her to moan loudly as my fingers dance along her.

Bringing my head back up, I slip my tongue out and lick her up, down, and all around as I pressure my tongue down onto her clit.

She grabs my head as I continue to twirl my tongue around her softness. Snaking my arm up her body under her dress, I slip my hand into her bra and begin to massage her breast while I keep my attack on her clit. Her sweetness is so strong here.

"Oh God, Valerio. That feels so good. Oh, keep going please," she moans.

I slip my hand back down and slide a finger into her opening. Crooking my finger, I rub against her core, while I begin to softly kiss her clit and tease it with my tongue.

I keep up my movements and groan when I feel her hand on the back of my head as she grinds into my face, forcing my tongue to press hard against her clit.

"I'm coming, I'm coming!" she shouts as she grinds my face into her pussy.

Suddenly, I feel her insides clamp down on my finger as she starts to spasm, a loud moan escapes her lips as she quivers, ending with her falling limply back into the bed.

"Oh...my...God." I sit up and watch the flush from her face slowly disappear. "That was the biggest orgasm I've ever had," she pants as her eyes flick toward mine. I wipe the wetness on my mouth away and grin.

"There's more where that came from. I told you that I wanted to show you how much I appreciated you. I think I did a pretty good job," I say with a wink, climbing into bed with her.

"You have to promise to do that again because that was better than anything I've ever felt," she murmurs with a tired sigh.

"I promise. Now if you will excuse me, I have a date with a cold shower." I get up off the bed as I flip the bottom of her dress back down.

"Wait, why are you leaving now?" she asks, propping herself up on her elbows to look at me.

"I told you that this was going to be all about you. I meant that. As much as I would love to see your lips wrapped around my cock, blowing me, I don't think that it's the right time for that just yet. Just like I would love to just slip deep inside of you and make love to you all night."

Her mouth drops open as her face turns beet red. "O-Okay." She wets her lips. "Are you sure?"

Oh God, you know how to make this hard for a guy don't you? I'm trying to be a gentleman and not force myself upon you, taking you like an animal, but you're making it hard. I close my eyes and try to force my straining erection away, but it fails.

I sigh. "There will be plenty of time later, but right now, tonight, I'm going to go take a cold shower. I'll never rush you into it, but ten more seconds here, and I'll give in if you ask me again if I'm sure."

Quickly, I walk to the door and unlock it, slipping out into the hallway. Rushing off, I make my way to my bedroom where I shut and lock the door behind me. With a flash, all of my clothes are stripped off and my aching cock is finally free from the waistband of my boxers. It bounces to attention in front of me, pointing towards my shower.

"God, I don't know how the good guys do this kind of shit. I wanted to take her right then and there. I wanted to make her mine and pump my seed deep inside her. *Fuck*...I need to stop thinking about that. At least I'm still thinking with my brain and not my dick," I mutter to myself as I walk into the bathroom.

In my large shower, I turn the water temperature on cold as far as it will go and hop in. My erection starts to fade, but the water does nothing to douse the fire she's lit inside of me.

# SIXTEEN

Kat

I take a sip of an ice-cold lemonade by the pool and soak up the last rays of the sun before it goes down. With the first day of September, summer is reaching its end. Nice days like this, days spent together bonding by the pool will come to an end soon enough. All of the boys are enjoying the pool while Valeria, Carina, and Illaria are playing in their small, roped off play area. The more they grow, the more I'm reminded...

The twins have become more comfortable in the water when I take turns with them, but they don't love it as much as Valeria who constantly asks me in her cute baby talk to "Leggo." She definitely needs to take some more lessons.

The sound of the door opening behind me makes me turn around. I'm half-expecting it to be Valerio, but I know he said he would be late tonight. I'm proven correct when I see Luca instead. "Valerio should be home soon," He reassures.

The sound of the water splashing in the pool stops, making me turn my attention back to them.

"Yay! Dad!" Vincenzo screams and rushes over to the steps. The rest of his brothers don't follow him and continue swimming.

"What about the rest of you boys? Are you boys ready to go inside?" I ask.

They stop splashing abruptly. "Already?" Emilio whines.

"Come on guys, don't give Kat a hard time," Luca says.

I shoot him an appreciative smile. "It's almost dinner time anyway and you guys still need your baths."

They sigh but immediately get out of the pool and run inside. After they're in, I grab Valeria out of the play area and the twins, who are getting heavier every day. Valeria runs inside ahead of me. I hurry after her and set the girls down inside, closing the door behind me.

"It smells great, Bernadette," I comment, taking a long sniff of the heavenly meal of spaghetti with meatballs.

She smiles. "Thanks Kat. Take your time with the kids. Dinner will be waiting when you're done."

We both know I'll be a while making sure all eight kids are clean.

---

BY THE TIME I finish up with the twins, I'm surprised everyone is sitting down at the table. Each kid has their plates already made and Valerio is sitting in his seat.

It's been about a week since we've spent a lot of time together, and I miss seeing him somewhere other than the dinner table. Every night I keep hoping he'll come in, but I suspect the exhaustion from the job is getting the best of him.

I place the twins in their high chairs and sit down, hurrying to make my plate so I don't make everyone wait longer than they've had to.

"Sorry for the wait," I say quietly as I finish.

"No hurry, Kat," he murmurs. "A king will always wait for his queen."

My face heats up as I lock eyes with him and find them staring at me like he wants to eat me as much as I want to eat this spaghetti.

I place the first bite of food in my mouth and eat slowly while everyone else seems to devour theirs. One by one, his men leave until it's just Luca, Luciano, and Alessio. As soon as the kids are finished, Valerio instructs Bernadette to take them upstairs and play with them for a while. Something he hasn't done in a while. What's going on?

My eyebrows furrow as I glance at Valeria's pouty face. I really don't mind, he should know that by now.

"I can do it, Valerio," I say quietly.

They always like to talk before it's time to put them in their beds and read them stories.

"Not tonight, Kat. We have some business to talk about," he states as he wipes his hands on his napkin.

Bernadette nods at both of us and rushes off with a twin in each arm and the other kids ahead of her.

As soon as she's gone, his mouth forms a smile. "Kat, I'd like you to take a trip with me."

My mouth drops open. "Me?" I ask, pointing to myself. He's never wanted to go far with me before.

"Yes, out of New York. Just the two of us. It might end up going a little long...all depending on...well..." He shares a look with his three men and then turns back to me. "We're going to California."

"Oh," I reply, not really knowing what to say. Not that I don't want to go with him, because a trip with the two of us sounds like a great time. Maybe it'll finally be time, but what about his kids? I can't just take him away from them.

"You've never been to California, have you?" Valerio asks.

I hesitate for a moment, to remember the correct answer. "No. I've always wanted to though."

He nods. "It's a beautiful state."

Yes, it is.

I glance at Luca. "Are you sure we should be going without you, Luciano, or Alessio?"

"I need them here to watch the kids. They won't let me down. Right?" Valerio says, looking from one to the other.

"Of course, boss," Alessio replies.

With no other reason left to keep me home, I respond. "Then I'll go." The idea fills me with a little nervousness because I have no idea why we're going, but will still be time that I get Valerio all to myself.

We share a smile, and then he shocks the hell out of me when he says, "Good. Can you pack a bag and meet me outside in fifteen?"

"Wait, wait. We're going to the airport *now*?"

"Surprise!" he says with a chuckle.

"Luciano and Alessio, help Bernadette put the kids to sleep. It's been a while since they've had you do it."

"Alriiiight," Alessio says with a groan.

"Don't act like you don't like to. You even make up their bedtime stories rather than read them," Luciano says rolling his eyes.

"Shut up," Alessio says with a glare but leaves the room to head upstairs.

Luca bursts out laughing, and Luciano cracks a smile before following Alessio.

With that, I stand up. "I'll get packed then."

It takes me ten minutes to get what little I have put away with my toiletries. I feel so guilty leaving, and apparently Valerio has the same idea because we both get to the staircase at the same time.

After a tearful goodbye and lots of hugs, we exit the mansion together and hop into a waiting car being driven by Luca.

As we leave the driveway, Valerio takes a phone call, leaving me to be lost in memories about the last time I went to California.

---

IT'S JUST past midnight when we arrive in California and head straight for the Beverly Hills Hotel. Check in is a breeze, and they seem to know exactly who Valerio is, not that I'm surprised by that.

We enter our suite, and I walk right past the gorgeous main room with a sitting area and dining table to the bedroom with a king-sized bed in the center.

I flop right in the middle and sit up on my elbow, watching as Valerio stalks in and closes the door with one hand while starting to take his suit jacket off with his other. His eyes jump to meet mine as he starts taking his shirt off, revealing his toned six-pack.

I can't help as my eyes trail down farther. He clears his throat, as he goes to unzip his pants. "We have a long day tomorrow, or should I say today. But I'd be happy to postpone that for something else."

His eyes don't leave mine, waiting intently for my

reaction.

After a moment of hesitation, I start peeling off my own clothes. "You're right. We should get some rest."

I turn around and not even a second later, I feel the warmth of his body behind me. He leans down to my ear and whispers, "Are you sure?"

A tingle of anticipation shoots to my toes. "Yes. We should definitely behave tonight."

I wouldn't want him to miss something important because of me.

He kisses a trail down to my neck and licks a spot that has me shivering with want and leaning my head into him, so he has more access.

Suddenly his warmth disappears from behind me. Turning around, I find him getting on the opposite side of the bed in his underwear. I get in with just my bra and panties on and lay with my back to Valerio. Somehow, I drift off, but not before feeling him behind me with his arm draped comfortably around me.

---

THE NEXT MORNING, I wake up the opposite way I fell asleep, facing Valerio. When I open my eyes, I find him staring right at me.

"You look so peaceful sleeping," he says, cupping my cheek and leaning forward to press a chaste kiss to my lips.

"Good morning," I say brightly, unable to help the smile beaming from my face. Somehow, I managed to sleep well. "What's the plan today?" I ask.

"Well first, breakfast. Then we need to get a rental car so we can get straight to business."

And that's exactly what we do after getting ready. It

wasn't easy convincing Valerio that we didn't need to take a shower together. I used my time to think about whether this trip involves seeing *him*. Not that I've ever met *him* in person.

Our rental car, a black Lexus, is driven straight to a mansion in Calabasas. It's behind a large iron gate, just like home, and a light gray color.

"What do you have to do here?" I ask.

He doesn't answer when we pull to a stop in the circular driveway. Opening the car door for me, he helps me out and keeps a tight hold on my hand.

I glance over my shoulder, a little nervous to see what's inside. But when we walk in the large French doors, I find nothing. A beautiful mansion, just as big as the one in New York. There's not a soul on the main level and no furniture. It's completely empty. But it doesn't smell like it's been left empty for a while. In fact, it smells clean.

"Are we waiting for someone?" I ask hesitantly, stopping in the kitchen.

Valerio smirks. "No."

"Then...what are we doing here?"

He locks eyes with me and pulls me to the sliding glass doors, leading out to the backyard with an Olympic-sized pool in the back.

"Do you like it?" he asks.

"I do. Is the upstairs as beautiful as the downstairs?"

"Yes," he responds with a nod, glancing from the pool to me. "Would you like to make this our vacation home? When we want to get away from New York with the kids...we can come here. Go to the beach and enjoy the sunny SoCal weather?"

My mind is stuck on the "our" part.

"Our vacation home? Valerio—" I stop, at a loss for words.

"I thought you'd love it, but I had to know for sure. I can put an offer in today."

My mouth drops open, and I can't stop the tears from leaking out of the corners of my eyes. This is the important business? Buying a house? Our vacation house?

I don't get to think another thought as he pulls me to him and kisses me so hard all I can think of is how good he smells and how good it feels to press my lips against his.

He pulls back abruptly. "Sorry Kat, I forgot one thing." His eyes narrow a little as he stares at the ground.

"What? What is it?" I ask anxiously as my stomach drops a little.

Slowly, he's gets down on one knee, simultaneously reaching into his jacket and pulling out a black box.

My hands start shaking uncontrollably as I bring them up to cover my mouth. His eyes shine with nothing but affection and love for me. Gently, he pulls open the box to reveal a shiny jewel. "Kat, will you marry me? Will you wear and be my black opal?"

The dark blue with hints of red, yellow, and lime green shine in the sunlight. What a beautiful jewel.

I'll never take it off.

"Yes," I softly reply. He takes it out of its box and pushes it onto my finger.

"I'm glad you didn't notice the only ring you bought is missing."

Grinning, I shake my head. "Actually, I did. I just thought maybe I misplaced it."

He leans down and presses his forehead against mine. "Mrs. Marchioni, I can't wait to marry you."

"I can't wait either." He presses his lips against mine as a happy tear slips down my cheek.

THE NEXT TWO weeks are nothing but a celebration. It's almost like we were able to have an engagement honeymoon. Our offer is accepted almost immediately, and then the wait for the house to close is on. During our wait, we spend every waking moment together. No business besides the occasional phone call to Luca, and the kids video call us every night. We simply enjoy each other's company, going to the beach and acting like normal people. It's a breath of fresh air.

He takes me to do all the touristy things to make sure I don't miss out on anything. By the time the two weeks are up, I love L.A. almost as much as New York City.

I never got to see this much of the city before, even getting to see the Hollywood sign and Chinatown. Valerio changes into a different man than the one I get to see in New York. Someone more free without so much weight on their shoulders. Every night we go to sleep and almost go all the way, but we end up stopping and going to sleep, cuddling with each other.

The first day after the two weeks, we go to the house and meet the agent who gives us our keys.

I can't keep my excitement down as Valerio hands them to me, letting me open the door.

Instead of staying on the main level, I run straight upstairs, going room by room. Twelve rooms, including our master bedroom on the second level.

Stopping in front of one of the rooms, I peer inside. The sound of Valerio's footsteps on the wood floor get closer. "What are we going to do?"

"About what?" he asks with a puzzled look on his face.

"This," I say gesturing to the room. "There's four empty

rooms, well three, if the twins want their own rooms. What are we going to do with them?"

He grabs my hand and places a kiss on top of it. "What would you like to do with them?"

"I don't know…"

"Well, let's not worry about that. After all, I have a feeling we'll have no problem filling the other rooms up."

He turns to leave without another word and my cheeks heat up. "Valerio!"

WE SPEND another few days talking to an interior designer about the exact vision I have for the house. It gives me some room to be more creative than I have been in a long time. By the time we're done, Valerio is writing a large check, but he doesn't even blink at the cost that the interior designer estimates will be needed to complete the job.

I feel a little guilty spending so much money, but he insists that I get it exactly how I want, so I'm comfortable with it.

The next morning, we're on an early flight back home. The whole flight we can't keep our hands off of each other. "Are you sure you don't want to be part of the mile-high club?" Valerio whispers in my ear as he yanks my shirt off and pulls me into his lap.

I straddle him with my legs and kiss him heatedly. "No, I'm not sure."

Beneath me, I feel his erection grow at my words, making me grind down and moan at the friction between us.

He pulls me down so his lips brush mine and press hard as he reaches around and grabs my ass to grind me against his erection. Panting between kisses and moaning when I feel his hands switch to my breasts, I almost don't hear one of the pilots say we're landing in New York City.

Abruptly we strap ourselves in, but not without continuing to gaze at each other with complete and open desire.

---

LUCIANO PICKS us up at the airport.

"Congrats, love birds," he says with a happier tone than usual as we hop in the backseat.

"Thank you. How are the kids?" Valerio asks. "They don't know we're coming home today."

"They've been great. Vincenzo is getting better at his math and Aurelio's reading has improved. Of course, they all miss you."

"And the clubs? Nothing from the Russians, right?"

"No, boss."

"Good."

We arrive at the mansion just around the time when they start getting up for the day.

Valerio and I go straight upstairs and stop by each kid's room, starting with Vincenzo.

I don't know if I'll ever get tired of seeing how much he loves his dad. I leave them to have their own moment, but what shocks me is when Vincenzo quietly says, "Wait, is Kat here? Did she...come back?"

"Of course. Come in, Kat," Valerio invites.

I peek through the door and Vincenzo gets out of bed, races right to me, and gives me a tight hug.

That hug is echoed by each kid. Valeria screams with delight at seeing me and then the twins. It makes my heart soar with joy.

Bernadette comes in just as we set the twins down in their cribs.

"Welcome back, Kat." She smiles at me, but her eyes are immediately drawn to my ring finger.

"Congratulations, my dear." Her words are spoken with sincerity, but the smile on her face isn't as wide as it was.

"Thank you."

"Kat, I'm tired, and I bet you are too. Bernadette can handle the kids while we take a nap."

Nodding, I let him press his hand on the small of my back and lead me out and down the stairs to his room, soon to be our room. Without even pulling our clothes off, we get in bed. Valerio falls asleep before I do. My eyes stay glued to the shiny ring on my finger.

The ring that changes everything. How long until he finds out my secret and this ring is ripped right off of my finger?

The thought shakes me to my core, but the heaviness of my eyelids gets to me, and I fall right to sleep.

# SEVENTEEN

## VALERIO

As the months go by and the holidays come and go, I keep expecting something to happen. Something to come and take Kat away from me, dooming me to spend the rest of this life alone. But nothing ever happens. When the new year comes, she's right by my side.

I've been able to go back to doing short business trips and Vincenzo actually seems okay now. It gives me hope that despite the fact that my kids have had to endure such a hard loss, the loss of their mother, that they won't feel sad forever.

Even though it's been over a year since she's been gone, I know somewhere out there, the answers to her disappearance exist. And while I'm not actively searching and trying to figure out what the next move is from the people after my family, I know sooner or later I'll find out. They'll come for me, for my kids, and maybe for Kat. Next time, I'll be ready. They won't be able to hide from my wrath when they do.

Until then, I'm going to celebrate this week. This week is the anniversary of finding Kat. One year ago, I was plotting my journey to Russia, assuming that they were keeping my wife somewhere there. And while I didn't find the mother of my children, I found Kat. I'll never regret going.

She's done so much for my family, tonight is the night to talk about celebrating her.

"Kat, what do you think about having a small party here to celebrate your one-year anniversary here?" I ask with a smile, hoping she thinks it's a good idea.

She flashes me a small smile and sits a little straighter in her chair. "I'd love to have a little party with just the family. I mean why wouldn't I?" she asks.

"Good. It'll just be us, the staff, Alessio, Luciano, Luca, and the kids. I don't want anyone else here to put a damper on that evening."

"Thank you, Valerio. I really appreciate you...giving me a place to really call home." Her eyes start shining with tears as she clasps her hands together on the table and touches her ring.

"I should be thanking you, you've shown me what I was truly missing in life," I softly reply.

She smiles, but there's something off about it that I can't place. Her fingers leave the ring and pick up her fork to continue eating. She must be nervous about our nuptials. It's not easy being the queen around here, but hopefully I'll be able to keep *them* away for a little longer until she's ready.

---

INSTEAD OF LETTING Bernadette handle the party details, I clear out my whole schedule, letting Luca, Luciano, and Alessio handle everything. I want this to be the best party for Kat. She deserves it. After living out on the streets for years, I'm sure she's never had a party just for her.

As I get back from one of my trips to the store, I come around a corner to see Luca and Alessio whispering.

"Have you seen the boss lately? It's like he's become a man possessed. He's been taking care of this party for her all by himself, like he doesn't trust anyone else to even help," Luca says in a hushed tone, followed by a few words he says so quietly I can't hear.

"I know. Do you think Kat has tamed the beast inside of him? What is my uncle going to say?" Alessio asks.

"It doesn't matter. He's still on vacation, and he's not due back any time soon."

They both nod and go down the hallway to the basement door. All I can think of is the fact that these are two of my best friends, forget about being my men. Are they even fucking happy for me?

Dejected, I push the disappointment away and bring the bags into the kitchen to be put away. I retire early for the night without talking to the men, who seem preoccupied with checking out a club one more time for the night.

At some point during the night, I feel the dip in the bed as Kat climbs in. The next morning, I wake up before she does and get ready. I finish my shower and walk down the hallway to the bed. Her normally content face is twisted like she's having a bad dream.

I lean down and kiss her forehead. "Kat," I whisper.

Her breathing quickens and one of her eyes crack open. "Hey."

"Baby, do you think you could leave the house with Luca while we set things up for you."

She nods and gets ready in a hurry but doesn't leave before sharing a long kiss with me.

"Thank you for doing this."

I wave as she leaves the room, and as soon as I wait an

ample amount of time, I head straight for the kitchen where I go to work. Bernadette patiently shows me how to make a nice lunch for her. While it's cooking, we decorate the whole main area. It takes us almost the entire time they are gone, but I finish just in time. I hear the front door open and Luca's voice booms out, "Hey Valerio, we're back! I hope everything's done..."

A minute later his face pops in and he eyes everything. "Wow."

He walks in, followed by Luciano and Alessio. I wait with bated breath to see the apple of my eye walk in and see everything I did for her. My heart is pounding, and the anticipation is killing me, and then she does. Kat walks in and sweeps her eyes over the whole area before landing on me. She walks straight for me and gives me a crushing hug.

"Happy one-year anniversary of you coming into all of our lives Kat. I can't wait for what the future holds in store for us."

"Valerio you didn't have to do all this for me," she says tearfully.

"Yes, I did. You have my whole heart Kat, right in your hands. That's something I've never been able to tell a woman. I'm in love with you and nothing will ever change that."

Her face turns red and then she's full on sobbing.

"I didn't mean to make you cry, love," I murmur as I cradle her in my arms.

She slowly stops, and I wipe her tears away.

"I love you too. I'm just so happy to be here. How about we get the kids and everyone in here and we have a nice dinner?"

Nodding, I glance at Luciano. "Can you get the kids down?"

"Not a problem, boss," he replies.

Giving Luca and Alessio the cold shoulder, I help Kat into her seat and sit down in mine without giving them another look.

As soon as all of the kids are in their seats, Bernadette sets the food on the table, and then takes her seat in between Emilio and Aurelio.

"Dig in!" I exclaim and help the kids get portions of the steaks I made. Just as I start cutting up Aurelio's, the ring of the doorbell sounds, making everyone freeze in place and become quiet.

"Who could that be?" Alessio asks after a long few seconds, breaking the silence.

"I can get the door, sir," Bernadette says, moving her chair back.

"No, please. Stay. I will get it." I stand up out of my chair and give everyone a small smile.

No one is supposed to come today. This had better be good.

Throwing open the front door, I find my aunt and uncles on the front steps.

My annoyance slips down a level. "I wasn't expecting you guys. Would you like to come in for dinner?"

They nod, but seem caught up in their own thoughts, murmuring to each other.

"What brings you over here?"

Domenico rubs a hand down his face, stopping at his chin.

"We thought we'd come to let you know that your parents are back from vacation and they're on the way here. Right. Now. "

"What? What the fuck do you mean? Why didn't they call me? How long have they been back?" I ask, looking from each of their faces and feeling my anger start to rise.

I'm not prepared for this. For Kat.

The sound of heels clicking across the tile catches my attention. Kat. I need to let her know.

Right as we meet in the middle of the room, I'm about to tell her everything not to say to my father.

Before I can even get a word out, the doorbell rings for the second time this afternoon.

"Shit." I glare up at the ceiling and take a deep calming breath.

Kat gives me a look and then sneaks by me and my aunt and uncles to open the door before any of us can get there first. Over her shoulder, I see both of my parents. My mom in a business suit with a happy expression, and my father, with a scowl firmly planted on his face. He pushes the door open and takes off his jacket, placing it in Kat's hands.

"You got a new maid, son?" he asks glancing at me and then to Kat.

"Get me a drink, will you? It was a long flight and we ran out of alcohol halfway back. Straight whiskey on the rocks and make it a double," he barks and pushes past her.

My mother rolls her eyes and places her jacket in Kat's hands as well, following my father.

And that's when the small sliver of control I have slips away.

"Stop," I state, gritting my teeth. Father turns around, eyeing me with a half-confused, half-pissed off face.

"You do not disrespect my fiancée. If you come into my house, you will show me and her some Goddamn respect. I am tired of you thinking that you can do whatever the fuck you want in my house!" I shout at him.

"Excuse me. Your *what*?" Father shouts back.

His gaze turns to Kat and shoots down to the ring on her

finger. The shiny black opal ring that proclaims her as my queen.

"I did not approve of any of this Valerio. I never received a call about you wanting another wife, or even being interested in someone. And who is she?" he says gesturing to her. "I refuse to allow this to happen. A stranger in my family. She does not get to wear that ring. Do you know how *they* would take it if you married a woman who isn't a part of the other families? They would be in open revolt because you are giving control to a nobody!" Father practically shouts in my face.

He stares into Kat's face and glares at her while still yelling at me.

"I will not allow this. I will get the other families, and I will make sure that I get the keys to the kingdom back."

My hands roll into fists and just as I'm ready to punch him, Mom touches Dad's shoulder.

"Dear, you need to stop. You are going way overboard with this, and I will not stand for it. We only just got back from vacation, and I want to have peace with my son. Now you need to apologize to Valerio. We interfered with his love life once. That's enough," Mom tells him sternly.

"That is most certainly not enough. We don't even know her. For all we know she could be a spy. No. I refuse to let this happen. I will not let my family and all we've built fall."

My father quickly turns to face me, and he glares at me with a look of hatred in his eyes. "Mark my words, I will make sure that this will not happen."

"Father, I am the boss now. If I want to marry her, I'm going to marry her. I run this family now, not you. I love her. I have never loved anyone like this before. And I'm not letting anyone take her away. So, keep threatening me. I will come out on top," I say in a low tone right in his face.

My aunt and uncles pull us away from each other before anything else can be said.

"Look, brother. You need to calm down. We've all gotten to know Kat. She is an amazing woman. She just wants to be happy and to make Valerio happy. You need to start caring for your son before he kicks you out of his life for good. You will lose Valerio. Are you hearing me?" Domenico asks calmly.

"It's no longer your way, brother. I *refuse* to let you come between these two," Aunt Evelina says flatly.

"Why should I give a shit about anything that you three have to say? I am the one who was in charge, not the three of you!" Father screams.

The three of them are unshaken by his words, only blinking in response.

"This is happening, and there is nothing you can do to stop this. I promise you just like I promised Kat. I will marry her. I love her with all my heart, and that's what matters to me now."

He nods to himself for a few seconds seemingly grasping what we've all been saying, until he turns to my aunt and uncles and rips into them.

"How could you three know about this and not tell me or check her out. She could be a spy for the fucking Russians for all we know. Sent in here to fuck with us or to take over. Why would you not do something about this? She could be working for the Cartel or even the people that attacked this family over a year ago!" He shouts at my aunt and uncles.

"We did check her out. We even had Valerio's men keep an eye on her," Oliverio replies.

"Do you really think that I wouldn't check out everyone who comes into my house? Do you really believe that I'm that fucking stupid to let just anyone around my kids?" I shout at my father.

He scowls at me again and seems to be about to raise his hand toward me.

Before he can strike me though, Mom puts her hand on his arm.

"You will not hit him no matter what. It is not your place anymore. Now you are going to hear them out because I do not want to say this again. If I have to repeat myself then you are going to be finding not only a new wife but a new life as well, do I make myself clear?"

I've never heard my mother talk like that but to hear it sends chills down my spine.

"May I say something?" Kat asks, surprising me and also my father from the way his eyes watch her.

"Yes, you shall, and it better be something good."

"I'm nobody, I'm not anyone important at all. I have no intentions of ever betraying Valerio. I love your son, and I would never betray or put him in harm's way. He's treated me like a real person here, and I won't give that up. I'm sorry if that doesn't fit in your plans for him, but I'm not going anywhere," Kat says with a fierceness that I haven't seen yet but is undoubtedly attractive.

"She has done nothing and asked for absolutely nothing from me, and I love her because she doesn't care about the families or the money or anything. She loves me for me and my children."

"You have my word that I will do nothing but treat him and his children with love and kindness. I know that my word doesn't mean much to you, but it means a lot to me and all I'm asking is for you to trust me a little. Can you please do that?" Kat begs my father.

"Grandpa, don't be mad at Kat," a small voice from around the corner calls out.

Vincenzo comes around the corner and stares at the floor.

"Kat has been nothing but nice to us, and I really like her. She has been here for us, even at times when Dad has had to go away for work. She has been here for all of us," he yells, unable to look into the face of my father.

"Vin, it's okay. Kat isn't going to go anywhere, I promise. She is going to stay right here," I tell him to calm him down. At the same time my heart is swelling with pride. It takes a lot of guts to speak up to my father.

Suddenly, Valeria runs out from around the same corner that Vincenzo was hiding behind and tugs on my father's pant legs.

"What is it, little Valeria? What's wrong?" he asks, staring down at her.

"That's Mama, Grandpa. Don't be mad at Mama."

My mouth drops open, and I look at Kat who glances at me.

He hesitates for a second. "Valeria, that's not your mother. Your mother is…gone."

"No! That's Mama! Don't talk bad 'bout Mama!" she says, her voice raising a few octaves.

I grab Valeria off the floor and hold her in my arms.

"My sweet girl, Valeria, Kat will be your mama, but never forget your other one, okay." I hug her tightly.

"Enough! I've heard enough from everyone at this point. I don't like it. I'm not sure I'm ever going to actually like it. However, I will agree to get to know her. I expect you to come over to our mansion more often as well as bringing the kids. That is non-negotiable if you want this to work. Do I make myself clear? I better because I am not willing to budge about letting this go," Father says without ever taking his eyes off me.

Whatever, that's fine by me if he's willing to let this whole thing go.

"Fine." I just want this to be done. I want the peace I had back. "What about you Kat?"

"Yes, that's fine with me. I want everyone to be happy and if that takes coming over to spend time with you then I will gladly do that." She smiles at me and squeezes my hand tightly.

I offer my hand out to my father, formally to shake my hand so he knows I mean business.

"Not so fast. This is going to be a trial period and how long it lasts is up to me. Only after I deem her in the clear will I allow you to get married to her. Not a second before, because you are clearly blinded by love, and I need to make sure whoever is going to be in charge of this family other than my son is someone that can be fully trusted. Those are my rules if she wants to become part of this family and you would be wise to follow them," he gives me a smug smile and reaches for my hand. Before he can grab it, I yank it back and glare at him.

"I am only going to say this once so I want to be perfectly clear so you can understand," I drop my tone of voice and speak calmly. "When I explode, I can be very dangerous, but it's the moments of calm that you should truly fear. I am the boss here. Not you, so no, I do not accept those terms. I will not tolerate any more fucking interference from you or anyone else. Do I make myself clear?"

I refuse to be pushed around anymore by anyone and if my father wants to be a part of my life and my children's lives then he is going to change because I am done acting like his fucking underling when I am the boss now.

His lips form a thin line, but he shakes my hand. A sigh of relief escapes from everyone watching.

"Now, Mother, it was a pleasure to see you. I'll be over to see you soon."

She comes over and kisses my cheek. "See you soon, my son." She kisses Valeria's head and shoots a welcoming smile at Kat before leaving with my father right behind her, followed by my aunt and uncles.

The moment the door closes, I've already made up my mind, and I hope Kat is fine with it. "Alessio," I bark, "I want you to call the minister and the judge because we're getting married next week. We need to start getting everything in order. Do I make myself clear?"

"Yes, boss, I will call them first thing in the morning. Do you have a particular day in mind?"

"I was thinking toward the end of the week that way we can get everything planned and put together during the week."

"Are you serious? You want to get married next week?" Kat stammers.

I set Valeria on the ground and Vincenzo grabs her hand.

"Kat, take a deep breath. It's going to be okay. Yes, I'd like to get married next week. But if you don't, we can halt everything and wait." I squeeze her hand and watch as she takes a deep breath and shakes her head.

"No, let's do it. I'm scared, and a little nervous, but I know this is right."

"It is," I say, and kiss my queen-to-be. No one is getting in our way.

---

"WHAT THE HELL do you mean you are out of blue irises. I

THE MAFIA'S BLACK OPAL

refuse to take no for an answer, and I don't give a shit how much they cost. I will pay any amount just make damn well sure that the flowers are here in time for the wedding. Got it?" I yell into the phone.

Slamming it down, I notice Kat standing in the doorway.

"Come in Kat. Sorry about that. I just want everything to be perfect for you."

She nods and strides in.

"You don't seem to be too interested in the preparations," I comment, making a note about the flowers.

She bites her lip. "It's not that I'm not interested. It's just that I'm really nervous about this." She twiddles the ring around her finger.

"I'm sorry I sprung this on you. I know that it isn't ideal, and you probably had a different day or month in mind. It's just I couldn't wait any longer. Now that my parents know, I feel like nothing should stop this now. Fuck what the other families think."

Her smile lights up the room. "Thank you for trying to give me the wedding of my dreams."

"Oh, that reminds me. Evelina is coming over within the next hour or so to take you shopping for your wedding dress. When you get back, we can do a small cake tasting. Until then, I'm going to be trying to deal with a DJ for the wedding which is something that I never really understood what the big fuss was about until now..." I trail off and shake my head, clearing it from all the thoughts of the past.

"Are you okay Valerio?" Kat asks sweetly.

"Yeah, I'll be okay. Let me handle the minor things and you and my aunt can take care of the dress. Okay?"

Kat nods and leaves, closing the door behind her.

Rubbing my eyes, I sigh.

Planning this wedding makes me think of my first one. It

was nothing like I hoped it would be. My parents and her parents came together and set everything up for us. She didn't even get to pick her own dress. The families were all there, and they approved of our match. Everyone seemed fine with everything except her and me.

God I'm so nervous. I've never been this nervous about anything before. This is driving me insane, and I can't do anything about it but wait. God fucking damn it, I just want to sign the paper.

Pulling out a bottle of scotch, I pour myself a small glass over ice. I sit back down in my chair and wait for the catering company to get here so we can get the cake tasting set up.

Thirty minutes after everything is set up, Kat and Evelina get back, coming straight to the dining room where the cakes are laid out.

"These all look delicious," Aunt Evelina says, eyeing all of them.

Kat nods in agreement. "Why don't you help us choose?"

"Oh, I couldn't," Evelina says glancing between us.

Smiling, I go around the table and pull a chair out for her. "Aunt Evelina, you can be our tie breaker. Sit, I insist."

She sits down immediately, pulling the chair up to the table. The happiness on her face is easy to see, but she sighs wistfully.

"You know I was in love once myself. Deeply in love. I just wish he had the balls that you had. You stood up to the former Don and not only that, you pretty much spit in his face by holding the wedding after he said he wanted a waiting period. I wanted him to fight for me, for my hand in marriage, and go against everything, but I guess that just wasn't in him. I'm happy for the both of you though." A longing smile comes across her face and fades quickly.

We end up choosing a more traditional wedding cake with buttercream frosting and lemon filling. Once everything is settled, Evelina excuses herself to go home, leaving me alone with Kat.

The next few days pass in a blur and the night before the wedding, it's just Kat and me in the house. Tonight, I let her sleep in her old room for the first time in a long time.

"Tomorrow, your life changes. Are you sure you want this?" I gaze into her crystal-blue eyes. "Are you sure you want me?"

She leans up, cupping my face in her hands, and stares deeply into my eyes. "I do. Are *you* sure you want *me*?"

"Always. I will make sure you want for nothing and you have my word on that."

"I love you so much, Valerio."

"I love you too, Kat. See you at the altar."

She grins and closes the door gently, leaving me to walk to my room alone. What did I do to deserve an angel?

# EIGHTEEN

## Kat

The coldness of the air wakes me up. Even rolling to the right feels weird. Something's off. I blink my eyes open to find no Valerio, and then I notice I'm in my old room and I start remembering.

Today's the day.

I'm getting married today, to Valerio.

A rush of excitement hits me followed by the nervousness of a soon to be bride.

But underneath, I remember today is the wedding, and he still doesn't know everything. How can I even tell him? I should've told him before today. What is he going to think of me?

What if I tell him, and he puts me in the basement to be interrogated? What a wedding day that would be.

Sighing, I get out of bed and walk straight to the kitchen

to find Bernadette on the phone. She waves at me as she speaks intently to someone on the other end. "They better be here in time or you'll be hearing from Mr. Marchioni."

She pauses for a second and then smiles. "Yes, that's what I thought." Pulling the phone away from her face, she presses the screen and sets it on the counter.

"Now, how're you my dear?" she asks and pulls me into a hug.

I lean my head into her neck and sigh. "I'm okay. But can I ask for a little advice?"

She pulls away and studies my face. "Of course, ask away."

I pause and think about whether I should ask. What if she brings this up to Valerio? He told me he wouldn't see me until I walk down the aisle per tradition.

"Please don't tell Valerio," I blurt, "but there's something he doesn't know about me. Something that...might make him hate me."

She frowns. "I don't think there's anything you could say that might make him hate you. He loves you. What's wrong? You can tell me."

Hesitating, I glance away and then back to her. "I can't say, but I have no intention of hurting any of his family. It's just something about me, about um... my past that he might not like."

She raises an eyebrow. "I thought you didn't remember anything."

"I lied," I whisper.

"Oh honey, you need to talk to him soon. The sooner the better." She gives me a quick hug and glances at the clock on the wall. "But not right now. Evelina should be here any minute to take you to the salon. Hurry and get ready!"

Oh. That's a nice surprise. I assumed I was doing my own

hair. Going to the salon isn't necessary at all, but since it's already planned, of course I'll go.

As soon as I slip on a pair of flats, a knock sounds at the door.

"Coming!" I exclaim and grab my bag.

Opening the door, Evelina immediately grabs me and pulls me down the hall. She glances around the corner and then leads me to the foyer and then outside. Pushing me into the waiting car, she heaves a sigh of relief. "Good. He didn't see you."

I nod in response. "I think he's mostly staying in his office or his room."

A picture of him in his black tuxedo pops into my mind. All six feet and four inches of him.

The car lurches forward, and I turn my attention to the front to find Luciano driving.

"Thanks for taking us," I state, glancing out of the window at the partly cloudy sky.

He grunts in response and when we arrive, he gets out of the car and helps both of us out.

The same lady who did my hair last time does my hair again. She gabs about how romantic weddings are and how I'm so lucky to be marrying Valerio. She does mine and Evelina's hair at the same time. This time, I ask for blonde highlights to give a different look in my plain brown hair.

"You are so gorgeous. I bet that gown is to die for."

It definitely is. This gown was everything I wanted. A stunning princess ballgown with a sweetheart neckline and a crystallized top with a long train. It's a dress for a queen, which I guess is pretty fitting since I will be after today.

"It is," I reply, just as she puts the finishing touch on my hair and hands me a mirror.

My jaw drops when I look in the mirror, turning both

ways to see how beautifully it is done. It's pulled up and back in a bun with a sparkling jeweled band around it.

"Thank you so much," I tell her, slipping out of the chair and giving her a hug.

"Oh!" She says in surprise but hugs and rubs my back.

Evelina gets out of her chair and grabs her purse from the table.

"You did an amazing job. Keep the change." Evelina stuffs a wad of cash into her hands and she starts to protest, but Evelina insists. "We'll be back again."

Luciano opens the doors for us, and I slide in after her. I'm about to tell Evelina thank you again when Luciano clears his throat. "Kat."

My eyes jump to his in the mirror. "Yes?"

"Valerio is lucky to have you."

Those words bring tears to my ears, and I remember how I haven't told him the whole truth.

He starts the car and pulls out of the parking lot. "I didn't mean to make you cry," he says softly.

"It's not you," I say, wiping my eyes before the tears can spill out.

"What is it, lovely?" Evelina asks, placing her hand on top of mine.

"I just...I'm just happy," I blurt, lying through my teeth.

She pats my hand. "You deserve all the happiness in the world. There's another reason why I wanted to take you on this trip, though. I need to tell you exactly what you're in for. Has Valerio talked to you about the families?"

A wave of anxiety goes through me at the thought of meeting them. Valerio mentioned that I'd have to meet them someday. It would be unusual for families to miss a wedding, which means today must be that day. *If they knew the truth...*

Shaking my head, I respond, "Not really. He just said I'd have to talk to them eventually."

"Well, today's the day," she says with a hint of annoyance. "Don't worry, Valerio will be right by your side. He won't let them chew you up and spit you out."

"That's comforting," I say with a fake laugh.

"As you know, we're the main family, but there are five core families and three side families. The side families don't matter as much as the core families, but they can be replaced by a side family at any time. The side families will be attending the wedding, but they won't have to formally introduce themselves like the core ones. The two that are always trying to get Valerio, and before then his father, Salvatore, out of his chair are the Palladino and Falco families. The Palladino family has two sons and a daughter. My father tried to get one of their sons to marry me, and that was the one time I flat out refused. The Falco family has a son and two daughters. The father is very controlling and an alcoholic. His son isn't any different, but his father believes their family should be in control. Then there's the Richetti family. They have one daughter, and they're bitter because Valerio was supposed to marry her, but of course Salvatore changed his mind at the last minute, pissing them the fuck off. The other two families are the only ones who are in good standing with us."

She pauses. "Well, now it's only one. The Santini family has three sons, their mother passed away a few years ago and their father has stepped away from everything so the three of them run everything for him. Finally, the Dioli family. They have one son and…had a daughter. They are not happy with Valerio, with him giving up on finding his first wife. I believe they are still trying to find her themselves." A look of sadness flashes on her face. "They're good people, but I don't think they'll be friendly today. You understand right?"

Nodding, I try and take it all in. Hopefully, I can keep everyone's name straight.

"Kat, I almost forgot. Who's going to walk you down the aisle. It's usually the job of the father and in some cases the mother but you don't, well, I'm sure you wouldn't want my brother to do it right?"

Shaking my head, I accept that I don't need anyone. I can walk myself down the aisle.

"I'll do it, if you'll have me, Kat," Luciano suddenly comments.

Smiling, I look at him. "You don't have to."

A small smile forms on his lips. "You're going to be my family. I'm sure Alessio or Luca would have offered too."

Pausing, I look at Evelina who nods, showing me that it's a great idea. "You're right. Thanks."

We finally pull into the driveway and up to the French doors. Taking a deep breath, I glance at the ring on my finger. It's almost time.

---

MY HANDS quiver at my sides as I wait just inside the double doors. The wedding is being held in the area to the right where there's a few less trees. It was decorated exactly how I wanted it to be. The arch has been ready for two days now.

Valeria has already walked down the aisle as our flower girl. She looked so adorable toddling down the aisle and throwing huge bunches of petals that she ran out halfway and then ran straight to Valerio.

I can only see him in the distance, but I can already see how sexy he looks.

Suddenly, I feel a presence next to me and glance over, jumping slightly.

Luciano chuckles. "Sorry I scared you, but are you ready? I think it's time."

"It sure is." I take a deep breath and force myself to remain calm. I'll tell him after the wedding, when we're alone. If he wants to get a divorce... who am I kidding, he'll kill me. Maybe that's just what I deserve for not saying anything for so long.

Luciano holds his arm out and I reluctantly hook mine in. He opens the doors. "Deep breath."

Nodding, he walks me out and around to the right side of the yard, leading me down a path to the aisle. I grip the bouquet of blue irises a little tightly in my nervousness. The beautiful melody of soft sounds gets louder as we get closer. Every person in all 200 chairs turns to stare at Luciano and me. Maybe I should've worn a veil after all. I grip his arm a little tighter in my hand, but he doesn't flinch. We walk steadily down, and I watch as Valerio's face gets closer.

The happiest smile I've ever seen him have is on his face. I know Luca and Alessio are at his side, but I see no one but him. As I stop in front of him, Luciano pries my fingers off of his arm and then places my hand in Valerio's and steps to the side. Valerio's aunt steps up and grabs my bouquet, so both of my hands are free.

My face heats up as there's complete silence. I can feel everyone staring at my back as I face the officiant with Valerio.

He smiles at both of us. "Welcome family and friends of the bride and groom. This is a very special day for Valerio and Kat. They mark this as the day they officially begin their lives together as one. A marriage is full of commitment. It is entered into with the desire and hope that it will last for life.

Kat and Valerio, before you say your vows, please confirm for me by saying that it is your wish to be married."

He turns to me first. "I do," I say, sincerely.

Valerio repeats the same words, "I do."

The finality of those words shake me to my core.

"Now for your vows, I understand that the bride and groom would like to say their own. We will start with the bride."

A shaky breath escapes me as I look away from the officiant and into Valerio's blue-gray eyes. The eyes I'll never get tired of seeing.

"Valerio, I'll never be able to thank you enough for saving me. For being my hero. When I was held captive, I never thought I'd be able to see the outside again. Just when all hope was lost, you came and..." A tear slips from my eye. "You rescued me and those other girls. You've given me the freedom to recover and find myself again. You've shown me love and given me a home and a family to love. You are the best man I've ever met, and I'm honored that you've chosen me to be your partner in life. I love you so much."

The last words come out just as I start full on crying. Valerio wipes my tears away and looks straight into my eyes.

"Kat, you are my sun, moon, and stars. I found you, God I'm lucky I found you. And you gave me the piece of myself that's been missing all this time. Your laughter, your smiles, they make any stormy day better. Your braveness, your determination, and your selflessness. It makes *me* want to be better. You've been there for my kids when I couldn't. Even when things are hard, you're always my bright spot. And I can't live without you. I'll never be able to let you go. I love you, always, my darling."

At his words, my heart clenches. I should've told him. Why didn't I just tell him?

"And now, we would like Valerio's kids to come up."

Vincenzo, Nicolo, Vittorio, and Emilio come up from the first row of chairs, followed by Aurelio who's clutching a pillow with two wedding bands in the center. Valerio's mother walks up with a twin in each arm and Valeria following her.

"Kat, marrying Valerio means becoming a mother to his children. Would you like to say a few words?"

I crouch down as they all crowd around me. The twins don't exactly get what's going on, but they're being quiet and watching me.

"Thank you for accepting me into your home and for letting me love your father. I will never ever replace your mother, but I hope that you'll let me love you like I would my own kids."

They stare at me with wide eyes and then all rush to hug me at once. Tears well up all over again, and I straighten up reluctantly, kissing the twin's cheeks and letting Valerio's mother sit back down.

We turn back to the officiant who talks quietly to Aurelio, who holds up the pillow as high as he can. I reach for the silver band and Valerio for the gold.

"Please place the ring on each other's finger."

We slide them on each other simultaneously and then turn back to the officiant.

"Please approach the table behind me and sign your names, Luca and Luciano, please sign as witnesses."

I sign first and then Valerio, Luca, and Luciano. We walk back into place before the officiant, who smiles at us. "Best wishes to you both. I now pronounce you man and wife. You may kiss the bride."

Valerio and I look at each other and then meet in the middle, kissing each other fiercely. It sets off fireworks in my head, and it's a long minute before we stop, reluctantly pulling away from each other. Suddenly I become aware of the eruption of cheers. Valerio grabs my left hand and walks me back down the aisle.

He kisses my hand as we reach the end and walk to the vacant area that we designated for pictures. "I love you, Mrs. Marchioni."

"I love you too."

I really, *really* do.

---

AFTER TAKING tons of beautiful pictures with Valerio and then a ton with his kids, we move off to the reception area where the cocktail hour is being held. All eyes turn toward us as Valerio walks straight toward the front of the crowd, where all of the dishes and platters are set up. Half of everything is already gone, and there's a small line at the bar. His hand stays firmly around my waist the entire time, reassuring me that he will be right by my side as the most important part of the reception happens, the introduction to the families.

Valerio's father and mother approach us and stand by Valerio's side. He lifts his right hand and places it on Valerio's shoulder.

"Welcome, Mr. and Mrs. Marchioni. Since we've all gotten a good amount of alcohol in our systems, it's time to greet the happy couple!"

He lets go of Valerio's shoulder and steps to the side with Valerio's mom.

Slowly, people from the crowd come toward us, some content to take their time, some anxious to get it over with, and some that just aren't willing. I take a deep breath and try not to fumble with my hands as the first group of people come up, giving me their congratulations and welcome.

The next group of people to come up is led by a man with a few gray streaks in his hair, a woman with curly black hair, and a younger woman with the same curly hair, only lighter.

The man reaches out to shake my hand first. "Congratulations, my dear. I'm Montrelle Richetti. This is my wife, Octavia, and my daughter Leone. We wish you great happiness in your marriage." He nods his head respectfully to Valerio who nods back. Octavia and Leone both shake my hand, though Leone refuses to even look Valerio's direction.

This isn't as bad as I thought it would be. After the people who came up with them are done, a larger group approaches.

It's headed by a man with a completely blank expression with three men at his side. He takes my hand and presses a kiss to it. Leaning a little close, he studies my face. "Congratulations, I am Paolo Santini. These are my sons: Federico, Marco, and Onofrio. If you need their service, they are happy to offer it. Right, boys?"

Those "boys" are all 6'3" and incredibly handsome. They bow respectfully toward Valerio and I.

"Anytime."

I glance toward Valerio who cracks a smile. "Good to see you guys. We need to have lunch soon."

They nod in agreement and leave. The next family that comes up is completely different. Heading them is a man and a woman with cruel smirks on their faces. "Welcome," they say simply. Turning away from me, they glance at Valerio. "Valerio."

They start to turn away, and I instantly feel the grip of his hand on my waist change. "Don't you have something to say, Martelli? Martina?"

They turn around and lift their heads up, scrunching up their noses. "We came didn't we. That should be enough."

"It is *not* enough. You will show my wife the proper respect she deserves. Introduce yourselves."

They turn their full bodies around and roll their eyes. "Martelli and Martina Palladino."

Without another glance, they turn to leave, muttering as they go, "A waste of time."

Left behind are two men and a woman.

"Valerio," both men say with a slight bite to their voice.

"Rinaldo, Silvio," Valerio says dismissively.

"Congratulations," the woman says with a fake smile as she looks me up and down.

"You may go, Riviera," Valerio thunders.

Their eyes widen, and they scamper away after their parents, with their whole party following after them, but not before shaking our hands quickly.

The heads of their family may want to insult us, but they certainly don't. Any of the core families can be changed, and they're all aware of that.

After, a few more people come up to shake our hands. A short older man with dark bags under his eyes and a woman with tons of jewelry around her neck, wrists, and fingers, with two younger women at their sides. "Congrats Valerio, so nice to see that you're well," the man states as he shakes his hand and then moves in closer to shake mine. Instantly, I can smell the overwhelming scent of alcohol. His smile changes as our eyes meet. It becomes a little wider and he hangs on to my hand a little longer than I'd like.

"Yes, I am in perfect health Dino. Renatta. Where's Dino Jr.?" Valerio replies briskly.

Renatta shrugs with a half-glance around. "He's off getting drunk, I'm sure."

The daughter to the right of the mother, the younger one, shakes my hand. "Hi, I'm Perla Falco."

The older one moves around her father. She's just as tall as I am with large, striking green eyes and hair only a few shades darker than mine. "Alessandra Falco."

Dino clears his throat. "Good wishes." He nudges his wife and they leave, with their daughters following them.

Their daughters don't seem that bad, but what about the son?

As our line of well-wishers starts to get smaller, I count on my fingers four out of the five core families down. Just one to go. And it's the hardest one.

My hands start to shake, and I clasp them together as they approach us. I know it's them because of the deep scowls of absolute hatred on their faces.

They stop in front of us, closer than all of the other families. Valerio doesn't move a muscle as the woman steps right up to Valerio's face. Her face twists as if she's going to smile, but instead she spits right in Valerio's face and steps back. Gasping, I look from her to Valerio.

The serious expression on his face shifts as he pulls out a handkerchief from his suit and wipes it away. "I'll let it go, one time. But if I were you, I'd never try that again," Valerio booms.

The man's face twists into anger as he gets right in Valerio's face. "You don't threaten my wife like that, boy."

"I'm not a *boy* anymore," Valerio states in a low tone. "Say it one more time and see what happens." His arm falls away from around me, but the man doesn't back away.

"I should punch you right in your pretty face."

Suddenly, a voice interjects, "Tonino, this is *not* the place for this. Valerio is your boss and you will show him respect."

My jaw drops when I hear the voice, and I have to blink a

few times to make sure I'm seeing things correctly, because it's Salvatore.

"Isn't it?" Tonino quips. "This woman is taking up the spot that my daughter deserved. Your son quit looking for my girl. My only daughter, gone for good."

"Tonino—" Salvatore starts.

"And you!" he yells in my direction, staring at me with daggers. "How is it that you get to raise the children my daughter bore, you get her seat, and you get her husband?"

Guilt envelopes me as his words process in my brain. No, it isn't fair.

Stepping back, I hope to get away from the true words he's screaming. I wish they weren't, but he's right. Wrapping my arms around myself, I turn slightly to the right, when Salvatore roars, "*E-nough*! This is your queen now, whether you like it or not and you will show her and my son some damn respect. Do you understand me?"

My eyes widen as I whirl around to stare at him. My eyes meet ones that are mirror images to Valerio's. His eyes soften slightly and then fix themselves on Tonino.

Without any delay, the family that hates me so much, finally speaks the words that can end this whole matter. The words that pour out of his mouth are sharp.

"Tonino and Emelinda Dioli. Our son, Francesco Dioli." They all turn around to leave and escape as far back into the crowd as they can. Only then do I realize that the whole crowd has been steadily watching the whole incident happen, not missing a moment of it.

The remaining people rush up to shake our hands and congratulate us, and finally, the hardest part is over. I sigh with relief as Valerio whispers in my ear, "Soon this will be over, and we'll be alone. I hope you're looking forward to that as much as I am."

I nod in reply and try not to let their reaction to us ruin the day. After all, it's not about them, this day is ours, and no one can ruin it without our consent.

A few minutes later, we're led to the tables for the early dinner. There are at least forty tables set out for guests, and one long table up front for Valerio and his kids.

At the closest table sit his parents, uncles, aunt, Luca, Luciano, and Alessio.

Valerio pulls out a chair right in the middle of the table for me and helps the kids to a chair each. His mom and dad have the twins so anything they need, they'll be able to get quickly without disturbing us. I'm not surprised by his mother's generosity, but his father...especially speaking up like he did.

I watch as he kisses Carina's chubby cheek and sits down next to his wife.

"Kat?" Valerio whispers, grabbing my attention.

As I turn to look at him, I can't help but notice how much joy fills his face. "There's one more thing, we have to make the official announcement so this can be official."

*Of course, they do it too.*

He stands up abruptly. "Before we have the first dance, we will do *la promessa*."

I rise next to him.

"Kat, please make your promise to everyone as their new queen." Valerio sits down, letting everyone's attention fall on me.

Biting my lip, I look at the crowd of people and find their blank stares a little overwhelming, but I step up to the occasion and stare at all of them, even the ones who don't like me. "I, Kat Marchioni solemnly vow to put the Italian Mafia above all else. I will protect the families from outside threats and promise that we will thrive and grow. I make this vow as your queen."

A long moment of silence follows, making me wonder if I said enough, when all of a sudden, a clap sounds, and another, and another. Valerio places kisses my cheek and snaps his fingers.

The soft sounds of a harp begin, and Valerio leads me to the middle of the grass area. Luca gets out of his chair and stands next to the end of our table to watch the kids. Everyone turns in their seats to watch us step onto the dance floor, a large square of tiles covering the center of the reception area.

When we reach the center, Valerio puts his arm around me and holds me close. "You are the most perfect woman in the world, and I'm ready to take you to bed. Can we leave the party without being noticed?"

I laugh softly, leaning my head against his chest. "No, I don't think we could. I'm ready to be yours in every way, Valerio."

He clenches me a little tighter. "Soon," he growls as he leads me across the dance floor.

A wave of heat passes through me, but I smother it and focus on enjoying the dance that ends a few minutes later.

We walk back to our seats, and as I sit back down next to Valeria who's playing with a flower she found in the garden, I can't help but worry. What if this is my last happy moment? What if my night ends in the basement instead of Valerio's arms?

I have to tell him. I can't wait any longer.

Clenching my hand nervously, I turn to him. "Valerio—"

"Dinner is now ready to be served!" The caterer announces.

He bluish gray eyes lock on my light blue ones. "What is it baby?"

"I...erm...I..." I babble.

His brows furrow as his eyes grow concerned.

A sick feeling comes over me. "I'm just hungry."

He smiles. "Good thing they're serving dinner now."

Nodding, I turn away and clasp my hands together under the table and twist the ring on my finger.

Yeah, good thing.

***

HOURS LATER, after everyone has gone home and the party has run its course, it's just us now. The kids have gone home with Valerio's parents and all of Valerio's men went to one of his clubs to continue the celebration.

It's almost ten when we walk inside the back doors, and I feel like there's a slow train coming, inching toward me about to hit me.

I haven't felt this nervous since seeing him for the first time. Maybe, just maybe, he won't completely hate me. I wring my hands together and jump when a hand touches my back.

"Kat? Is everything okay?"

"Can I um...can we talk in our room?" I ask hesitantly.

I don't give him a chance to reply. I start walking and every step fills me with dread. When we finally reach our room, I'm almost gasping for air.

I step out of my heels and walk down the hallway to the bathroom, switching the lights on as I go. Behind me, I can hear Valerio's soft steps following right behind me.

I glance into the mirror at myself in my beautiful dress. I

place my hands on the counter in front of me and stare at Valerio's eyes in the mirror.

"Can you unzip me?" I ask quietly as my hands begin to shake.

Without reply, his hands go to my back. The zipper slowly glides down, exposing the small bit of my back to the cold air.

"I can turn the heat on, if you're cold. Or maybe..." He leans down to my ear. "I can warm you up."

My dress falls away leaving me in my white bra and underwear with garters. In the mirror I watch as his hand reaches around and just as he's about to touch my breast through the bra, I grab his hand to stop him.

"Before you touch me, you should know who you're touching."

The air between us becomes cold and frigid. "What do you mean, Kat?"

Closing my eyes, I struggle to form the words.

"Kat." His voice is low and dangerous.

I gulp a little. This is probably the worst position I could be in. Caught between him and the bathroom counter.

"My name isn't Kat...at least not my full name."

There's silence, and I can't meet his gaze in the mirror.

"Katya Krasnoff. That was my name."

The silence continues on endlessly, without even the slightest sound, so I just continue.

"You're not dumb so you can probably tell by my name, I'm Russian. My family...I have a family. My parents work for..."

"Are you fucking serious Kat? Your parents work for *him*? Did you work for him?" He asks incredulously.

"I cleaned up around the house. My dad is one of his men.

Not one of his main men, and my mom is one of the maids. I used to help her."

"What else? What else have you been lying about?"

The hurt and anger in his voice has me regretting waiting for so long.

"Tell me, Kat."

I open my mouth to say the rest, but nothing comes out. I'm terrified. If he's reacting like this to what I've already told him, I don't know how he'll react when I tell him everything else.

Tears fill my eyes, dropping down my face to the counter below.

"So, you've never had a memory problem. You knew all along and this whole year...you never said a word. I trusted you. I defended you from everyone. Was my father right?"

He backs away from the counter, finally giving me room. "And on our fucking wedding day! What kind of shit is that, Kat?"

"I'm sorry," I squeak out. "I was afraid, and I don't want to lose you."

"Fucking tell me everything, Kat. Ev-ery-thing," he enunciates dangerously.

The words I need to say are stuck in my throat. Tears pour down my cheeks and I shakily say, "That's it. There's nothing else. I was taken while I was out shopping for groceries. I went alone, late at night and was taken before I could even get in my car."

If he knew the whole truth, it might change the way he sees me forever.

"So you weren't just on the street. Are you sure that's it?" He asks, clenching his fists.

I nod my head and he stalks to the counter, stopping right next to me. "How do I know you're telling the truth?"

"I guess you don't…" I trail off, wiping my eyes.

He stays quiet for a moment. "Kat, do you love me?"

Nodding, I finally look at him and stare shockingly into wide tearful eyes. "I do."

The tears in his eyes strike me to the depths of my heart. I've never once seen him like this.

"Don't lie to me anymore about anything. Please. I can't say I'm surprised, because I always had a feeling you were hiding something. Somehow, I was able to convince myself despite my instincts that you were telling the truth about your past. But if you thought that…that I'd kill you if you told me this…I wouldn't have. I might have left you in the basement to question you for a day, maybe two. But I wouldn't have killed you."

"Am I going in the basement now?" I ask, ready to accept the fate I've been fearing all day long.

"No. But this better be it. I don't know what'll happen if I find out there's something else you aren't telling me."

He'll never find out. Just nod. *Nod.*

Nodding, I reply, "There's nothing else."

He takes a deep breath and runs his hands through his hair. "Now that that's over…"

A weight off my shoulders is lifted, and I can finally breathe again.

Turning me around, he presses his lips onto mine and asks in between kisses, "Katya Marchioni, will you come to bed with me?"

The sound of my full name, my full *new* name, makes a wave of heat pulse through me. "Make me yours, Valerio."

Those words are enough for him to pick me up and carry me bridal style and oh so gently to our bed.

He lays me down right on the edge and then tosses off the

bedspread so there's only sheets. With hurried hands, he throws off his tuxedo jacket and unbuttons his shirt.

His eyes glide from my long legs to my lips, and if it's even possible he's quicker, getting his shirt and pants off in a flash. I back up to our large headboard, watching as he crawls on the bed, following me.

"I've been waiting so long for this, baby," he says, finally stopping directly on top of me, but holding himself up with his hands on each side of my head.

His lustful eyes travel to my bra that cup my breasts. With one hand he pulls my left strap down, and then switches to my right. Slowly he pulls the bra down on the left and then the right, leaving me fully exposed to him. He growls in delight and bends down to catch a nipple in his mouth. I gasp and watch as he sucks it into his mouth. His talented tongue strokes it. With the hand not holding him up, he grabs my other nipple between his fingers, twisting and pulling it, eliciting a sharper gasp from me that has the wetness between my thighs starting to pool.

He switches between them, giving equal attention to both. In between us, I can feel the hardness of him pressing against my stomach.

"Hurry," I moan.

He lets go of my right nipple to say, "No, I'm going to take my time."

His lips catch mine, and he presses his tongue in, rubbing over mine. The faint taste of cinnamon hits my tongue. The gum he chewed after eating dinner.

I wrap my tongue around his, and our tongues clash together, dragging around each other until he breaks away. Inching down, he moves to my ear. He leaves a trail of kisses all the way down to the bottom of my neck, until he stops, sucking on my neck hard enough to leave a mark that without a doubt will be noticeable tomorrow.

His new position makes me feel his length more acutely. I move my hips up and down, making him groan into my ear. An excited shiver goes to my toes, and I do it again just so I can hear that sound.

The suction on my neck suddenly releases as he grasps both of my breasts in his hands and moves his body against mine roughly. "Do you see what you're doing to me? You're making me hurry."

My orgasm starts building as I picture his length moving inside me.

I moan and ache to have his lips again, but he moves his hips away. A warm hand pulls my underwear down, taking them off completely along with my garters. With sure hands he pulls my legs apart and stares right at my core. It's not something he hasn't seen before, but knowing that finally, this is leading to more, has me tingling all over.

His heated gaze lowers and he thrusts one finger inside, testing me to see how ready for him I am. I moan unabashedly as he starts fucking me with his finger. "You're so wet, Kat. Wetter than usual. You want me inside you now, don't you?"

"I do," I moan out.

He puts another finger in, stretching me more.

"Hurry," I urge him as his fingers slide in and out easily.

He pushes a third one in, making me lurch off the bed. His free hand clutches me, holding me down against the bed. "Please Valerio, we've waited long enough," I moan out. He leans his head down and I feel the slide of his tongue along my clit. With a tug, he pulls the fingers out of my opening and licks his tongue over them, drinking all of me in. "I will never get tired of the taste of you," he declares, meeting my eyes.

I almost orgasm at that, but finally, he pulls his boxers down and yanks them all the way off, throwing them like they're the most annoying thing in the world.

I'm met with the vision of his eight thick inches. I don't even have to ask before he's lying on me again, but this time, my legs are spread open, and I'm oh so ready for him.

Our first time. Finally.

Tears of happiness leak out of my eyes as I feel the tip of him pressing against my entrance.

He places his hands on either side of me and presses his forehead against mine. "You came into my life unexpectedly," he whispers. "You stayed here, in this house, knowing who I was and some of the things I've done. And somehow you saw me..."

He presses into me slowly, inch by inch. It's been so long that it aches a little. "You saw someone capable of love. God, I tried, I tried my hardest..."

He presses in deeper, "not to let you in, but I couldn't. You grabbed my heart and let me steal yours, and now I couldn't let you go even if I wanted to, Kat..."

Only then do I notice he's fully in, seated inside me. I wrap my legs around him and moan at the feeling of fullness. His fiery eyes search mine, regarding me, when his hips jerk, and I moan as a delightful tingle of pleasure runs through me.

He moves his chest off of me to get a better angle and thrusts his hips slowly, moving inside of me, causing the tingle to build. Suddenly, he captures my mouth in a kiss and with every tangle of our tongues, his thrusts start getting faster, making me moan into the kiss. He fills me to the brim with his cock and the faster he goes, the more I want.

Breaking off the kiss, I wrap my hands around his broad shoulders. "More."

His eyes light up, and he thrusts in harder, deeper, faster, more than I can take, and the feeling inside me that's been building explodes. It takes me higher than I've ever been before. He groans as I orgasm around him but keeps up the pace. "I'm going to come Kat, I'm going to come inside you, fucking finally."

"Valerio," I say, breathlessly.

"I'm coming," he says, closing his eyes and plunging one more time, all the way in so he's fully seated. I feel the warmth erupt inside me and gasp at the feeling.

His chest heaves as his eyes open and he presses a kiss to my lips. "I love you," he murmurs fervently.

"I love you too."

He gently pulls himself out of me, leaving a feeling of emptiness. As the high wears I off, I take my bra off, leaving me completely naked. Moving off the bed, he grabs our bedspread off the floor and puts it over me. I scoot over a little to make room for him and cuddle against him as he puts the bedspread over himself. "Good night, baby."

He places a strong arm around my shoulder, pulling me in so I'm right next to his heart. Right where I belong.

"Night."

He falls asleep before I do. The small bits of guilt still linger inside me for not telling him the full truth. *Maybe one day he'll be okay with the full truth.*

I watch the slow rise and fall of his chest and then his perfectly chiseled face for a good while in the darkness before finally drifting off myself.

# NINETEEN

## Valerio

Waking up slowly, I notice that a hand is deftly stroking my now rock-hard cock. My eyes shoot open to find Kat lying next to me, bobbing her hand up and down my shaft.

"Good morning," she purrs with a slight grin as she continues to move her hand up and down.

I stretch my arms out behind me. "Kat, you're playing with fire. If you keep stroking me..." She rubs the head masterfully and I choke out, "I am going to ravage you and you won't be able to stop me." Gripping her other hand inside of mine, I squeeze it as a warning.

"Maybe that's what I want," she says with a mischievous grin.

"I won't be gentle like last night," I reply, my control barely hanging on. I glance down at her perky breasts. Her rosy nipples are hard and just begging for my tongue to suck them.

Her eyes go to my cock and she licks her lips. "I want you inside of me, right now. I want you to claim me as yours from now till forever."

At that, I can't wait any longer. In one move, I roll her over and pin her down, causing her to squeal in shock. I force my lips onto hers, holding her tight as we kiss like it's the last thing we'll do. "You know I could really get used to being woken up like this," I say between kisses.

"I'll have to do this all the time then," she says playfully.

Slipping myself in between her legs, I line up my cock with the entrance of her pussy. Slowly, I rub up and down her wet slit, teasing and tantalizing her. Her love juices glisten along my shaft as I rub it up and down her.

"You're already ready for me. You are the perfect fit for me." I hold back a little, sticking only the tip of my cock slowly inside her, even though it's killing me.

"Don't tease me, just do it please. Take me. I want you deep inside of me." And then I get an evil idea. I slip just a bit farther into her and start to make shallow strokes in and out, teasing her entrance. She starts to moan as I tease her further and further. As I keep making the shallow strokes, I cradle her perky breasts in my palms. Cupping them and continuing to tease her, I keep making shallow strokes just deep enough to tease her but not satisfy her. She tries to arch her back as I lean forward to tease, attempting to force me deeper inside her, but I can feel her do it and pull out quickly.

"Not yet, baby. Not yet. I want to tease you until you're crazy with need for me. Beg me a little more," I whisper into her ear.

"Please...please don't make me beg..." Kat gasps, biting her lower lip softly, looking at me with hooded eyes.

"Uh-uh, I am going to make you *scream* for me." I keep teasing her, slipping the tip of my cock back inside her, but this time, instead of shallow strokes I rub it up and down the inside of her entrance.

"Please, please just thrust deep inside me. I want it so bad," she begs softly.

And because I can't wait any longer, and I want to satisfy her, I give in. "With pleasure, baby." In one thrust, I bury myself deep inside her. My cock throbs as I bump softly against the entrance of her womb. I grab her legs and lift them up, pulling her ass closer and forcing myself deeper inside of her. She drags her fingers down my back, leaving scratch marks that I can already feel welling up. I continue to thrust into her as she wraps her legs around me, forcing me to press against the entrance of her with every thrust. Her moans are like music to my ears.

While thrusting, I use my hands to grip her tight ass cheeks and thrust harder and harder. "You feel so fucking good," I groan. "You're gripping me so tightly."

"Oh God, yes, Valerio, keep going. Go faster," she says, meeting my thrusts. "I want you to come inside me again."

"I know you do," I yell while impaling her against my cock. I pull out only to flip her over and thrust myself deep inside her from behind. She moans loudly at the intrusion, panting, but meeting my every thrust. She angles herself perfectly, pushing her head and chest into the bed while raising her ass. I ram as hard as I can and a loud slapping sound fills the room every time our bodies meet.

I rub my hands along her ass cheeks and finally to the crack where I rub my thumb against her puckered hole. I can just barely hear a muffled beg. "Please Valerio, I want to look you in the eyes when you finish inside me."

Carefully I flip her back over onto her back.

"You know what happens the more times I finish inside you right?" The thought lingered in my head the first time.

She runs her soft pink tongue over her bottom lip. "I know." She pulls me into a deep kiss, and I thrust myself back inside her, groaning as her body tightens up. Feeling the building tension, I pump harder and harder against her perfect body. Suddenly, her moans get louder, until she starts quaking in my arms. Reaching the top of her climb because of what I'm doing to her.

As she starts to come down, I move my thumb over her clit. "Valerio," she gasps.

"I'm going to come inside you Katya," I groan and finally go over the edge. I feel myself erupt deep inside her, and after staying in place to watch her beautiful face, I slip out of her.

I watch as a little cum leaks out when I do and push it back in. She makes a pleasurable sound.

"We've never really talked about having children, Kat, and I know I have a lot of them, but I'd love it if we had one." The image of her carrying my child in her belly makes my cock stir a little, but I need to rest, if only for a little while.

I settle myself on the bed next to her, waiting to hear her answer, but she gives none.

"Do you not want one? You're such a great mother to my kids."

She smiles. "I love your kids Valerio. If it happens, it happens. I don't plan on letting you wear a condom anytime soon."

Changing the subject, I grab her hand. "Before we do anything else, let's take a shower together." Before she can protest, I grab her ass and pull it toward me. She yelps in surprise, and I pick her up, wrap her legs around me, and carry her against my chest as I walk down the hall to the shower. With one hand, I open the shower door and step inside. I don't want to let her go, but I do, to turn on the shower.

It's large enough so we're both at separate ends with two shower heads for each of us.

Just a quick shower. I lather myself up with soap, going from head to toe. When I get to my lower half, I remember exactly what I was doing a few minutes ago. The image of her laying with her ass in the air makes me rise to attention. I imagine just what it might be like to bury myself deep within her tight puckered hole. God her tight ass would feel amazing wrapped around my thick cock.

Turning around, I let the water hit my back and my eyes are immediately drawn to a beautiful view, Kat is bent over washing herself, her legs showing not only her beautiful pussy but also her tight puckered hole.

My cock hardens as I think about burying myself in each one of her holes. I lather up my body and notice her glance back at me while I'm lathering my abs. Her eyes heat up and she smiles a little as she moves her hands over her breasts.

I stalk toward her, never taking my eyes off of her. I back her against the wall and take her lips in a bruising kiss. She puts her arms around my shoulders and I quickly pick her up. We mash our mouths together, grinding our lower bodies together as the warm water cascades over us. She bites my lower lip and sucks on it softly as my hands cup her ass. Testing the waters, I work a finger over her tight pucker, rubbing my finger around the ring. We continue to kiss and make out as I slip my finger slowly inside of her up to the first joint.

Kat notices that my cock is already rock hard. "You enjoy my other hole."

"Someday, maybe you'll let me inside it."

Her face turns a little pink. "Maybe," she replies. "Until then, use the other one. And hurry." This time, I don't wait. I line my cock up with her tight slit and plunge deep inside of her. I hold her against the shower wall, slippery as it might be, and start to thrust inside of her.

"Oh God this feels so good, even better the second time," she moans.

She clutches me tightly to her and our bodies slide together easily. I guess we're not getting clean just yet.

I bounce her up and down on my length. We do it wildly, unable to keep our voices down. I'm glad the bathroom is deeper into our room where no one can hear her moans but me.

Changing positions, I move her while she's still impaled on my cock to the floor of the shower and thrust inside her, holding my hands on her hips. She surprises me by moving them and placing them on her shoulders instead for more leverage. It allows me to get deeper inside her, hitting her womb once again.

Her eyes start to glass over as she tightens. "Not yet, baby," I whisper.

I bring her up in my arms, standing up and move her ass so she's bouncing on my cock. She wraps her arms around my neck, pushing her breasts against my chest. It makes me move my hips faster. I can't take much more.

"It feels too good," Kat says, as her walls tighten around me and she lets out a loud moan, her orgasm finally washing over her.

Her face is so beautiful when she does. I feel myself start

to swell. "I'm going to come, Kat. Tell me to come inside you."

"Come inside me, Valerio. Come right now."

Obeying my queen, I thrust up, as far inside as I can and let myself finish inside again. Groaning, I shallowly thrust until I'm completely spent. I let her down gently, pulling myself out of her.

As soon as I do, I'm already missing the feeling, but I know it's time for us to actually get clean.

"Let me wash your back," I murmur.

She walks to one side of the shower and allows me to lather it up. I have to stop myself from grabbing her ass. "All done."

She turns around and smiles at me. "Is this how it's always going to be when we shower together?"

"More than likely," I say with a smirk, and pull her against me.

She sighs. "Guess we better not waste more water." She steps back and turns the dial off on one side and then goes to the other to turn that one off.

"Let's leave before we try and do more and hurt ourselves," she says with a giggle.

———

SOMETHING STILL BOTHERS ME, so I tell her I'll be back and go into my closet to call Luca.

He answers right away. "Yes, boss?"

"Luca, there's something I've been wanting to ask you."

"Okay...go ahead. I'll tell you anything you want to know," he says obediently.

"Are you...do you like Kat?"

He scoffs. "Of course not. I mean she's hot but she's yours—"

"Not like that," I growl into the phone, angry at the image that comes to mind. "I want to know if you think she's right for me."

He laughs. "Man, I have never seen you this happy. Well, not since we were younger and we had more freedom to run wild. But she brings out a different side of you."

"If you think that, then why did I hear you whispering to Alessio about her?"

The other side of the phone is silent. "I just…I know that you love her and she loves you. It's a wonderful thing to find your soulmate. My dad never had that. I know your parents have a great marriage, but I've been able to see your relationship happen right before my eyes. It's a little hard because I know it'll never happen to me."

"You don't know that, Luca."

"I do. And I know Alessio feels the same. You know, for whatever reason, no girls have ever really shown an interest in him. We're both just jealous, man. Don't let us ruin your happiness."

"Thanks for always being there for me Luca. I know you were born into this position, but you're my true brother and you wear the Marchioni name proudly."

Luca laughs, but I know hearing that from me makes him feel good. "Good to hear. Now go back to fucking your beautiful wife. I'll be here to talk anytime, but you'll only have this after-wedding bliss for so long."

"I will," I say with a chuckle and hang up.

I'm about to open the door to the closet and leave, when a feeling comes over me. I know I should trust her, but after her admission last night, I have to know. No, I need to know if she's hiding something.

I speed dial another number in my phone. This time Luciano picks up. "Boss?"

"Luciano, I need you to find whatever you can on Katya Krasnoff."

"Boss, is that her real name?"

"It is, and it's of the utmost importance that you not say a word about this to anyone, not even Luca or Alessio. This stays between the two of us. Report back to me as soon as you find anything."

"But boss—"

"Luciano," I say in a low tone.

It's not like him to not go along with my orders.

There's a small pause, making me question where his mind is at, but he eventually responds, "I'll do it and get it done fast, boss."

"Good."

I hang up the phone for the second time, but stay standing in my closet.

Damn she's got me on a hook like a fish. Me. The Italian mafia boss. Any other woman would be in the cellar for lying to me like that. As much as it hurt, as much as it would've been smart to take a step back, how can I? As long as Luciano never finds anything, everything will be fine. I have enough enemies. I don't need my wife being one of them.

And that Russian bastard, he doesn't know I have one of his former workers, but I wonder what he'd do if he found out.

She'd be dead that day. He'd consider her an enemy for defecting to the Italians and fear that she'd spill every secret she heard.

*Over my dead fucking body. He'll never find out.*

I leave the closet in a hurry. When I get back, she's watching TV. I swallow my guilt and snuggle against her.

"Everything okay?" she murmurs.

"As long as you're here with me," I reply and hope that nothing comes back that I don't already know.

If something does, what am I supposed to do? I'll have to cross that bridge if something comes out.

# TWENTY

## KAT

I can still hardly believe that I, Katya Krasnoff, am actually the queen of the Italian mafia. Staying that first day was the best decision I've ever made.

Valerio gets back in bed, propping himself up on his elbow as he stares at me. It's not a lustful stare, but a thoughtful one.

"Is something wrong?" I ask carefully.

"Kat, about the Russian thing…"

Fear rises in my stomach at the reintroduction of my past, and I reply, "Yes?"

"Did you hear anything while you worked there? Did he ever make plans with you in the room? Are they planning on moving against us even with the treaty in place?"

"No," I reply, answering honestly to only one of his questions.

His eyes narrow slightly. "Are you sure?"

I nod solemnly. "Yes."

His eyes bore into me, as if he's trying to detect a lie. I swallow a little, waiting for him to say something else.

Anything else. Finally, his eyes relent, smiling the same as his mouth does. "My family is everything. I will do anything to keep them safe. I will also do anything to keep you safe. Nothing and no one will ever take you away from me. Do you understand me? I will always find you."

He cups my cheek and takes my mouth in a deep kiss that has me gasping in pleasure when he's done.

It doesn't matter, he's not looking for me. Why would he? Someday though, I hope to see my family again. Until then, they'll go on with their lives and be okay.

***

AFTER LOUNGING AROUND with Valerio for an hour, enjoying the rest of our first blissful morning as a married couple, my stomach grumbles.

Valerio raises an eyebrow. "Are you hungry?"

"After all that exercise, I'm starving."

He smirks. "I'll go get us something, you stay here and relax." Rising from the bed, he heads straight for the dresser and grabs a pair of pants from the first drawer, tugging them on. I'm a little sad to see that firm ass of his gone from my view, but he always looks great in whatever he wears.

"Thanks, baby," I respond, and snuggle my head into the pillow. I'm so sleepy. I could take a little nap while I wait for him.

It feels like I close my eyes for only a few minutes when they shoot open at the sound of the door opening. I sit up, pulling the blanket over me as Valerio sets a tray with an omelet, sausage, and French toast in front of me. "This is a lot just for me. Do you want some?"

He shakes his head. "You go ahead and eat. I'll wait until we get on the plane."

Chewing a piece of sausage, I gulp it down. "The plane? Where are we going?"

He sighs. "I was making your food when Luca came to tell me that my father wants me to leave with him on a trip to Italy. The Sicilians need me to come and tell them about you."

A piece of omelet gets lodged in my throat at that. "Are you...are you going to tell them the truth?" I ask, twirling my fork around.

"I have to. They preside over us," he replies, running a hand through his hair. "But I'm not going to worry about that right now because I'm not leaving with my dad. He's giving me two weeks before we have to leave for Italy, but right now, we're going to pack up and go on our honeymoon."

I heave a sigh of relief. "Well that's good. Where are we going?"

He smiles. "I'd rather surprise you. Just finish your breakfast so we can get going."

Nodding, I eat the rest of my food as he throws clothes and toiletries in our bags. By the time I'm done, he's gotten everything packed up. Anything we've forgotten we can always get where we're going.

"I'm done," I say, pushing the tray to the end of the bed.

I move the bedspread aside and get out of bed. "I'm ready." But why is it so cold? Valerio bursts out laughing and I glance down to find I'm still naked. "Clothes would be helpful."

I walk down another hall to my closet and pick out a pair of black jeans and a gray sweater to go over my pink bra and panties.

In the closet mirror, my hair's a mess. In fact, if I had to describe it, I'd say it's sex hair. Slightly damp from the shower, but all over the place. I brush it down and throw it in a messy ponytail. To make things easy, I choose a random pair of sneakers and pull them on.

I walk out and back to the bed area, when Valerio's phone rings. He answers is quickly. "Yes, we'll be out in a minute." He touches the screen and then shoves it into his pocket, with a quick tug he grabs our bags. "Luca's waiting."

The excitement of going away again with just Valerio drains the sleepiness out of me completely. I leave our bedroom first and walk quickly to the hall. Bernadette is in the foyer to see us off. "Have a good trip you two. Be safe," she says, giving me a motherly hug.

She hugs Valerio too, and then he ushers me out of the door and straight for the waiting Range Rover.

After we're both strapped in, Luca hits the gas and we're hurrying to the airport. "You never know, Salvatore might change his mind."

"You're right," Valerio says, grabbing my hand in his. Squeezing his hand, I watch as we approach some traffic on the way to the airport. Valerio squeezes back and leans down, speaking softly with plenty of promise in his voice, "We have another opportunity to become part of the mile-high club."

The closeness of Luca and knowing he might've heard Valerio makes my face turn red. "Shhhh."

Valerio laughs and gives me a peck on the lips. An evil thought goes through my brain and I let go of his hand to reach down and cup my hand around his junk. "Right now, I say yes, but it's too bad we're stuck in traffic. I might change my mind when we get there."

He growls. "Luca, hurry up and get to the damn airport!"

"I'm going boss. Keep it in your pants for a little while longer."

Oh God, so he *did* hear.

———

*Two weeks later*

ON THE BEACH, I'm lying on my towel, soaking up my last few rays of sun when I feel a few drops of water splash beside me, signaling Valerio's return from the water. Only a few other people are on the beach, and they're all spread out quite a distance down from us.

"How is it? I should go out there one more time before we go back to our room."

"Great, and you should. You're going to miss it when you get back."

"I'm going to miss all of this," I reply. "Can we get a house here too?" I ask, half-jokingly.

"Sure."

I open my eyes and pull my sunglasses down to look at him. "Are you serious?"

He shrugs. "Why the hell not? You love it, I love it, the kids will love it. Next time we come here we'll go house hunting."

Smiling, we meet each other in the middle and share a mind-blowing kiss that goes straight to my toes. "Let's go down together then."

I pull my sunglasses off and leave them on the towel, as I get off the ground and head toward the ocean.

Valerio and I have spent the past two weeks talking about everything before I go back to New York and he goes to Italy. I already knew a lot about him, but what I didn't know was the connection between the mafia there and here. There used to not be one, but twenty-seven years ago, a connection was formed. The Sicilians are no one to play with. They are the ones who run everything. They preside over the New York mafia because all Italy is the motherland. Most things have to be run through them and agreed upon by the family there.

Twenty-seven years ago, Valerio's father, Salvatore, married the heir to the Sicilian mafia, causing the two to merge together forever.

"Women are our most precious treasures. They are queens, and so it has always been tradition that the woman leads, and the man follows. My mother will always have more authority than my father in the states, and somewhat even here in Italy." Finally, the pieces come together about his parents not being here for so long. At some point in the future, his mother will have to spend the majority of her time there once she takes over, and only a small amount here.

It had me wondering what will happen when his mother has to step down because he doesn't have a sibling to take over after her. And the simple truth is, we'll have to rule from both places, half of the year there, and half of the year here, until Vincenzo is old enough to take over from us here.

It was a lot to realize, but I've come to the conclusion that where Valerio goes, I go, wherever that may be.

We run up to a small wave and let it hit us straight on. It pushes us back, letting the cold, salty water, rushes over us.

"Do you know how sexy you look right now?" Valerio asks, moving behind me and putting his arms around my chest.

"No, but I know I love you."

"I love you too, which is why I've been thinking about something. I don't know how long I'm going to be away in Italy. I don't go there often. I think we should extend our honeymoon a little while longer so we can fully enjoy it before you don't see me for a while."

Whirling around, I stare into his smiling bluish gray eyes. "You want to stay here longer? And piss your father off?"

"Fuck him, and no. I don't want to stay here. But there's a cruise leaving in three days from Barcelona. How do you feel about a two-week European cruise?"

My heart swells with joy. This man. But the kids…

"Your kids are going to be away from you longer then."

His eyes sadden. "I feel bad, but this honeymoon is once in a lifetime for us. I'll do what I can to make it up to them when I get back from Italy, but when you get back, make it up to them for me, please? I feel horrible that we're going to miss Vittorio's birthday, so do something special for him."

"I will," I vow. "Whatever he wants, he'll get."

"But I know it won't replace having me there. It seems like I'm always missing out on one of their birthdays. I'm surprised they're so happy every time we call them."

"That's because they love you, and they know you're doing your best. And once you get home from Italy, you won't have to leave again for a while, right?"

He sighs. "I hope not. But I could be called away anytime for one reason or another. This is our life, Kat, and I wish I had a set schedule like other people, but I don't."

He pulls me to his chest, holding me tightly to him as the water lulls around us.

---

*Another two weeks later*

THE LONG FLIGHT home is almost over, yes, we're finally going home. It seems like we've been away for so long, but it's only been a month. The European cruise was just as fun as Hawaii, only we got to see so much more. Those few days where we were out to sea, we stayed locked up in our room, even when the maids came to clean it. We couldn't get enough of each other, and I know I'm going to miss it when he's gone. The other days were spent on land, in Greece, and also Italy, which may or may not have been a mistake, have been great.

We both discovered a love for painting and agreed to do some of our own at home. It was a wonderful trip, and I don't regret taking it one bit, but halfway through, all I wanted to do was go home. And now that we finally are, I'm excited.

The only thing that ruins it is him having to leave a few hours later.

"One more hour," the pilot says over the loudspeaker.

Valerio smiles at me and gets on his phone. Suddenly, out of nowhere, the plane rocks. It jolts me in my seat a little, but we've been having turbulence off and on for a little while. It wasn't easy to sleep last night on here, and I'm completely exhausted. My mouth opens in a yawn, and I go to put my hand to my mouth to stifle it when my stomach twists.

Oh, God. I knew I shouldn't have eaten that burrito.

I get up from my seat and move to the back of the plane to the bathroom.

As soon as I close the door, the contents of my stomach rise out of nowhere. I fall to the floor as it erupts out of my mouth, barely making it into the open toilet. Grabbing a piece of toilet paper, I try to wipe my mouth when I get the same sensation again and throw up a little more and heave until there's nothing else to come out.

With the piece of toilet paper, I wipe my mouth and then throw it in with the vomit and flush it all away. Completely drained, I collapse against the wall.

I haven't thrown up like that in a long time. Not since…

Somehow, I get the energy to pull myself up using the handle of the door and walk out to our bags. I glance at Valerio who's still on the phone talking animatedly.

Deep inside my carry-on bag, I grab the thing I'm looking for, a test, and some perfume. I shove both of them in my pocket and walk slowly back to the bathroom. The stench of the vomit hits my nose as soon as I open the door. I spray like crazy to get rid of the smell and then read the instructions for the test. I can't believe I'm actually taking one of these again.

I was supposed to get my period a few weeks ago, but I never got it. This test was supposed to be for when we got home, but I guess I'm taking it now.

After completing the directions, I place the cap back on it and set it on the small sink area. I flush the toilet and then sit on the floor to avoid looking at the test and watching the result appear. If this is positive…God, I knew it was possible. And it was going to happen sooner or later but now of all times?

With a deep breath, I pull myself up and glance down. The result is simple and clear to read. There's no squinting. The second line is strong.

I'm pregnant. With Valerio's child.

Grabbing it, I push it down into my pocket and wash my hands. I have to tell him.

Unconsciously, I rub a hand down my stomach. A baby. I walk out of the bathroom and sit down next to him. He pats my hand and squeezes it. The phone call goes on forever, until the pilot announces, "We are now beginning to land, seat belts please."

His seatbelt is already on, so I hook myself in. He hangs up the phone and pushes it into his jacket pocket.

"You okay, baby? You look like something's bothering you."

"I-um..." his eyes stare into mine. Just say it, he'll be thrilled. The ring of his phone interrupts my next few words. He looks at me apologetically and scowls at his phone before answering, "We're about to land, Father. Can't this fucking wait?" After a pause, he responds, "Fine, go on..."

It'll just have to wait until we get off the plane. Our baby...another prince or princess.

# TWENTY-ONE

## Valerio

The plane touches down in New York after a rather long flight. I can't wait to get home and see the kids, if only for a short time. Getting off the plane, Kat and I walk down to the waiting Range Rover. Other than extending our honeymoon by two weeks, I've never missed any business trips or anything having to do with the job. I know the old man won't be happy, though. When we get in the car with Luca, he immediately turns around. "What the hell were you thinking, doing that?"

"I know it was a spur of the moment thing, but listen, Kat and I only get one honeymoon. What all did the old man say when he found out?" I ask, not really caring about how much he's freaking out.

"Valerio, he's super pissed off. I haven't seen him that

pissed in a long time. He's been taking it out on the men," Luca says with a lower tone.

"What happened? Is everyone okay?" Kat asks.

"Yeah everyone is fine at the house. It's just the old man said he needed you and because you took so long to get back, you guys are running out of time. He must've had something really important for you to do."

"Running out of time for what? What the hell is going on Luca? What aren't you fucking telling me?"

"Look, all I know is the old man isn't happy and wants you to come over right away."

"Okay, take us home really quick then."

On the drive home, all I can think about is why the old man would want me and be so pissed off. The only thing that I can think of is that either one of the families is in open rebellion or something to do with the Sicilians. If one of the families was in open rebellion, I'm pretty sure that Luca would flat out tell me. Fuck that only leaves the Sicilians and if they are the problem, then we all have some big ass problems.

"Fuck. It has to be the Sicilians. It just has to be, but why would they want something now?"

"What do you mean?" Kat asks with a puzzled look.

"I think that the Sicilians might want to meet up with us, which is something that I don't really like the idea of. The core families there are a little different than our own, here."

"Okay. So apologize to your father and get going. Don't let me keep you here," Kat states.

"I'll be gone for a while. I wish they'd come here, but it's been ages since they have. They don't like leaving their homes in Italy. We have to give them respect because they are the old families and without them, we would lose support of everyone."

Once we get home, I notice that my father's car is parked right in front of the door, and I can see him waiting inside for me.

As I get out of the car, he gets out and rushes over to me, grabbing me by the collar of my dress shirt.

"Do you have any idea how much trouble we are in if we don't meet with the Sicilians by tomorrow?"

"No. What the hell is going on?"

"They want to meet to discuss the ongoing problems with the Russians as well as the ongoing problems with the families."

"Just let me spend a little time with the kids."

"No. You should've thought about that before. You have one hour and then we have to go back to the airport."

I push him away from me. "I don't think so. I'll be there in two hours and no less than that."

He scoffs angrily, but there's nothing he can really do since I'm the boss.

Kat and I bring our bags into the house, and I drop mine by the door itself.

She brings hers to the door of her old room which is odd. She has been kind of odd since we landed, but I'll have to forget about that for now.

"Let's go see the kids in the playroom before I have to go again," I say to Kat.

"Yeah, I'm sorry you have to leave again, but at least once you get back you won't have to leave again for awhile right?"

"Hopefully," I reply.

We make our way to the playroom where all the kids are building with blocks to see who can build the highest tower.

When the kids see us, they jump up, leaving the blocks happily to assault us with hugs. Kat seems a little apprehensive of the kids, only giving them half-hearted hugs.

This needs to be taken care of now. "One sec, kids."

I pull her aside and get straight to the point. "Hey Kat, are you okay?"

"Yes, why?" she asks, her brows drawing together.

"Are you sure? I mean you've been acting a little strange since we got off the plane. Is it because I'm going to meet with the Sicilians?"

She smiles, but it's not her usual one, leading me to believe something is really wrong. "I'm fine Valerio, I promise."

Turning away, I finally give the attention back to my kids. They help me with my own tower, and even though I'm having fun with them, I can't stop thinking about Kat being odd. She's barely looking at the kids. She's definitely not okay. I need to ask her again.

"Kat...are you..." I start

"Valerio, I told you I'm fine. That answer won't change so please just drop it because I'm not going to say any more on it."

"Fine, though I don't like this. I'm going away and you're not telling me the truth. I thought we were going to be honest," I say, staring into her eyes.

My tower falls and Valeria waddles over to me and hugs me in her tiny arms. "It's okay. Towers fall. Vin says we can do it again. I love you, Daddy."

Her sweet voice reminds me that I still need to tell them. "I love you too little one, but I have some bad news."

All of the children turn to look at me.

"I have to go now. I have to leave again. Maybe for a week or two, I'm not really sure."

Nicolo stands up quickly. "But why are you leaving? You just got back. This isn't fair," he frowns and pouts.

"It's a business trip, son. I have to go on it. There is no way I can't go."

They all hold their heads down, making me feel guiltier. Valeria tears up and says, "Don't go, Daddy."

"Sweet pea, he has to," Kat says to her.

I sigh and shake my head. There's nothing I can do. I give all of them a big hug and then walk out. It's hard with every step, but I'm doing this for us, for our family. Going back to the main floor, I go to the kitchen where Bernadette is waiting with dinner ready. I grab a Tupperware container and fill it full of food, enough for me to eat on our trip and then walk out the door of the kitchen to head toward the front door.

My children are there at the door waiting for me. I stop and pat my hand on Vittorio's head.

"I'm sorry, that I missed your birthday Vittorio. You are really getting taller, you've almost caught up to Vincenzo."

As I turn to Kat, I give her a kiss although she has a look on her face like she needs to tell me something.

"Are you sure you're okay?" I ask one last time, hoping she'll actually give me an answer before I leave.

"It's nothing I promise," she says, but her crystal-blue eyes say something completely different.

Nodding, I head outside to where my father is waiting in front of his own car. Getting into the car, I watch as my father gets into the other side of the car. Neither of us in the driver's seat.

"So, if you aren't driving then who is?" I ask curiously.

"I am," a voice calls out right away.

"Oh hey, Lucio, it's been a long time since I've seen you. Let's get going then," I say a little briskly.

Not that I don't like Lucio, because I do. I'd just rather be inside with my family. Lucio is my dad's right-hand man, like

Luca is mine. The title is passed down from father to son in the case of my family.

I can't say that I'm happy about going to Sicily, but it's a pretty good trip for being something that I don't have to pay for. We do it the old-fashioned way, not taking our own plane. As soon as we get on, we notice that there aren't a lot of people in the seats at all. In fact, there is nobody on the plane at all other than the pilots.

Lucio, my Father and myself, all get into our seats and wait. Soon the plane is taking off but things just feel out of place and weird.

"Hey Old Man, did you buy out the plane?"

"No, I didn't but I feel just as odd about this as you do. Trust me, I noticed right away as well. So did Lucio."

"So, what are we gonna do about this? I mean this can't just be a coincidence? This has to be something that either the Russians set up or one of the families set up right?"

"It could just be a coincidence. I mean there isn't any actual problem so far right?" I ask.

"Just be prepared because we might need to leave or jump out of the plane as soon as possible. So, Lucio know how to fly a plane?"

"Not really but I could figure out pretty quickly. I've flown smaller planes before but never something this big. I hate to think that we could all die due to me, but honestly I'd blame the other families before you put a blood curse on me."

"It's okay. I'm sure that this is just a weird occurrence," I mutter, more focused on just getting the show on the road.

A voice comes over the loudspeaker. "Hello passengers. Sorry that you are the only ones flying to Sicily today. However, this trip wasn't supposed to happen. The three of you were the only ones who bought tickets. Thus, we did not want to spare anyone for the flight attendants."

Well that is finally a good answer, at least this isn't a set up to try to kill us.

We finally arrive in Italy and find a car waiting for us at the airport. It takes us directly to an old church, which is odd because I never knew the meeting place to be a church before. Generally, it's at the main family's house, which in this case would be my grandparents, Marcello and Gemma Sinagra.

When we walk in, they're facing the doorway, already waiting for us. My grandparents are in their early sixties. Both of them have gray hair, but they're both in great condition and their minds are strong. Grandmother has always held herself a certain way, I'm guessing it's how she was trained to act. My grandfather is a little more laid back.

Grandma Sinagra looks down her nose at my father. "It's been a long time since you brought your son, Salvatore. Now, we were supposed to talk business before, but never got the chance."

He bows to them. "I am no longer the head of the family in the states. Valerio is, don't you remember? We talked about this the last time we were here giving you an update about his missing wife?" my father replies.

"Oh yes that's right. Poor girl. How did the search go for her?" Grandma Sinagra asks, straight to me, ignoring my father.

"Not good. I spent months searching for her. I reached out to an associate I have in Interpol to ask if she could find her, but even they had no luck. It's like she just vanished without a trace. I couldn't find the guys that took her nor could I find even a shred of evidence about the location of where she was taken." The words just pour out of me and I feel ashamed. Not that I didn't find her, but that I might be perceived as a failure in the eyes of my grandparents.

"So, you stopped looking for her knowing full well that if you did, it would cause strife with the lesser families? You willingly took a risk that could have endangered our family's name and made an enemy out of another one of the core families?" Grandpa Marcello asks, a small twinge in his voice that I can't quite place.

"Yes, Nonno," I reply with my head bowed down. I know that he can have me replaced by Alessio quickly enough, seeing as this position should be his, or by anyone he decides because he is one of the original families.

"Well all I have to say about that is good. Put those lesser families in their place. They are beneath us, and they need to learn that. We are better than them, we are the ones in charge and that's all there is to it," Grandpa Marcello says with a small smile.

"Wait, so you aren't mad that I gave up and ended up marrying someone outside of the families?" I ask.

"Oh no, on the contrary, while we were surprised, it is in fact your life. This is something we have to tell you though. You need to keep an eye out because the lesser families are going to be gunning for you now, and if you let your guard down for too long they *will* strike," Grandma Sinagra replies.

"Yeah. We ended up flying on a plane that had nobody on it. It seemed very out of the ordinary, but it was explained away," Father replies.

They ignore him completely, keeping their attention on me.

"So, tell us about your new wife. A nice good Italian girl, I hope. We know that you were here in Italy with her and you didn't even come to visit us," Grandma Sinagra replies. "We could have met you near the cruise port."

I hesitate to answer, thinking about whether to tell them at all about Kat's full background. The more I think about it, the more I realize that they might not be as understanding as I am. They have a longer history with the Russians than we do. They might even try to use her against the Russians. I'd hate for her to become a pawn in this stupid war. I need to protect her. As much as I want justice for those that the Russians have killed, we have killed just as many as them of theirs.

"I'm sorry Nonno e Nonna. I meant no disrespect. The only reason we didn't is because we were on our honeymoon. I didn't want to interrupt that. And like lovebirds, we couldn't keep our hands off of each other. She's a wonderful woman who I ended up rescuing from a human trafficking ring. She was so quiet and she had suffered so much with no place left to go. So I let her stay with me and she helped me take care of my children as well as kept me from doing stupid things. I started to fall in love with her slowly but surely. There was nothing that I could do to stop it. She's kind, and she loves me for me, not as the head of the Italian mafia."

I glance up at them and finally get out what I've been feeling. "I can't help what I feel, especially when I'm around her. We took an extended honeymoon because I wanted a little more time with her, just us. She is my everything now, along with the kids."

Grandpa Marcello nods. "I understand and I hope you understand us. While we are happy as your grandparents, we have to tell you that there will be backlash from that family after the disappearance of their daughter. No matter what happens, your family will stick beside you because that's all we can do to keep our power and our family safe."

"Besides, love happens when you least expect it, doesn't it, Marcello?" Grandma Sinagra asks, sharing a secret smile with him. "Anyway, let's actually get down to business. What are we going to do about the Russians and the Cartel? Because we can't appear to be weak at any point. If we do, they will swoop in and try to take us out at the earliest chance they can."

"I know. I've met with both the Russian boss and the Mexican boss. I wanted to sit down with them and make sure that the pact will be kept for now. As for the Mexicans, he wanted to see *me* which was more of him trying to figure out what was going on with me and mine."

"Why would you do something so very stupid as going to meet them without letting us or your father know what was going on?" Grandma Sinagra snaps, looking at me like I'm stupid.

I calmly reply, "I had it handled, and I still do. There is nothing they can do to me without drawing attention to themselves or without dragging the other sides in to attack them. Those that fuck with me or fuck with anyone that I care about is going to unleash a demon that they don't want to fuck with. Everyone is so scared of the Russian because they think that *he* is so dangerous and fucked up right? They haven't seen anything yet."

My grandparents and my father and his secondhand man all stare at me and then nod in unison.

"You can't do anything stupid right now though, anything you do can give the other families an excuse to create a coup against us and we can't afford that. Yes, we can always replace them with the other families outside, but it's not worth doing that until we absolutely have to," Father says.

I nod and let my temper cool. No need to pick a fight with my own family if I don't have to. Plus, they would just decide that I was being ungrateful or disobedient.

"Isn't there any way this can all be settled today? I just want to get home to my lovely wife and keep her and my children safe. The more time I spend here, the less I spend there with them. Tell me what you want me to do about the Russians, and I will take care of them."

Father grips my shoulder. "Son, it's not that easy. I hate the fact that we can't just wipe them all out, but it would break the pact, and it would be fair game on our men and our territory."

"You're right, but that doesn't change the fact that I'd like to do something about all this and the most I can really do is just get prepared and keep an eye out for someone who is gunning for me."

"There is something that you can do and that is what we need to talk about right now. You need to sleep with both eyes open and keep an eye on what is yours because right now, you are in the cross hairs of at least ten different groups of people."

I watch as my grandparents just stare at my father and his right-hand man.

They give him a look, and I notice his face drops as he frowns.

"You are going to need to stay here for a week or so because we need to discuss with you everything that you are going to have to do to navigate your way out of this mess that you have fallen into," Grandpa Marcello remarks with a frown of his own.

"I don't want to stay here, I just told you that my new bride is at home with my kids and I don't want to leave them alone any longer than I absolutely have to."

"Don't argue, Valerio. This is for the best. That way we can strategize and make sure that we don't make any stupid mistakes that could lead to our downfall. This is for the family, especially since we don't have a female heir."

I completely forgot they have never really cared for my

father, and they blame him for a lot, even things that might not be his fault. My parents were never supposed to fall in love and being able to only produce one child has only given them reason to not like him more.

"First off we will have to go back to the house. We wanted to make sure we wouldn't be followed. Who would think that a mafia meeting would be held in a church?" Grandma Sinagra looks at the three of us. "Now you are going to come home with us and stay in the guest rooms that we have had made up already."

Father doesn't protest, and I follow his lead. Anything to get this over with.

"I will go with you as long as I can call my wife and talk to her first."

Grandpa Marcello nods. "That's fine, just don't take too long. We need to get back to the house as soon as possible because if we don't, we risk drawing too much attention to us. The last thing we need is to have all but one important person in our family die."

The core families here are capable of it. They'd shoot all of us and then take over. Or at least try to and argue between the lot of them about who would be the main family.

Walking away from them, I pull out my phone. I wait for her to pick up and as soon as she does my heart feels at peace. "Kat, I love you. I can't talk for very long, but I wanted you to know that I'm okay. As of right now, I'm staying for a week. "

"Okay, do whatever you need to do. I promise everything is going to be fine. I'm handling things here," she says with a tone of authority.

It makes me feel a swell of pride.

"I know, baby. Do you think you could put the kids on the

phone? All of them? I'd really appreciate it, Mrs. Marchioni," I say seductively into the phone.

She giggles and I hear the smile in her voice as she says, "Anything for you, Valerio."

I talk to each of my kids individually, even though the twins aren't talking in full sentences, it's great to hear them try and talk. Their voices make me miss them so much, and all I want is be home with them.

To forget about it, I tell them stories of the wonderful place that I'm in. How beautiful and majestic it is. I tell stories about how when I was a young lad, I always wanted to move here and have my own place without having to deal with any of the other families just my own little house with a vineyard or something that I could call my own without anyone or anything getting in my way.

I feel a tap on my shoulder, and see my dad motioning at his watch, signaling that my time is up.

"Listen, I'll talk to you soon," I say to Vincenzo.

"Okay Dad, I love you."

"I love you too, son. Can you put Kat on the phone?"

A moment later, she's back and I tell her quickly, "I have to go. I'll call again soon. Love you."

"I love you too," she says in a sad tone that makes me not want to hang up.

I put my phone away and go back to my father, Lucio, and my grandparents.

I'll get this settled soon, as soon as possible so I can go back. Sometimes I understand exactly why Domenico doesn't want the job, but what I can't understand is why Alessio wants it so much.

"Let's go, son," my father says, grabbing me by the shoulder and leading me outside.

The sun shines brightly as we walk out, and I'm in awe all

over again. I love it here, but I just wish my family was here with me.

I will handle all of these other crime families and anyone who messes with us. If I can actually keep a good handle on everything, I won't have to come back out for a while for business reasons.

I can almost hear Kat telling me not to be so hard on myself, but I can't help it. I will show those fuckers that the Italian mafia is on top. The pressure is on.

# TWENTY-TWO

## KAT

The instant Valerio leaves, I regret not telling him, even if I would have had to say it in front of everyone else. Maybe he won't be gone that long. The kids stare dejectedly at the door and move to go upstairs back to their play area.

"Wait kids, gather around," I call to all of them.

Carina and Illaria are walking perfectly now, and they toddle toward me when I crouch down. "Your father and I have been gone a while, and we're sorry. To make it up to you, we're going to have nothing but fun while he's gone. Of course, school work needs to get done and I know it won't be the same, but what do you guys think?"

They all cheer and start yelling at the same time to ask what we're going to do.

"Since we missed your birthday, Vittorio, you get to choose the first thing we do. What would you like to do?" I ask, looking at him.

His large blue eyes blink at me. "I like roller-skating."

"Oh. Why don't we go to a roller-skating rink tomorrow then?"

He cracks a smile and grabs me around the neck, hugging me tightly. "Thank you."

"Until then, why don't we go and do some arts and crafts?" I ask.

Valeria claps excitedly, jumping up and down. "Yes, yes, yes!"

I glance at all of their faces and find all of them smiling. I hope that…

Tears start to well in my eyes.

"We go up?" Carina asks pointing to the stairs.

Nodding, I follow her and the rest of the kids up the stairs.

---

*Three months later*

THE TOILET in the master bedroom and I have become best friends, but I'm hoping that time is almost over. It's been hard waking up every morning and puking my guts out. It's also been hard being without Valerio during this time. I did my best to be careful to hide it from everyone, but I knew a secret like my pregnancy would be hard to keep.

One morning I was with my "best friend", throwing up, and then as soon as it was done with, I went to brush my teeth.

I made the mistake of going to the kitchen and smelling the eggs that Bernadette was making for the kids for breakfast, an instant regret when I felt the bile building in my throat. I rushed to the nearest bathroom, unfortunately not my own, but the main bathroom everyone uses on the main floor.

And even more unfortunately, someone was already there, washing their hands when I burst in and threw up all over the floor in the bathroom.

Over my tear-filled eyes, I looked up the dress shoes to the pants to the shirt, and finally to the face of Luciano. His eyes were disgusted at first, but he managed to piece it all together in a second and was instantly grabbing the cleaning materials to clean up the mess I didn't mean to make.

After he was done, he picked me up and helped me to my room.

"Does Valerio know?" He asked.

"No. I didn't really get a chance to tell him…"

"While he's gone, I'll get you anything you need, just call."

Those words echo inside my brain as I rub a hand down my stomach to find the small bump there. It feels like it's getting bigger every day. Luciano bought me a few baggy shirts to hide it, but I'm still fitting into my regular jeans and pants fine.

Luciano has been great, taking me to the doctor at the clinic nearby and making sure I don't get too tired out from the constant fun with the children. The throwing up has slowed down, and I'd like to think as I get to the end of my second trimester, it'll stop completely.

I didn't think Valerio would be gone this long, but by his last phone call, he should be coming back later this week. He's not happy about being away for so long, but there was really nothing he could do. During his absence, Emilio and Nicolo have both had their birthdays. Bernadette helped me have parties for both of them. We went to a trampoline park for Emilio's and Luna Park for Nicolo's.

But by coming home next week, by the end of the week, he'll be missing another one, Vincenzo's birthday this time.

Last year, he was home before his birthday was over, but not this year. This year he'll miss it completely.

I walk into the family room to find Vincenzo and Vittorio watching cartoons on TV.

"Hey guys, it's finally warm enough to swim. Do you guys want to go out?"

"Only if you swim with us," Vittorio comments, eyes glued to the TV still.

I glance down at my bump and palm it through the shirt. I wish I could. "Sorry guys, I can't."

"Why not?" Vincenzo asks, turning his attention away.

"I don't really feel well enough to swim."

He gets up from the floor quickly and touches my arm. "Do you need to lie down or maybe go to the doctor's?"

His concern melts my heart, and I place my hand on his head to ruffle his hair. "Thanks, but I'll be okay. It'd make me feel better if I saw you guys swimming."

He smiles and looks at Vittorio. "Let's go get our suits on and see if Emilio and Aurelio are done with their lessons."

Vittorio nods, and they take off running up the stairs. Ten minutes later, Vittorio and Vincenzo come back with sad looks. "They can't yet, not for another hour."

I pat both of their heads and walk down the hall to find Bernadette. By the sound of it, she's watching TV in her own room. I peek in and find her doing exactly that.

"Do you think you could help Emilio and Aurelio get into their swimsuits in an hour as soon as they're done with their lessons."

She nods and smiles. "Of course, Kat. You need to rest."

"I'm going to go outside and watch—" I start, but then her words process in my head.

She gives me a knowing look. "Did you think I haven't been paying attention? Your face is a little fuller and you've been wearing baggy shirts."

Instantly, I feel the need to explain. "I'm sorry I didn't tell you."

She rises from the bed and pulls me into a hug. As soon as she does, she looks down. "I definitely feel that bump. Don't worry, dear. I'm assuming it's because Valerio doesn't know. I'm not offended at all."

"Only you and Luciano know. And he wasn't supposed to know either."

"May I?" she asks, hovering her hand over my stomach.

Nodding, she places her hand down. "Wow...another baby. What a blessing for you two. I'm so happy for you, and Valerio is going to be overjoyed."

And also angry that through all of our phone calls, I haven't even given him the smallest hint that I am. "I better get out there and let the boys get some exercise."

She nods and her smile widens. "I'll go up to get the other boys and girls too as soon as they're done."

"Thanks," I say as I close the door. I hurry back to the boys, afraid I've taken too long and they've changed their minds and gone back to the TV, to find them right around the corner, waiting for me, each on one side of the man I've been missing for three months.

My mouth drops open. "Valerio!" He smiles and we lock eyes.

"Surprise, baby!" He holds his arms out and walks to me to give me a hug. And though I ache to feel his embrace, I know as soon as he does, he'll feel my stomach too.

Did Bernadette know he was coming home early? Why didn't she tell me!

I place my hand out to stop him. A wounded look flashes on his face. "One second, honey."

I glance around him at Vittorio and Vincenzo who are talking excitedly about all the things they want to do with him now that he's back. "Kids," I say interrupting them.

They stop abruptly and turn to me. "Do you think you could go upstairs and tell your brothers and sisters that he's home?"

They nod quickly and take off up the stairs, yelling "Dad's home!" over and over.

"Is something wrong?" he asks, crossing his arms and watching me carefully with his eyes.

Instead of answering, I walk to our room. He follows after me. As soon as he comes inside, I lock the door behind us so we won't be disturbed.

"There's something I have to tell you," I say, biting my lip nervously and facing the door.

"Kat, you're starting to scare me."

I fold my arms around myself and turn around. "Valerio, I'm sorry I didn't tell you earlier, but there was never a right moment before and, well, just hug me."

His brows draw together and he leans down to grab me in his arms. The second he does, he freezes. "You smell good," he murmurs. "Really good. But is that what I think it is?"

He backs away, staring at me with an awed expression. I lift my shirt up and show him my baby bump.

"Kat! You should've fucking told me. I would've made them let me come home to you. Baby, we're going to have a baby! I didn't know it would happen this fast." His hands immediately come down to my stomach. "Do you know what it is?"

I shake my head. "Next week is the appointment to find

out, but I think I'd rather let it be a surprise. For my...I mean I'd just rather be surprised."

He smiles. "We can tell everyone at dinner."

"Well, not everyone," I say sheepishly, pulling my shirt back down.

"Who else knows? Don't tell me fucking everyone knows but the kids."

"No, I wouldn't do that. Bernadette is just observant, but before her, Luciano knew. He helped me while I was throwing up my stomach contents every morning. I'm still a little sick but nowhere near what I was."

"Then we'll announce it at dinner to everyone, but right now, I've been missing my life," he says in a low tone. His eyes shine with desire as he moves his hands over fuller breasts and down to my hips. Leaning down, he catches my lips in a deep kiss and runs his tongue across my lips before I give him entrance.

Opening my mouth, he thrusts his tongue in and moves his over mine sensually. I move my hands around his shoulders, pulling him in even closer as my body starts to respond to him.

He breaks the kiss to take my shirt off and backs me up to our bed. I lay back, my belly thrusting into the air as I feel his hands pulling my jeans off, and then my underwear. His eyes fill with lust as he sees me bare to him. He throws his jacket and shirt off and unbuttons his pants to reveal his length, already fully hard and ready.

"It's been way too long Valerio, I need you inside me, now," I tell him.

I turn over carefully, getting on my knees and keeping myself partially off the bed. He places one warm hand on my back, and the ache to have him inside me starts. A finger probes my entrance, testing my wetness. He makes a pleased sound. "You're already so wet, my Katya."

He thrusts a finger in, and another. Moaning, I move my hips back and wiggle them. "Please, enough."

"Whatever you want my queen," he says as something larger replaces them, pushing right inside me. As soon as he's fully inside, he thrusts forward. "You're so fucking tight. I've missed this."

"You're finally home," I moan out as I throw my hips back, meeting his thrusts.

His thrusts keep hitting a spot that makes me pant and quiver, aching and craving more. "Harder, give me everything you have, Valerio."

He groans, stroking inside faster, and then my orgasm washes over me, leaving me quivering and shaking. "I can't... I can't hold it off any longer." His hips slow inside of me, shallowly moving until he stops, and I feel his warmth filling me from the inside.

This is what I've been missing these past three months. I love this man with everything I have, and now we're going to have a baby.

"I won't be leaving again, I promise," he says solemnly, helping me turn over onto my back. "I can't miss any more of your pregnancy. Your first child and you've been dealing with it alone. Rest here, I'm going to go see the kids."

Nodding, I watch as he gets dressed again and leaves, leaving me alone in our room.

---

AT DINNER, everyone is seated and dinner is at the formal dining table. His father is sitting at the end of the table with his right-hand man, Lucio, and his mother

Valentina on the other side. Next to Lucio is Oliverio, then Evelina, and Domenico, his wife, and his two younger kids. The kids, Alessio, Luca, and Luciano occupy the other seats, along with Bernadette, who's smiling ear to ear.

Valerio stands up. "Before we eat, I'd like to make an announcement."

Nervously I look away from the watchful eyes that look between us. Valerio glances down at me with a wide smile. "We're having a baby."

"Another?" Salvatore thunders.

"Sal, be nice. This is her first child," Valentina scolds, and then smiles at me. "Congratulations. I can't wait to have another grandchild."

"Wait, so I'm going to have *another* brother or sister?" Vincenzo asks, almost unbelieving. His other brothers start chattering and next to me, Illaria laughs at all the noise while Carina looks at all of us with a puzzled look.

"Correct, bud," Valerio answers, over the noise.

His aunt murmurs her congratulations while his uncles come over to hug both of us. Lucio stays sitting, staring at me, like he's seen a ghost.

I give him a questioning look, and he looks away, staring at his empty plate. I gaze at Valerio to see if he noticed, but he doesn't seem to. I wonder what that's about.

"Let's eat then!"

---

LATER, after the kids are put to sleep and Valerio's done having a celebratory drink with his family, he crawls into bed next to me, throwing his arm around my body, his arm protectively pressed around my stomach.

"Do you know what was up with Lucio?" I ask, carefully trying not to step on someone's toes.

He breathes in deeply. "Honestly, I'm not sure. I did notice him acting weird, and he did drink a lot, but he did before every time I announced the birth of my children. I've never thought to ask him. If I had to make a guess, it might be because Luca's mother walked out and left him."

My heart fills with sorrow. "It must hurt him to see us pregnant."

"Don't worry about it, Kat. You don't need to be stressed out about it. Go to sleep and relax," he says, breathing in deeply as the words leave his mouth.

Slightly, I move my shoulder, to see the smallest part of his face and find he's already fast asleep.

I fall asleep feeling happy that there's one less secret on my shoulders.

*Three months later*

A LOUD RINGING pulls me out of a deep sleep. I reach out to the right to find Valerio's shoulder and find he's already sitting up, reaching for the reason for the noise, his phone.

"Hello?" A short pause. "There's what? Hold on, hold on. We'll be right there. Don't call the police."

He throws his phone on the bed and rushes down the hall to his closet.

"What's going on?" I croak in my sleepy voice.

I pick up his phone to see it's two o'clock in the morning.

"My biggest club is being robbed. At this time of night

318

there's a ton of money, and if these fuckers get away, we're going to lose a lot. Don't worry this won't take long." He takes a gun out and stashes it in the holster at his side and pulls a jacket over it.

He rushes out the door without closing it behind him.

"Be safe," I say to the empty room. I lie my head back down against the pillow, hoping to get back to sleep since it's been harder to sleep with this giant belly here. It won't be long now, only a month and a half.

Breathing in deeply, I feel myself starting to slip away when in the silence of the night, I hear the clear sounds of gunshots.

My eyes shoot open and dart to the door.

No, *no*. Not now. Not here. Not again.

I put a hand over my stomach and sit up, sliding carefully out of bed and grab my phone from the nightstand. The kids. As fast as I can run, I run to the rooms closest to the kitchen and knock on each of the maid's door, the last one being Bernadette's.

She throws the door open first and then rouses the other maids out of their beds. "Something is going on, you need to go upstairs and get the kids to the safe room," I say gravely.

"Come on girls, let's go get them and hurry," Bernadette orders. The girls look at her fearfully and then run back the way I came and up the stairs. Bernadette and I follow them to the double set of stairs, and I urge Bernadette to go up.

The safe room is well hidden, a room on the third level. They'll be safe there, and I'll join them as soon as I see if Valerio's parents are still here. They've been staying with us to spend as much time together before the baby comes because shortly after, they're going back to Italy.

Glancing down at my phone, I go to the app for the security cameras and find the one for the front gate at the end of the street. My jaw drops in horror when I find it broken open and all of the men guarding it strewn around. They must almost be here.

Suddenly, a hand touches my shoulder and I whirl around to find Valentina holding a gun and Luciano behind her.

He puts a finger to his lips and points upstairs. "Go," he mouths.

"What about you? Are you the only man here in the house?" I ask, dread filling me.

He nods gravely and motions for us to go without him, dooming him to the fate of the men at the front gate. Suddenly outside, we hear shouting and the sound of a barrage of gunshots, followed by silence.

I rush up the stairs with Valentina right behind me, and as soon as we get to the top, the door bursts open. Valentina pushes me away from view and starts shooting down at the men. I hear screams from a few of them and the sound of bodies falling. I cover my mouth and stare as she tries to fire more, but she's out and moves back to fire reload.

Suddenly, a few shots are heard from downstairs, and I know by the screams of the men that it's Luciano firing on them this time.

*This can't be happening.*

Suddenly, in their broken accents, I hear them say, "Man down. Look for the pregnant woman."

"I can't believe this is happening again," Valentina says angrily.

I back away and eye the staircase leading to the third floor. No. I can't. It's too late. Valentina turns toward me with sorrowful eyes as we both hear the footsteps of their boots walking up the stairs and then her eyes widen as shots ring out and she falls to the ground right in front of me.

"No! Valentina!" I run forward and collapse on the ground next to her as she stares up at me with tears in her eyes.

"I'm sorry we couldn't protect you, honey," she says, holding my hand.

A few intruders stop in front of us. "Katya Krasnoff, you are to come with us or we will take you by force."

Tears pour down my cheeks as I watch my mother-in-law wince from the pain. "I'll come," I respond, because I don't know what'll happen if I stay. Will they just take me like they said, or will they try to find the kids?

I won't take that chance. Slowly, I move off the floor and two men each grab ahold of my arms. One of them wrenches the phone out of my hand and tosses it to the ground next to Valentina. I turn my head and watch as she struggles to grab it.

As I walk down the stairs, I see another body lying around the corner of the hallway leading to my bedroom. Luciano. And he's not moving.

I sob, brokenly and angrily. "What do you want with me?"

But they don't reply. They never reply.

# TWENTY-THREE

Valerio

**W**onderful. In the middle of the fucking night, the club is being robbed. Is it some random robbers? Or is this the Russians or the Mexicans trying to fuck with me?

"Luca, Alessio, take some men and head around back. If they try to escape that way you guys will cut them off, preventing them from escaping. Got it?" I shout trying to mask the rage in my voice.

"Got it, Valerio. Come on men, get your asses moving!" Alessio and Luca shout at a group of my men.

Fucking hell, who would be stupid enough to fucking try to rob from the Italian Mafia? Who in their right fucking minds would stop and think that this would be a good idea. I mean seriously, if you have a death wish, there are other easier ways to go about it other than fucking with the Mafia.

I'm gonna make sure these men's deaths are slow and fucking painful for trying to rob from me.

"Make sure these stupid shits don't escape, I want to make sure that they realize just what the fuck they've done before we kill them." I smile as I think about all the different ways I can torture them into realizing that they made one of the biggest mistakes of their lives. I pull out a silenced Beretta and make my way to the door. Behind me are my father, Salvatore, and some more of my men.

I wait for everyone to get their firearms out and ready before I charge in with my weapon drawn. Once inside with father following right behind me, we find that the robbers are trying to escape through the back doors, exactly where I sent my most trusted men.

Once they realize they are caught, they quickly surrender to us, throwing down what weapons they have. We quickly strip them of their masks and notice that they are Caucasian. Not Russian or Mexican. Damn, I can't say I wasn't secretly hoping it was him.

"Please don't kill us."

"Yeah please, we'll do whatever you want we promise."

"Yeah what they said," the men call out to me.

Their cries for mercy have me rubbing the bridge of my nose. "Shut the fuck up before I put a bullet between your eyes right now."

I grab my father. "We need to question the dancers, see if they overheard anything or noticed anything off about these fuckheads." I nod toward the dancers on the stage, and they quickly stop to come and answer my questions.

The dancers all say the same thing, that they came here and once they came inside all they did was wave around their weapons and yell 'this is a robbery'. That's really odd. Why the hell wouldn't they trash the place or take the cash from the register tills? They didn't take anything either which is also odd because we have a lot of expensive stuff all over the place here that tweakers could easily pawn for a bunch of quick cash for drugs if that's what they really wanted...

But hearing they didn't do any of that doesn't make much sense right now.

I need to know exactly what's going on. I go over to the men and fire off a round into the air. Pushing my barrel into one of their legs makes a sizzling noise as his pants leg starts to burn from the hot barrel. The man screams and tries to get away.

I stare into his beady eyes. "Now we are going to play a game where you guys tell me the truth, and I don't splatter your brains all over my carpet."

"We don't know anything, I promise!" one of them shout.

"Why the hell did you bust into a Mafia establishment and try to rob the place? I mean fuck, you could have easily stolen anything up front including from the cash registers and yet you didn't. You didn't take the easy money when you could have been in and out in just a few minutes instead of being here when me and my guys show up."

The same man who shouted gulps, and the one next to him speaks up, "Well we heard that there were fancy gems hidden in a safe, but we never got a chance to go for them."

Salvatore frowns and pulls me aside. "They are lying through their fucking teeth. I can smell a lie when I fucking hear one and that smells like a mountain of crap."

"Something isn't right here. We need to get the men and go back to the house. These guys must have been a fucking distraction of sorts, and we fell for it hook and fucking sinker."

My heart sinks as his words process, but it makes more sense than them coming here for nothing.

Calmly, I motion for my men to gather up. "This is a distraction. Kill these fuckers and have three people stay behind for the fucking cleaners. Everyone else, get your guns ready and let's go because something isn't right."

The whole way home, I'm anxious and scared to death for what I'm about to find. Please let my family be home and asleep in their beds. The fucking car isn't driving fast enough. I swear to God if I got hit again, I'll make it my life's work to find these fuckers and torture them until they die from the pain inflicted.

"What the fuck is taking so long? I don't care if you need to plow people out of the fucking way just get me back home right fucking now!" I shout.

"Valerio, losing your cool right now isn't going to do anyone any good so please just take a deep breath and wait for us to arrive before you decide to blow a gasket. Now I know you are fucking afraid of losing your wife or your family but right now, they need you to keep your fucking cool." Alessio grabs me by the collar, snapping me out of the rage.

"Fine, fine," I grumble. "I understand so can you kindly take your hands off of me now?"

"Oh yeah, sorry about that."

I keep my cool until we start getting close to my house and my heart drops when we get to the front gate and it's wide open with some of my men dead just inside.

I hope out of the car quickly and rush over to the men and notice that a few of them are still alive, just dying.

"What the fuck happened? What happened to you guys? Are the people still fucking in there? Answer me you fucking useless peon!" I scream while shaking one of the guys.

"Boss..." he chokes out, "I'm sorry, boss, there was a horde of these guys." He coughs up some blood and manages to keep talking. "We tried so very hard boss...we tried...." I watch as the life goes out of his eyes.

I rush back to the fucking car. "Rush to the main house right now, I don't give a shit if it's a trap or not we need to fucking get there right now."

They punch it to get to the main house, but in my heart, I know it's too late. I can see the carnage all around my property. This wasn't a fucking snatch and grab, this was a full fucking invasion where they butchered my men and wanted to make a point that no matter how many men I have, it won't be enough to stop them from coming in and taking whatever the hell they want. We manage to make it to the main house and my heart fucking drops once again. The French doors are wide open and there are several bodies outside, and I can tell there's a woman's body among them. I can't quite make out who it is and I think if I see it's Kat, I'll go into a full on rage that won't be stopped. I'm going to lose it here and now.

"Valerio, before we go in there, you need to address your men about this," Alessio says.

I'll make it fucking simple then. "Men, if you find any of them, you put a fucking bullet in their brain okay? I don't care if they are begging for their fucking life. I don't care if they say they have a family. I don't even fucking care if they are a man or a woman. You put one right between their fucking eyes after saying I sent you to do it," I shout.

I watch as they get out of the car a little ways before the front door, and they make their way around the building checking out the sides of it. Taking a deep breath, I ready my nerves and decide to go to the front door and see who is right there.

Both Salvatore and myself leap out of the car and rush over to the body. When we get closer to it, we realize it is my mother's body. Checking her pulse, it's faint but it's there, she's alive and I am so thankful for the fact that she is alive. If my mother had died due to me, then I'd never be able to forgive myself.

"Who the fuck did this? What the fuck happened!" I scream out to the sky.

My father calls 911 right away. The only thing I can go through in my head is why the fuck would anyone come after not only my mother but after all of my men and my family. Is it because I married Katya or is it because I pissed off one of the other families. Or is it just because they think that they can get away with this. So many thoughts run through my head. The only thing that I keep coming back to is that this is all my fault and whoever did this is going to fucking pay. I will hunt them down until they are broken and bloody and make sure that on the last breath they take, they don't pray to God, they pray to me because God isn't listening to them anymore.

I will make them remember the name Valerio Marchioni because it's the last name that's gonna come off of their lips. My face is going to be the last one that they see. I will show them that they poked a sleeping bear and now the bear has been unleashed. They will fear me and they will run, and when they run, I will chase them down to the ends of the fucking earth. They will never escape, not this time. Nothing they can do this time will free them from the fucking monster that is going to be coming after them.

"Father, I don't know what to do. If they took her too, what am I going to do? I couldn't find her before, how am I gonna find Kat. How am I going to save her if I couldn't the last time this happened?"

"Snap the fuck out of it Valerio, you need to be strong right now not become a sniveling little bitch. Grow the hell up and be a man. If you don't, I'll take back over the family and you can go live in a fucking apartment or some shit. They got your mother and I'm pissed off too, but you don't see me screaming at the world."

"Fuck you! I just want to make sure that I am here for my family and that means Kat too, you fucking asshole."

"No fuck you! If it wasn't for *you*, your mother would be okay right now. So why don't you shut the fuck up for once and check the fucking house before I kick your fucking ass."

I can't argue with him about that, if it wasn't for me, my mother wouldn't be hurt. This *is* all my fault. Please let Kat be somewhere inside the house.

Before I move past, my mother manages to reach out to me.

"Valerio. They took her...I tried to stop them but..." she whispers and then passes out.

No...no...oh God no. It's happened again, and I wasn't here to stop it. I failed again and this time they took my wife *and* my unborn child. I can't handle this, I can't handle the feeling of failing again. I love her too much to just lose her like this.

Father slaps me. "Valerio! Snap the fuck out of it! You have your children counting on you and the longer you stay in your own damn head, the worse things are gonna get for them, so hurry the fuck up and get in there. I've got your mother. The paramedics will be here soon and I'll make sure she gets the best treatment once she is settled. We will meet up and figure out where to go from here, got it?" Father yells at me.

"Fine, I'll go find out what the inside looks like. Just keep everything on lock out here and make sure that nobody comes out unless it's the kids or me. We don't know who we can trust anymore."

I try to psych myself up to go inside, but it just feels wrong no matter what I do. It just feels wrong to try to feel good or strong when I am anything but. How stupid can I be that I sent all my best men and myself to the fucking one place where we'd be too far away from my wife and kids to be able to help if something went wrong. My grandparents warned me that an attack was probably going to happen against Kat, but I didn't want to listen to them because I figured I could protect her better than anyone else. My grandparents can be harsh, but in reality all they want is what's best for me and I spat it back in their face essentially by only partially listening to what they had to say.

Fucking hell. This is a worse than the fucking last time this happened. This time I'm actually madly in love with my wife, and this time, they also took my fucking unborn baby that she was carrying. If anyone touches him or her, I will pump them and their families with lead.

And then I remember the safe room. They have to be in the safe room. My children need to be brought out of there right now. They need to be led to safety and this is not a place that's safe anymore. I don't even want to be here anymore if all I'll be able to think about is how multiple times people have broken in, killed my men, stolen my wife, and fucked me over. Why would anyone want to stay here after all that has happened? Why should we?

Walking into the house, I look around and see blood all over the place, but not a lot of bodies anywhere. Slowly I move, clearing room by room and notice that people aren't all over the place, but there is an awful lot of blood on the floor. I clear each room in the front half of the first floor and then head upstairs where I see a body around the corner leading to my bedroom. A body that looks way too familiar for comfort.

Please God, don't let it be him. As I get closer, I find it is. Luciano. It looks like he gave his life to save either my children or Katya. I will forever be grateful for his sacrifice. I walk away from his body and clear each room upstairs. I find them exactly where I thought they'd be, in the safe room.

"Oh, thank God you are okay," I shout but they look frightened.

"Where's Mama?" Valeria asks, glancing behind me.

"Yeah what happened to Kat, Dad? We never saw her when the shooting started. Bernadette and the other maids came in and made us lock the door until she came back for us, but she never came back. Did they take her like they took Mom?" Vincenzo asks with tear soaked eyes.

"I'm sorry, Vinny, I'm sorry everyone. I don't know where Kat is. But I'll tell you this, kids, I'm not going to give up on her. I'm going to find her and make those bad men who took her pay."

I lead the kids outside and put them in two of the empty SUVs and have them taken away. Please let nothing happen to them on their way to the safe house. I go back in and search through the rest of the rooms and find not another soul.

I hate that there is nothing I can do right now to find Kat, but I'm going to bring in the best detectives to find clues to her whereabouts. They will search the house, security feed as well as anything else they want so that I can find out where the hell she is.

They are going to remember the day they fucked over Valerio Marchioni, and it is going to be a day that everyone will talk about so that they know not to fuck with me every again. The love of my life. My son or daughter. God, how could I be so fucking stupid?

"Valerio, are you okay? Everyone's getting a little worried," Luca shouts from outside.

"Luca, get Alessio and come in here," I shout back.

Luca and Alessio walk in, and I lead them to the right hallway where they see Luciano's body.

"Oh God, man why? Why! He never meant to go out like this. It's not fucking right that he gets taken out by some shitty kidnappers," Luca shouts.

"I can't believe he's gone. We will have to have some drinks later in his name. I can only trust you two and Father," I say somberly.

"Yeah he didn't deserve this, but at least he is in a better place now. No more wars or fighting for him. You really can't trust anyone else, can you? You don't know who is actually out to cause problems or to cause situations that will benefit themselves instead of putting the family first."

"Guys, gather every last man I have outside. Get everyone together. It's time to make a statement to them so they don't start defecting."

Before they do, I walk over to Luciano and try to feel for a pulse, desperately hoping for a miracle, only to be surprised when I find one.

Running outside, I yell. "Luciano's alive. Get an ambulance here quickly!"

After the ambulance has taken him away, all the men gather in front of me and I start talking. This can make or break me. "Men, you all have been around me through thick and thin. We lost friends and family today, but we will not forget those that we lost nor will we forgive what has been taken from us because when it comes down to it, we must come together to take care of each other. If we don't, then they have already won by dividing us."

"I'm promising right now that they are going to pay for the fucking mess that they put us into. They took two of my wives and my unborn child, it's time to hunt their asses down and rip them the fuck apart. There will be no safe place for them to hide. They might run, but I will follow to the ends of the earth if I have to. I will make sure of two things right now. I promise to come back with Kat and the heads of the kidnappers on spikes."

I am shaking because of all the rage that is building up inside of me.

"I almost lost my mother today, and I almost I lost a best friend in this conflict. I could have lost my children if it wasn't for the maids saving them by taking them to the safe room. I could have lost everything again, and all in one day. So, I am saying this right now so everyone can hear. I don't care if you stay, I don't care if you go. The only thing I care about is making sure that I find and rescue Kat, my unborn child, and that my mother and best friend pull through. If those things happen, then honestly I could care less about the people involved as long as they didn't try to interfere anymore. I need Kat in my life and there is no substitute for her. I don't want to find someone to replace her like so many people think I did before. I did not try to replace my first wife, in fact, I tried my hardest not to fall for Kat, but it was really the first time someone has shown me true love. If you'd like to leave, thank you for your service and goodbye."

With a deep breath, I finish.

A rush of emotion, of gratefulness hits me as I hear clapping from all around. My men are cheering me on and whooping. I guess they made up their minds on whether they were gonna stay with me or not. Now, I just need to find some time or clue as to who took Kat and go from there.

---

IT'S BEEN one whole month since I last saw Kat. Once again, it's like my wife has disappeared off the face of the earth, and there is no evidence anywhere of her being here or her being taken other than by us.

The good news is that my mother is almost fully recovered from her wounds and will be getting discharged from the hospital soon. I asked Father for help, but he said only when your mother is back to full and is able to come home will he be ready to help. The other good news is that Luciano survived the attack. He was severely injured, but he is alive and bedridden until he heals a bit more.

My kids have all more or less shut down on me. They miss Kat so much and things just aren't the same...again.

Why couldn't they have taken me instead of her? Why did they have to take anyone at all?

*To weaken me.*

Valeria and Vincenzo are the worst of them. Valeria is inconsolable, nothing I do makes her smile or happy and all she does is cry. As for Vinny, he is so angry all the time now which I don't blame given the circumstances. He has every right to be made all the time.

I refuse to just give up though. Unlike before, I have a ton of people out there looking for her everywhere. It's only a matter of time before someone finds her and then we have a nice big barbecue where the kidnappers can be the ones getting roasted. And if I do find Kat's body, I will force feed them their own dicks after I cut them off with a dull knife. I'm not giving up. I'm not going to surrender. I even have my aunt and uncles out there helping with the search. We have to find her. There is no other option. It's just going to take some time. Only, she's nine months along now and she could go into labor at any point. She might already have gone into labor.

Fuck. I'm going crazy and so are my kids. We need to find her and soon. And hopefully the men so I can finally know who's fucking behind this. I hope it's soon because my kids are going crazy and honestly, I am too.

My phone starts vibrating in my pocket, and I take it out to find a call from my father.

"Hello?"

"Valerio, it's me, your father."

"Yeah, I knew it was you due to the caller ID. What's the update on Mom?"

"She was released into my care today. She'll be okay, and now that she is okay, I can put all my focus into finding your wife. I want you to come down to the club today. There are some people there who want to meet you."

"Yeah, okay sure. I'll come down. Anything to get my mind off of this whole mess even for a little while."

Driving down to the club later, I pull in to see a number of different types of expensive cars.

Going inside, I see a bunch of people of different nationalities all seated at one big table along with my father.

"Good, I'm glad you could make it, I was just telling my friends here about the new Mafia boss and how wise it would be to get on his good side."

"Who are these people, Father?" I say glancing at all of their faces. They all have serious looks.

"They are bounty hunters. They find people who are hiding or missing and bring them back. I've told them all about your missing wife, and they think they might be able to help or at least track down someone who does know something that you can learn and use to find Kat."

"Thanks Dad. Even though we've never been able to see eye to eye, I'm glad you could help me with this and try to find my wife." Without a second thought, I turn to the group of them. "You're all hired. Let's go find my wife."

# TWENTY-FOUR

Kat

I can't believe they were able to get me again. This has to be the same group of people who did it the first time. They forced me in the car, a man roughly covered my eyes, with a blindfold, but didn't knock me out. We traveled far, I think. By the time we stopped somewhere, I had to use the bathroom bad. Someone grabbed me by the arm and pushed me forward. My feet touched the doorway of a building, and I was taken to a room somewhere to the right.

Before taking off the blindfold, they forced me out of my clothes and put a gown on me. As soon as it was on, they pushed me onto a bed, the only bed in the room, and chained my ankle to a bedpost. The man who took the blindfold off is not the same man who put the blindfold on. "You will stay quiet, or we will kill the baby."

It's what he says every time he leaves, in perfect English,

unlike the men who had me in the car. They all spoke to each other in a different language, and when they talked in English, I could barely understand what they were saying.

This man is also the only one to interact with me. Giving me food and unchaining me to go to the bathroom connected to this room. Neither room has windows, like it's meant exactly for captives. I always take my time in the bathroom since it's the only time I can get up and move around. If I take too long, he bangs on the door, and then it's back to the white walls.

When I was first taken, the room I was in had one window, and I was able to see that I was in a small house in the middle of a field. It could've been anywhere. Now, I don't know where I am. Am I still in New York?

I don't know how long it's been, but time seems to drag on. My belly gets bigger every day, and I'm afraid that soon, my water's going to break.

I keep hoping that this is all a nightmare. I can't possibly be away from home again, but I wake up and find it's real. Every hour I hope something changes, somehow, he'll slip up and not unchain me. I keep looking at the door expecting to see Valerio walking through. I can't stand the thought that I'll never see him again. After everything, meeting Valerio, falling in love with him and his kids, getting married, and now this baby, all of it, ripped away. If it takes as long as it did the first time to find me, though, I don't know what's going to happen. What did he think when he got back and saw his best friend dead, his mother possibly dead, and me gone? He must be furious. And his kids, what are they thinking?

Suddenly, I'm pulled out of my thoughts by the door opening. The same bald head peeks through, but I glance behind him to find him pulling along a woman with ropes

THE MAFIA'S BLACK OPAL

tied around her wrists, a blindfold around her eyes, and a piece of cloth tied around her mouth.

In his empty hand, he has a chain similar to mine. But the thing that makes me balk is seeing her pregnant stomach. It's a little smaller than mine, but she's still well along in her pregnancy. He sets her down on the floor, chaining her to the opposite bedpost.

He takes the blindfold off, and I find she has light piercing blue eyes, with a hint of green in them. They angrily stare at him as he moves to take off the cloth covering her mouth.

"You will not make a sound. If you do, I will come right back and rip that baby from your womb."

Her eyes grow furious and she wrenches at her wrists, trying to pull the rope off.

"Stop now or the cloth stays in your mouth," he barks.

She makes a frustrated sound, but complies. He removes the cloth and backs away, leaving the room after a glare in her direction.

Sighing, she finally looks in my direction. Her eyes widen as she eyes my belly. "You're pregnant too," she whispers.

Nodding, I bite my lip. "I was eight months along when they took me."

"I was six and a half months," she says, staring down at her stomach with a worried expression.

Questions are lingering at the tip of my tongue. Who is this woman? Would it be rude to ask?

"This is the second place I've been, because I wouldn't cooperate at the other one. I thought maybe I'd be able to escape on the way here, but a lot of men were with me when I was being moved."

"This is the only place I've been," I reply. I wonder if I had put up a bigger fight when they chained me here if I'd be moved too.

"Are you having a boy or a girl?"

"I don't know. I kind of wanted it to be a surprise, but now I wish I knew," I say rubbing my stomach and feeling the baby kick around. "At least I know they're alive."

She smiles. "Mine wouldn't show me. Just kept hiding themselves from me and my husband."

Her husband must be looking for her too. If he finds her, then I'll be found too! A wave of excitement fills me. Now there's double the chance that we get found. "What's your name by the way?"

She glances at her hands and pauses for a moment. Her hesitation lasts so long, I almost think she's not going to tell me, until she finally says, "Kitty. What's yours?"

I can't tell if it's her real name or if she's lied, but I'll take her at face value. It doesn't really matter in the long scheme of things. "Kat. My husband is looking for me too."

"Then we have a fighting chance." She lies back on the floor and turns away from me. There's nothing else to do but wait, so I relax and close my eyes.

At some point, I hear the door opening again and find my bladder is full, feeling like it's ready to pop.

The man goes straight for Kitty. "We found another location for you. Do you need to use the bathroom before we go?"

"No," she responds, staring at her wrists.

"Are you going to come quietly, or do I have to put this cloth around your mouth?" He asks, pulling the same cloth she came in with from his pocket.

She shakes her head and he unlocks the chain. Pulling her up easily, he goes to walk when out of nowhere, she bends her head down and bites his arm.

"You fucking bitch!" he screeches and slaps her.

She recoils in fury and spits in his face. "You'll be sorry about that! You know who my husband is! He will kill you the moment he finds me. And as for your boss, he'll find himself in the cage soon enough."

"Shut the fuck up before I knock you out!" he yells.

She doesn't say another word and allows herself to be pulled out. Glancing back at me one last time, I can see the sadness mixed with anger, and then the door is closed behind them, and I'm alone. I'll probably never see Kitty again. I just hope she and her baby stay safe. I say a silent prayer for both of us.

I cross my legs together to keep the pee from leaking, and sigh with relief when the man comes back after a while. He unlocks the chain and gets ready to point at the bathroom, but I'm already hobbling off the bed and waddling to it. All the while, my bladder is ready to explode.

After using it, I sit on top of the closed seat and think. They must have wanted to move us to keep us apart. If one gets found, the other won't be discovered. She didn't cause a fuss this time, so that can't be why they moved her. That's the only thing that makes sense.

I stay sitting on the toilet for a long time, until I finally hear the harsh pounding on the door, making me jolt. Back to the bed it is, then. They'll be feeding me soon.

Opening up the door, I walk straight back to the bed, and he places the chain around me again. He leaves, and I expect to get a little time before the nasty oatmeal stuff comes, but he comes back almost immediately. This time, another man is behind him, with a bag in his hand.

"This doctor is going to check and see how far along you are. You are to obey his every command." Without a second glance, he leaves.

He stalks over and pulls my underwear off. I can't imagine I smell very good, but he doesn't seem to care as he uses his instruments to look down there.

"Nine months. You'll be giving birth soon. Good. Then we can get rid of it and get out of this damn state."

So, we are still in New York! That statement gives me hope. But it's been a month...is Valerio still actively looking for me? I have to hope that he is, if not for me, for this baby.

"Don't look so happy, you'll never be found. Who would think to look here?"

Valerio would. He's smart enough to figure out whatever kind of cover they used to hide this place. He smirks cruelly and goes to the bathroom to wash his hands in the bathroom. "How do you live with yourself?" he calls from the bathroom. "You know, knowing what you did."

I freeze and stare at my stomach. Inside of me, the baby shifts, possibly due to the added stress of that question.

Don't reply. Just ignore it.

"You are one of the most heartless women in the world. Does your husband know?"

And then I can't take it anymore. "Of course, he does," I bite out.

He walks back into the room. "Okay. Whatever you say, Katya."

Hearing my name in his mouth makes me cringe, but he walks out of the room, leaving me alone. Just as I start to get off the bed, the other man comes in and says, "Tsk tsk tsk. Both feet on the bed." He attaches the chain back, and I'm back to where I started, with no one.

The doctor's question rings in my head. Does your husband know?

I'M ROUSED from a deep sleep by the sound of shouting. My eyes shoot open as I watch the door. Screams and shouts of anger, and then, the sound of something large breaking. And then shots, tons of shots are fired. I wrap my hands around my belly and scoot all the way to the wall.

The noise rings in my ears until abruptly, the shouting becomes faint, and then the boom of the guns is gone. I stare in horror at the door as the knob slowly turns. The door opens slightly, and I'm face to face with a familiar face.

His black hair is smoothed over a little more than usual, like he had a hat on or something, but his eyes brighten when he sees me. "Kat."

"Luca," I whisper.

He opens the door fully, and then backs out of the doorway. "Valerio! She's here, hurry!" His shout brings a happy swell to my heart and a few seconds later, I'm met with the face that's occupied my dreams.

Valerio covers his mouth upon seeing me and rushes to the bed. He cups my face in his hand and starts speaking lowly in Italian, eventually switching to English. "I actually found you. I didn't fail this time."

Glaring at the chain around my ankle, he calls out, "We need a key. Look in all of the pockets!"

He sits on the bed and pulls me up to him, holding me tightly like I'm precious and can break easily. "You have no idea how long this month has been. I thought I fucking lost you Kat, forever. I haven't stopped looking for you since that night. I only sleep every other day and even then, it's not very long."

I watch his hands shake a little and notice the deep bags under his eyes. Alessio runs into the room with the key, and Valerio unlocks the only thing keeping me here.

I move my leg to get out of bed so I can finally get out of

this place and go home, when Valerio stops me. "Don't. Let me take care of you, amore mio." He gently moves his arms under me. "Put your arms around my shoulder."

Nodding, I strain up and wrap my arms loosely around, and he picks me up, carrying me away from the world of hell I endured for a month. When we walk out, I see the carnage from the battle that was won to get me back. Tons of bodies are strewn around in the hallway outside the room I was held in. Blood covers every wall and organs are strewn around. Not a soul is alive. And it looks like Valerio paid extra attention to make it that way.

It's only a few more steps until we're outside, and I'm met with more bodies of men. They must have kept a lot here. But more than that, I'm finally able to see where I was hidden. A forest, deep in one. The sun is almost completely blocked out, making it dark. The sun's rays are only able to peek through the cracks between the leaves.

Three cars are on the small dirt road, and Valerio walks to the first one. Ever so gently he sets me in the backseat and straps me in before getting in beside me.

"One second, Kat," he says getting on the phone.

"We need to get all of this cleaned up today. We can't burn it down, so we'll have to get the bodies out and then scrub everything away so there's no trace of anything left. Get it done."

I stare out the tinted window at the small house. My room wasn't the only room. After a few minutes, I realize he's off the phone. "There were no other girls in the other rooms?"

"No. You were the only one...why? Was there someone else with you before we got there?"

"A while ago, yeah. There was a woman."

He sighs. "I'm sorry we weren't able to rescue her."

Leaning against his shoulder, I smell the faint scent of his cologne and the hint of cinnamon from the gum he was probably chewing. He wraps his arm around my shoulder and kisses my head.

"She was pregnant, Valerio."

He takes a sharp intake of breath. "I'll have my men keep looking for her. I can't make any promises though."

I nod and know there's a next to nothing chance of finding her. But then, I thought the same for me. It's possible. I'll have to hope for the best for her.

Suddenly, he reaches in his jacket pocket. What he pulls out makes me gasp. He hands me the one thing I've been missing. The thing that's become a part of who I am. The black opal ring he got me, signifying me as his queen.

"I found it on the nightstand, exactly where you left it. I wasn't sure if I would ever be able to give it back to you again. I decided to bring it with me on this trip. Maybe it brought me good luck. All I know is I'm fucking glad, Kat. Everything is going to be okay now."

I hold my hand out and watch as he slides the ring back on my ring finger.

It solidifies the fact that I'm going home. I can be free again. A sob escapes my mouth. This baby is going to be born and live. I got so lucky.

"I know, baby, I know," Valerio whispers to me. "We're going home."

# TWENTY-FIVE

Valerio

Kat collapses into my arms and cries her eyes out. The only thing I can think of doing is just wrapping my arms around her and holding her until she gets it all out. The only thing that is running through my mind the entire time she is crying in my arms is how I want to find the person that is truly behind this and make them pay pound for pound. For every single tear that has come out of my beautiful Katya's face, I am going to take a pound of flesh for it. Let's see how long they last once I start ripping them apart with a pair of glowing red tongs.

I got so lucky when I found that guy in an alleyway in the back of one of my clubs. Who would have thought that someone who was hanging out there would have information that lead to Kat's location? He told me that I needed to look in the forested areas of Upper New York, but before I could ask anything more of the guy, he took off running but that was okay. He had given me a lead, and that was all that I wanted.

"We ended up pulling in quietly once we found the place that they've been keeping you. We waited and waited to make sure that nobody was coming other than the guys that were here watching you. Once we felt ready, we drove around back and opened fire with a ton of automatic weapons. We made sure to shoot every man there because there would be no way in hell that any of these guys would give up their boss if they even knew who he or she was. This kind of thing plays out like a shell company. They get bought by another company working for a company that so on and so forth is owned by another big company that could get in trouble for buying said thing."

"So, what are we waiting for, can't we go home right now?" she asks, wiping her face.

"No, we can't. We have to wait for the new group of guys that I have coming. They're going to clean up the base and act as the people who were hired. That way if the big boss does show up, then we will find out who it is."

"Oh, that makes a lot of sense. So, when the new guys get here..."

"The ones that are already here with us are going to take us home," I finish for her.

I think about all the issues we have had trying to find her and all the problems that happened that day. I hate whoever is behind this, and I am going to make sure to find this fucker and torture them until they beg me to end their life. When they do, I am going to give them a revolver and lock them in a meat locker chained up. The revolver will have no bullets so they have nothing to do but starve and dehydrate to death.

"You've been quiet, and you haven't told me about the

kids yet? I had Bernadette take them to the safe house. I didn't want anything happening to them. I gave myself up after your mom got hurt and Luciano got hurt and well, I just want to know if they will they ever forgive me?" Kat starts crying again softly.

"Kat, the kids have been quiet and unresponsive since you were taken. The only one who hasn't been has been Valeria who has been crying non-stop and begging for you. The kids aren't mad at you Kat, they miss you. They all miss you. It hasn't been the same at the house without you, and I have even thought of moving completely because of how much bad blood I have with that house now. But I wanted to wait till you got home to make a decision on that because we are husband and wife, and I'd never take away your input or opinion on what we should do."

Kat smiles and leans her head against me. "I love you, Valerio."

"I love you too, Katya."

While we cuddle together, enjoying the fact that we've gotten another chance to live and love, the new men show up, and we're finally on the road home. My men and I took a lot of lives today, but it's worth it to have my wife and my queen back. She is my everything and I refuse to lose her again. And the baby is just fine.

I wonder if she would be willing to carry a gun to protect herself. Those guys got fucking lucky that I changed my plan at the last minute and wanted to just get Kat out of here. The monster in me wanted them to be tortured, but it's more important for Kat to feel safe again.

"Are the kids going to be okay?" Kat asks with small tears in the corners of her eyes.

"I'm sure they'll be fine once they see that you're okay and healthy and happy to be back. You know they love you more than me, right?" I laugh and give Kat a huge grin.

"They do not, they love you more than me."

"Uh huh, right."

"Well I can't wait to see them. I've missed them all so much. Especially little Valeria and the twins. They've really grown up right in front of my eyes. I just want to hold them tight and never let go as soon as we get home."

I can't wait to get home and surprise the kids with the fact that Kat has been rescued. They're going to be so happy now that she is back. I also can't wait to show her to my mother and my men who helped me rescue her, staying by my side instead of leaving when they absolutely could have. I wouldn't have blamed them. No one wants to be under a weak Mafia boss.

I hate the fact that she has to go through so much shit just to end up with me, but at the same time, I can't stop loving her with all of my heart. My kids...our kids love her. There is nothing in this world that could tear me apart from her I would tear the heavens asunder if it meant getting her back and now that I have her, I will fight like the Spartans to keep her safe.

There is a moment of silence and then Kat turns to me.

"How is your mother doing Valerio? She got hurt because of me, and I'm really worried about her. I didn't want anyone to do what they did, and if anyone died because of me, I could never live with myself. So please tell me that everyone is okay and that nobody died for me. I really need this right now. Valerio please tell me that she is okay."

I think for a second about her question.

"My mother is okay. She was released after getting some work done on her to make sure that there was no permanent damage. However, there were people who did die for you more or less. We lost a lot of the newer recruits who gave their lives trying to protect the compound. They refused to go down without a fight, and they took out quite a few of their men from what I could gather about all the blood with missing bodies. Mom is okay though. She's already back at home and has been relaxing far more with my father. He stepped up too you know? He helped me out a lot in finding you. He even brought in some old school bounty hunters to help find you. Granted they didn't really work out so well, but the important thing is you have been found and you're safe now."

"And what about Luciano?" she asks with a sigh, looking down at her hands.

"That's a different story. He's not dead. But he's not fully healthy yet. He had a lot of internal damage and the only reason he is alive is because the ambulance came so quickly. A few minutes later and he probably would be dead. He's currently in the clinic right now. There isn't a set date for him to get out yet."

"I am so sorry, I didn't want any of this to happen, and now he's lucky to be alive all because of me." Tears start welling up in her eyes.

"Kat, it's okay. He wanted me to let you know that he doesn't blame you at all and none of this was your fault. He would have done that anyway because he would have wanted to keep the kids safe. You don't have to worry at all. It's okay, I promise you. We're almost home, so just relax and calm down a bit okay?"

We spend a few moments in silence before I hear a wet sound and my feet feel soaked, like they've just been in a puddle of water. I turn on the backseat light and look down to see a lot of liquid all over the floor. Kat gasps and looks at me.

"Either I just peed myself and I have a urinary tract infection or my water just broke and I'm in labor now," Kat says with a sheepish smile.

Well, shit. "Hey! Driver! Change of plans. Head to the clinic right away."

"I know where we are, and it's probably going to take us about thirty minutes to get to the clinic."

"That's fine just please hold my hand and keep holding it okay?" she says in a shaky tone.

"Yeah that's no problem, baby. I'm not going anywhere. You never have to worry about that ever again," I promise her.

"Don't worry, everything is going to be fine. Just squeeze my hand when it hurts. We'll be at the clinic before you know it." She starts squeezing it hard, indicating a contraction. My hand is already in pain, but it's worth it if it helps her. "You sure are gripping my hand pretty tightly," I joke.

"Sorry the contractions are so damn painful," she says apologetically, and then clutches her stomach with her free hand. "Oh God, I can feel it coming."

By the time we reach the clinic, my hand is red and the bones are hurting because of how badly she has crushed it. She's really much stronger than she looks. It makes me really proud knowing how strong she is, inside and out. While my hand hurts, I don't mind it that much.

I'm going to be a father again, and this time with the love of my life, Kat. I can't wait to be able to bring them both home so our family can be whole again.

Nine children. I'm going to be the father of nine. But for Kat, this is her first. I couldn't give her a baby shower, but I promise to do everything else right by her. "Katya?"

"Yes Valerio?" she asks, wincing through another contraction.

"I can't wait for you to give us our child. You're going to do great *amore mio*, and I'll be right here." I squeeze her hand with my crushed one. "I will cherish you and our child forever."

---

## Kat

WINCING, as the next contraction starts, I slowly sit on the bed assigned to me in the clinic. This is actually happening.

The nice nurse from the front desk helps me change into a gown. "Please lay down so we can get all of your vitals."

I take a slow, even breath and lay back against the pillow as she checks me over. Maybe I can get an epidural before this progresses further. Valerio's right hand touches mine comfortingly. He looks at me a little nervously, but mostly he's trying to smile so I can forget the pain.

"I'm going to check and see where you are."

She gasps. "You only went into labor less than an hour ago, but you're already at a ten. This is pretty fast," she comments. "We better hurry and get you ready to push."

Moving to the doorway she calls out, "Doctor! She's at a ten already. The baby is coming."

The contractions suddenly get more painful, and I feel the urge to push. But the doctor still isn't back. "Valerio," I cry. "It hurts. I need…"

The pain down below suddenly increases tenfold. The nurse comes back with the doctor behind her. "Kat, so glad to see you. Oh dear, you've lost a little weight. Let's see what's going on."

She peers down below my hospital gown. "Oh. Yes, you're definitely ready to push. I'm sorry we never got you into those birth classes, but don't worry. I'm here. We're going to do this. Ready?" She glances up at me.

Nodding, I look at Valerio who offers me his hand. I gladly grab it and clutch it.

"And push, one, two, three…" the doctor starts, counting all the way to ten. I take a breath and then go back at it on her orders.

Each and every time it feels like I'm ripping apart until finally she says, "The head is crowning. One more push, and we can get the head out."

Hearing that makes me gather all the strength I have, crushing Valerio's hand in mine, and pushing for ten seconds with all of my might. The distinct sound of a small gush is heard, and Valerio peeks over. "Oh my God, Kat. The baby's head is out. You just need a little more."

I take a deep breath and wipe the sweat off my face with my free hand. This is it. I just need a little more.

"One…two…three…" the doctor starts counting as I push again. It takes one more push after before I see the doctor's hands move down, and then suddenly, the pressure down there is gone. A loud and angry cry erupts. The baby is out, and he or she is crying. Thank God.

"And a baby is born at…" she glances at the clock. "7:09 P.M. Dad would you like to cut the umbilical cord of your son?" She holds him up, and I cry tears of joy at how beautiful he is with wisps of black hair, just like Valerio's.

Valerio grabs the scissors from the nurse and cuts the cord. "He's so beautiful Kat, our little boy."

"We'll take him and check to make sure everything's fine and then we'll bring him back," the doctor says with a smile.

I just hope everything is okay with him. How would I forgive myself if he weren't okay?

"Baby, I love you," he says, kissing my lips.

"I love you too."

And now our love has taken form.

---

THIRTY MINUTES LATER, the nurse brings back my baby and sets him against my chest. All the while he's been gone, I still haven't been able to think of a name. Of course, we thought of a few when I was still pregnant, but even then, we couldn't come to a decision together.

"What do you think about Vikenti?" He asks.

Something about the name seems strong to me. It's meant for a prince. "I like that."

He breathes a sigh of relief and watches as Vikenti's lips twitch slightly. "Our two worlds, the Russian and the Italian have come together. I never thought I'd say that."

I laugh and gently kiss his little head.

"I'm sure his siblings can't wait to meet him."

Clearing my throat, I nod. "Yes. Why don't you go and get them?"

He frowns. "You really want me to leave you?"

"It's for the kids' safety."

He pauses for a moment. "You're right. I need to be with them when they travel in case of an emergency. I'll be back as soon as I can." He kisses my forehead gently, and then Vikenti's.

After he's gone, I hold Vikenti close and feel tears threatening to spill over. I thought I've already cried enough today, but I guess I haven't. "I'm sorry," I whisper to him.

WHEN VALERIO GETS BACK, he doesn't just bring the kids, who are out of their minds with excitement about seeing me and their new brother. He brings his parents, uncles, and aunts with Domenico's children. Luca and Alessio come in too, taking a peek at him.

His mom gets out of her wheelchair, standing up to look at him.

"You sure know how to make sons, Valerio," she says with a laugh. "Vikenti is going to be a looker when he's older, just like these boys here."

The only person missing is Luciano. I need to see him, he's here after all.

Suddenly it comes back, his parents, they know now. They have to know. When the men came to get me, they called me Katya Krasnoff, not Kat Marchioni.

I stare down at Vikenti and rest him against my chest.

"I'm sorry everyone, I lied to you all." Valerio's hand touches my shoulder. Maybe to stop me from talking, or maybe to encourage me. Either way, I keep talking. "I was afraid, scared that I would lose Valerio. I'm Russian. I know and remember the history between our people well. I even worked for the enemy, but that's not the case anymore I promise. Vikenti is —"

"Half Russian, half Italian," Salvatore finishes and stares at him. "May I hold him?"

I gently gather him and hold him out to his grandfather.

"Kat, I may be a harsh man, but I will never ever hate my own blood, and that's what Vikenti is. He's just as much Valerio's as he is yours. But I want you to know I don't hate you, not at all actually. In fact, I thank you for going willingly with them and saving my other grandchildren. Valentina told me. I can't say that finding out you were Russian didn't bother me for a while, because it did, but it's something that I have to accept. You are part of the family now. You are the queen. I will defend you against anyone."

His words make me remember the wedding, how he stood up and didn't allow the Dioli's to act out any more than they did.

"Protect the family. I will always protect this family," he states, and hands Vikenti back to me.

"Thank you," I say softly.

Salvatore actually smiles at me. "Now I think we should let you two rest. It's been a long day. You too, Valerio. Get some rest. I'll take the kids back to the house with us, don't worry."

"And I'll go," Alessio adds.

Valerio nods. I wave goodbye to the kids who are reluctant to leave again after only just seeing me again. With some nudging, they all walk together, holding hands, next to their grandparents and Alessio.

Domenico and his wife leave afterward with their two kids, and then Oliverio.

The only two left are Luca and Evelina.

"Your son is so beautiful Kat," she says softly. "Please can I hold him for a while?"

"Of course," I say and gently place him in her waiting arms.

She stares down at him and then starts crying openly. "He's so precious."

Valerio smiles, but behind him I see Luca, with a scowl looking at them. Something seems to flow through him because his face turns neutral, and he walks to the door, facing it. "I'll be back soon." The door closes after him when he leaves.

The only thing I can put together is that seeing her like that reminded him of his mother. The mother that abandoned him and left.

My heart aches and I glance at Valerio, sharing a look with him. He nods, seemingly understanding.

A few minutes later, Vikenti starts crying and Evelina glances up at us. "He's probably wanting his mother."

She places him back in my arms and steps back. "I'll be back to help you guys with anything you need tomorrow."

When she's gone, I murmur, "I think she's lonely."

And then, for the first time, I get Vikenti to latch on to my breast for the nutrients and nourishment he needs. Luckily, it works, and he starts sucking away.

Breathing a sigh of relief, I finally relax. "You're a natural at this Kat," Valerio comments, smiling proudly at Vikenti.

I guess I am.

---

THE NEXT DAY I'm feeling completely rejuvenated and well rested. Well enough to get Vikenti and see Luciano. It's a little bit of a walk, and I'm a little sore, but I manage well enough. When I get into the room on the other side of the clinic, I hear soft snores and approach the left side of the bed quietly.

Should I wake him up? He probably needs all the rest he can get.

I run down his entire body, seeing each place a bullet went in by the wrapping around both of his upper arms, around his shoulders, his lower right leg, and stomach.

His normally brushed down hair is in all directions, and his face is a little thinner than what I remember.

If I bother him, he'll tell me.

"Luciano," I whisper.

He doesn't seem to hear so I whisper a little louder, "Luciano."

Slowly, his eyes blink open and then widen when he sees me. "You're okay! Kat, what are you doing out of bed? Is Valerio still here?" he asks looking around me.

"He's at home with the kids, but he should be here in about an hour."

He stares at the bundle in my arms. "He told me you had the baby. Vikenti right?"

"Yeah," I softly reply.

His lips press into a thin line. "I'm sorry I didn't stop them from taking you. I failed again."

"Everything turned out just fine, and that's what counts. You did your best, and Valerio doesn't fault you for that."

Valerio's most serious man smiles and lets out a breath he seems to be holding for a while. "When you're all better, you can hold your new nephew."

"Thanks, Kat."

I turn around to leave, when his next words stop me in my tracks. "Kat, your secret is safe with me."

Whirling around, I clutch Vikenti to me. "What do you mean, my secret?"

"You know," he says, narrowing his eyes at me.

I laugh a little. "No really, what do you know?"

He glances at the baby in my arms. "You are my queen, and though I feel as if Valerio should know, I know why you haven't told him. He told *me* to look into you after you told him your name. I told him exactly who you were, the daughter of one of his men and a maid at that Russian bastard's mansion. But make no mistake, I know everything."

I close my eyes and murmur, "Thank you, Luciano."

Opening them, I find him leaning back to rest, his black

hair flopping back with him. "If you ever need to talk, I'm here."

Nodding, I leave before Valerio comes back and finds us talking about this.

I'll tell him eventually, some day. If Luciano can find out, he can too. And the only person he needs to hear it from, is me. Just not *now*.

# EPILOGUE

*One month later*

Kat

Since I never got to have a baby shower for Vikenti, we decided to have a party, just for us, for our family. The baby shower would've included all the women from the other core families, but this party, it's just for us. As much as I wish it was outside so the kids could have plenty of room to run around and play, we're having it inside because it's December. It's cold. And it just might snow.

Suddenly, the doorbell rings.

Everyone in the sitting room freezes.

I glance around at everyone. Salvatore, Valentina, Domenico, and Farfalla. Evelina and Oliverio are here too.

And of course, Luca, Alessio, and Luciano are here, but they wouldn't need to ring the doorbell. Who could that be?

I shoot a quizzical look at Valerio who says, "I'll get it." A look of seriousness crosses his face before walking around the corner to the door.

It opens, and I expect to hear the sound of Valerio's deep voice. Instead, there's nothing but silence. We all look at each other, and Salvatore starts to get out of his chair, when from around the corner, two people walk in, with Valerio trailing behind them.

Valentina jumps up from her chair. "Mother! Father! What are you doing here?" She runs and hugs them while I panic. My eyes widen as I look at Valerio.

He shrugs. "Grandmother, please have a seat." He pulls out the chair he was sitting in and lets her sit down. He runs to grab one for his grandfather.

"Kat, these are my grandparents, Marcello and Gemma Sinagra."

Gemma stares blankly at me while Marcello nods in welcome. Her hazel eyes stare directly into mine. "Kat is short for?"

My mouth dries out and I stare back. My mouth starts to open, and just as I'm about to respond, Salvatore clears his throat. "Mrs. Sinagra, it's just Kat."

Her eyes flash with something I can't place, and she turns her head slowly to look at him. "Did I ask you?"

"Well no—"

"Then shut your mouth," she says, and turns back to me.

I straighten up and fix her with my best smile. "My dear, please call me Grandma Sinagra."

There's a moment of silence and his grandfather says, "You can just call me Grandpa Marcello, sweetheart."

I smile at him. "Would the both of you like to meet Vikenti?"

She perks up, "Of course."

And then, weirdly enough, the doorbell sounds again. Once and then two more times.

Valerio frowns. "I'll be right back."

"Were you expecting more company, dear?" Grandma Sinagra asks Valentina.

"Well no, Mother, we weren't."

Valerio comes back, leading the way this time, and his eyes widen and look from his mother to his father. He mouths, "We're in trouble."

He rushes to get two chairs for them.

Completely confused, I look behind him to find an older woman and man, both the same age as his grandparents as soon as he moves out of the way.

"You have to be shitting me," the older man says, walking into the room.

"What the hell are you two doing here?" the woman asks.

Valentina's parents stand up. "We came to support our daughter and her family."

"And we came to support our son and his family," the older woman in the doorway says.

"My daughter was the one who got shot! What happened to your son huh? Where are his scars?" Grandma Sinagra yells.

"Now, let's all calm down," Salvatore says, looking from Grandma Sinagra to the woman in the doorway. "Mother, come in and sit down."

She glares at Grandma Sinagra and sits down in one chair while the older man sits in the other one.

Valerio scratches the back of head and grins. "I guess you

get to meet both of my grandparents today, Kat. This is Adriano and Gianna Marchioni."

"It's so nice to meet the both of you," I say.

"Be honest dear, it isn't," Grandma Sinagra says with a scoff.

Grandpa Marcello and Adriano lock eyes, glaring at each other.

I glance at Valerio who calls up the stairs, "Kids come down!"

Loud, thundering footsteps sound and in come all of the kids.

Everyone except Soren and Caelia hug each pair of grandparents. They only hug Salvatore's parents.

To keep the distraction going, I cross the room to Vikenti's bassinet and pick him up. His blue eyes are blinking up at me as he wakes up from his nap. He's a pretty quiet baby, preferring to observe more than scream. I stop in front of both pairs of grandparents and look to Valerio for help on who gets to see him first.

He shrugs.

After they get their last hug from Valeria, they both spot Vikenti in my arms.

"Oh, let me see the doll," Grandma Gianna says.

"No, let *me* see him, dearie," Grandma Sinagra says.

I stand frozen in my shoes and glance down at Vikenti who slips his tongue out and moves his mouth. "I umm…"

Suddenly, they both jump up, and hold their arms out for him in front of me.

The longer I take, the more frustrated they look. After they see I'm not budging, they turn toward each other and start arguing again.

"Tell your wife to sit down," Grandpa Marcello says.

"Why don't you tell yours to?" Grandpa Adriano responds crossing his arms.

Valerio comes up behind me and whispers, "I love you, baby. Thank you for staying. Whatever comes at us, we'll be ready, guns blazing if we have to. I will protect you and our family."

A hand goes over my butt and squeezes.

"I love you too. Thank you for finding me...times two and being my true love." He laughs and pulls me around for a kiss with our son nestled in my arms between us.

# THE ITALIAN MAFIA

Valerio Marchioni - The current Italian mafia boss of New York

Katya Marchioni (Krasnoff) - The current Italian mafia queen of New York

Vincenzo Marchioni - Oldest child between Valerio and his first wife

Nicolo Marchioni - Second born child of Valerio and his first wife

Vittorio Marchioni - Third born child of Valerio and his first wife

Emilio Marchioni - Fourth born child of Valerio and his first wife

Aurelio Marchioni - Last born son of Valerio and his first wife

Valeria Marchioni - First born daughter of Valerio and his first wife

Carina Marchioni - Older twin and seventh born child of Valerio and his first wife

Ilaria Marchioni - Youngest twin and youngest child of Valerio and his first wife

Vikenti Marchioni - Newborn son of Valerio and his second wife, Kat

Luca Marchioni - Best friend and secondhand to Valerio

Luciano Marchioni - Best friend who was adopted into the family

Alessio Marchioni - Best friend and oldest cousin who should rightfully be the mafia king

Salvatore Marchioni - Valerio's father and previous New York Italian mafia king

Valentina Marchioni - Valerio's mother and previous New York Italian mafia queen. Eventual queen of the Sicilian mafia.

Domenico Marchioni - Older brother of Salvatore, uncle to Valerio

Oliverio Marchioni - Younger brother of Salvatore, uncle to Valerio

Evelina Marchioni - Younger sister of Domenico, Salvatore, and Oliverio

Farfalla Marchioni - Wife of Domenico

Soren Marchioni - Domenico and Farfalla's secondborn son

Caelia Marchioni - Domenico and Farfalla's only daughter

Adriano Marchioni - Domenico, Salvatore, Oliverio, and Evelina's father, previous mafia king of New York before Salvatore

Gianna Marchioni (Vitali) - Domenico, Salvatore, Oliverio, and Evelina's mother, previous mafia queen of New York before Valentina

Marcello Sinagra (Voltolini) - Current Sicilian mafia king, father of Valentina

Gemma Sinagra - Current Sicilian mafia queen, mother of Valentina

# AUTHOR NOTES

Tiffany:

Thank you so much for reading our very first co-write together. This story has been in my heart for a while. The main points of the story hit me one day in the car and James added to them, thus we decided on a co-write. Kat was super interesting to write. Maybe one of the most complicated characters I've written so far. If you're wondering what's coming next, that's super secret, but rest assured I won't keep you hanging for long. I hope you enjoyed the journey.

James:

Thank you for reading our book, I hope you enjoyed it. Valerio isn't your typical mafia boss bastard. He has a family, kids that he cherishes. More than anything, he'll put them first. I enjoyed writing him a lot and he's the foundation for everything coming soon. As for the future, I can't say just yet, but there's a hint in the book about it. Thanks again!

# ABOUT TIFFANY RANSIER

Tiffany Ransier is a multi-genre author. She loves writing twisty, heart-stopping novels. She has a love for diving in to different worlds and making theories about books and shows. She lives in SoCal with her parents and younger brother. Her boyfriend is James Ransier, another author. They are the parents of an adorable Siberian Husky/Shiba Inu mix named Peg. When she's not writing or reading, she's baking or swimming in her pool.

Stay in the loop and never miss a release!

Newsletter: www.TiffanyRansier.com/newsletter
Website: www.TiffanyRansier.com
Join my reader group! We'd love to have you:
https://www.facebook.com/
groups/JamesandTiffanysReaders/

facebook.com/TiffanyRansier

twitter.com/authtiffransier

instagram.com/authortiffanyransier

bookbub.com/authors/tiffany-ransier

goodreads.com/TiffanyRansier

pinterest.com/TiffanyRansier

amazon.com/author/tiffanyransier

## ABOUT JAMES RANSIER

James Ransier is a multi-genre author. He loves working with all of the different characters and worlds he creates. He lives in SoCal with his girlfriend Tiffany Ransier, another author. They have a beautiful dog named peg who is a Siberian Husky/Shiba Inu mix.When he's not reading or writing, he likes to spend his free time playing video games.

Stay in the loop and never miss a release!

Newsletter: www.JamesRansier.com/newsletter
Website: www.JamesRansier.com
Join my reader group! We'd love to have you:
https://www.facebook.com/
groups/JamesandTiffanysReaders/

f facebook.com/AuthorJamesRansier

🐦 twitter.com/authorjransier

📷 instagram.com/authorjamesransier

BB bookbub.com/authors/jamesransier

a amazon.com/author/jamesransier

g goodreads.com/JamesRansier

## ALSO BY TIFFANY RANSIER

Vibrant Awakening

When Twilight Met Jacek

Alaska (coming soon)

ALSO BY JAMES RANSIER


Recipe of Love

Song of Love (coming soon)

CPSIA information can be obtained
at www.ICGtesting.com
Printed in the USA
LVHW041233260623
750802LV00006B/543